fated
to the
vampire
prince

ainsley james

Book One of The Vampire Prince Duology
A SANGUINEVERSE NOVEL

Published by Ainsley James Books, LLC

Chesapeake, Virginia

ISBN (paperback): 979-8-218-81336-9

ASIN (ebook): B0FR6FW96D

First Edition

Cover design by the author

Interior art by @elleillustrationss

Printed in the United States of America

Content Warning: This story contains sexually explicit material and darker themes. For more information and a full list of content trigger warnings, please visit:

www.ainsley-james.com

To every eldest daughter who dulled their spark to survive in a world that told them they were too much:

Darling, you are fire.

And fire is meant to burn.

CHAPTER 1
VOIR

CLAIRE

I spotted him across the ballroom and couldn't look away. His golden hair was carelessly pushed to one side, and he wore a smirk that looked like he'd just awoken from a very good dream.

But I didn't think anything Prince Bastien of House Allard did was careless, and he certainly didn't dream. He was a vampire, just like all the princes who ruled the Unified Territories. And tonight, it was my duty to become his next *sanguine partner*—the person he exclusively feed from for the next year—bound to him by contract at the conclusion of his Sanguination Ball.

I was repulsed by the idea of getting close to him, but I had no other choice. This was my fate. And if I failed... Suppressing a shudder, I touched the side of my neck, just above the black lace choker Mama bade me to wear. The vein in my neck throbbed, keenly aware of all the reasons I had to be afraid of a vampire.

Blackness crowded the edges of my vision, and queasiness

churned in my stomach. I stared at the floorboards, trying to slow my breathing.

Just thinking about the word *blood* made me lightheaded, which was something I struggled with over the years. Now, I had no idea how I was going to convince a vampire prince that I was the one he was searching for. What if I swooned at his feet during my interview? That would put an end to my mission pretty damn quick.

My sister snapped open a paper fan and waved it in my direction. The cool air chilled my skin but did nothing to quell my nerves. "Don't look," Seraphina muttered, "but *the Duke himself* is staring right at you."

I glanced up to find the pale blue eyes of Prince Bastien, the Duke of Roselyn, watching me from across the ballroom. His gaze cut through the pack of hopefuls crowded around him.

The eyes of my enemy.

Yet everything inside me stilled. My breath, my thoughts. I swear, even my heart skipped a beat. He was painfully, hauntingly beautiful. And like all predators, those eyes were crafted to lull me into a false sense of security. The longer he stared at me, the more time slowed. The people around me fading. Dulling. Blurring into the background. The chamber music and conversation fell to a low buzz.

I shook my head to clear it, but that didn't help. It was like I was underwater, and the only thing I wanted to swim toward was *him*.

A disgusting concept.

"*Enchanté, my dear*," said a silky voice that was so close, I swore it was whispered in my ear. I looked around for who'd done it, but no one was nearby. A musical laugh hummed in my ear, and my attention snapped back to the vampire.

It couldn't have been him... but by *Diana*... it was. He was speaking to me. *Inside my mind.* It was terrifying. And yet, I was elated. Against all odds, I must've done something right. I'd caught his attention.

"*Care to join me on the balcony?*" The voice slid into my mind like a guest. "*You look like you could use some fresh air.*"

The Duke pointed to my left, and I followed his finger to a set of ornate doors. I struggled to find words, but I wet my lips and whispered back to him, "*Is this for m-my interview?*"

His mouth didn't move, but I heard his reply just the same. "*Yes. And no.*"

The bubble of hope expanding in my chest popped. *What did that mean?*

I had to secure this job as his sanguine partner. I'd made a sacred vow to my coven, and even though I had no concept of what I was getting myself into, the fact remained. I might be a witch without magick, good for nothing but tending the gardens and feeding the crows. But I had to be better—different—than the girl I'd been if there was any hope of avenging Gran and the countless others who'd died at the hands of dark magick. The vampires had failed to maintain the balance of good and evil.

I had to become a spy.

The vampire broke eye contact, and my senses screamed back to life. The music. The chatter. My sister beside me. It returned so fast that I was dizzy all over again.

"I told you *not* to look," my little sister said through her teeth. She fluttered the fan faster, blowing the fine hairs framing my face so they caught in my eyelashes.

"Telling someone not to look is daring them to do it," I bit back, tearing the fan from her hand. "And stop waving this thing in my face."

A swell of guilt rose in my throat. I wasn't mad at Sera. I was just... nervous. Something I couldn't afford to be.

I untangled a lock of silver lilac hair from my lashes only to find the Duke of Roselyn chuckling like he'd heard our whispered conversation from across the hall. I swallowed hard. If he could speak to me from across the ballroom and distort the noises of the guests, then surely, he could hear *everything*.

A good thing to know for someone who wished to deceive a vampire.

Clasping his hands behind his back, the vampire strolled toward the set of ebony-stained doors he'd pointed to, casually shrugging off the questions of those around him. He glanced back and gave an encouraging nod, beckoning me forward. The look on his face was curious, but I was wary.

I didn't want to follow him. I was scared of what might happen. But at the exact same time, it was all I wanted to do. There was no room for fear.

"I have to go," I told my sister.

My attention drifted over her shoulder to the dais. If I impressed him during the interview, I'd be summoned before the court to complete the sanguination ritual. *Whatever that meant.* Mama was scant on the details. All I knew was that there was no turning back once the contract was made.

I would be his for the next year. And he would be mine to spy on.

I took one step forward, and Seraphina blocked my path, hands planted on her hips. She looked so different without her white hair, which she'd charmed to match my lilac hue as a disguise before arriving.

"Why are you acting so weird? You can't start freaking out now. You vowed—"

"Shh!" I said, silencing her before she could say something to give us away. I opened the fan and held it between us, blocking our faces from the vampire. "I can't explain what just happened, but he spoke inside my head and invited me to the balcony."

"He spoke inside your head?" she repeated.

I could feel the Duke's attention through the thin black paper fan. Something told me he wasn't accustom to waiting. "I think he wants to interview me." Her bow-shaped lips parted. Clearly, she was just as surprised as I was. "Wait here for me, okay?"

She gently took the fan and folded it, then playfully tapped the side of my cheek. "You can do this, Claire. I know you can. Just be confident."

I offered her a wry smile. "Thanks, Sera."

My little sister was everything I wasn't. A witch born with the Magick of the Light in her veins. One of Diana's chosen daughters. Trained to hunt the sources of dark magick on earth and destroy them. She'd take over our family coven when Mama stepped aside.

I wanted to protect her from the Dark Witches. The same ones our vampire monarchs had never held accountable for murdering innocent Witches of the Light.

I hated Prince Bastien Allard and his brothers for what they were and what they failed to do. But if I wanted to learn his secrets, I had to pretend that I was entranced by him, like the rest of these soft humans fawning for the right to be his pincushion. Straightening my spine and rolling my shoulders back, I strode across the ballroom with slow, deliberate strides, trying not to trip over the hem of the black lace gown.

At my approach, the vampire opened one of the doors and held it for me. I lingered at the threshold just long enough to meet his curious gaze. Like the other vampires, he wore a cere-monial black frock coat with gold trim that made him appear dark and severe. But the Duke added something extra—a black leather holster that cut across his muscled chest. Nestled against it was a jeweled dagger.

It was the kind of weapon you wore not for battle, but as a

statement. A promise. I found myself wondering what kind of promise he meant to keep with it here, at a ball thrown in his honor.

Before I lost my nerve, I dipped my chin and stepped out into the cool night air. Wind kissed the exposed skin on my cheeks and arms, and I resisted the urge to wrap myself in a hug as I walked to the stone railing that overlooked Château Corbin's famous hanging gardens. They were surely beautiful in the light of day, but now, in the dark, the bushes and trees looked as monstrous as the gargoyles sitting atop the buttresses.

As monstrous as my midnight companion.

I didn't hear his approaching steps, but I felt him standing behind me. It was as unsettling as walking in a graveyard at night. *If the gravestones intended to drain your blood.*

On the weeklong voyage to the capital, I'd devoured every scrap of information Mama had packed on the vampires, but didn't learn much. Rumors more than facts. Save for the bit about their diet. I'd never seen one up close before, much less been interviewed by one, but I imagined that a vampire would want someone soft and sweet to feed from.

Unfortunately, I'd never been either of those things, preferring plants and books to people. But I supposed there was a first time for everything.

Steeling my nerve and fighting against every reflex in my body screaming to run, I turned around, coming face to face with the Duke of Roselyn. The moon was a spotlight on him, bathing him in an eerie glow. What I knew about him I didn't like, but what I didn't know held my curiosity.

"Your Grace," I said, dipping into a curtsy.

When I lifted my chin, I found him contemplating me with a strange look. He shifted his weight, leaning heavily on the head of his cane, which looked much more ornamental than functional. I held my breath in my chest.

"I make you uneasy," the vampire said.

It wasn't a question, and he wasn't wrong. He did make me uneasy. Everything from his devastating beauty to his stillness to the fact that he could talk to me without moving his lips from across a ballroom gave me pause.

Instead of trying to lie, I stayed silent.

After a long moment, he asked, "Why are you here?"

There was no hint of accusation in his tone. Still, I had the unnerving suspicion that he knew exactly why I was here. A bolt of terror struck me in the stomach. The old me would've started to cry. I never took well to Mama's sharp questioning. But I couldn't be that girl anymore. Now that I'd left Prideaux Hill, I had to be stronger.

I swallowed the hot press of tears and breathed through the terror, then told him the only truth I had. "I came," I said, finding my voice, "for *you.*"

My hands trembled, and I clasped them together, refusing to look away from the cold depths of his eyes. A frozen moment passed between us. Him, unflinchingly still. Me, wearing a new kind of confidence as armor.

He broke eye contact first, but his gaze trailed down to my neck, lingering on my lace choker. I wondered if he could hear the blood in my veins or the sound of my heart beating faster, but I didn't dare to ask.

Another beat of unnerving silence passed. A muscle in his jaw feathered, and then a flicker of confusion passed across his face.

"I see." The words came from somewhere deeper in his chest. More growl than anything.

Had I said something wrong?

I swallowed hard and closed my eyes, silently praying to

the Moon Goddess for help because I couldn't mess this up. He *had* to choose me. I just didn't know how to convince him. This was the first time I'd even spoken to a man who wasn't family.

"If I make you so uneasy, how will you endure a year at my side? If I disturb you so thoroughly, just standing on a balcony, how will you follow me into battle?"

I opened my mouth, but no words came. It was a fair question. Many others found him captivating and were willing to leave their families for a chance to be in his service. Plenty who didn't have an aversion to the very thing he wanted. Blood.

My desperation rose, and I touched the rough lace around my neck. Mama's choker reminded me of what was at stake.

Bastien smirked at my discomfort, like the arrogant vampire he was. But I couldn't give up that easily.

"Anyone who meets you is uneasy, Your Grace," I rushed to say. "You command the largest army. You live in the biggest castle besides this one. If I wasn't uneasy, you would have reason to be suspicious."

He considered me for a long moment. As he did, he shifted slightly, allowing a thick shaft of moonlight to illuminate his chest. My gaze snagged on a glow of pulsing red light, barely visible from behind the strap of his leather holster. Once I'd seen it, I couldn't look away.

It drew something deeper than attention.

Collecting my courage, I stepped forward and lifted my hand to the pulsing light. Before I could touch it, he grabbed my wrist, twisting it until I yelped. His grip rough against my skin. "What do you think you're doing?"

He held me in place, eyes searing into me with murder.

I realized he assumed I was reaching for his dagger. "No, Your Grace. It's—"

The red light flashed brighter, staining our hands with its

crimson glow. He released me and quickly removed a gold chain with a pulsating stone from under his shirt.

Each throb of light was like a heartbeat.

The vampire tucked the gem back inside his shirt and repositioned his dagger over it. Hiding the glow. When he looked back at me, his eyes were stone cold. "I will not be taking you into my service, if that's what you came here for." He tapped his cane against the stone as if to accentuate his point.

My throat was thick with desperation. What was I going to do? I couldn't lose this job. I had to convince him I was a worthy partner. "Please, Your Grace. Prince Bastien. I beg you to reconsider."

I tried to reach out to him, like the soft, dutiful girl I was pretending to be, but he backed away.

"Do not seek an audience with me again," he growled.

"No!" I cried. But the sound only echoed in the cold night air.

I was alone. The Duke of Roselyn was gone. I stared blankly at the open door, trying to order my thoughts.

I'd promised my family I'd get this job or die trying. And... *I'd failed.* He'd rejected me. Something about it stung worse than being ignored. If he'd never invited me for an interview, I could've died quietly outside the castle with Sera beside me.

But that wasn't my fate. The tingle of magick burned against my lips, and a whole new kind of terror took hold of my heart. The choker tightened as the conditions of the vow I'd made to my coven were fulfilled, the lace turning to piercing barbs.

The pain was all-consuming. A thousand tiny blades. I reached for the stone railing to steady myself, even though nothing inside me felt steady. Especially when something warm and wet rolled down my neck and landed in a splatter beside my hand. I sucked in a sharp breath at the sight of red.

Blood.
The spell was ready to claim my life.

CHAPTER 2
MOURIR
CLAIRE

I thought the spell would provide me a quick death, but apparently, Mama hadn't granted my failure that kindness.

Another drop of blood landed beside my hand, and a sickening wave of dizziness broke against me. Partly because I couldn't stand the sight of it, and partly because I was going to die here, at Château Corbin, on some *Diana*-forsaken balcony, miles away from my family home where my spirit could be at peace.

Tears streamed down my cheeks as I collapsed against the railing. I had so many regrets. Most about my failings as a sister and a daughter, but at least Seraphina wouldn't have to see me like this.

The sharp sound of metal striking stone came from behind, and once again, I *felt* his presence. Slowly, I turned to find the Duke of Roselyn mere inches away, staring at me with those cool blue eyes of his.

He was back. *Why?* I searched his face for an answer but found only an emotionless mask. He grabbed my chin in his cold hand and tilted my head to the side, examining my neck, which caused the searing pain to spread. I swallowed a scream as tears raced down my cheeks.

"Who did this to you?"

When I didn't answer, he released his hold on me, but the pain didn't. A breath passed. The barbs dug deeper. Another wave of dizziness had me stumbling right into his arms. He drew his dagger and slid the cold blade between the lace and the thin skin covering my throat.

My eyes went feral when I realized he was going to cut the choker off, which wouldn't work. It would kill us both. This wasn't just a scrap of lace, but an enchanted object. No one but Mama or a true Prideaux witch could remove it.

"No! Don't!"

His hand stilled, the blade waiting against my throat. We stared at each other for a hot, tense moment. Tears leaked down my cheeks. Fear gathered in my chest. I was waiting for him to say something, *anything*. Instead, he pulled the dagger away and brought the bloodied blade to his lips. He dragged it across his tongue, sucking the tip, staining his lips red. The sight of my blood turned my knees weak. He fitted his arm around my waist, holding me upright.

When I looked into his eyes, I wondered if this monster would be the last person I'd ever see. If he'd be the last one to hold me. I hated how desperate that thought felt.

"Your blood is tainted with magick," he rasped. "Did you know that necklace is cursed?"

I didn't dare answer.

"How foolish could you be?" the vampire continued. His voice was dark. His expression pinched. "Magick isn't something to meddle with."

As if he cared. Vampires didn't concern themselves with humans, even though it was their promise to keep the balance of power and protect innocents from evil. It was hard to focus on my hate when red tears leaked down the front of my dress.

Live, live, live, my heartbeat sang. *Live long enough to avenge your family. To protect Sera.*

"Please," I pleaded, meeting his cold eyes. Knowing this was my last chance. The pain made words nearly impossible. "Help me. Save me."

The shadows around his eyes darkened, and his incisors lengthened into sharp points that peeked out from beneath his top lip. He wasn't my savior. He wasn't going to make this better. He was going to drain the rest of my blood and leave me for dead. Fear sharpened all my senses, and I struggled to escape his grip, but Bastien's hold on me was absolute. His fists like manacles around my arms.

"Who are you?" he demanded.

Before I could respond, the door to the balcony was thrown open, and Marius, the High Prince of the Unified Territories, loomed behind us.

Now I was alone with two vampires.

Like Bastien, Marius was in his monstrous state. His eyes were coal black and shadowed, and his fangs were bared. Bastien released his crushing hold on me, and I fell to my knees. I scraped my palms catching myself on the rough stone floor, but the pain didn't stop me from crawling away, needing to put space between me and the two brothers who looked like they wanted to tear each other apart.

"Dammit, Bastien. I know you don't want to be here, but how could you feed from a girl without a contract? In the middle of your Sanguination Ball?"

"I have done no such thing," he snapped back, turning to glare at me with murder in his eyes. "This girl is bewitched."

I wasn't technically bewitched, but I didn't think revealing that would help.

Turning to the moon, I said a silent prayer to Diana to protect me. If the vampires discovered I was sent from the Prideaux Coven as a spy, I'd be thankful that the collar would kill me before they tortured me into providing information.

"Don't test me, brother," Marius cut in. "The proof is in front of me. Her blood is on your lips. The law dictates death for a vampire who feeds without contract."

Death? *No.* If Bastien died, I would too, and this would all be for naught.

"I know the law, and I did *not* break it," Bastien refuted. "I tasted her blood to confirm the presence of magick."

Marius snarled. "I won't hear your excuses. This has caused enough scandal for one night. I quelled the outrage of the nobility by announcing that you've chosen her as your next sanguine partner, and that this was a mutually agreed-upon *taste test.*"

The magickal barbs retracted, relieving me of the worst of the pain. I couldn't believe my luck. The High Prince was forcing his brother to accept me. Finally, something had gone right. I pressed my lips together, thanking the Moon Goddess.

As if he could sense my relief, Bastien glared at where I sat huddled on the cold stone. "I refuse to take this woman as my sanguine partner." He spread his arms wide as if in invitation. "I'll gladly accept death over suffering her presence in my castle for a year."

The smile on my lips wilted. *He'd rather die than be around me?*

The old wounds his statement poked hurt more than the fresh punctures on my neck. Something must be truly wrong with me if I could be born without magick, and if a murderous vampire would rather die than spend a year with me.

I didn't belong anywhere. Not truly.

"Stop being dramatic," Marius said dismissively. The

shadows around his eyes receded along with his fangs, a serious look replacing his threatening one. "I need you in the west, expanding our territory. Or here at court, ruling beside me, if you ever see fit to track down your mate."

He playfully slapped Bastien's shoulder.

"I'm a warrior, not a politician, as I frequently remind you," Prince Bastien snarled. The courage of his conviction sent a wave of adrenaline through me. "If you're forcing me to accept this woman only to placate the sniveling aristocracy, then I suppose you'll have to kill me."

I couldn't believe the nerve of this self-righteous vampire. It must be nice to have had such a long, full life that he could throw it away over something this trivial. But my life was still on the line, and I very much wanted to live. If only to make up for my inability to fight dark magick alongside Sera.

I contemplated the vampires, unsure of what to do next. They were a portrait in opposites. Marius, with his short black curls and deeply tanned skin. Bastien, with his chin-length pale blond hair and blue eyes. One built for parties and courtly appearances, the other for war.

Marius offered me his hand. "Come, poppet."

I knew what had to be done. I had to continue to play the part of the terrified human girl who was desperate for this job. I swallowed hard, trying to beat back the fear as I glanced at his long, spindly fingers. After a moment of trepidation, I clasped his hand and allowed him to help me to my feet.

Prince Marius cast a look at his brother once I was safely at his side. "If you choose to ignore my offer to spare your life, then I will make sure this girl is well cared for, in accordance with our laws. She'll be sent to your castle, where she'll live in your room. As is her right."

I was being used as a pawn, but Prince Marius had no idea I was playing a different game.

"You cannot be serious!" Bastien interjected, stepping forward to glower at me. "That necklace of hers is responsible for your unhappy nobles. Mark my words, she's nothing but trouble."

I huddled closer to Prince Marius, continuing to play the part of the terrified girl covered in her own blood. Truth be told, I didn't need to act very much. I was scared of what Bastien might do. With his lips and his teeth and his hands and that cane.

He was dangerous. A killer. And he wanted me dead.

Marius draped a protective arm around my shoulders, shielding me. "If the girl bought a magickal necklace to bleed for you, then all the better. She's a cunning little thing who is willing to do whatever it takes to secure this job. Appreciate the gesture, Bastien."

The vampire set his cool hand on the side of my flushed face, commanding my attention while speaking to his brother. "We love a willing and dedicated sanguine partner, don't we? Someone desperate to gift us with what we so badly desire."

I hid my disgust behind a demure smile, which Marius seemed to appreciate. This vampire thought me soft and sweet, like a ripe grape ready to be juiced. He was completely unafraid of me. But he should be very afraid of what a sweet grape like me could learn. Of the things I could whisper to my family. And of the vengeance we planned to take on their beloved Dark Witches.

His ego would be his undoing. These vampires thought everyone was thankful to serve them. It made them careless, which was exactly what Mama had taught me.

Bastien growled like an animal about to strike. The sound caused another bolt of terror to land in my gut. I tensed as he stepped closer, walking into another shard of moonlight. With Diana's gentle glow clinging to the silver white of his hair, I couldn't look away. He was so strikingly handsome it stole my breath. Terrifying and alluring at the same time.

"I don't trust her," said the Duke, striking his cane on the ground. "You can't force me to accept this arrangement."

My hand trembled as it floated to my neck. The memory of the death I narrowly escaped fresh in my mind. Bastien tracked the movement, his pale blue eyes following like a hunter stalking his prey.

A smirk crested Marius's lips before his hand fell from my face, and he turned to his brother. "You're right. I can't force you to do anything you don't wish to do. If you want to die for your crime, then fine. I'll cut off your head. But the girl will live in your castle and drink your wine and live handsomely while your bones rot away in a mausoleum. Few will mourn you. Least of all her."

He paused, turning to me. "Will you mourn the Duke of Roselyn while you lay on his silky sheets?"

Bastien watched me carefully. I didn't know what to say, so I simply shook my head.

Marius laughed musically. "After all this, who could blame you?" He touched the side of my cheek, trailing a long finger through something wet, which I assumed to be blood. "She'll enjoy her days, serving Tyson, who *will be* the next Duke of Roselyn after your untimely death."

"I will not allow it," Bastien seethed.

The High Prince merely shrugged. "This death won't be like our first one, brother. When I cut off your head, you won't come back."

A flicker of relief passed through me. If he was dead, I'd still be protected as his sanguine partner. If he was dead, I could spy on the new Duke of Roselyn without enduring the feedings. And if he was dead, it would mean there was one less vampire in the Unified Territories.

And yet, the red smear on Bastien's chest drew my gaze and refused to let go. He'd tried to save my life. And when I stopped him from accidentally killing us both with his chivalry, he'd hauled me against him like he'd rather hold me in his arms than let me die alone. But he hadn't come to save me. He'd come to save himself. An important distinction.

I wanted to spit at him. I wanted to slap him. But deep down, more than anything, I wanted someone to hold me like that again.

Marius clapped a hand on Bastien's shoulder. Imploring. "I need you, brother. I need your leadership. Your army. I need you to hold the line against the Lawless Lands. You've heard the reports, same as me." He shook Bastien once. A smile breaking across his face. "Stop being dramatic and do what you've pledged to do."

A moment passed. Wind howled through the trees. The torches hanging beside the balcony doors flickered. I waited for his decision, holding as still as a corpse.

But what would that fate be?

The blade, *or me?*

CHAPTER 3
FALLIOR
BASTIEN

Death would be the easier option, all things considered, but my brother was right. It was my responsibility to lead the army and hold the boundary between the Unified Territories and the Lawless Lands. Hector and Chastity, the leaders of Light and Dark beyond our borders, were closer than ever to accepting terms of protection. But the situation was tenuous. Factions inside the covens still didn't trust vampires, and it required a skilled negotiator.

After centuries of diplomacy, I wasn't about to hand ownership of my castle to my whelp of a nephew, Tyson. I had to overcome the *problem* this woman presented. I'd been mate-less for centuries. Now, five hundred years later, she appeared. It all seemed too suspicious, but Marius wasn't listening to reason.

A year would go by in a blink, and if I kept her at arm's length, I could get through this and move on with my life. The pull of a mate bond couldn't be as strong as my free will.

The one benefit I could see was that she didn't appear to

know who she was to me. And neither did my brother. *Thankfully*. While we'd once been as close as true brothers, we'd drifted further apart over the centuries. As the High Prince, his job was to rule and play nice with nobles. Mine was to hold the line between our people and the terror that reigned beyond it.

Yet, despite our differences, he was still my brother. Not by birth, but by death. *Mon Sang. My blood.* I'd sworn to do anything for him. Which was why I drew in a long breath and forced myself to look this woman in the eyes. "Fine. I'll accept her into my service."

I watched her for a moment, tracing the shape of her lips as they parted in surprise, reveling in the flush of color that stained her cheeks.

"Splendid!" Marius replied with a clap of his hands. "Now, take..." He twirled his finger in the air. "I'm sorry, but what is your name, dear?"

She glanced between the two of us. Then, haltingly, said, "Claire. My name is Claire Donadieu."

A cool breath of air wrapped around my shoulders and rustled through the long strands of her hair.

Claire.

Her name was its own kind of magick. There was no other way to describe it. Forever, my attention would be attuned to the sound of it. My senses sharpened whenever it was spoken. My desire for her absolute.

I closed my eyes and drew in another steadying breath. I didn't want this. I didn't want to be fated to anyone. Had I known when I saw her across the ballroom that the intense need to speak with her was the pull of a mate bond, I would've run instead of giving the bloodstone—my mate-identifying rune—time to recognize our connection.

When I opened my eyes, I found Marius dabbing the dried blood from Claire's neck with a damp towel that he'd procured from a steward, cleaning the worst of the mess the choker had made.

I had to swallow a growl at the sight of him touching her. Even though I loved my brother, a vision of tearing his arm from the socket and beating him with it flitted through my mind. My fingers tensed, and adrenaline coursed through my limbs. I watched him tend to her the way I should be. When he was finally done, Marius captured her hand in his, holding it as he escorted her to me.

I had to keep this new protective desire in check. If my brother discovered the truth—that Claire was my mate—I'd be forced to give up my castle to Tyson and live here in the capital. Pandering to gossiping courtiers, hosting expensive parties, and listening to petty disputes. A sentence worse than beheading, in my opinion.

My brother offered me Claire's hand with a grin. I merely glared at him. Marius sighed in frustration. "Bastien, it's time to take Miss Donadieu to the dais, claim her as tradition demands, and put this whole mess behind us."

Claim her. *Yes.* That's exactly what I wanted to do. To claim her as mine. To make us one body. One breath. The longer I stood in her presence, the stronger it became. The pull was unlike anything I'd experienced before.

Fight, damn you. Fight back. I was stronger than some base desire. I knew nothing about this girl, and I was suspicious of the little I did know. I could do this. I just needed to remind myself of what was at stake.

Her deep brown eyes met mine, wide as a fawn, and the bond between us deepened. I could feel her heart beating in my chest, and I could smell her fear as keenly as I could smell the apples ripening on the trees in the orchard below.

She was afraid of what came next.

My instinct was to offer words of comfort. To take her in

my arms and tell her she would be safe. Because I'd make her safe. An instinct that I had to fight against with all my willpower.

Chest tight, I slowly lifted my hand and waited for Marius to place hers in mine. When he did, a pop of something that felt like magick stirred between us. A jolt of heat that I felt in every corner of my body—the first ounce of warmth I'd experienced since my death.

I tried to look unaffected because I knew Marius was watching me. Studying my reaction. He might come off as a playful host, but there was a reason why my brothers and I named him High Prince. He was cunning. And I knew he was suspicious of my intense opposition to Claire. However, Marius wasn't the one I was worried about at the moment.

Claire was grimacing at the place our bare skin touched like my flesh had just burned her, and I wondered if she had felt it, too. The snap of magick. If the stories were true, she should be able to feel the pull of our bond. I hoped in this case the stories were wrong. Or, that, because her blood was tainted with magick, she was temporarily immune to it.

My attention shifted down to her throat and the black lace choker coated in blood. I used the sight to fuel my anger. I was only in this situation because she so unwisely dabbled in magick.

Falling back on the courtesies Marius expected of me, I placed my free hand behind my back. "Shall we give the people what they want, Miss Donadieu?"

"Oh, we're going now?" she asked, her voice wobbling. "You're going to claim me r-right away?"

I narrowed my eyes. "That's how this works. I drink from you, and they all clap. The first bite seals our contract. That's what you want, isn't it? For me to drink your blood?"

Say no. Say you want to run away.

The scent of her fear intensified. My need to comfort her became almost unbearable.

Instead, I instructed myself to focus on how angry I was. She had thrown the fate of so many in jeopardy just by daring to be in my presence. If I let my guard down for one minute, for one *second*, everything I'd worked to build would come crashing down. I hated her for who she was and for ruining what little peace I'd found in this life. To my surprise, focusing on anger seemed to work. It cleared my mind. If I could only stay angry, I could survive this.

"Yes, that's what I want," Claire finally said, even though the scent of her fear was omnipresent. The fragrance clinging to my clothes and sticking to my tongue. "Okay, I'm ready."

"Then follow my lead."

The attendants opened the balcony doors for us, revealing a massive crowd of nobles. Drinks in hand. Glasses raised. Marius strode forward, making his announcement of the imminent joining between Claire and me.

"Oh wow," Claire muttered under her breath when everyone cheered. "Are they all waiting for us?"

I shifted my gaze to her face, hoping to watch her squirm under the pressure, but instead was captivated by the way moonlight streaming in from the stained glass windows illuminated her lavender hair with an iridescent glow. It was breathtaking. The world could've been burning, and I wouldn't have noticed.

"We are the entertainment," I forced myself to say.

"That's really intimidating," she replied, still staring at the crowd.

Meanwhile, I was staring at her. At the way the light caught her hair. "Yes," I said, the words dripping from my lips, "it's all very intimidating."

Somehow, I forced myself to tear my focus from her and

carry out my duties despite everything in me screaming to claim her mouth as mine, to seal the bond between us with a kiss.

Step by step, I led us to the dais at the front of the ballroom, where the rest of my brothers and their sanguine partners stood waiting. Tibitha, the woman I'd been feeding from for the last year, stood off to the side next to my second-in-command, Natalia. Unsurprisingly, my niece looked miffed that I'd selected someone without consulting her. Claire's hand trembled as I guided her up the stone steps, and my anger wavered.

"If this is too much—"

"I'm fine."

She wasn't, but I couldn't let that thought consume me.

I knew this was why our laws forbade taking your mate as a sanguine partner. The bond was consuming enough without their blood running through your veins. The elders warned it made us too impulsive and rash. But I didn't have a choice. I'd have to force myself to drink from Claire in front of an audience because my only other options were death or admitting the truth to Marius, which would destroy everything.

The violins played while I bowed to Marius. Claire, following my lead, curtsied. I tried not to take notice when the swell of her breasts strained against the black lace bodice of her gown as she did.

"As all good matches begin, so does the one between my brother, Prince Bastien of House Allard, Duke of Roselyn, and Miss Claire Donadieu. With a first bite." He canted his head to the side and grinned coyly. "Or rather, a second, in this case."

Soft chuckles sounded from the crowd. Others whispered, clearly offended that I hadn't chosen their daughter as my sanguine partner.

Claire's cheeks flushed at the attention, and I felt the

thrum of her heart beating faster against my chest. Pulsing from the bloodstone I wore on a thin gold chain around my neck.

I wanted to get this over with, but dread coiled tight in my gut. I'd only had a taste of her blood, and I was already fighting myself not to drag her into a corner and finish what I started. If one drop could unravel me this much, what would happen when I took more?

Still, tradition demanded a show. I took her hands, like we were about to dance, and spun her in a slow circle before pulling her into my arms. She gasped in surprise, her fingernails biting crescents into my arms.

I guided her down until her silver lilac hair brushed the red carpet and my nose was buried in the warm hollow of her throat. Gasps came from the crowd. *Oohs and aahs.* This was the spectacle they all wanted from their rulers.

I drew in a breath of her delicious scent and held it, letting it fill every corner of my chest. Part of me ached to sink my teeth into her and drink until I knew every secret she carried. Another part of me feared that if I did, there'd be no pulling back—that I'd lose the control I'd kept for centuries. But there was no escaping this. I had to show the courtiers and Marius that nothing was amiss.

And while all this was swirling inside my head, I could tell by the clammy sheen of sweat on her skin and fluttering pulse that she was terrified. I waited for the change to happen. For my bloodlust to be triggered. For my incisors to drop and my eyes to blacken, ready to feed.

But... nothing happened.

CHAPTER 4
TOUCHER
CLAIRE

I held my breath, waiting for him to strike like I was about to jump into the frigid, white-capped rapids of the Starfall River. But instead of feeling his incisors on my neck, I felt like I was floating—drifting in a current, and the only person I wanted to listen to was *him*. The wailing of the violins disappeared along with the low conversation of the crowd.

I swallowed a curse. The wretched vampire was in my head again. Without moving my lips, I asked him, *"What are you doing?"*

Silence.

"Well?" I prompted him.

"Your fear is inhibiting my ability to transform." Each word sounded like it cost him something. *"I need you to relax—to want this—or it won't work."*

How was I supposed to relax while in such a compromising position? On stage? In front of hundreds of people? Much less *want* him to bite me.

"I can't relax. It's not possible."

He growled in frustration, and the sound vibrated against

my ear, sending unexpected little bolts of pleasure down my spine. *"You have to make everything difficult. Don't you?"* he gritted through his teeth. Even his voice in my head sounded exasperated.

"I'm not trying to make things difficult, Your Grace, but this whole thing is unnatural. The people. Your brothers. I've never been around so many strangers in my life."

Why had I given him that truth? I needed to be more careful with my words. Much more careful. The less he knew about me, the better.

There was a pause, and then he said, *"Fine. Let's try something else."*

"Fine."

I had no idea what I just agreed to. What else could he do to get me to relax?

Bastien expelled a deep breath against my neck, causing a wave of tingling pleasure to roll down my spine. I had to hold back a gasp. Slowly, he moved his lips to my earlobe, then breathed again. The smooth line of his mouth grazed the shell of my ear. I shivered in his arms. Never before had I felt such things. I hated this man. Was terrified of his bite. But by Diana, something inside me *wanted* him this close. If only to feel his breath against me once again.

"Wh-what are you doing?" I asked.

He hummed against my skin. *"Trying to appeal to another one of your instincts."*

Another instinct? Did he mean...?

Oh. *Oh.*

Before this moment, I'd never so much as spoken to a man outside my family, let alone had one press his lips against my neck. I'd had crushes on boys from afar, but that's all they ever were. I was no good in a marriage alliance with a neighboring coven, despite my mother's status. I was told she would never force me on a man of worth because I couldn't defend myself or my children from dark witchery. Which meant I rarely left Prideaux Hill because I was too much of a burden to protect when we traveled.

I was often alone, content with tending the ravens and the garden, because I accepted my fate a long time ago. I was destined to be a spinster. Untouched and undesired by anyone. But the Duke's mere breath had awakened something deep inside me I hadn't known was there. A desire to be desired. He sighed against my skin again, this time adding a small satisfied sound. My breath stumbled.

"Much better. Your fear is dissipating. Now, if it's okay, I want to try one more thing." His words were slow and soft in my head, and I swallowed hard as another hot pulse of heat rolled through me.

I hated myself for letting him make me feel this way, but I needed to seal our pact with a first bite, as much as the act revolted me. This was how I became a spy, proving to my family that I could be useful, even if I didn't have magick. I had to want him to bite me.

Everyone was watching. Waiting. Wondering what was going on. *"Okay. Fine,"* I said begrudgingly. *"Do whatever you think will help."*

His lips ghosted down my neck like a lover's might, and I pretended he was someone else. Someone with a heartbeat. Someone warm and sweet. When his cold tongue licked a slow trail up my throat, from my collarbone to the choker, my body turned to dough. Despite the people all around, I'd never felt anything so *satisfying.*

"Good, very good," he purred. *"Now tell me to bite you."*

"Do it. Bite me."

His lips closed around my skin, sucking gently, before I felt the pressure of teeth. My hand flew to the back of his neck, fisting sections of his hair as the bite deepened. I arched into him. His grip around my waist was like steel. Yes, there was pain, but there was also... *pleasure.* Waves of it rolled through me, starting low in my core and traveling up to my belly button in slow, warm strokes. However, the tug of desire couldn't stop me from imagining what he was doing.

Swallowing my blood.

As soon as I remembered that red stain on his lips, the stage spun. I struggled against the lightheadedness. I wasn't strong enough to fight back against my phobia. A cold sweat broke across my brow, and my grip on his hair loosened. Wishing I was stronger, I looked toward the crowd, searching for my sister, needing to see Seraphina's face. She would tell Mama I'd done what I'd set out to do.

They couldn't say I was good for nothing. Not anymore.

The last thing I remembered before blackness squeezed out my vision was a blur of lilac hair and the sound of my name.

When I awoke, I was being carried down a set of stairs. A hand was fitted under my knees, another held a silk cloth against my neck. My head resting against a chest. Tilting back, I realized Bastien was the one carrying me. Everything came back in a rush. The dais. The people. His body against mine. His breath. *His tongue.* Shame heated my cheeks. I'd let a vampire lick my neck. *Diana, help me.*

"Put me down," I managed to say.

"Gladly," he answered. "This is the second time you've bled on my shirt."

As if the wealthy vampire was worried about one shirt. Irritation and shame made me bolder than usual when I snipped back, "Don't say that word." I didn't want him to inadvertently make me pass out again. Now that I was in his service, I needed to be a sponge, soaking up every bit of information on the vampire.

"What word?"

I gritted my teeth. "*Bled*."

The vampire reached the base of the stairs and turned a corner that led into a long hallway lit with wrought-iron candelabras. The flickering light sent shadows across the art on the walls.

"Why not?"

"Because it makes me sick."

I tore the silk cloth from his grip and held it against my neck. Temper smarting. Shame twisting like a snake in my gut.

"What do you mean *it makes you sick?*"

His question was like hitting an old bruise. I'd explained this to many family members over the years, including the midwives who asked me to help in the birthing beds, the healers who asked me to remove arrows or set wounds, and the huntresses who demanded I skin hares. I couldn't do any of it without passing out, humiliated time and time again for being useless in every way imaginable.

"I can't explain it, but every time I hear that word, I get dizzy."

Bastien stopped in front of a door and kicked it open. I let out a gasp as he strode inside and kicked it closed. The door hung loose on broken hinges.

Inside, the room was dark, save for the light coming in through the crack in the door. He lay me down on a velvet settee before striking a match, lighting a candle, and setting it on the small table beside me. Shadows flickered to life between us. I swallowed hard as he studied my neck. Then he wrestled the silk cloth from my grip and held firm pressure against his bite mark.

"And what happens if you see it?" he asked. "Do you swoon?"

"Sometimes," I answered. I noticed a smear of red still staining his chin, and fresh sweat broke out on my forehead.

"You understand this position entails talking about and seeing the very thing that makes you ill?"

I hugged my knees to my chest, putting more space between us. "Does it? I thought I was applying to be your royal dog walker."

He let out a chuckle that held no humor as he stood and reached for a pitcher sitting on a sideboard. He poured a measure of water into a glass and then offered it to me. "I can't wait to enjoy a year's worth of your so-called humor in my castle."

I took the glass, holding it to my lips. "Are you always this cheerful, or is it just with me?"

I drank deeply despite the pain in my throat. The vampire watched me as I did. He held his answer until the glass was empty.

"What you see is what you get. If you want to back out now, I'll understand."

Oh no. He wasn't getting rid of me that easily.

"I'm not backing out."

"Of course you aren't." He refilled my glass, then glared at me until I took another sip, tracking the movement with his head canted to one side. "Consent is essential to this process, and if the feedings make you ill..."

"I need this job, just like you need me. I can handle it."

Bastien leaned down so that our noses were mere inches apart. Fear crowded into my senses, but I pushed it back. I wasn't going to let him intimidate me. "I do *not* need you. Make no mistake."

I held his gaze, not giving an inch. He was lying. He did need me. We'd sealed our pact, and now he had no choice but to keep me. He might not like me or trust me, nor I him, but we needed each other. Just for very different reasons.

"Claire!" someone screamed off in the distance.

I sat up straight, my attention turning to the door. No one knew my name except Sera. The muffled sounds of struggle had me on my feet despite the lingering nausea.

"Get your hands off me!" Grunts. "Claire!" the voice screamed again. "Claire! Where are you?"

CHAPTER 5
RETROUVER
CLAIRE

My heart leapt into my throat at the sight of a female vampire clutching my little sister by the root of her hair.

"Look what I found snooping around," the vampire said teasingly. She wore her dark brown hair in a braid that coiled down her shoulder like a snake. Her blouse was ivory satin inlaid with pearl buttons and detailed with gold appliqué. Most surprising, however, were her trousers—perfectly tailored to her long, lithe body.

She was beautiful. The only thing amiss was the red welt on her cheek. Sera grunted as the vampire dragged her inside the room.

An angry scream tore from my throat. "Let her go!"

Before I could think better of it, I snatched a candelabra from a nearby table and ran toward the woman, intent on doing as much damage as I could, but I was stopped by Bastien.

He caught me around the waist and pulled me back against his chest. "Not so fast, Miss Donadieu." He plucked the weapon out of my grip, then set it back on the table. "This is my niece, Lady Natalia. She's my second-in-command," he explained. His lips moving against my ear. Voice low. "You'd do well not to attack her again. Especially when I'm not around to stop you. Understand?"

I tried to squirm out of his grip, but he only held me tighter. "Stop." At the command, I froze, my skin heating despite his coldness. "I'm assuming you know this woman," he asked.

"Yes. Of course. She-she's my *everything,*" I said, tears burning in my eyes as Natalia dragged Seraphina across the carpet. "Stop hurting her!"

Natalia snorted. Her red lips quirked in a frown. Her tiny nose crinkled in disgust. "Does *my everything* have a name? Something you call her in polite company."

"If only there were polite company around."

I bit my lip. I shouldn't have said that. Mama would be disappointed. I was supposed to be acting soft and sweet. Docile, even, to earn their trust. That was the point of the mission. But it was hard to act sweet around these vampires, especially when one of them had a fistful of my sister's hair, and the other was intent on hating me.

"Watch your tongue, *Miss,*" Natalia said, giving a sharp tug on Sera's hair that made her yelp.

"Stop!" I cried. Desperate to do whatever it took to get her to let her go. "Her name is Sera Donadieu. She's my little sister."

Natalia paused, canting her head to one side. "A Donadieu? From the Nightfall Convent?"

We both nodded. Sera wincing as she did. Seeding the lie. Since I couldn't bring my own parentage scroll to the Sanguination Ball without giving our plot away, I had to forge one. The most uncomplicated identity to assume was that of a girl without parents. *Donadieu* was the surname given to the orphans of Nightfall, the land south and west of the capital. The convent not far from Prideaux Hill. The orphans housed at the convent were those of dead soldiers, more often than not. Victims of the vampire's relentless pursuit of territory.

"Well, well," Natalia said, an eyebrow lifted. "Two little orphan girls." She shifted her attention to Bastien. "Uncle, you've truly outdone yourself this time." Her smile flattened. "I thought we agreed no more strays at Château Rose."

"This stray bit my leg when I tried to leave," Bastien quipped.

Bit him? If I remembered correctly, he was the one who bit me.

Natalia laughed dryly, then pointed to the red welt on her cheek. "Looks like bad behavior runs in the family."

Sera gave me a sheepish grin, and I tried to hide my shock. She'd slapped a vampire. A brave but reckless move. Something worse than this could've happened to her, and I would've never forgiven myself.

I shifted in his grip, but Bastien's hand flattened against my stomach, holding me still. The back of my body flush against his. He was too close. *Much too close.* The intoxicating aroma of bergamot and fresh pine wound its way through senses, reminding me of cool nights beside warm fires.

I focused on my hatred of him—on the fact that I was now a spy, and my job was to collect information about his knowledge of the demonic relics and their whereabouts. "Please, Your Grace. Tell the Lady to release my sister. She only wanted to ensure I was okay. I'm the only family she has."

There was silence, and for a second, I wondered what he was planning to do with her. Whether she'd be taken prisoner or if they'd extract justice for striking a vampire noble. Instead, he relaxed his hold on my waist. I used the opportunity to put space between us, daring to take a step closer to Sera, who was too proud to beg for her own freedom.

"Lady Natalia, let the girl go."

Thank Diana.

"As you command, *Your Grace*," Natalia said, releasing her hold on Seraphina's hair.

My sister rushed to me, wrapping her arms around my middle and squeezing me tight. I smoothed my hand over the back of her head, hoping she wasn't in too much pain.

"Are you alright, Clairey?" Sera asked in a whisper.

I choked on a sob. Sera was the only person in our coven who treated me like I wasn't broken, and the only one I'd do absolutely anything for. I nodded. "Yes, I'm fine. Just a little sore. How are you?"

"No worse for the wear," she replied. I could hear the hint of pride in her voice.

From the corner of my eye, I watched Bastien walk around us to stand beside Natalia. The two of them spoke in Sanguisi, the language of vampires. I took Sera's face between my hands, my gaze tracing every inch of her to ensure she hadn't been harmed. Sera did the same, but when her attention narrowed on my neck, she sucked in a sharp breath.

"Oh, Claire." Tears sparkled in her eyes. "That looks *awful*."

I didn't want her to be sad. I wanted her to be proud. *I'd done it.* Against all odds, I'd been taken into the Duke's service. I would endure a thousand bites if it meant finding the location of every demonic relic for her. Once I did, Mama and the coven would destroy them, and at last, Sera would be safe. She wouldn't have to lead our family's war against dark magick. She could live a blessed life practicing her gift in peace.

As I stared into her eyes, I watched her brown irises turn bronze, like a shield catching the light of the sun, just like they always did when she was casting a spell. Before I could stop her, the tingle of magick tickled over my neck, easing the worst of the pain caused by the choker.

I couldn't believe she dared to use magick in a room full of vampires. It was so, so reckless. And all because I couldn't do it myself. The shame welled inside me until tears flooded my eyes. She shouldn't be wasting her magick on me. Sera still needed to make it back home in one piece, and this time, she'd be traveling alone. The full moon was a week away, and she wouldn't be able to recharge her powers until then. I leaned my forehead against hers in a silent *thank you*, but the moment was short-lived.

"I wonder how two orphan girls came to own such fine dresses," Natalia said to Bastien in the Common Tongue, loud enough for us to hear.

I took Sera's hand in mine. Mama had prepared us for their suspicion. "The dresses were donated to the convent by the Dame of Nightfall for any girl wishing to attend your Sanguination." I ran my hand over the smooth black lace covering the boning of the bodice. "With a few modifications, we were able to make them fit."

The best part about this answer was that it wasn't a lie. The Dame of Nightfall, a member of the human aristocracy, donated dresses each month to orphan girls who desired the income of a sanguine partner. With a bit of planning and a lot of magick, our coven was able to secure these two.

The vampires stared at us like they weren't sure what to make of our story. "The Dame is in attendance tonight," I offered. "Question her if you wish."

Natalia went to move, like she was going to do just that, when Bastien gave a slight shake of his head. "I have no desire to remain at Château Corbin, questioning nobles. Now that I have my new sanguine partner, we ride for Roselyn."

He reached inside his pocket and removed a small coin

purse. With a thoughtful look at my sister, he tossed it to her. Sera caught the leather pouch with a curious look. Inside, there were gold and silver coins. Both of our mouths dropped.

"Your Grace?" Sera asked.

His pale blue eyes flicked from me to my sister. However, his hard, chiseled features remained stoic. "Considering the circumstances, I'm assuming Miss Donadieu would prefer you to have her first month's earnings. She will want for nothing at my castle, and that purse will provide you with enough money to return to Nightfall comfortably."

To say I was shocked by the gesture would be an understatement, but I told myself it didn't mean anything about Bastien other than he had a conscience. If he believed Sera and I were orphans, then perhaps he felt guilty. His warmongering had left countless children without parents. Either way, when Sera brought Mama the extra coin, it would be of great help as they plotted their next moves. It meant more weapons. More rare ingredients for potions.

"I guess this is goodbye," I said, trying to be strong. Sera melted into my arms, hugging me tight.

"It's not goodbye. It's see you soon," she whispered.

I looked at her one last time, at the stubborn upturn of her nose, and nodded. With her head held high, my sister followed Natalia out of the room, turning to wave one last time before disappearing down the hall. I pressed my lips together, trying to keep the sob buried in my throat. The vampire didn't make a move to comfort me. He simply waltzed to the door, picked up his cane, and waited for me with an expectant look.

When I didn't move, he expelled an annoyed breath. "Miss Donadieu, are you coming?"

CHAPTER 6

DEVOIR

BASTIEN

The sound of hooves beating on paving stones and the creak of wheels came. Moments later, my coach appeared. Its black carriage and riders a welcome sight. *Unlike the woman beside me.*

The one whose heartbeat was pulsing inside my bloodstone. The one who was marked by my bite. I'd never been more conflicted in my life. Somehow, I'd taken the blood of my mate and hadn't lost my head. However, I'd lost something much more precious. My free will. I realized I no longer belonged to myself. But to her.

The blind panic I'd experienced when she'd fainted in my arms was something I never wanted to experience again. And yet, with her phobia of blood, it seemed an inevitability. In the short term, I'd avoid feeding from her. I'd gone hungry before. Then, when we arrived at Château Rose, I'd ask Imogen for answers.

My fingers grazed the throbbing stone hiding under my shirt, the one that had named her my mate. As I did, I caught myself studying the way the moon shone on her hair, turning

39

the loose lavender strands into a rainbow of color as they whipped around her heart-shaped face. She was an infinitely beautiful problem. I hated the thought, despised myself for thinking it, but couldn't look away.

I knew I made her uneasy. I could tell by the way she held herself and the way she kept shooting sidelong glances in my direction. If she hated me, all the better. It would make resisting her easier.

The coach came to a grinding halt and a footman hopped down, making a fuss over opening the door and preparing the steps. Claire hugged her arms against a sudden gust of wind, and I struggled to hold back a smirk. If she thought this was cold, she was in for an awakening. My castle was tucked away in the northwestern foothills of the mountains. Snow decorated the pines nearly year-round and the wind was unforgiving.

I suppose it would be my responsibility to keep her warm. Marius's voice lanced through my unhelpful thoughts. "Why is my general leaving so soon?"

So much for stealing away while the party raged on. I'd done my due diligence by attending the ball, as Marius demanded, and now it was time to go. Two members of my family accompanied him—my brother Claude and his son, the little wretch, Tyson.

My *heir*.

Marius stopped short of where we stood. A glass of red wine in one hand, the other resting on the hilt of his sword. Subtlety had never been his strong suit.

Claude and Tyson stood beside him, looking as much alike as father and son could. Dark brown hair and bronze skin. They both had the air of vampires that lived far too comfortably. Their strength earned by practicing in the training yard, not real battle.

Taking a sip of wine and eyeing Claire in a way that made my fists clench, Marius continued. "I thought you'd stick around for a dance or two. Make small talk with the courtiers. You know, reassure the people that they're in good hands."

Make small talk with courtiers? Perhaps the wine had washed out his good sense. I wasn't someone who offered reassurances. I was good at two things: building alliances and ending lives.

Dried leaves swirled around our feet. Even this far south, the usually warm air had turned crisp. "The seasons are changing. I have little time to send troops through the mountain passes before they're iced over. I cannot linger."

Marius and Claude exchanged looks, and I wondered what they'd really come to say, especially with Tyson in tow. He had his eighteenth name day this past year, and appeared a man grown. In Tyson's case, I suspected the spoiled boy would take a millennium to actually mature.

I introduced Miss Donadieu, who curtsied and smiled. I wasn't sure if the money I'd given her sister had muzzled her, or, if in the aftermath of our first bite, she realized she was in over her head.

Little did she know, Natalia was arranging for her sister to be followed by a scout. I didn't like loose ends any more than I liked small talk.

"The Viscount is eager to ride with his uncle and learn more about the lands he's to inherit. Whenever you see fit to find your mate and return to the capital."

I stilled, barely daring to breathe, not wanting to give anything away. "I've explained that won't be happening. I don't think the mated life would suit me the way it suits Claude." My lip curled in the suggestion of a grin.

"Same old Bastien, I see," Claude deadpanned. "Content to die alone in that frozen wasteland you call home."

"If my life is so unappealing to you, then withdraw your petition to have your second son appointed as *my* heir."

He eyed me sharply. "We may be immortal, but none of us will live forever. The treaty must be upheld and you are heirless."

"I have trained Lady Natalia."

Claude ran a frustrated hand through his coal-black hair, a color he hadn't been born with, but *reborn* with. A physical manifestation of the family allegiances we sacrificed to become what we are. As if the change in our deadened hearts hadn't been enough.

"She is Josse's child. His *heir*. If she would only..."

"Enough," I snapped.

The following silence was dark and hollow. We'd disagreed on this many times before. I'd been outvoted in favor of a male-only inheritance. The urge to argue the ridiculousness of it rose inside of me, but Claude pressed on, side-stepping the real issue once again.

"Take Tyson with you," he demanded. "He's the best fighter in the training yard, and has run out of challengers."

I snorted in response. My family didn't find any humor in it though.

Claire, who had been quiet, was watching me with big, brown eyes framed by thick lashes. The look she gave me stole my breath. In an instant, I was consumed by her. My attention sinking to the luscious curve of her lips. My own parted, desperate to taste her—to seal our bond. I regarded her neck and the lace choker that was coated with dried blood, and my suspicion resurfaced.

Why would an orphan girl dabble in magick? Didn't she understand the consequences? There was something about her I couldn't place. That necklace left too many questions unanswered. I was going to have my hands full with her. There was no doubt about that. Babysitting a spoiled princeling while trying not to lose myself to the mate bond was going to be impossible.

"These aren't sparring matches in the ring, boy," I told my nephew, tearing my attention away from Claire. "The Lawless Lands are just that. *Lawless.* The witches who reside there don't live by our treaty. They are still at war with one another. The Light and the Dark. We are the only thing standing between our people and safety. Are you ready to cross blades with a demon, to die if necessary, to maintain that balance?"

Claire's heartbeat drummed faster against my chest, and I set a hand over it if only to ensure the light wasn't visible from behind my dagger. She wasn't just nervous. I could feel her fear deepening. She was afraid.

Good. She should be.

Tyson pretended he wasn't. He puffed out his chest, which made me laugh. The boy responded with a hard glare that didn't intimidate me in the least. He had been born a vampire, raised with the comforts of the capital. He didn't have the humility that came with suffering a human death, or an appreciation for delicate peace that made us what we are.

"I'm well aware of the dangers, Uncle. I'm ready for the challenge. Hector and Chastity will concede to our terms, and when they do, we'll win more land to rule." He paused, then added, "Ever since I've been named your heir, my little brothers have been begging me to get them a castle too."

Win more land? Is that what he thought this was about? *Palaces for lordlings?* In a single, vicious motion, I swept my cane out and cracked it across the back of his knees. Tyson's legs buckled, and he hit the stones hard, the air whooshing from his lungs. Before he could scramble upright, I caught him by the throat and hauled him up until his boots barely scraped the ground. Darkness bled into my vision as the monster within slipped its leash, baring its teeth.

The courtyard went silent, save for Tyson's choking breaths.

"You think this is a game?" I snarled. "That we bleed so your brothers can decorate another castle?"

Tyson gripped my wrist, trying to pry my fingers off his windpipe. But he wasn't nearly as strong as I was. No. Few were.

Claire let out an audible gasp, and that one little noise had me tilting my chin in her direction. Her fear curled around my senses, distracting me. Her heartbeat racing once again.

She wasn't just afraid. I was scaring her. Something uncomfortable twisted inside my chest at the realization. I gritted my teeth, squeezing Tyson's neck harder. So what if I was scaring her? If fear drove her away from me, all the better.

If I let down my guard and gave in to the mate bond, this *boy* would become the Duke of Roselyn, in charge of holding the line between our lands, and I'd be banished to this gilded place—*with her.*

I couldn't let that happen.

I regarded my nephew with disgust. In all his well-kept southern finery—the royal blue of his father's crest, the gold chains and rings and silk trimmings—the boy looked hopelessly unprepared. He wouldn't survive an hour in the Lawless Lands. Nor would the soldiers respect him. This war was *my* burden. Not his. I'd been fighting for hundreds of years. Forging alliances he couldn't hope to understand.

"The Duke of Roselyn does not conquer land for castles, boy. We have a higher purpose."

"Enough of the theatrics, Bastien," Marius drawled. "We only ask out of courtesy. Tyson will accompany you. He needs to be tested."

I cursed under my breath as I shoved the little wretch aside, resigning myself to my fate for the second time this evening. I knew I had to take him with me. If I tried to challenge Marius and it came to crossed swords, there was a chance he'd see my awakened bloodstone and know the truth: that I'd taken my mate as my sanguine partner, against our laws, and sought to deceive him.

It was best to take the boy with me.

"I can't protect him from his own foolishness," I told Claude, who nodded.

"All I ask is that you train him as you've trained Lady Natalia. Teach him how to lead, Bastien."

My lip curled, and I shook my head. Restlessness coursing through my limbs. There was nothing I could do to make Natalia my heir—not without Josse's blessing, which meant I was done with this conversation. It was time to leave. "Call for your sanguine partner and your trunk. We leave for Roselyn immediately." I spat at the boy's feet. "Keep your ridiculous courtly attire here. You won't need it where we're going."

My nephew fled in a flash of shadow, his father behind him. I watched him go with a sinking feeling in my gut. No good would come of this. Marius, content with his trouble-making, waved his wine glass in the air.

"I hope to see you at the next Sanguination Ball. Until then. Brother. Miss Donadieu." He bowed. "Adieu, *mon sang*."

Once he was gone, I seized Claire's hand and guided her toward the coach.

"Get in."

She shot me a look that would've made a lesser man cower. "You don't need to take your bad mood out on me. I didn't invite your nephew."

"Get in, *please*," I added through my teeth.

Claire rolled her eyes, but did as she was told. A footman

handed me the reins to my horse, Lucien. His black mane a welcome sight. With one easy motion, I mounted.

"Aren't you riding with me?" Claire asked, pausing on the topmost step of the coach.

Me? Ride? In the carriage? *With her?* Absolutely not. Generals didn't ride in carriages.

"I ride with the guard." My lip curled in a reluctant smile. "My nephew can keep you company."

Before anything else could be said, I motioned to the footman, and he snapped the door shut. I didn't want to see her reaction. I didn't want to see her at all.

CHAPTER 7
CRAINDRE
CLAIRE

We rode at an unforgiving pace for three days, never stopping except to change horses. When we did, Lady Natalia would force a skin of water into my hand and demand I drink. Otherwise, none of the riders spoke to me.

I saw Bastien only briefly during that time. There was never an opportunity to exchange more than a glance with the vampire I was supposed to be spying on. Sometimes, when I couldn't sleep, I'd open the curtains and watch him: a lone figure in moonlight, riding beside us, hair unbound and bright against the dark. His jaw set. His mouth a hard, tempting line. I wondered if his necklace was still pulsing like a heartbeat, and what that meant, but I knew he'd never humor my curiosity.

Frustrated, I closed the curtains and let out an exasperated huff, which drew the attention of my only companions: Bastien's nephew and his sanguine partner, a young woman named Lady Okeri Djannelle. A human noble who'd grown up in the capital.

More often than not, Tyson was grumbling about being

locked inside a carriage instead of being allowed to ride. Lady Okeri listened to his bellyaching with mild disinterest as she massaged a sweet-smelling cream on her mahogany skin until it glistened.

Neither seemed interested in me except in fleeting bursts, like when they produced a deck of cards and wanted to play to pass the time—some game from the capital they called *Dépouiller*, which took me the better part of a day to learn. They said it was more fun with strong drink and more people and quickly lost interest.

I didn't mind when they ignored me. I was used to being invisible. It was the daily feedings that were more difficult to ignore. At sunset, when the last rays were streaking through the sky, Lady Okeri would set her hand on Tyson's cheek and examine him.

"You need to eat," she'd say without fail.

He'd make some joke about being 'full of himself' that he likely found funny, but Okeri didn't. And neither did I. "Laugh all you want, Tyson, but no matter how full you claim to be, by sunset you look weak."

This caught my attention. From the corner of my eye, I watched them locked in debate about this perceived weakness, wondering if vampires needed blood *every day* to maintain their strength. Swallowing hard, I wondered if Bastien expected to feed from *me* that often.

Okeri tilted her head to the side, pulling back her curly hair, and offering herself to him. "I can't stand that sickly look in your eyes. Just do it."

Gripping the side of her neck, Tyson pulled her close. "If you insist."

I looked away in an effort to avoid swooning, but there was no escaping the way Lady Okeri gasped when his lips found her neck or the sound of him swallowing mouthfuls of her like she was sweetened tea on a stifling day.

A sheen of sweat broke out across my brow and my hands began to shake. I didn't know how I was going to endure the same once we arrived at Château Rose, so I put it out of my mind.

In the hours I spent in silence, I stared out the window and thought of Sera. Hoping my little sister made it back home without doing something reckless. At night, when I could sleep, I dreamed of seeing her again in the graveyard outside our house. Watching her cast spells under the light of the full moon. Happy and whole.

My dreams never remained sweet for long. They'd weave into nightmares that left me drenched in sweat. Images of a graveyard turned bloody, of bodies littered between grave-stones. And of a wolf with piercing eyes coming to claim Sera's life.

On the morning of the fourth day, when I had a terrible crick in my neck from sleeping on the tufted bench and barely exercising my legs, we stopped at a small inn on the bank of a lake that looked as big as the ocean, just as the sun was setting.

I'd studied enough maps to know this must be Emerald Lake. And by the sun's position, I knew we were near the northern bank, just south of Swift River. Nearly midway between the capital and Château Rose.

Part of me was excited to be allowed out of the coach for a proper meal, but another part of me was terrified of what was waiting: the Duke of Roselyn, and his teeth.

I searched for the moon's shape in the sky, wanting to say a small prayer to Diana, asking for her protection. The moon would be full in three nights' time, and when it was, Sera and my family would be able to recharge their magick. But luck was against me. The sky had turned into a riot of colors that reminded me of wildflowers in spring. Pinks and blues and pale purples, all reflected on the smooth surface of the water.

When the door to the coach was opened, goosebumps lifted on my skin, pebbling my flesh in the bitter chill of the evening. My companions exited first; I followed after, my arms hugged tight around my body, teeth chattering as I descended the wooden steps. My aching legs stiff as I stepped onto the dirt road in front of the inn.

A wooden sign out front read *"Tooth* and *Hare,"* and was adorned with a picture of a bloody rabbit in the jaws of a wolf.

How... *pleasant.*

"What a dump," Lady Okeri said under her breath, gesturing to the sod-roofed building. Her voice carried a rich tenor that made her sound so sure of herself. "The Duke can afford better accommodations than this."

I thought the inn looked quaint, and I was especially interested in the line of smoke puffing from the chimney, which meant warm food and a cozy fire. The smell of roasting meat hung heavy in the air, and my stomach growled.

Tyson shook out a long fur-lined cloak and settled it around Lady Okeri's well-defined shoulders. "I'm sure he *could* find better accommodations, but my uncle prefers to watch us squirm so he can call us soft. It's all part of the test, you see."

Offering her his arm, Tyson escorted his sanguine partner toward the inn. Their heads bent together in laughter, chuckling over some private joke. The long royal blue cloak emblazoned with the golden sigil of House Allard flowing in her wake—a moon, a blade, and a coiled serpent encircled by twelve small stars.

Absently, I wondered what it was like to be that close to someone—other than my sister. Or to have a man place a cloak around my chilly, exposed shoulders and make light of this bad situation with me.

I found Bastien scowling as he shouldered a pack. I knew I would never have the kind of relationship with my vampire that Okeri had with hers, which was fine by me. I didn't want the Duke to be my friend. I hated him. I despised being in his company. And he clearly despised being in mine.

After watching Tyson with Lady Okeri, I'd been expecting Bastien to come for me, but he hadn't. Instead, the past three days had been a reprieve from his irritating presence.

At the same time, something inside me stirred. Something deep and dark that he'd awakened at the ball. His white shirt was a ruin of dirt and sweat that clung to the muscles of his chest. The sleeves pushed up his corded forearms. His black trousers and riding boots snug against the thick lines of his legs. He gathered the tangled strands of his hair into his hand and tied them off, pulling every sharp line of his face into focus.

My attention narrowed on his lips, which were the only thing soft about his face. The memory of those lips ghosting over my neck infiltrated my thoughts, and warmth filled my cheeks. That night, when I'd asked him what he was doing, he replied, *"Trying to appeal to another one of your instincts."*

He'd been trying to make me *want* him. And the scariest part? It had worked. I couldn't remember wanting anything more. Except, perhaps, magick of my own. It made me wonder if there really was something wrong with me. Something broken. Something that repelled Diana's light from within if I could harbor such desire for a vampire.

I stewed on this thought for a long time. After three days in a cushy cage, I decided my inexperience was to blame. Bastien was the first man to touch me. To make me feel wanted. Of course it tugged on some primal instinct. Besides, it wasn't like I meant anything to him. It was all for show. So he could drink my… blood.

I shook the thought from my head and strode forward, ready to be inside the warmth of the inn, when a woman appeared at the door, wearing an apron and holding a wooden ladle. I stopped dead in my tracks—my breath stilling.

Her long, fiery red hair marked her for what she was. A Dark Witch.

Diana, protect me.

I stumbled back, knowing that prayers wouldn't help me now. Witches of the Darkness kept company with demons. Their power was unnatural. An affront to the power of the moon. She'd kill me where I stood if she knew who my mother was.

"Rabbit stew and crusty bread for your companions, Your Grace, and bitter red wine for you!"

I backed up a pace, then another. Keeping company with vampires was one thing, but I couldn't break bread with a Witch of Darkness. It would likely be poisoned. Maybe that's what my vampire overlord had planned. Me, face down in a bowl of soup.

My chest locked tight, breath scraping against my throat. The witch's eyes found mine, and I couldn't look away. Did she know who I was? Could she smell what I was? The enemy, sent to spy upon her evil deeds and sniff out the location of her precious relics.

It was too much to leave to chance. I needed to get out of here. I needed to hide. But there was nothing around except thickly wooded forests that were likely crawling with Dark Witches, and the lake, which likely concealed water demons.

I didn't have magick. I couldn't defend myself.

With a million terrible thoughts swirling in my head, I retreated for the safety of the coach. At least if I was in the coach, I could bar the door. In my haste, I nearly tripped but managed to stay on my feet. My pulse pounded in my ears so hard I could barely hear my own ragged breath. The coppery taste of iron coated my tongue, as though blood was already filling my mouth. The world tilted with each step, my vision tunneling until the coach was the only thing I could see.

I stumbled on the top step but caught myself, reaching for the rail, when a hand closed around mine, yanking me back.

CHAPTER 8
HAUNTER
CLAIRE

I knew who it was without looking. No one's hand was as cold as Bastien's. "The inn is this way," the vampire said, his voice laced with amusement. I tried to pull my hand away, but his grip was iron. As I struggled against him, his smile faded.

"Stop."

The command rippled through me. I froze in place. My eyes snapped to his. The humor in his expression had fled, replaced by a curious look as he studied me. "You're cold," he said, softer now.

He reached into his pack and extracted a long cloak lined with ermine fur, and swung it around my shoulders. It was the same style as the one Okeri wore, but black. His fingers brushed over my bare collarbone as he fastened the clasp at my throat. The touch of his hand, the sudden weight of the cloak, the faint scent of pine and earth on his skin pulled me back into my body. But only barely. This cloak could keep out the cold. Not curses.

"Something is bothering you. Tell me what it is." His deep

voice managed to hold an edge of command despite being whisper-soft.

For a moment, I considered keeping quiet. If I said nothing, maybe we could eat, sleep, and leave without incident. Maybe the witch would never suspect what I was. But her flaming hair burned in my mind. My pulse throbbed so hard against Bastien's fingers, I knew he could feel it. The longer I stayed silent, the more it felt like my fear was filling the space between us.

"Tell me," he repeated.

He wasn't just asking. He was giving me the smallest of choices—speak or let him drag me inside.

I swallowed hard, the words scraping my throat as they fought their way free. "Dark Witches run this place," I said in a hush, lest they hear me. "We can't stay."

He considered me for a moment, head canted to one side. "Shreesa means us no harm. Her family has run this inn for generations. These witches practice their craft quietly and within the bounds of the law."

Anger rose in my blood. This was the problem with vampires. They always sided with darkness. If he genuinely cared what they did—he'd be acting differently, which was why I had to know what he knew about the demonic relics. My coven would fix this. "That's what they want you to believe," I said through my teeth.

He narrowed his eyes. "You're afraid."

If I wasn't so angry, I might've laughed. He would be afraid, too, if his family graveyard was filled with the bones of those killed by dark magick. While I couldn't offer *that* explanation, I could play up my false identity as an orphan.

"Yes, of course, I'm afraid. I was raised at Nightfall. The convent has no love for Dark Witches and demons. I'd been told stories all my life of how they eat children."

Bastien cracked a smile. The quirk of his lips softened the rest of his face. "The nuns only told you those stories to scare you into behaving."

I straightened. Furious he was making light of this. "Sister Vera said she'd seen one eat a child whole."

A half-truth. My aunt wasn't a sister of the faith, but she swore she saw a Dark Witch's jaw unhinge like a snake, showcasing a mouth full of pointed teeth.

Bastien chuckled at that. "Well, as noble as Sister Vera is, I can assure you Witches of Darkness don't eat children." He put his arm around my shoulders, pulling me close against his side, and wheeled me around to face the inn. "But they do make excellent stew. I think a hot meal will do you good." He paused, then added, "As your duke, I am mandated to provide for your well-being."

I glared up at the vampire. He was wearing the same half grin he'd sported when he invited me to the balcony. Charming and debonair. Accustomed to getting his way with a wink. But his good looks wouldn't work on me again. I knew his dark side. The one that was temperamental and mean. "I'm not going in."

"Miss Donadieu," he said, bending down to bring his face level with mine. His voice a low purr. "Do you think anyone here is as frightening as me?"

I lifted my chin. Trying to be brave. "You're not frightening."

On one hand, it was a bald-faced lie. A part of me was very afraid of his fangs, his strength, and his coldness. But on the other, there was something reassuring in his eyes that let me know I was safe. No one here could hurt me, so long as I was with him.

He cupped my chin, holding me in place when I tried to look away. "I swear on my life, no one will eat you."

I contemplated the vampire staring into my eyes and the vow he'd made to keep me safe. It opened the well of guilt that lived in the pit of my stomach. All my life, I'd been told I was a liability. Without magick, I couldn't hope to survive outside our family property, especially not around Witches of the Darkness. I'd been told it was too dangerous to take me on hunts because that meant one of my family members would be tasked with defending me, and it would make the party weaker.

When I offered to learn other skills, like explosives or archery, I was laughed at and told to stay out of sight. Now, I was far outside of the safety of Prideaux Hill, sent on a vow to spy for my family. Which meant doing things that I was afraid of.

I studied the Duke, searching his face as I'd watched Lady Okeri do with Tyson. He was trying to hide behind his smile, but I could see that he was weakened. His eyes were shadowed and cheeks more sunken after days without eating.

Good. If he was weak, all the better.

I swallowed hard. For a heartbeat, I considered digging my heels into the dirt and refusing him. Would he drag me inside anyway? Leave me out here in the gathering darkness as punishment? Behind us, the forest loomed like a wall of black teeth, and the lake glimmered like an open maw, daring me to run.

Mama would tell me to stop being so emotional and act logically. It would be foolish to pass up this opportunity to learn more. If the witches were practicing dark magick, they must have a demonic relic hidden on the property. It was my job to find it and get word back to my family so they could strike. I knew what I had to do, but I didn't like it one bit. I pressed my lips together and nodded. "Okay. Fine. I'll stay."

Bastien's thumb stroked across my cheek. His gaze

thoughtful. "There's some measure of bravery in you." He released his hold on my chin, frowning. "Or maybe it's stubbornness."

An awkward beat passed between us. Neither of us moved. A chilly breeze blew the fine hairs around my face. "Maybe it's both," I replied.

"Indeed."

With a stony expression, he offered me his arm, and with hesitance, I took it. Walking with halting steps toward the entrance of the inn. My heart was a drum in my chest, beating out a too fast rhythm when we entered. I forced myself to pay attention to every little detail. Inside, it was warm, and smoke from the fire burned my eyes. Magicked lanterns hung above trestle tables, overflowing with food, drink, and Bastien's guard.

I counted three red-haired women moving through the dining room, serving drinks and stew. Surely there were more lurking in the shadows. I caught one of the witches staring at me, and a bolt of fear lanced through my heart.

"Do you want to wash before dinner?" Bastien asked, speaking close so I could hear him over the sound of a lute and the low hum of conversation. "I had your trunk brought inside."

I hesitated. While hiding upstairs to collect my nerve sounded appealing, I needed to take control of my fear. No one was going to hurt me. They wouldn't dare. And as disgusting as I was after four days on the road, so was Bastien. And so was his guard. Even Okeri and Tyson were seated beside the fire. Her, eating. Him, sipping wine.

If I was going to earn an ounce of credibility, I had to show strength. "No. I'm fine. I-I should eat."

"Look at that. Something we agree on." He gave me a pleasant smile. I scowled back at him. Bastien guided me to the back of the establishment, close to the fire and a grimy window that overlooked the lake, where Natalia sat waiting.

She was enjoying a glass of wine with one of her booted feet propped up on the bench. She was the kind of beautiful that was sharp and intimidating. With her thick braid and high cheekbones. However, the red welt Sera had given her was healed.

I sat across from her, avoiding her eye, and Bastien took his place beside me on the bench. I wanted to ask Natalia how Sera got off after the ball but was distracted by the presence of two Dark Witches. My pulse, already pounding in my ears, quickened like I was running uphill. A young witch with copper hair set a glass of wine down in front of the vampire and placed a mug of what appeared to be mead before me. I had no love for the sickly sweet flavor and turned my nose up at it. Another witch set down a trencher of bread covered in steaming hot stew, which was arguably harder to ignore.

She handed me a fork and said, "Enjoy, Miss." I recoiled. Sliding closer to the vampire beside me. My shoulder pressed into Bastien's, his thigh a solid line against mine. Even through layers of wool, I could feel his unnatural coolness.

My fear of these witches was as real as the chunks of meat in the stew, and my insides crawled with disgust despite how hungry I was.

When the witch left for the kitchen, I tracked her movement. When she was gone, I shifted in my seat so that I was no longer touching the Duke. I skeptically eyed a pair of witches as Bastien passed them a silver coin. He shouldn't be paying them. He should have their heads on spikes outside his castle gates.

One of the witches pointed to the itchy scabs on my neck—the ones that Mama's choker had cut into my skin—and muttered something to the other. "We can have Granny prepare a poultice for those wounds to prevent infection, Miss."

"No!" I replied too loudly, wary of anything they might give me. But the strange looks I was receiving from my vampire companions forced me to clarify. I lifted my hand to the choker, playing my part. "No more dabbling in magick, I meant to say. I've learned my lesson. I can heal on my own."

Bastien covered my hand with his, his fingers curling around my palm, and gave me an encouraging squeeze. I stared at the place where our hands were joined, unmoving. He didn't say anything. Didn't apologize, or tell me I was being irrational. He just *touched* me. His presence warmed my entire body, despite the temperature of his skin. It was strange having this vampire comfort me when I was scared. No one did that for me. No one but Sera.

I reminded myself that he wasn't doing it for my benefit but out of self-interest. He was hungry. Above all else, I had to keep that in perspective. He was using me just as much as I was using him.

"A poultice isn't magick, Miss," the witch tried to clarify. "Just a bundle of garden herbs steeped in Gran's special tea."

Gran's special tea, indeed.

At least she still had *her* Gran. Mine had been *killed* by one of them: a dark spell fired directly at her chest, turning her heart to graveworms. Bastien dragged his thumb across the back of my wrist in a slow, soothing motion. I drew in a steadying breath, and refocused on my mission. Not the comfort his touch elicited.

I didn't believe the witch for a second. She was just saving face in front of the Duke. All my coven's healing magick was born from the power in their blood and the gift of Diana's blessing from the moon, like when Sera performed the pain relief spell. I didn't want to be infected with whatever demonic magick they infused into their healing salves.

But just because I took it didn't mean I'd have to use it. I swallowed my fear and my malice and offered the girl a smile that I hoped looked more like a snarl. "In that case, any help would be very welcome."

She curtsied and hurried off. My grin flattened as soon as her back was turned. The words were sandpaper on my tongue. Asking a Dark Witch for help, even if I didn't intend to use it, went against everything I'd ever been taught.

Bastien removed his hand from mine once they were gone, and I quickly placed mine in my lap. He went back to ignoring me, conversing with Natalia in their language. Even though I didn't understand Sanguisi, I could tell by the way they were talking and shooting glances at the boisterous red-haired woman with the ladle that it was about her. What did he call the witch? *Shreesa? Yes. That was it.*

I didn't let my attention linger on her. Instead, I decided to take in my surroundings. To the right was a set of stairs across the dining room, and to the left, a door that likely went to a kitchen. Other than the floating lanterns, there was little in the way of magick happening out here. The stuffed crows, bats, owls, and elk adorning the walls were a strange decor choice, but seemed harmless. I spied several smaller buildings through the grimy window, all with orange light glowing from their windows. I wondered if that was where they hid their relics and did their dark witchery. From everything Sera told me, the Dark Witches concealed the relics in unlikely places, guarded with protection spells and traps.

Without magick, I couldn't hunt for them and undo the spells, but I was very good at being invisible. After years of being turned away from countless coven meetings, my curiosity demanded I learn to be silent. I'd gotten so good at it that my grandmother had called me the *Ghost of Prideaux Hill.*

A sudden rush of sadness made my throat constrict. Now, *she* was the ghost. It was easier to be angry than afraid. And I was very angry with these agents of darkness. I sat silent for a time, alone, even in a room filled with people, allowing the web of thoughts in my head time to untangle. I was jolted back to the present when Bastien's cool breath grazed my temple, his lips so close to the shell of my ear. I pressed mine together and closed my eyes to keep from gasping.

Each one of his slow exhales against my skin did something to me I couldn't explain. It was the same reaction I had the night of the ball. A warm pull of desire inside my core that curled its fingers around some primal need. He hadn't even touched me, but the soft place between my thighs reacted as if he had. A buzz of anticipation had me squeezing them together.

I had to do something to stop my body's reaction to him.

"Eat," he commanded.

The word a whisper against my skin. A slow wave of desire rolled through me, sending heat into my cheeks.

I ran my tongue across my lips and straightened. I had to be stronger than this. I had to be the spy I swore I'd be. Not a simpering girl.

After cleansing my hands with one of the hot towels, I picked up my fork, lowering it to a piece of meat. Pretending it was a red-haired witch when I stabbed it. "Did my sister make it out of the capital okay?" I asked Natalia, while trying to convince myself to put what the witches *claimed* was rabbit into my mouth.

The vampire took a sip of her wine. Her clever eyes dragged from Bastien to me. I noticed that while she drank, he abstained; his glass was untouched. "Absolutely," she said, twisting the long stem between her fingers. "I packed her inside a coach myself. She's likely nearing Nightfall now." Her attention returned to Bastien. "If they rode as hard as we did."

I didn't miss the annoyed tone in her voice. And apparently, neither did Bastien.

"The harder we ride, the faster we return home. And for that, I will not apologize."

Natalia scoffed. "Just because I agree with you doesn't mean I like it." She drained the last of her thick red wine and set the glass down on the table. "If you'll excuse me, Uncle, I'm going to have my dinner." Glancing at me, she added, "You should do the same."

My hand stilled. I swallowed hard. Yes. Of course. His dinner.

"This conversation isn't over. Don't forget."

Natalia glanced over her shoulder at Shreesa. "I never forget, Your Grace. It's why you despise my counsel so."

He gave an irritated grunt. "Go. Eat. We'll speak later."

She disappeared without another word. Once she was gone, the Duke sighed, rubbing his temples before lowering his forearms to the table.

I slid a forkful of food into my mouth. The meat was well-seasoned and juicy. Spite was the only thing keeping me from moaning. I chewed slowly, savoring the flavor, as I tried to understand what *hadn't* been said between the two of them.

I'd been kept out of enough conversations to read between the lines. And I could tell that Bastien and Natalia had been arguing, likely about the witch, Shreesa, and they were going to meet up later to discuss it further. I speared another bite of meat and shoved it into my mouth. That seemed like a conversation I wanted to observe.

If Bastien thought I was going to stand meekly by his side while he plotted with Natalia, he had another thing coming. Tonight, the Ghost of Prideaux Hill was going to haunt a new locale.

CHAPTER 9
PENSER

CLAIRE

The inn grew rowdier as evening stretched on. Bastien's guard—composed mostly of human soldiers—was clearly enjoying the well-earned night off. They approached us where we sat to exchange a few words with the Duke. I, however, sat in silence, gazing out the window at the cluster of log homes crowded beside the lake, contemplating how to proceed.

I propped my chin in my hand and crossed my legs, nervous energy coursing through me. I was running out of time to come up with a plan. If Bastien caught me spying on him and Natalia, it would do little to forge the trust I was supposed to be gaining. I was playing a dangerous game with a vicious enemy. A game my family had been fighting for centuries. We were so close to eradicating the last sources of dark magick in the Unified Territories.

Still, doubt prickled in the back of my mind. How could I avoid being heard by a vampire? If I was caught and he sent me away, would Mama's choker kill me? Unable to hold still any longer, I turned from the window to find Bastien studying me.

He immediately focused on the table when he realized he'd been caught. Picking at a scratch in the wood with one of his long fingers.

I didn't know why, but the fact that he had been watching me caused a burst of heat and adrenaline to flush my cheeks. Which *infuriated* me.

The peace House Allard claimed to protect was a farce. My coven knew the truth. The vampires sided with Dark Witches more often than not. The fact that we were sitting inside a Dark Witch's den was proof enough. So why? Why did the vampire's attention make me feel so... warm?

I went to pick up my mug of mead, just to do something with my hands, but the vampire pushed the mug out of my reach. Gaping at him, I said, "I'm thirsty."

He reached across the table, grabbed a pitcher and a cup, poured me a glass of water, and then pushed it into my hand. Lifting a brow, I took the cup and drank slowly, letting the cool liquid slide down my throat and watching him as I did.

Why the refusal? I considered the full glass of wine sitting in front of him.

I'd heard Mama lecture Sera a hundred times about how important it was for her to practice restraint, although she rarely listened. Did Bastien have the same philosophy? Did he want to remain sober because he was in charge? It was a plausible explanation. But why disallow me?

Then it hit me. He didn't want alcohol in my veins. Maybe it would affect him too. I let that thought bounce around in my head. How could this play to my advantage? If alcohol affected him as it affected me, then perhaps other things would, too.

A wicked plan took shape in my mind. One that might help dull his senses so that I could spy on him later tonight. The only problem with my plan was that it wouldn't affect Natalia, so I'd still need to be careful, but something told me she wasn't as attuned to me as he was. Besides, she had drained a glass of wine at the table. Maybe she'd have another after her feeding.

It wasn't a perfect plan, and I had no idea if it would work, but it was worth a try. When I finished my stew and chewed as much of the black bread as I could stomach, I found the Duke staring at me again. His steady gaze was impossible to look away from, almost like there was a tether connecting us.

"Are you ready?" Bastien asked.

What he left unsaid made my spine straighten: are you ready... *for our feeding.*

His lips would be on me again. Those soft lips. And his hands. Holding me tight to him. Crushing our bodies together. Taking what he so desired from me. The thought caused something hot to twist in my stomach.

I was the only person who could satiate him. This powerful, strong warrior. This prince. He might deny it, but he *did* need me. And knowing that I was desired and needed was a feeling I'd never had before. A heady, intense throb that was impossible to ignore. But my family needed me, too. They needed me to keep my head and not allow whatever strange desire was burning between us to ruin my mission. And familial obligation overrode everything else, especially this feeling.

"Yes," I replied as casually as I could.

Bastien stood, offering me his arm. I stalled to collect my thoughts by taking another gulp of water. I needed time to procure some ingredients from my trunk, and I couldn't have him sinking his teeth into me beside the fire.

"Could I freshen up first? I'm filthy."

Bastien clenched his jaw, his throat bobbing as he swallowed. "Of course. Whatever makes you more comfortable." He inched his arm closer to mine, and reluctantly, I took it.

A jolt of excitement tore through me as I set my hand on

the crook of his arm and let him guide me to my room. As we passed through the crowded dining room, making our way toward the staircase, heads turned. Rowdy conversation dulled to whispers.

When we approached where Okeri and Tyson were seated, his nephew stood, nearly pushing his chair into the hearth fire. "Your Grace," he said with a bow. Lady Okeri curtsied. Bastien waved him off with a grunt and a dismissive hand. The sour look on Tyson's face made me smile, and I dipped my chin and covered my mouth with a hand so as not to offend him..

He caught me smirking, and a smile kicked up one side of his lips. "Didn't you enjoy your time with my nephew?" he asked as we ascended the stairs.

I took a second to consider how best to answer and decided on the truth. "I've never met someone so... spoiled."

Bastien laughed, and, *by Diana*, the sound was deep and musical. Almost as entrancing as his scent, which carried notes of bergamot and fresh pine. "Something else we agree on."

He paused in front of a door and extracted a key from his pocket. Nerves twisted in my stomach as he unlocked it and opened it for me. Inside I found my trunk beside the bed. I was sure his guard had searched it, but Mama had planned for that. However, it wasn't the only trunk in the room. An unfamiliar black trunk sat beside mine. One that looked much more lavish, with gold detailing and buckles. And that bore the sigil of House Allard.

Suddenly, my throat ran dry. "Your Grace, whose trunk is that?" I asked.

The vampire cleared his throat. "It's mine."

My mouth fell open, and I couldn't stop a surprised breath from escaping my lips. There was only one reason why his trunk would be in my room.

"It is customary for sanguine partners to share a room with

their vampire when traveling. For your protection," he explained. All humor gone. His face a stoic mask.

While his intentions might be noble, they did nothing to quell my nerves. "We wouldn't want to go against tradition, would we?" I said. I ran my fingers through my hair, wanting to scream. I hadn't planned to share a room with him.

"You should know that I have no use for a bed, so there's no need to share."

I nodded and forced a smile, as if that solved everything. "Could you give me a moment of privacy?"

"Of course." He closed the door behind him. I expelled a tight breath that did nothing to relieve the ache in my chest. Share a room. *With a vampire?*

Diana. How was that going to work?

Flustered, I crossed the room quickly and opened my trunk. Now, more than ever, it was imperative that the sleeping draught worked. Rummaging through folded garments and supplies with shaking hands, I searched for the damned vial, tossing dresses and skirts on the floor, but the only thing I could think about was sharing a room with Bastien. How could I sleep with him looming over me? I couldn't.

When my fingers closed around something smooth and cool, I wrenched it free, grateful it hadn't broken in travel. "By your light, please let this work, Diana," I prayed. Uncorking the small blue vial, I dripped three drops of a sleeping draught on my tongue, letting the floral-tasting liquid soak in.

I knew exactly how this draught affected me. I had thirty minutes before I'd be battling its effects. Bastien needed to feed on me during that time, which didn't seem like a problem, considering he was standing outside the door. It seemed smart to plan for contingencies. All would be lost if the draught lulled me to sleep while I was out spying. I needed something to counteract the effects. Thankfully, Mama had instructed me to pack a small apothecary. I found the pouch of telareyon root powder, which I could take after Bastien fed. It would negate the tiredness and give me the energy to carry out my mission.

I quickly changed my clothes, donning a sleeping shift and robe, and splashed some clean water from a basin on my face, toweling off the droplets. The telareyon root tucked safely inside my pocket.

Everything was ready. *All that remained was letting him bite me.*

My skin prickled with anticipation of the press of his lips, the sharp sting of his fangs, the rush of warmth that had left me weak-kneed. At the very same time, I wanted to run from the room and let the lake swallow me whole. Desire and dread battled inside me, tightening my throat until it was hard to breathe.

I looked at myself in the mirror, smoothing the wispy strands of silver lilac hair around my face. There was no going back. I drew in a deep breath through my nose, reminding myself that I couldn't pass out. I had to maintain my constitution through this. I had to push aside this phobia so that I could spy on the vampire and learn more about the relics.

I'd seen what a body cursed by dark magick looked like: I'd smelled cursed flesh charring from the inside out, seen grave-worms in my Gran's heart, and heard the wails of my aunts, uncles, and my mother. All the while, vampires like Bastien watched on. Taking no action against these wicked witches. I'd promised my sister I'd do anything to keep her safe. Brave, beautiful Sera. The Witches of Darkness must be stopped at any cost.

Even if I was that cost.

CHAPTER 10
PICORER
CLAIRE

I opened the door to my bedchamber, bracing myself for the vampire to sweep inside, pin me against the wall, and sink his teeth into my throat, but he didn't move. He just stood there, staring like he'd forgotten how to breathe. His eyes traced a slow, languid path down my body, heat blooming everywhere his gaze landed—like a hunter setting snares, trapping me in place.

He was drinking me in, but not the way I'd braced for. His gaze lingered on the swell of my breasts. My nipples tightened beneath the thin fabric of my shift, as if coaxed into hard peaks by the weight of his stare. I rolled my shoulders back and lifted my chin, trying to ignore how delicious it felt to be desired and pretend to be unbothered by him.

"Please, come in, Your Grace." The words left me in a bare whisper, but I knew he could hear me as if I screamed it. I stepped out of the way to allow him inside.

The sound of my voice seemed to jolt him from his daze.

"Your robe…" he replied.

He closed the distance between us in two slow steps. My

breath caught as his hand found the loose fabric, pulling the edges together over my chest. The whisper of silk against my skin made me shiver.

Then his long fingers found the sash, easily threading the ends to make a knot at my waist. His knuckles brushed my stomach as he worked. The faintest touch, but it sent an unexpected shock through me, rolling down my spine and pooling low. My thighs pressed together instinctively, my body betraying me, turning warm and slick despite the danger of what came next.

For someone whom I despised so deeply, his touch ignited something I couldn't ignore.

When Bastien was done with the knot, he tested it to ensure it was secure by slipping a finger under the sash and tugging, which I wasn't expecting. I gasped, my hands splaying out on his hard chest to catch myself. He steadied me with a hand on my low back, holding me flush against him.

I tipped my head back, lips parting as I looked up at him. The hunger in his eyes nearly undid me. My toes curled against the soft carpet.

"This isn't the convent. You would do well to knot your robe."

"I'll keep that in mind, Your Grace," I said. Not sure what else to say.

"Good."

Every muscle inside me tightened and melted against him at the same time. He didn't pull away, nor did I, but something stiffened between us. Something hard that pressed against my stomach. Something that my body instinctively leaned into. I forced myself to steady my gaze on his, taking in every inch of him to distract myself from that hardness. Trying—and failing—to ignore it.

This close, his eyes were as clear and blue as the water that lapped at the shore near the Falls of Amara, my favorite place in the whole world. Especially when the sun kissed my bare skin, and the breeze was warm. Right now, he was making me feel warmer than the sun ever had. My attention drifted to his mouth. To the way his lips were parted. I shook my head to clear the fantasy. *The sleeping draught.* It was already working. My thoughts unraveled into dreamy wisps. Ill-conceived fantasies. I needed him to take his fill of me before I was too tired to think straight.

"Aren't you going to come in?" I asked, my voice breathy and much higher than normal.

He hesitated for a moment longer, then released his hold on me. Stepping back and running a hand through his hair. "Get your cloak. And put on some slippers. I want to show you something."

Confused, I took a step backward, trying to relieve myself of the effect his scent and his body had on me. I had to keep my wits about me. "But what about our feeding? You need to eat, don't you?"

His reply was not hurried. His gaze ticked down my body and back up again, as if he were assessing me. "I'm not hungry."

I squinted, recalling what Lady Okeri had said to Tyson. "But you look weak."

"I assure you, I am *not* weak, Miss Donadieu. Now, if you'll be so good as to follow me."

I bit my lip, trying to think. I needed to act. I'd already drank the sleeping draught. Desperately, I reached for his hand. His skin, while cool, was rough and calloused from days in the saddle. I lifted it to my neck. The fire crackled. The muffled sounds of those still drinking could be heard below.

"Your Grace" I said, "Please. Let me do my job."

"Your heart is racing. I can feel it." His thumb skated across my throat. "Just here."

He leaned in, and I had no idea what he meant to do. *Just bite me,* I thought. But he didn't. He just got closer. And closer. Until my only thoughts were of his lips and how desperately I wanted to feel them against mine. A terrible, awful thing to think.

Bastien dropped his hand from my throat. "I said, *follow me.*"

He didn't wait for me. I couldn't believe he was leaving, just like that.

"Where are we going?" I called after him as he disappeared down the long hall, quickly toeing on my slippers.

He didn't reply.

Cursing under my breath, I was forced to chase after him as he made his way down the stairs and through the tavern, passing those dedicated to their drinks. They all cheered and raised their glasses as the Duke of Roselyn strode out the back door.

Racing after him, I struggled to keep up with his long strides as we exited the inn. I was grateful for the cold, which was probably the first time in my life I'd ever thought such a ridiculous thing. It was keeping me awake almost as well as the telareyon root in my pocket, and it gave a reason for my cheeks to be pink besides his presence.

Bastien pointed at a nearby wooden building. Low light shone from fogged windows, and the only sign of life was the line of smoke puffing from the chimney. The front door a stone's throw from the black lake.

"Why are we going there?" I asked. My brain conjured images of torture devices where these evil sorcerers put Witches of the Light to the question. "And why are we walking so fast?"

Frigid dew soaked the hem of my robe, chilling my ankles.

Bastien didn't slow his pace. "We're going to the bathhouse."

"A bathhouse?" I repeated.

Off in the distance, I saw an ancient witch standing on the porch of one of the small homes. All of a sudden, the inn seemed much safer. I lowered my voice. "Your Grace, why are we going to a bathhouse?"

I laced my arm through his and pulled myself against him, feeling safer with a blood-drinking vampire between me and her.

He angled his chin toward me. Humor lighting his icy eyes. "Didn't you take baths at the Nightfall Convent?"

"Of course I took baths," I said defensively. "Just not in a special house or in the company of..." My thoughts broke off, and I unwound my arm from him, hugging it to my chest. I gazed at the grass. "A male."

He stopped in front of me, and I nearly ran right into him. My damp slippers skidding over the slick grass. His glare was hard and cold. "I'm only *accompanying* you, not bathing *with* you," he clarified. "And I'm doing so because it's my duty to protect you from the evil witches who fed you stew and offered to make you a poultice for the wounds that magickal necklace created," he said, gesturing to the choker. "That necklace is the reason you and I are in the mess we're in."

There was something accusatory hiding behind his tone, and I knew he didn't trust me. Nor I him.

Bastien might be a beautiful monster, but he was still a monster. I recalled what Mama had told me. To be polite and subservient. That's what they want. A pleasant pincushion. "You're upset with me."

He made an amused sound in the back of his throat, but nothing in his face was playful. "You're insightful."

"I thought I was stubborn. Or perhaps, brave."

While the moon refused to shine on the lake, Diana's light didn't shy away from him. It hung on his every feature. The silvery glow illuminated one side of his face, and in this light, the Duke of Roselyn looked otherworldly. Beautiful, and at the same time, terrifying.

"Those qualities are not mutually exclusive," he said.

The one good thing about this battle of wills was, like the cold, it was helping me fight the sleepiness lurking behind my eyelids. *We needed to hurry this along.* Bastien backed up several paces, easing his way toward the entrance of the bathhouse. I followed him. Wondering what he was thinking and why he'd really brought me here. Was it only for a bath? Fear rose inside me once again, and I wrung my hands together, trying to work out the nervous energy.

"What makes you so insightful and brave, Miss Donadieu?" His attention drifted to the strip of lace around my neck. "What drove you to purchase a magickal necklace that could have killed you?" He paused. "What do you need from me?"

He'd brought me out here to question me, I realized. To force a confession. Well, I wasn't giving up that easily.

"Safety," I said, exasperated. "Security. Money. All the reasons a woman becomes a sanguine partner."

These were lies, but I knew it was the truth he wanted to hear. The truth I'd been taught to give.

Faster than I thought possible, he whirled me around, the solid wood slamming against my back as his body caged me in. The wind left my lungs in a whoosh of breath. His hand gripped my chin, forcing my attention back to his face.

Suddenly, I wasn't as cold as I was a moment ago.

His eyes narrowed. "You are far too innocent to have chosen me on your own. My castle is the furthest north, closest to the border, where snow falls year-round, and you shiver in an autumn chill. You could've picked a different vampire's ball to attend; one whose temperament and castle were better suited to your delicate nature."His chest rose and fell against mine, each breath a brand on my skin. My lips parted on a tremor I couldn't suppress. "Someone coerced you to put on that necklace. Someone instructed you to target me. And I want to know *who*."

CHAPTER 11
TROMPER
CLAIRE

I struggled, but it was no use. "Let me go."

"First, I want an answer. Who did this?"

I struggled to find a reply, unsure what spawned this sudden line of questioning. Had his men found something in my trunk that gave me away? Was this the end? Was that why he dragged me out here? To turn me over to the Witches of the Darkness? And what about Sera? My fists clenched when I recalled the way Natalia had treated her.

Even though I wanted to tell the Duke every terrible thing his kind did and why I'd given up my life at Prideaux Hill to come here, I held my tongue. I knew I was supposed to be submissive or, at the very least, fearful, to earn his favor, but I couldn't stop the humorless laugh that tore from my throat.

"You are just as insufferable and pigheaded as your nephew, Your Grace."

I shouldn't have said it, but what was done was done.

The vampire's lip curled, and a shadow of the monster he truly was made itself known. The shadows under his eyes darkening. Fear rose inside me. "And why is that?"

His kind were all the same. Self-serving and obsessed with the war waging outside the Unified Territories instead of focusing on the people within their borders. He should be protecting innocent Witches of the Light from the likes of Shreesa.

"The fact that you are a duke with a castle and guards and money, while I'm forced to sell my... my *blood* so my sister and I can survive, is what makes you insufferable." My words came as sharp as the barbs on Mama's choker, even though I had to fight against the dizziness that word invoked.

"Had my father not died in your war," I continued, giving him half-truths that came with real pain, "I wouldn't be here. The gold you gave Sera will change her life, and that's all that matters to me. Helping my sister." I drew in a steadying breath, then added, "No one put me up to this, but *you.*"

The power of my admission had the shadows around his eyes retreating. It seemed I'd struck a nerve with my vampire companion.

"Now," I said, holding his gaze even though I was trembling with adrenaline and fear, "are we going inside? Or are we going to stand out here and bicker with your hand at my throat?"

He released his hold on my chin like I'd slapped him before putting a foot of distance between us. "I didn't mean to imply..." he started, then stopped. Searching the grass for an answer. "You must understand..." he tried again. Another excuse falling flat.

I crossed my arms, waiting.

His gaze lifted, and I was surprised to see apology warming his icy eyes. "I hurt you."

"You flatter yourself, Your Grace. It would take more than words to hurt me."

His eyes widened, and I wondered why.

"I-I just..." Bastien cleared his throat. "I've had over five hundred sanguine partners. Each one unique. Some witty. Some kind. Some were half as beautiful as you." At this, my cheeks warmed. He took a step closer. "But they were all of *my* choosing. This time, you and that necklace chose for me. I'm sorry for questioning you so sharply, but as you can see, I'm still furious."

"A lot of choices were made for me, too. So, excuse me for not feeling bad about what I did. Next year, when you're done with me, you can pick whomever you want and forget all about *this mess*."

His lip curled. "Fine."

"Fine."

Nothing was said for a hot, tense moment. We simply stared at one another. Seething. Finally, Bastien extracted a key from his pocket, and I stepped aside so he could unlock the door. He let me in before following after, closing it quickly and securing the bolt.

By Diana. Everything inside the bathhouse was black. The walls. The candles floating above the rectangular pool. The glassy black stone tiles decorating the ceiling and floor. Even the towels laid out beside the steaming surface of the water. All of it as black as a twisted soul.

I didn't need magick to know this bathhouse was powered by demonic energy. The unsettling presence of dark magick hung thick in the air. Thicker than the scents of this place, which were unfamiliar and strange to me. The sweet aroma not unpleasant, but I didn't want to breathe too deeply for fear of what it might do to me.

It was unnaturally warm inside, and I knew no wood stove was powerful enough to maintain this temperature and heat the pool. This was the work of a demonic relic. One I very badly wanted to find and smash to pieces, but I felt *sluggish*. The heat weighing on my eyelids. I couldn't endure the sleeping draught's effects much longer. Not in this place.

The vampire was seated on a small chair, removing his boots and socks. He glanced up at me as I approached, and I stilled. Something had changed between us. I wasn't sure what, but after our argument, there was a shift in energy. Not that I thought any better of him, *because I didn't*. He was still insufferable. His lips were pulled into a tight line, and his jaw set. Clearly, he was still angry. But it didn't make him any less striking.

No, not at all.

His deep, musical voice echoed in the small space. "Yes?"

I cleared my throat. My fingers seeking out the telareyon root in my pocket. "I'd like to do our feeding before I bathe," I said. Maintaining my calm despite the light-headedness threatening to consume me. I had to be strong. "Should we get started?" I asked, glancing around for a good spot.

Bastien rose from the seat, barefoot, and slowly padded over to me. He stood out among the darkness of the bathhouse, with his white shirt and straw-colored hair, and at the exact same time, blended in. Like he belonged in dimly lit places. Cast in shadows. Removing the tie that had held back his blond hair, he let the chin-length strands fall loose around his face.

My throat ran dry as I watched his thick muscles flexing through his shirt.

"I already explained that a feeding won't be necessary," the vampire said.

I forced calm into my voice even though I was mentally screaming. It had to be now. "Aren't you hungry? You haven't eaten in days."

Something that could've been mistaken for humor lifted one corner of his mouth. "Worried about me now, are you?"

My mouth opened, but no words came out.

He canted his head to one side, contemplating me. "Take your bath. Soak in the bubbles." I opened my mouth to argue, but Bastien raised a hand. "You've chosen to trust me with your well-being for the next year, and now, while I won't go so far as to say I trust you, I understand your motivations for being here. So, let's not ruin the moment with debate."

Had my defiance earned me his respect? Perhaps the Duke didn't just want a soft and sweet pincushion to sink his teeth in. Perhaps he wanted a woman with a spine. Maybe that's what had changed.

"I'm going to the steam room," he said, grabbing a towel and tossing it over his shoulder. "I'll be back soon."

It looked like the vampire wanted to say something more, but instead, he ran his long fingers through his hair and stalked away. I watched him leave with a mix of emotion tumbling inside me.

Who knew how long he'd be gone. And he didn't intend to eat. By *Diana*, I was failing, and I couldn't keep doing that. My family was trusting me. I had to get him to feed from me. Maybe if I tempted him, he wouldn't be able to resist. So, as much as I hated begging a vampire to do anything, it was my last resort. "This room has plenty of steam, Your Grace. Please," I said, desperation bleeding into my voice. "I don't want to be alone."

It seemed to work. He turned to face me, concern etched into the corners of his eyes. "You're nervous."

Trying to sell my fear, I said, "A little."

"What are you nervous about?"

I rounded my shoulders and made myself smaller like I sometimes did when I was in trouble at home. "That I'm failing you," I said quietly. "A sanguine partner is supposed to keep her vampire strong, isn't she? If something happens tonight because you're weak..." I let the words trail off.

My gaze skated down his body. The steam had saturated his clothes, causing them to stick to his muscular torso. I swallowed hard, and told myself I didn't want him here for any other reason than practicality.

"You are truly worried that I won't be able to protect you?"

Our eyes connected, and a warm pulse of heat traveled from the tips of my ears down to the base of my spine. My breath shallow. My thighs drawing closer together. I nodded once.

CHAPTER 12
DÉNOUER

CLAIRE

I dragged my hair off my sweat-slick neck, baring myself to him like an offering. "If you would only eat, Your Grace."

Bastien's jaw flexed, and his fangs glinted white in the dim light, sharp enough to make my pulse stutter. He closed the space between us with one slow, predatory step. "You don't know what you're asking for, Miss Donadieu."

I tipped my head back. "Yes, I do."

One hand fitted around my waist; the other cradled the side of my neck, his thumb grazing the frantic beat of my pulse. "Your blood makes me—"

His breath hitched.

"Please," I whispered.

"It's so tempting. Especially when you beg."

I swallowed hard, clutching my robe, my body caught between terror and something far worse—*want*.

"I'll bathe on the other side of the pool," he said finally, his breath ghosting my skin. "And if, when I'm done, you still wish it—if you still want *me*—I will feed."

His pledge did nothing to ease the tension inside me. If anything, it made it worse. When he released me, I nearly stumbled from the sudden absence of his touch. His long strides carried him to the shadows at the far end of the pool. The candles caught him in pieces—shoulder, hair, the long line of his back—before darkness swallowed him again.

As much as I was loath to enter this water, I needed to be quick about it. I fumbled with the knot he tied, but it held fast. After another failed attempt to get the knot loose, I whispered into the darkness. "Your Grace?"

A breath later, he was standing in front of me. I knew how fast he could move, but still, I gasped.

His shirt was already off, and, oh, Diana, his body was just as perfect as I imagined. Thick muscles. Strong arms. Broad shoulders. His smooth skin was marred with ropey pink scars, but it didn't make him look any less attractive. Instead, it added to his allure. This was a warrior. A man battle-tested. He'd taken lives and left the battlefield with only cuts. My eyes caught on the gold chain at his neck, and the bright red crystal pulsing like a second heartbeat. It was impossible to look away from the glow. I could feel it in my own chest, answering the wild thrum of my pulse.

"Did you need something?"

The question barely registered. *Yes. I needed something.* My gaze dragged back up to his face, my lips parting on a breath I couldn't seem to draw fully.

I smoothed a trembling hand down the front of my robe, remembering the knot. "I-I can't untie this."

He rolled his lips together. "Do you want me to..."

"Please," I answered quickly.

He lowered to one knee, putting his face level with my stomach. A duke, a predator, kneeling before me; the sight knocked the breath from my lungs. How many times had he ever been on his knees for anyone? I'd wager not many. I drew in small sips of air through my nose to calm my heart, but it wasn't working. It was racing, throbbing against my ribs like it wanted to leap into his waiting mouth.

Wordlessly, his fingers brushed against my belly as he made quick work of the knot. I watched in rapture as he twirled the loose satin sash around his finger before letting it unravel to the ground.

"Done," he whispered.

I shifted, and the folds of my robe opened, exposing the thin cotton sleeping shift beneath. My nipples pinched despite how warm it was and sweat prickled down my back. Every inch of me very aware of him. His attention had my lip quivering, and I fisted sections of the robe to steady my hands, but it was no use.

"Do you need help with anything else?" he asked, still on one knee, looking up at me through impossibly thick lashes.

The soft place between my thighs ached for him in ways I didn't know it could. I wanted his help relieving the ache, and somehow, I knew his deft fingers could handle the task. I could only imagine what it would be like to feel his palms glide up my legs as he lifted my shift. Until... I closed my eyes and tried to push the image out of my brain.

The vampire might not be able to read minds, but I was aware of his ability to sense my desire. He'd told me as much the night of his Sanguination Ball. He knew exactly what I was feeling, so why was he still on his knees looking at me like that?

Did he... desire me? Did he want to touch me... *there*? As soon as the thought entered my head, I chastised myself. I shouldn't be thinking like that. He was a monster. I was disgusting for even imagining such a thing. "No, Your Grace. That was all."

He hesitated for a moment before he stood, then he said, "Very well. Enjoy your bath, Miss Donadieu."

My name lingered in the hot, sticky air between us before it was the only thing there. Like a shadow, he was gone. Absorbed into the darkness of the bathhouse, somewhere just out of my sight. But I knew he hadn't left. No. He was still here. And, perhaps, still looking at me.

My breath stuttered, and I quickly removed the robe, setting it beside the pool, then toed off my damp slippers. The only thing left was the shift. I squeezed my eyes shut and told myself he wouldn't look when I undressed. He was a duke with some amount of decency. But what if he did? What would he think of my body? Maybe he'd think I was just as imperfect as I felt. Or maybe—just maybe—he'd have a different opinion.

Again, I shoved the thought away and pulled the night-dress over my head. I'd never felt more exposed in my life than standing in the near dark with a vampire across the room, completely naked. But I didn't let it stop me. I lowered myself in, step by step, until the warm water covered my breasts. As much as I hated to admit it, it felt good. I glanced in the direction of the vampire, but it was so hard to see little more than shadows in the dark. The little splashes of water coming from across the pool my only indication that he had also gotten in. Images of water beading down his bare chest infiltrated my thoughts. Clearly, the sleeping draught had done more than induce sleepiness.

Frustrated, I chose a bar of soap that smelled of lavender and a black washcloth, then set to work cleansing my body and face. Dragging the cloth carefully down my neck and chest. The rough cotton was teasing as it slid across my nipples, and I tilted my head back, dipping my hair into the water. Every move felt like pouring honey from a cold jar. My limbs were heavy. My eyelids drooped. It was getting harder and harder to fight sleep in the warm water.

I suppressed a yawn as I set the cloth aside and grabbed the jar of shampoo—working some between my palms before massaging it into my lilac hair. I leaned back into the water to rinse it out, and as I did, I stared up at the black ceiling. I was so tired, and the water was so warm. Maybe I could close my eyes for a second. Just long enough to rest. No. I forced them back open. I had to stay awake. I had to fight. Bastien would be done soon, and then he'd feed, and I'd take the telareyon root. But I was so incredibly exhausted. I'd barely slept on the ride here, and all I wanted to do was rest.

My blinks grew longer. Candlelight danced across the glassy black ceiling tiles in a mesmerizing pattern. On my next blink, my eyes stayed shut. My tired brain conjured the image of Bastien on the night of his Sanguination Ball. Of the way I felt in his strong arms. Of the way his tongue dragged up my neck. And then, how everything around me dulled when he'd opened the connection between us and spoke inside my head. I remembered feeling like I was underwater. Like I'd jumped in, head first, and he was the only thing I wanted to swim toward.

Except this time, I didn't swim.

I simply let the warmth cradle me until I drifted off to sleep. As I did, I dreamed I saw a man wreathed in fire and a woman bathed in brilliant white light calling me home.

CHAPTER 13
CHOISIR
BASTIEN

Bringing Claire to this place was infinitely stupid.

My mate was bathing across the pool, *naked*, and here I was, trying to pretend she wasn't.

My mind kept running circles around every interaction with her. Every touch. Every look. I'd been winning the fight against my urges until she'd asked for help untying her sash, and I immediately dropped to my knees for her. It had taken every modicum of restraint not to push up the hem of that little nightgown and taste her. Had she told me to make her come while I was on my knees in front of her, I would've forsaken every vow I'd made to myself and the laws that prevented vampires from fucking their sanguine partners. Parting her with my tongue and stroking her pleasure. Licking her sweetness until I found the exact right way to make her scream. Sliding a finger inside her just to hear her choke out *Your Grace* while she writhed on my hand.

But I had other problems besides temptation. My bloodlust was becoming harder to ignore. Especially when she begged for it. I'd never been thirstier in my life.

By the gods, *I was ravenous.*

I filled a cup and poured water over my hair, rinsing the soap and wishing my thirst for her could be ignored. While my kind could move in the sunlight, it drained our power and weakened us. Restoring it with human blood was the only way to become strong again. If Claire were anyone else, I would've already satiated my need. But she *wasn't* anyone else. I had to figure out how to avoid drinking from her, but I was running out of time. I couldn't wait to ask Imogen for ideas.

So here I was, giving my mate a chance to change her mind about the feeding while red-hot bloodlust dripped down my throat and the desire to claim every inch of her body surged in my veins.

The bloodstone pulsed with each slow beat of her heart, letting me know she was relaxed. No trace of fear hung in the air. I resisted the urge to turn around and look at her. To see her long, wet hair clinging to damp skin. To watch soap bubbles slide between her breasts.

Pounding my fist against the tile, I gritted my teeth and forced myself to think straight. Despite our mate bond, I didn't trust her, and she clearly felt the same way. As much as she tried to hide it, there was animosity in her eyes. And that animosity fueled my suspicions about her. If she blamed me for her father's death and the hardships in her life, then that left room for hate to become action.

I leaned against the pool's edge, bracing my forearms on the tile, and hung my head, cursing the gods for their sick sense of humor. Why had they chosen this woman to be my mate? Why couldn't I have been left to live alone? Wasn't I doing enough for my family and for the land I swore to protect? One would think so.

While I struggled with the unfairness of my situation, a cold finger of dread wrapped itself around my heart, unsettling me. My vampiric senses heightened, and I listened for any movement around the bathhouse or within it but found nothing. Nothing but this building sense of dread. Something was wrong. *Very wrong.* But what?

Grabbing my bloodstone, I saw the truth: the light had gone out. I turned it back and forth to see if my eyes were playing tricks on me. But no. It was no trick. The light had gone out for the first time in twenty-five years. That would only happen if... I turned, searching for Claire, but didn't see her figure amongst the steam.

Had she...?

I didn't allow myself to finish the thought. I dove underwater, swimming hard, when I saw her floating beneath the surface, unmoving. This was my fault. I was too distracted. Too in my own head to notice her struggling. I got my arms around her and clutched her to my chest as I climbed out of the pool. Water dripped from our naked bodies. She was limp, and that scared me more than anything ever had.

"Miss Donadieu! Claire, can you hear me?"

Her head lolled to the side, but she didn't answer. I laid her down to assess her. Blue lips. Chest still. If I didn't breathe air into her lungs and restart her heart, she was dead. But sealing my lips to hers would solidify the mate bond, and there would be no turning back. I'd never be able to deny her. I'd be at her whim. Her mercy. Which wasn't what I wanted. I had to save her, but there were serious repercussions if I did.

For the longest second of my life, I considered letting her go. If I did nothing, I'd be free of her. Of the temptation. Of the problem she presented. Of all the ways she could ruin the life I'd built for myself. Water beaded down my chin, dripping onto her pale cheeks like tears.

My heart twisted with anguish, and I knew I couldn't let her die. She was a complication in my life, but I couldn't be responsible for her death. I had to save her. Lacing my fingers together, I pressed them to her breastbone, compressing her chest and forcing her heart to beat. After, I pinched her nose and lowered my lips to hers, hovering over their perfect bow shape for just a moment—just long enough to feel the weight of this decision—before carefully tilting her chin back and fitting my lips to hers.

The tingle of magick buzzed between us, and my whole world came to a halt. Then slowly, my world began rotating around her, like she was the earth and I was her moon. Some primal urge tore through me. Something I couldn't fight. Mine. *She was mine.*

And she needed to live.

I gave her two full breaths before going back to compressions.

"Come on, Claire. *Wake up.* You have to wake up."

I pressed my lips to hers again and again, blowing life into her lungs. On my sixth attempt, when I was starting to lose hope that I wasn't going to save her, my bloodstone flickered back to life.

I stopped compressions, and Claire coughed up mouthfuls of water. I eased her onto her side so she didn't choke. Pulling wet strands of her hair from her face and tucking them behind her ear. When the worst of her coughing subsided, I rolled her onto her back, and her eyes fluttered open.

"What happened?" she asked blearily.

This time, I chose you.

She didn't need to know that. No. She could *never* know what I'd done. "You drowned," I said in a shaky voice. Hovering over her. Protectively caging her body with mine. "But you're alright now."

"Drowned?" she repeated slowly. She sounded confused and could barely keep her eyes open.

But still, she touched the bloodstone dangling between us. The one that was beating in time with her heart. I held my breath for fear she'd figure out what it meant. She rubbed a thumb over the stone, regarding it carefully, before her eyes shifted back to mine. Warm and brown and absolutely captivating.

"Why did you save me?" she asked. "I thought you hated me for not giving you a choice."

Her question struck at the heart of my struggle. A struggle I had to keep to myself. I pushed another strand of damp hair from her face. My fingers trailed down the side of her cheek until they grazed the edge of her lips. The urge to press mine against hers again rose inside me, but I pushed it back down. "You're irritating enough to be interesting. It would've been foolish of me to let you die."

She tried to laugh but ended up coughing up more water. I watched her carefully, making sure she didn't choke. When the fit passed, Claire wiped her mouth with the back of her hand and met my gaze. Holding it with so much curiosity, I wished I could read her mind.

"So, according to you, I'm irritating, interesting, brave, stubborn, and insightful."

I lifted a brow, unable to control the smile that quirked up one side of my mouth. "Are you making a list of the things I've called you?"

"Maybe."

What an interesting creature.

She was leaving off twice as beautiful as anyone I'd ever met. But, maybe she was keeping that to herself. Gods knew I was keeping plenty more descriptions of her behind my teeth. Sexy. Delicate. Strong-willed. Tantalizing. *Stop it, Bastien.*

"I'm so tired," she said.

"Then sleep," I replied. "Trust that I'll take care of you."

Her eyes fluttered shut, and they didn't reopen. I double-checked that her heart was beating and that she was breathing, then sat back on my heels, trying to catch my breath.

I'd been pushing this brave young woman too hard. She hadn't seen the world outside the convent, and I had to treat her more gently, no matter how suspicious I was, because this couldn't happen again. Especially now that I'd sealed our bond. I'd never be able to live with myself if she died in my care. Whether I liked it or not, Claire was under my protection, which meant getting her into dry clothes and back to the inn.

Trying to be as respectful as possible, I eased a hand behind her head and lifted it enough to slip the cotton nightgown on. It took longer than I thought it would to get her arms through the shift and pull it down around her body. Claire's limp arms and legs weren't helping the process. And neither was my bloodlust. Every time my fingers touched one of her throbbing veins, my mouth salivated, and I had to force myself to focus on her health. Watching carefully for signs that her heart might give out again.

After easing her arms into each sleeve of the robe, I tied the sash in a knot, then fastened the cloak around her shoulders. Once she was dressed, I dashed to the other side of the pool to dress myself, then returned as quickly as I could to her side. Sliding one arm under her knees, I hoisted her up against my chest. Reveling in the pink tint that had settled in her cheeks. She was alive, and right now, that's all that mattered.

Her warm body curled against me as we left the bathhouse. Her damp hair soaking into my shirt. Her cheek resting against my chest. It felt good to carry her. It felt right to be this close to her. Nothing had changed. And yet, everything had.

When I opened the door to the inn, we drew stares from my guard, but no one dared say a word as I walked past them and carried Claire up to our room. I laid her carefully on the mattress, then sat in the armchair by the fireplace, turning it to face the bed.

The room was dark, save for the firelight, but I had no trouble seeing her face or hearing her breaths. Grabbing a book and thumbing it open, I contented myself with reading while she slept, but I found myself stealing glances over the top of the book, unable to tear my attention away from her for more than a few seconds.

She was restless in the sheets. Tossing and turning. Kicking the covers off. Then there was the little noises she made. Soft moans and sighs. Then I heard my name slip between her lips.

"Bastien. No, don't stop."

Something inside me roared with pleasure. I wanted to know exactly what I was doing in her dream that she didn't want me to stop. I gritted my teeth and banished the thought from my head. This was how I was going to spend the next year of my life. Having her close but needing to keep her at arm's length.

It was for the best.

There was a sharp knock at the door, and Claire stirred. I extracted my pocket watch and checked the time, cursing when I realized I'd forgotten my meeting. I set the book down and crept toward the door, not wanting to wake her. Cracking it open, I found Natalia waiting for me with her arms crossed.

She opened her mouth, likely to chastise me for being late, and I raised a finger to my lips. I slipped from the room, loath as I was to leave Claire for more than a second, and stepped into the hallway.

"We'll be staying an extra night," I said in a voice that allowed no argument. "Inform Shreesa that I'm very sorry, but I must speak with her tomorrow."

Natalia stuck her hand on her hip and flipped her long braid off her shoulder. "You were adamant that we hurry back to Roselyn. Now, you wish to linger? And since when do you cancel meetings?"

"Since when have you questioned my orders?"

"Since you started acting strange," she snapped. Her glare shifted to the door, then back to me. "And by the gods, Uncle, you look like hell." I waved her off, but Natalia narrowed her eyes. "You haven't eaten. Have you?"

"Natalia—"

"Does this have something to do with the orphan girl and your morality? Because I'll bleed the girl into a goblet and force-feed you if I have to."

"You will not touch Claire," I growled. Each word laced with the promise of violence. This was the first time since Natalia joined me at Château Rose that I'd threatened her, and the shock was plain on her face.

"How familiar of you to use her given name, Your Grace."

I ignored her needling. "You have your orders."

Frustrated, I retreated inside the room and leaned against the door. Watching Claire as she twisted in the sheets. This woman was going to be the death of me.

CHAPTER 14
RÊVER
CLAIRE

I lay on my back, staring at a sky peppered with a million shimmering stars.

"It's so beautiful," I whispered.

The deep voice of a vampire answered. "Yes, it is."

I could see him watching me from the corner of my eye, and my cheeks burned with heat. Pointing to a constellation, I told Bastien all about the brave witch the sky, a story I'd been fond of since I was a girl.

When I was done, he captured my hand and drew it against his chest, holding it there. The gesture drew my gaze away from the sky to tangle with his. Ice-blue eyes stared back at me, inviting despite their usual coldness, drawing me in like all the heavenly bodies above us.. Captivating and alluring—just like the curve of his lips.

"You are an exquisite creature," he said, thumb stroking the back of my hand in a way that made me feel like I was sinking into the ground.

Slowly, he pressed a kiss to the top of my hand before rolling onto his side and drawing me to him, molding our

97

bodies together. His hand fit against the small of my back. I felt so feminine in his arms and welcomed the press of his body. He brought his lips an inch closer. My back arched, and my chin tilted up, closing the distance between us until we were barely an inch apart. Anticipation of what would happen next had me trembling. I didn't just *want* him to kiss me. I *needed* it. Needed him. Needed to be closer.

There was a question in his eyes, and I answered by snaking my hand around his neck, stroking his skin with my fingers. The air was alive with the passion crackling between us. Slowly, ever so slowly, Bastien lowered his lips to mine, and the chaste touch of our mouths shattered everything inside me, like the sky exploding with stars.

He parted my lips, urging them open, and I invited him into my mouth, tasting him as he slowly mated our tongues together. Deepening the connection between us until I was so far into him I thought I might get lost.

I welcomed the feeling. I wanted to get lost with him.

His hand traveled up my waist to cup my breast, teasing my nipple between his fingers until I moaned inside his mouth. He swallowed the sound, devouring it like it was the only thing he needed to live when familiar voice sliced through the balmy night air. *Mama.* She was angry. I could tell by the way she was calling my name.

Breaking off our kiss, I dug my nails into Bastien's chest and pushed him away. I shouldn't be kissing this man that I hated. And I really shouldn't be liking it so much. This was wrong. But nothing about kissing Bastien felt wrong.

As I looked into his eyes, a strange pressure built in my chest, like the air had gone thin. The stars overhead blurred, then reformed into a thousand gleaming points that all seemed to aim at me. Pain unlike any I'd ever experienced lanced through my throat. And when I looked down, the lace choker was glowing red-hot—burning through my skin. Smoke curled from the wound, and when I opened my mouth to scream, no sound came out.

Bastien reached for me, but his hands turned to smoke before they could touch me. The ground cracked beneath me and I was falling—falling into a pit of shadow that swallowed the sky, the stars, and him. Everything. I sat up straight, trying to catch my breath. My chest tight, and my cheeks flush. My hands wrapping around my throat.

The vampire appeared at my bedside in an instant. "It's alright, Miss Donadieu," he said. "You are safe. You were having a bad dream. That's all."

His silky voice wrapped around my shoulders, calming and reassuring, and I tried to settle my nerves. The kiss, Mama, the starry sky, the smoke—it was just a dream. No, not a dream. A nightmare.

Bastien eased himself onto the edge of the mattress and sat beside me. "Do you often have such vivid dreams?"

I shook my head, trying to clear my thoughts. "No, I don't. I sleep relatively light..."

Suddenly, I realized what caused this dream. *The sleeping draught.* Nightmares were a side effect. The dream had nothing to do with my lust for the vampire, but from the potion. This was all chemical. But if that was the case, why couldn't I remember anything after getting into the bath?

"How long was I asleep?" I asked.

He canted his head to the side, regarding me with a strange look in his icy eyes. "What do you remember about the bathhouse?"

I blinked, shifting my gaze to the fire. Trying to recall what exactly transpired, but every time I reached for a memory, it vanished.

"It's fuzzy," I admitted. "I remember you *yelling* at me, and

I remember getting in the tub, but past that... *nothing*." He grunted thoughtfully but said nothing else. "Did I fall asleep when we got back to the room?" I asked, trying to fill in the blanks.

The vampire shrugged. "More or less."

I studied his face, trying to puzzle out his meaning, and realized how gaunt and drawn his features were. His cheeks were hollow. His eyes rimmed red and bloodshot. His lips paler than they'd been at dinner. "Don't take this the wrong way, but you don't look so well, Your Grace."

His face remained impassive as he said, "Occupational hazard of being in charge."

No, that wasn't it. He wasn't overworked. He was hungry. Starving. A memory materialized. Last night, I'd asked him to eat, but he hadn't. Instead, I'd fallen asleep. "Last night," I said, slowly, as if trying to recall a dream. "You were supposed to feed from me."

His look somehow darkened, smoldering hotter than the fire. "You're tired. It's the middle of the night." His attention dropped to my neck. "I am capable of waiting."

Even now, when he was nearly ill with hunger, he offered me a way out. It was thoughtful for a bloodthirsty vampire. I wanted to help him if only to lull him into a false sense of security around me. "I can handle it," I said stubbornly.

"As the lady wishes," he replied cooly. I watched his Adam's apple bob in his throat as he swallowed. "Lay back," he instructed. "I have an idea."

"What kind of idea?"

"One that might make feedings easier on you. I don't want you to swoon again."

Slowly, I reclined back against my pillow with my brows pushed together, wondering what he had planned. As soon as I was comfortable, he positioned himself at the foot of the bed, sitting on his knees, staring at me with longing in his eyes. The force of his attention was unlike anything I'd ever experienced. Except in my dream, when he'd devoured my mouth. It was such a real feeling that I could almost taste him. I shook my head to clear the thought.

"Do you trust me?" Bastien asked, shifting forward.

That was a complicated question. But the answer that rose to my lips felt simple. "Yes."

"Then I'll feed from your femoral artery this time. It should be easier on you."

For a second, I blinked at him. My femoral artery? "You're going to bite me... *there*?" My eyes shifted to my thigh as I said it. His gaze followed.

"Yes."

His hands slid under my knees and dragged me closer. I yelped, startled. "Wh-what are you doing?"

"Elevating your legs so you don't pass out." His voice was so calm, so matter-of-fact, as if this was the most ordinary thing in the world.

"Oh." My heart thudded so hard I was sure he could feel it. The position was terribly intimate, leaving me open to him in a way that made heat flood my cheeks.

He leaned in, close enough that I felt the brush of his breath on my inner thigh, and I swallowed hard. "Is this alright?" he asked, his pale eyes flicking up to mine, waiting.

A thrill of excitement tore through my body, but I told myself this was just business. He was hungry, and it was like deciding whether to use a spoon or a fork. It made no difference to him, neck or thigh, so why should it matter to me? I nodded, understanding his plan, and Bastien eased both my legs over his shoulders.

As he did, the icy blue color of his eyes disintegrated into blackness, and razor-sharp fangs peeked from between his lips, the monster inside him awakening. A part of me was terrified of his transformation. The part that hated him for who he was and what he was about to do to me. But another part of me *was not.*

Bastien's lips moved to my thigh, dragging across my skin in a way that sent me reeling. My back arching. Fingers twisting into the sheets. His tongue followed, wetting my skin with one long stroke. I squirmed, and my thighs clamped around his neck before I could stop myself. He gave me a wicked grin, showing off his sharp teeth, and then twined his fingers with mine as he gripped the bedsheets.

"Breathe, Miss Donadieu," Bastien said in a silky voice. "I haven't even done anything yet."

Lies. He knew exactly what he was doing to me.

"Spread your legs a little wider for me, *chérie.* I promise I'll be gentle."

The command went through me like lightning, and my body obeyed before my brain could catch up. My knees parted another few inches, baring more of me to him, and heat flooded my face. I tipped my head back against the pillow, dragging in a deep breath, then slowly exhaling—anything to keep my head clear while he was this close.

"Good. Very good. You're doing so well," he whispered. "Seeing you like this makes me so hungry."

There was some monstrous part of me that wanted this. It chased away the part of me that was afraid, until I was hungry too. Hungry for him. I hated myself for even thinking such a disgusting thing. Hated my body for reacting this way.

"You don't have to watch. In fact, it might be better if you closed your eyes."

Maybe. But I found I couldn't look away. Seeing his face between my legs like this only intensified my need for him. For him to touch me, to kiss me. All he'd need to do was turn his head a few inches and…My breath was short and tight, my chest rising and falling as I imagined just that.

"Tell me you want this," Bastien murmured, his breath teasing my inner thigh, each word a stroke of temptation. "Tell me you need to give yourself to me as badly as I need you."

"I thought you didn't need me, Your Grace."

He growled low in his throat, a sound that vibrated through my entire body as he pressed his lips to the tender flesh of my thigh. His right hand slid higher, holding me exactly where he wanted me.

"I lied."

My breath stuttered. His confession broke something inside me wide open. My body demanding more of *this*.

I barely felt his teeth as they pierced my skin. Nothing more than a prick of a thorn. But after a few seconds the pain melted into a sense of… *release*. Of… *pleasure*. Intense, unyielding pleasure snaked through me, seeking out new places to tantalize.

My skin pebbled with gooseflesh. My nipples peaked. One hand twisted in the bedsheets, the other tightened in his. Squeezing his fingers as my back arched off the mattress and a moan tore from my throat. His name trembled on my tongue, and I bit it back, terrified he'd hear the truth in it.

I shouldn't be acting this way. *Not at all.* Bastien was drinking my *blood*. It was unnatural and disgusting, and I was a terrible person for even liking it.

As soon as the word *blood* entered my head, I had to remind myself to breathe as a wave of dizziness rolled through me. But just as I was feeling flush, Bastien's teeth retracted, and he pulled back an inch, licking my thigh to catch the warm drips that rolled down my skin.

His tongue, so close to that sensitive place, made me shudder. Our eyes connected as he lifted his chin an inch, staring at me hungrily over the mound of my sex. The shadows around his eyes had retreated, and he looked like the beautiful man I'd seen across the ballroom once more.

I'd done that for him. I'd helped him. No, I'd... *sated* him.

Bastien dragged his tongue over his lower lip. "I've never tasted anything half as delicious as you."

The compliment struck at some dark chord inside me. The part of me that wanted to be desired and devoured by this man. The part that wanted him to touch me. I shoved that feeling to the side once more. Attraction had nothing to do with reality. I was on a mission. Feeding him was the price I had to pay to collect information.

"And to think," I said, trying to sound witty to cover up how needy I felt, "you almost died just to get out of this arrangement."

He made an amused sound before removing my legs from his shoulders and pulling the hem of my shift down, covering me. "How are you feeling? Dizzy?"

The way he asked the question almost made me feel like he cared. *Almost.* But I knew better. Bastien could never care about me. Nor I him.

I was a spy. He was a killer.

CHAPTER 15
DEMANDER

CLAIRE

After our feeding, I grew drowsy and fell into a fitful sleep that stretched well into the afternoon. My dreams were peppered with thoughts of my mission, Bastien, and this unsatisfied need he'd left me with.

When I awoke, my back and neck aching from lying in one place too long, my thoughts were a tangled mess. All night, I'd imagined a vampire kissing me. Touching me. Doing lurid things to my body that I should be ashamed of.

I lay in bed, staring at the wooden ceiling, trying to sort out my thoughts, and I kept coming back to one thing: I'd never felt desired. Not just from men. My family didn't desire my presence and had deemed me unfit to be of any use to their war except as bait. All because I'd been born without a trace of magick. But Bastien desired me. Last night, he'd told me he *needed* me. Something dark unfurled inside me again.

My hand slid under the covers to my thigh, just above the place he'd bitten me. I found no wound, just some tenderness. All evidence that he'd fed from me was gone, but still, I was plagued with thoughts of the unsatisfied ache in my core.

An ache put there by him.

I blew out a long breath. I didn't come here to be wooed. I came here to find out what he knew and help my family destroy the Dark Witch's source of power. Last night, I'd failed to spy on him, but I had learned that there must be a relic under that bathhouse, its demonic power concealed from my eyes.

My family needed this information much more than some vampire needed my blood. I told myself, "I just need to stop thinking about him." Yawning, I stretched and forced myself into a seated position, when suddenly I realized I wasn't alone.

"Your Grace!" I yelped in surprise. Bastien was sitting in the same chair, cradling a book in his long fingers. A smirk twisting up his lips. My cheeks heated with embarrassment. This was worse than my moan of pleasure during our feeding. This was admitting that I couldn't get him out of my head.

I wanted to bury myself under the covers, but pride and anger kept me sitting upright. Didn't he have something better to do than watch me sleep? He was the Duke of Roselyn. Couldn't he bother Lady Natalia or his guard with his frustrating presence?

He set the book down and rose from the chair, picking up his cane as he approached me. He'd changed into different clothes: a fitted black riding coat buttoned over a white frock shirt, his long legs clad in riding trousers and tall boots.

Had I not known Bastien to be one of the twelve vampire princes who held castles and ruled over this land, I wouldn't have believed it. His attire was modest. No jewels or gold adorned his clothes. While there was nothing princely about his attire, I couldn't deny there was a certain regal air about him. Blond hair fell around his face, framing a strong jaw and soft lips. I knew just how soft those lips were. Hours ago, they'd been on my skin. Pressed against my trembling thigh.

I swallowed hard, barely daring to breathe. I had to stop letting thoughts of him control me. He was nothing to me. Nothing but a means to an end. When Bastien stopped at my bedside, I leaned back against my pillow, gripping the sheets and lifting them to my chin. *As if the vampire hadn't seen more than his share of me last night.* I wondered if he wanted another feeding. Why else would he linger?

"Can I help you, Your Grace?"

He contemplated me for a moment. Tilting his head to one side and letting his icy blue eyes slide down my frame in a way that set my core on fire. With his hands folded atop his cane, he said, "I'm not here because I want something. I'm here because... after our feeding, you fell asleep so quickly," he said. "I was concerned."

Concerned. I turned that word over in my head. Was Bastien trying to say he'd been worried about me? No, that couldn't be true. He didn't care about anyone. If he did, he would hold the Dark Witches accountable for their crimes. But something in his eyes told me that, against all odds, he did care about me. Even if he didn't want to.

I didn't know what to say. No one wasted their time worrying about me. Having someone care was strange, and I was unaccustomed to this kind of attention. So I dismissed it. "You didn't need to go to such trouble, Your Grace. I'm fine."

He gave the barest shake of his head. Jaw clenched. "You misunderstand me," he said through his teeth. "I needed to stay. Had to stay. You are mine to protect. Mine to care for." Each word was clipped and came out as if he wished they weren't true. I gripped the bedsheets tighter. "Miss Donadieu, your health and welfare are *my* responsibility." He cleared his throat, then tapped his cane against the wood floors. "As part of our contract, of course."

As part of our contract. *Of course.*

He was here out of obligation, not out of need or care. I was a burden to him, too. Wasn't I? He never wanted me in the first place. This was all obligation. That realization helped put things in perspective, and I was finally able to set aside the way he was looking at me. I tucked a strand of wild lilac hair behind my ear, then sat up taller, pulling the sheet up with me. "Well, as you can see, I'm quite well. If not a little hungry. Don't feel like you need to keep concerning yourself with me."

He pressed his lips together, holding back whatever sharp words were waiting behind his teeth. Instead, he offered me a glass of water. I stared at it for a moment before taking it. "I'll have food brought up. You need to eat."

I drank a sip, letting the cool water wet my dry throat. "Thank you."

Bastien nodded once before strolling to the door with his cane tucked under his arm. When he reached the handle, he stopped and cast a look over his shoulder. I lifted my eyebrows, wondering what else the vampire wanted to say and wished he would leave.

"After you eat, Shreesa will attempt to remove that cursed necklace."

The glass slipped from my hand, rolling off the bed and crashing to the floor, shattering into a million tiny pieces. I clutched the lace choker as if to prove my loyalty. "I already told you that will not work."

Shame welled inside me, hot and fresh. On the heels of my dream, my mother's voice was loud inside my head, criticizing me for being such a foolish girl and a pitiful excuse for a Prideaux woman.

"What did I do to deserve such a useless, magickless daughter like you? Tell me!"

I wouldn't have an answer. Only an apology. I was so sorry I wasn't the witch she'd hoped I'd be.

Bastien was back at my side in a blink. He brought his face close to mine. "Tell me who did this to you and why you're so afraid of removing it." His voice was a rough scrape over my skin. A demand.

I fell back on the lie Mama had told me to say if this question was asked. "No one did this to me, Your Grace. I wanted to put it on. To secure this position."

"Then who sold it to you? Who worked the spell?"

"I-I don't know their name," I stammered, "only that I bought it willingly and didn't ask many questions. They told me once I was collared, the magick was permanent. And it would kill me if I took it off. Or if I tried to leave before the year was up." I drew in a shuddering breath, bowing my head and forcing myself to say the next part. "Please, Your Grace. I know I'm not very bright."

I blinked back my hurt at being commanded to say I wasn't intelligent, but if Mama thought it was important to mention.

"The vampire is a disgusting beast," Mama had said, *"but he's not stupid. He'll see that you aren't very bright. It will make sense that a foolish human girl like yourself could stupidly buy a magickal necklace without asking questions."*

I heard a crack, like the sound of wood splintering, and when I found the strength to look up, Bastien had crushed the wooden bedpost into pulp. His face was just as monstrous as when he transformed into a vampire, but without the shadows. My eyes widened, unsure why he was suddenly so furious. "Tell me who put these ideas in your head!" he demanded. The force of his conviction causing the fine hairs on my arms to rise. "Was it the convent sisters?"

I said nothing. Pressing my lips together until they hurt.

"If it was the sisters," he continued, seething, "I'll have Marius shutter that damned place. I don't need the Nightfall

Convent to help me protect orphans if this is the result. I'll care for them myself."

He threw his cane across the room, and it smashed a porcelain pitcher. I recoiled into the covers, but the vampire wasn't done. He was breathing heavy, his chest heaving.

"Give me a name, and I will have them excommunicated from the faith."

My gaze left his face, traveling to the shattered pitcher and the broken bedpost. Why was he so mad? I didn't understand. I wasn't very bright. Otherwise, Diana wouldn't have shunned me. There was a reason I wasn't given the gift of magick. It was difficult to admit, but there was no other explanation for why my hair was lilac instead of white and why I couldn't cast spells.

And, oh, how that truth burned in the back of my throat like hot tears. I swallowed them back. Forcing myself to confront the seething duke. "No one put the idea in my head," I told him, closing my eyes and turning toward the fire. Clutching my throat. "I'm not smart. You said it yourself. It was foolish of me to meddle with magick I didn't understand."

Bastien cupped my chin and forced me to meet his gaze. I didn't find anger in his eyes, but something else. Something I couldn't explain but that melted into me. "Anyone with eyes can see that you are very bright, and I will not tolerate you calling yourself anything less in my presence. Do you understand me?"

His hand traveled to my cheek, holding me more tenderly. I didn't move. Didn't dare to breathe. He was so close. "You did what you thought was best to care for your sister, and I can respect that. However, the wounds that choker left behind are deep and must be cleaned. I could taste the faint tint of infection in your blood." When I tried to protest, he shook his head.

"How you've been able to endure as much as you have since the night of the Sangination Ball is no small miracle."

It wasn't a miracle. It was magick. Sera's numbing spell.

She was out there, somewhere, trusting me to be the older sister she needed. The full moon should be rising either tonight or tomorrow—depending on how long I'd been asleep. She would be able to recharge her powers and finish the ride back to Prideaux Hill safely.

His thumb stroked over my cheek as he continued. "You don't need to be scared of me or these women. But you do need to be honest. If not with me, then with them, as to the spell used to bind the necklace. They can help you."

Help me?

Whatever warmth had been building between us froze. He wanted me to be honest to a strange witch who likely conspired to murder my Gran? The ones who would kill Sera on sight? These were witches who consorted with demons, and everyone knew demons were evil and couldn't be trusted. Bastien just wanted to learn more about my necklace and was manipulating my emotions to accomplish that goal. That's all this was—skillful interrogation by a master of lies.

I gathered my nerve and pushed his hand off my face. "Those witches are evil, and their magick is rooted in demonic power. I want nothing to do with them."

He growled low in his throat, but I didn't flinch. I had to remain strong. "You will let them clean the wounds," he said, rising to his feet. At his full height, Bastien towered over me. "If they fester, you'll die far more painfully than if the choker had killed you."

I scrambled to my feet, standing on the mattress to match his height, dropping the sheet I'd clutched in my fists. "Bring me a rag. I will clean them myself."

He leaned in. Too close. His breath kissing my cheeks. "You are stubborn."

I was painfully aware of what his closeness did to my body, and was helpless to stop my nipples from pinching against the cotton shift.

I set my hand on his hard chest and pushed him back an inch, relieving myself of his delicious pine scent, and the feel of his breath against my skin. "You're the one who told me it was foolish to dabble in magick, Your Grace. Why should I allow more of it into my life?"

After a few tense moments where nothing was said and the only sound was our heaving breaths and the crackle of the fire, Bastien snatched up the cane he'd thrown and straightened his jacket.

"Protect whoever did this to you," he said, wagging the end of his cane at me. "But the wounds must be cleaned, and Shreesa *will* be the one to do it."

CHAPTER 16
ÈTRE MORT DE PEUR

CLAIRE

When he was gone, I snatched a pillow off the bed and hurled it at the door. I would've preferred to throw something much heavier at his smug face—like a sword. Too bad I didn't have one.

Breath coming in short gasps, I reached for another pillow, intent on throwing something else, when my gaze snagged on the sash of my robe. It wasn't tied the way I would have tied it in a simple bow. I lowered the pillow, my anger cooling into confusion. Slowly, I set it aside and reached for the knot, tugging experimentally. It didn't give. I frowned, both hands working at it now, but no matter how I pulled, the knot held tight.

By Diana, it was the same kind of knot Bastien had tied earlier. Some knot surely designed to keep prisoners from escaping. Had he tied my robe a second time? I didn't remember that. My stomach dipped.

What else didn't I remember?

I grew restless the longer I tried to answer that question and came up with nothing, so I forced myself to get out of bed, sidestepping broken shards of glass, splinters of wood, and porcelain dust, and lowered myself into the chair Bastien had occupied by the fire. Hugging my knees to my chest.

I reached for glimpses of what had transpired while staring into the flames. As hard as I tried, there was nothing. Nothing... *except*—I lifted a trembling hand to my mouth, delicately tracing the outline of my lips. There was no memory, only a strange feeling that we had... I shook my head and lowered my hand. No. *No*. That wasn't real. I'd only dreamed our kiss. Yet, I couldn't shake the strange feeling that his lips had touched mine.

A spark of something akin to excitement ignited in my stomach before anger had my hands curling into fists. I was just disoriented. Over the past five days, my world had turned upside down, and I was doing things I'd never dared to think about. Staying in a den of darkness. Rooming with a vampire. To make matters worse, I was failing at the one thing my family trusted me to do: *spy on Bastien.*

Just thinking his name caused a torrent of emotions to churn in my stomach. I knew I was supposed to be acting submissive and sweet, like a flower waiting to have its petals picked to lure him into trusting me—it's what Mama had told me to do—but at every turn, I was failing at that, too.

Something about the man drove me mad.

Rubbing at my temples, I melted into the chair, watching the fire popping and hissing in the hearth. The wild flames made me think of my little sister. Sera believed in me. She believed I could discover the information necessary to destroy dark magick. And if she believed in me, I had to believe in myself. Besides, I'd learned a few valuable things.

A soft knock startled me from my thoughts. "I have your breakfast, Miss," called a voice from the other side of the door. "And the treatment His Grace requested."

By treatment, she meant *black magick.*

My hand drifted to the lace choker once again. Bastien had demanded I eat and allow the wounds to be cleaned, and Mama wanted me to be compliant and meek, but doing so challenged everything I was taught about their kind.

As much as I wanted to send Shreesa away, I knew I couldn't. I was already allowing a vampire to take what he wanted from my body, I supposed this was all part of my sacrifice. To be touched and prodded by enemies so my family didn't have to endure such shame.

"May I come in?" the witch asked.

"Come in!" I called, the words sticking in my throat.

The woman bustled inside with a wicker basket in one hand and a tray in the other and closed the door. My heart accelerated to a galloping beat as soon as it was shut. Fear prickled along my spine and nervous sweat broke out over my skin.

I assessed her like a fox sizing up a hen, even though she was the one with teeth. Shreesa was a middle-aged woman with thick red hair and a round face. I thought she looked kind, but I knew looks could be deceiving, especially with Dark Witches.

All it took was one spell, and she'd transform.

When Shreesa saw the broken pitcher and bedpost, she clicked her tongue. "My, my. This is quite the mess. What was His Grace in a rage about this time?"

She cast me a sidelong glance. Her thin lips curling into a knowing smile. But what she knew, she didn't say.

Extracting a slender wooden stick from her apron pocket, she chanted in a language I didn't know. As she did, her eyes glowed red, just like a demon's. The hair on the back of my neck stood on edge as the charge of magick reverberated through the room, and the smell of something sweet lingered in the air. Instinct had me out of my chair. I flipped it over to shield myself, cowering behind it. Then I snatched an iron poker from beside the fireplace for good measure.

The broken items put themselves back together like a jigsaw puzzle. Then she crouched to my eye level. "Didn't mean to scare you, Miss. I forgot His Grace told me you were from Nightfall, and Damien knows how the sisters love to spin tall tales about us."

Her eyes stopped glowing blood red, and she shoved the thin wooden wand back into her pocket; my grip on the iron poker loosened a little. "Did they tell you we have a mouth full of sharp teeth? The better to eat disobedient children? That's always been my favorite story."

She thought my fear funny, did she? Slowly, I stood from behind the chair, but I didn't drop my weapon. I'd heard the stories about Dark Witches my family allowed me to hear and those they didn't.

Of the viciousness. Of the inhumanity.

"Sister Vera said you can grow long claws and sharp teeth. That you are just as monstrous as the demons you worship."

Or as the vampires that protected you from justice.

Shreesa's eyes held a hint of sadness when she said, "There's a kernel of truth in every story."

Righteous anger had me taking a step forward. "So you admit it. You are a monster."

She set her tray on the dresser and offered me one of the muffins. I didn't move. I was petrified. I was furious. I was out of my element in every way. But I stood my ground because that was what Prideaux witches did.

"All magick is monstrous if wielded by the wrong kind of witch, child."

What a ridiculous thing to say. My family's magick wasn't

monstrous. It was a gift from the Moon Goddess, Diana. *A blessing.*

Those who had Diana's gift, the Witches of the Light, didn't transform into beasts. They were good. And used their magick to protect themselves. "And you think you're the right kind of witch, do you?" I asked, clutching the fire poker like I was ready to swing it at her.

I didn't know what I meant to do, only that I didn't want to be defenseless when she showed her claws. But Shreesa didn't move to attack me. She simply ran a hand down the front of her apron.

"I try to be," she said, then cleared her throat. Looking at me like I was nothing more than an exasperating child. "Now, why don't you sit down so I can clean those wounds? That's what His Grace wants. That, and for you to eat."

I didn't want to eat her food or let her touch me, but I had to calm my anger and quiet my fears, no matter how hard it was. This was my chance to question her. To be the spy my family needed.

Setting down the fire poker would be easier if Bastien was here and I knew I was safe. But he'd left me alone, even though he'd committed to protecting me. I shouldn't be disappointed or surprised. I was used to being alone.

Slowly, I took the muffin and lifted it to my nose. It was warm, and it smelled more delicious than anything I'd ever eaten. Cautious, I took a small bite. It was filled with autumn flavors. Pumpkin. Cinnamon. Hearty oats. Shreesa stepped around me and righted the chair I'd knocked over. I took another bite as I studied her, hating how much I liked the fluffy texture and sweetness.

The witch patted the back of the chair, encouraging me to sit down while she busied herself with little pots and bundles of herbs inside her basket. With one eye on the witch, I lowered myself into the seat. The poker resting on my lap, just in case she got any ideas.

Shreesa hung a kettle over the fire, whistling softly as she returned to her basket and extracted a bolt of linen and cut it into strips. If I was going to ask her questions, I needed to get started. I watched her for a few more moments, then asked, "How do you know the Duke?"

Shreesa raised a brow. "Eat another bite, and I'll tell you."

For the sake of my curiosity, I took another bite.

She gave me a cheeky smile. "Our inn has always been a stop for those traveling between the north to Château Corbin," she began, using a blade just as short and stubby as she was to cut needles from a bundle of rosemary, releasing its fragrant aroma.

"The Duke is old enough to have known every witch in our graveyard, and he's been good to all of us."

I let my gaze return to the fire, gripping the iron poker so tight the rough metal scraped my palm. Bastien had always favored Dark Witches. It shouldn't surprise me.

The kettle started whistling, and she rushed to take it off the heat. pouring its contents into a small cauldron before sprinkling in herbs, and adding a vial of essential oil. "Even though we don't live within his territory, His Grace has listened to our concerns, even when others would ignore them."

"And what were those concerns?"

Shreesa let out a sigh. "He's helped us out here and there with land disputes and hunting infringements, appealing to the Duke of Lakeland on our behalf. But most importantly, he always brings us back a gift from the Lawless Lands to keep our magick alive."

My mouth dropped, and a sick feeling rose in my throat. "He brings you demonic relics?"

"Yes, child."

By Diana, Bastien wasn't just turning a blind eye to their crimes. He was replacing every relic my family destroyed with a new one. My shame and disgust for my strange urges quadrupled. I'd thought about doing inexcusable things with a man who wasn't just turning a blind eye, but who was actively aiding them.

No. Not a man. *A vampire.*

Shreesa dipped the strips of linen into the cauldron, steeping them in the herbal concoction she'd prepared. "I know the Nightfall Convent teaches you to worship Diana and to see her Witches of the Light as protectors, but they have all but destroyed our way of life."

My temper boiled over, and I threw the muffin into the fire, then lifted the iron rod, pointing the sharp end at her heart. She simply let out another long sigh. It made me even angrier to know she didn't see me as a threat. My vision tunneled until all I saw was her unflinching face.

"Get out," I said between clenched teeth.

Without another word, the witch did as I commanded. When she was gone, I paced back and forth across the small room, poker in hand, seething.

I thought I'd come here to spy on Bastien and discover the location of the relics, but it was clear to me there was another thing I needed to do. A more important thing. Bastien wasn't just a monster—he was the hand that fed the fire. If I couldn't destroy the relics, I could destroy the man who kept bringing them back.

CHAPTER 17
SOIGNER

CLAIRE

An hour passed, and my temper had cooled, but my conviction hadn't wavered. I had to kill Bastien. If Mama had heard what Shreesa said about the relics, he'd already be a corpse. The light gone from his eyes. His body limp.

Some strange feeling soured my stomach at the thought of seeing his lifeless form, and I wondered if it was because of the bond between us. My blood now lived in his veins, and perhaps a tiny part of me didn't want him to die. But it was a small part. There were a million reasons why I had to follow through with this plan.

I was packing my trunk when a knock made my breath catch. Without looking, I knew it was him. I could feel his presence on the other side of the door. Surely, he'd come to yell at me for not listening to him. I bid him enter, and Bastien slipped inside the room and closed the door.

I lifted my chin and forced myself to look at him. It was hard to hate something so beautiful. So perfectly put together. With soft lips that could speak such pretty words. Lips that I swore I tasted, if only in a dream. But he wasn't just a pretty package. Bastien could snuff out a life like he was blowing out a candle. He was a killer, *a demon*, and I was the soft prey to sink his teeth in.

I trembled where I stood, filled with such hate and such desire. One I understood, and the other burned against my will. We simply stared at each other. The air charged with unspoken words.

"Say something," I commanded him. Yell. *Rage*. Raise a hand. Fuel my hatred with your vicious nature.

But he said nothing. And by Diana's light, I wanted to scream. I didn't want to pretend anymore. I wanted to hurl accusations at him and make him answer for being on *their* side. I wanted to make him explain why he treated the Dark Witches with so much care but never did the same for us. I managed to keep my words behind my teeth, unable to set aside the pretense that I was nothing more than a simple orphan girl who wanted a chance to better her life.

Bastien stalked across the room, and I braced myself for what he might do. He was a vampire prince, and I'd disobeyed him. I was no stranger to violence—the back of Mama's hand or the crack of a switch. But he didn't do any of those things. He simply pushed the back of the armchair against the bed, then he retrieved the little cauldron of herbal tea the witch had left behind.

I didn't move, and neither did he. He commanded me to sit with his unwavering gaze. I wrung my hands together, trying to decide how to proceed. Did I let this happen? Did I let him wash my wounds? Or did I tell him to go to hell?

Without another word, he opened the connection between us, muting every sound—including the crackle of the fire and the distant sound of voices below—and I was helpless to stop the connection's influence on me.

It was like he could burn everything away except the sound of his voice inside my head. Not compelling me to act but forcing me to listen. "I was wrong to leave you alone with Shreesa. I see that now."

His voice was matter-of-fact. And the sound of it inside my head had the same effect on me that his tongue had on my neck. Weakening my knees and causing a tingle to settle low in my core.

He continued. "And for that, I'm sorry."

He was apologizing? *To me?* For failing to keep his promise? My lips parted, and disbelief had my brows drawing together. *Why?* He didn't need to take care of me. He didn't need to keep his promises. I didn't want his help. I could fend for myself. But the words died on my lips, and when he beckoned me forward with a finger, my traitorous feet shuffled toward the chair of their own accord.

My eyes never left his as I sat, hands folded in my lap. He stared at me with an unreadable expression—those long lashes of his beating like butterfly wings.

"Lean your head back against the bed," he instructed.

I hesitated for a moment, then did as he asked, slowly tipping my head back until it made contact with the soft quilt. My throat open and exposed for him. My chest straining against the boning of my bodice. I shouldn't let him do this, but for whatever reason, I didn't stop him.

With care, the Duke pulled a sopping wet strip of linen from the cauldron and brought it to my neck. The tea dripped onto my skin. Each tepid droplet had me wringing my hands together and squeezing my thighs tight.

Slowly, he wrung out the cloth over my skin, causing rivulets of lukewarm tea to race over the lace, saturating the material. Some of the liquid pooled at the base of my throat. Some puddled on the floor. Some funneled down my cleavage. The sensation and the surprise had me gasping, and I moved to grab a rag to clean my dress, but Bastien stopped me.

Our eyes connected, and the intensity of his look stilled my breath.

"My dress," I explained, worried that the tea would stain the delicate blue fabric and ruin it. I only came with a handful of dresses appropriate for a vampire court.

Once again, he spoke to me inside my head, and it was like he was whispering in my ear. The rasp of his voice was as soft as lace.

"Don't worry about your dress." He eased me back. Then carefully placed the strip of linen over my neck. *"I've sent word to have dresses made for you. When we arrive at my castle, you'll have so many gowns, you could ruin one every day for five years and still not wear them all."*

The connection between us reverberated inside my chest and the force of his promise echoed in my heart. He reached for another strip, repeating the process all over again until the front of my gown was soaked through, and even the fire couldn't stop gooseflesh from covering my skin. I shouldn't be trembling like this, but I couldn't stop myself. My back arched as he set the second scrap of linen over my neck and grabbed a third. More drips. More shivers. More breaths catching and hitching before expelling in a rush of air. More of his focused attention. More eyes tracing my body as he reached for yet another.

"Tell me, Miss Donadieu," he said. The low tenor of his voice unfurled around me like a warm embrace, *"Is this experience as bad as you imagined?"*

I didn't know what to say. It wasn't like anything I'd ever imagined. I hadn't expected him to be so adamant. Or so... *attentive.*

I swallowed hard, knowing my dress was a ruin. Knowing I was a ruin.

"Not every experience you fear is worthy of it," he said. *"No one thing, or person, is all bad."*

Bastien wiped his wet hands on a cloth before walking around the chair to face me. *"The road ahead is rough. I should feed before we leave. But I will abstain if you do not consent."*

I should say no. I should make him suffer. Maybe he'd get sick enough that I could take him unaware. As much as I knew I had to kill him, I selfishly wanted to feel the euphoria that came with his mouth against my thigh.

Once he was dead and I returned to my coven with his secrets, I'd return to being no one—the *Ghost of Prideaux Hill.* The magickless witch who no man of worth would want. This pleasure was all I'd ever get, and I'd have to live with my shame forever.

That's all I'd take from him—this pleasure, his secrets, and his life.

I nodded and consented to the feeding.

Bastien sank to his knees in front of me. His hands gripping my calves. His skin cold through my thigh-high nylons. I lifted my head to witness him on the ground before me. His teeth dragged over his lower lip, and my thighs snapped back together as a pulse of desire rolled through me. Everything inside me clenching tight.

Those blue eyes. Those soft lips. Those strands of pale hair falling around his face.

His pledge resonated inside my chest, but it wasn't his words or false promises that I wanted. No. His rough, calloused hands dragged up to my knees, spreading my legs apart inch by inch. Hate and desire lived inside me, and right now, desire was winning.

He lifted my skirts just as carefully, letting the material

slide up my sensitive skin until the dress was around my waist. Every place his gaze landed burned, and the soft flesh between my thighs dampened. Turning slick with my need.

Carefully, he unhooked the garter holding up my silk nylons and peeled them down. Then lifted my legs over his broad shoulders before settling between them. The ghosting touch of his lips came next, following by the wet stroke of his tongue. The shadows under his eyes darkened, and his fangs appeared. Then came the full-body release of his bite.

I melted into the chair, knowing that each time he did this might be the last. And I decided to relish every moment of it.

We left for Roselyn at dusk. The coach swaying as the horses tore off into the night. Our vampire guard riding alongside.

Once again, I was accompanied by Tyson and Okeri, but I paid them little attention as I stared out the frost-stained window, contemplating how I was going to kill a vampire. The thought plagued me for hours, and every time I decided on a way to end his unnaturally long life, an ache formed in my chest that I didn't quite understand.

I rubbed at my breastbone, trying to ease the tension. This was the right decision. I just needed to stop being such a coward and choose a path. I was no warrior, so cutting off his head wasn't going to work, and I didn't think I could poison his food without killing myself in turn. I'd proven that much during my failed attempt to slip him a sleeping draught that only resulted in me falling asleep.

The only option was to get close enough to him that he let his guard down. And right when he thought I was the person he could trust and confessed all his secrets, I'd strike.

I rubbed my hand along the tender spot on my thigh where he'd fed from me hours ago, remembering the ecstasy he'd coaxed from me. Of the moan that had torn from my throat halfway through. Of the feeling of his lips kissing and sucking at my skin.

The problem with getting close to Bastien was that my body always wanted more than just his nearness. It wanted to be looked at and desired and touched. It wanted to experience things that filled my cheeks with heat and my head with lurid thoughts. I licked my dry lips and crossed my legs to relieve the growing ache between my thighs.

Was this the answer? Was giving my body what it so longed for the way to lull him into a false sense of trust? Perhaps so. Yet the thought made me equal parts excited and terrified. What if I was no good at wooing him, and I only pushed him away with my awkwardness?

Leaning my forehead against the cold window, I closed my eyes and expelled a long breath as images of me and Bastien entwined filled my head. It wasn't wrong to think these things if it was for the right reason, was it?

CHAPTER 18
FANTASMER
BASTIEN

espite Shreesa's inn marking the halfway point between my château and Marius's, the second leg of our journey up the mountain roads was slower. We'd spent the past two weeks inching along. The colder it got, the more we needed to stop and allow the horses and humans in our company time to rest.

The sun's rays were dulled by heavy clouds, but traveling during the day depleted us. Each night, we made camp at dusk. And each night, after my nightly meeting with my council, I returned to my tent to greedily feed from Claire as she lay upon a bed of furs.

Truthfully, I didn't need to eat every day, but I couldn't stop myself. Not when my mate was right there, so warm and soft. If I was feeding, I could throw her trembling legs over my shoulder. I could kiss her thigh. I could twist our fingers together. I could wipe clean the wound and ensure she ate. I could keep her company and learn more about her before she drifted off to sleep.

Under the guise of feeding, I could be close to her. But touching her and holding her and stealing laughs late into the night wasn't the only thing I wanted. I needed her. All of her. Needed to be inside her. Claiming her. Pleasuring her. Fucking her. Coaxing more than little whimpers from her lips, but screams that shook snow from the branches. Giving myself to her over and over. I needed to hear her say my name. Needed to feel those soft thighs around my waist as I came deep inside her.

And yet, I couldn't. But it didn't stop the temptation. The scent of Claire's desire was nothing compared to seeing it soaked through her undergarments every single night when my face was between her legs. It was torture. If only my enemies had this information, they'd know exactly how to bring me to my knees. I'd give up blood for a month for a taste of her sweet pussy.

The slow smile that had spread across my face shrank, and I berated myself for being so weak-minded—for being so pathetic. The need to claim her was an instinct I had to ignore, but doing so was like holding a lid over a boiling pot. The pressure building inside of me.

At times of weakness, I considered showing her my bloodstone and confessing the truth. That we were meant to be, if only we wanted it. But I *didn't* want it. *Couldn't want it.* There was too much on the line, and Tyson's presence was a constant reminder of that fact. If I gave in and told her the truth, I'd lose it all. *To him.* And he was incapable of doing my job.

At the same time, she was all I could think about. Even now, as I sat in this very important meeting with people I cared about and respected, I was distracted. My vampiric senses focused on my tent—on her. I could feel her heart beating inside my bloodstone, yes, but I wanted to know what she was doing. If she was thinking of me. If she was touching herself. Satisfying that ache I knew she had. The same ache I had.

I gritted my teeth imagining the scene, wanting to relieve that ache for her. But it was impossible. I couldn't deepen my feelings for Claire more than they already were. No, they weren't *feelings*. They were primal instincts. Urges put in my head by the gods that got the better of me each time I tried to keep them in check. Her blood in my veins making it all worse.

"Your Grace!" Natalia shouted, slamming her hand down on the table. "We need your thoughts on the matter."

Every eye around the table was on me. Curious stares that portrayed confusion or disappointment. Tyson was reclining back in his chair, arms crossed, one leg kicked out like he was comfortable at my table.

I shook my head slightly, trying to bring my focus back to the meeting, and looking around for context clues. Another map had been rolled out in front of me, one that was of the south, specifically the land around Château Blanc. I didn't know why the conversation had turned Nightfall.

I rubbed at my temples, realizing I hadn't heard a word that was said for some time. I was distracted, which seemed to be my new normal.

Natalia sighed. "What do we tell the Duke of Nightfall? My father requests you attend his Sangination Ball in four months' time. Will we be making the trip?"

I cleared my throat and turned my attention back to the map, trying to order my thoughts. My first inclination was to say no. The cold was setting in, but that didn't mean the witches of the Lawless Lands went to ground. It was too risky.

However, Josse's land also encompassed the Nightfall Convent, which meant I could take Claire to see her sister. The thought of her face when she saw her sister again made my heart swell. Besides, I'd like to inspect the convent myself. I suspected Claire wasn't the only one who had been mistreated.

However, it wasn't practical.

I lifted my gaze to my council and folded my hands. "No. We will not attend. Send our regrets. I'm sure my absence won't surprise Josse in the least."

Chuckles went around the table. Natalia made a note before calling for a page to send a raven to Nightfall. She was trying to hide her excitement. Ever since she'd been named unfit to be her father's heir, she preferred to stay away.

Once the task was handled, I hoped all business had been finished so I could return to Claire, but, I could tell Natalia had more to say. I could tell by the way she tapped her quill against the page.

"Well?" I prompted, rubbing at my temples.

"What of Shreesa's plea, Your Grace? How are we to handle allegations that the Prideaux coven is doubling down on their pursuit of demonic relics? She claims another has been taken. They're worried."

I made a tight fist. After all we sacrificed to seal the Blood Treaty, I grew weary of these continued hostilities. "We'll make good on our promise to bring more from the Lawless Lands on our next trip. Send word to Chastity."

This was my only solution for keeping the balance of power. paying the Witches of the Lawless Lands—those who still made deals with demons—for relics.

Natalia's scowl deepened. "That will only last so long if they are being targeted. Shreesa says they don't have enough magick to bind familiars, and all the beasts have died."

I stared at the map, thinking hard. As much as I wanted to hold the entire realm together by sheer force of will, I couldn't.

"Angelina Prideaux doesn't have the resources or the support to do little more than raid," I said. "I'll send word to the Duke of Lakeland, doubling down on my position that he strengthen his forces, and in the meantime, we'll send a patrol to protect Shreesa's home."

She made another note. "Very well. We'll treat the symptom, not the problem. *Yet again.*"

"I am *not* the High Prince," I scolded her. "I can only do so much."

"Uncle Marius would give you the crown if you would only take it."

I scoffed. "Is there any other business?"

"Yes, Your Grace."

I inclined my brows.

Natalia waved to the guards standing watch at the tent, who escorted in a human man. He was tall, well built, with dark skin and dark hair, and the sly, charming smile of someone who always got what he wanted. He bowed when he stood before my table.

"Your Grace, this is Alec. He claims to have seen *things*. Things that shouldn't be possible."

I inclined my chin, interest piqued. "Well, Alec, what have you seen?"

The man cleared his throat. "I was working at the Veraleese Inn, which is in Nightfall, Your Grace, when I saw..." he hesitated, "I saw two men who seemed *strange*. As a pillow whisperer at the inn, I see many people come and go, but none like these."

My nephew chuckled behind his fist. I shot him a chilly glare.

"Tell the Duke the interesting part," Natalia prodded.

The man wetted his lips and drew in a breath. "I know this is going to sound mad, but I swear Your Grace, on the night of Diana's moon, I saw these strange men with a woman, and they weren't treating her as a woman should be treated. So, I intervened, but before I could stop them, they attacked me and ran off into the night. When I went to help the woman, she transformed into a werewolf, scratched my arm, and raced off after them."

Laughs went around the table. My advisors clearly thought this was a ludicrous story.

Tyson drank deeply from his cup of wine. "Or he's lying to get a free ride in your court. Word of your hospitality stretches into the south, Uncle. He's clearly pandering to your altruistic nature. Not even the strongest Witches of the Light can transform into a wolf. It is but a rumor. A legend."

All hint of humor fled the tent. Silence fell. While I took counsel from advisors, no one in my court spoke for me. I motioned to Destinee, a hardened warrior. "Commander Gris, escort the viscount out of this meeting."

Tyson sat up straight in his chair for the first time. "Uncle, I offer my opinion."

His father asked me to teach him how to lead. The boy had much to learn in humility. He could thank me later for these valuable lessons. The look on my face didn't change. "Leave, or let Commander Gris toss you out."

With a huff and a flourish of his royal blue cloak, Tyson stood and stalked out of the meeting. Natalia was beaming with glee. "This was the same inn a *certain someone* was followed into."

She was being purposefully coy, so I slipped inside her mind and heard her tell me, *"Miss Donadieu's sister. Seraphina."*

My ability to slide into minds was a gift few other vampires possessed. I couldn't hear thoughts, but I could speak directly with someone. However, I'd never felt it as deeply as the bond I had with Claire.

"This woman who allegedly turned into a werewolf—what did she look like?"

"Like all Witches of the Light, Your Grace. Long white hair. Glowing gold eyes. A mean look on her face."

I canted my head toward my niece. *"See, Claire's sister had lilac hair. Not white."*

"Hair can be charmed!"

There was no use arguing with Natalia when she thought herself right. So I returned my attention to the man with the impossible story. "You said she scratched you. Where is the wound?"

He lifted his sleeve to show a set of ugly claw marks. They were too big for a common wolf—perhaps a bear.

A shocked silence settled over the meeting. I steepled my fingers, considered the man in front of me. He could be lying, which I found unlikely. Or, he could be embellishing a story because he was looking for a new home, as Tyson suggested.

"Do you have a family?"

He shook his head. "No, Your Grace. I was orphaned. Was on my own until I was sixteen. Started working in the kitchens at the inn, but I'm a shit cook. However, my other talents earned me a better salary."

A survivor. Someone who did what it took. "Do you wish to return to Nightfall, and to your position at the inn?"

Alec shifted his gaze from the floor back to me, surprise lighting his reddish-brown eyes. "No, Your Grace. Not after what happened. If it pleases Your Grace, I'd like to offer you my services."

Natalia scoffed. "Does this mean we're taking him with us?"

I had a habit of taking in strays, as Natalia put it. The unwanted. The runaways. The ones who had nowhere else to go. Those cast aside for being too much or not enough.

I saw myself in them, because I'd been that runaway. Afraid of the power in my veins. Of what my magick could do when I was angry. I rubbed my thumb across an old wound on the back of my wrist. One that not even my vampiric skin fully concealed. A reminder of the past.

The court could keep their polished heirs and perfect nobles. I preferred the company of those who had been through fire and lived to tell about it. The ones who chose loyalty because they knew the taste of betrayal. They were scrappier. Hungrier. Fiercer in their devotion. And twice as kind as those who'd never been made to bleed for their place in the world. *Like my nephew.*

So no—I had no intention of changing my ways. I'd rather build a court of lone wolves than fill my halls with sheep.

I contemplated the man, then made a decision. "I demand acceptance and respect of all who enter Château Rose. In my home, you will encounter those from different walks of life, or who worship differently than you. If you pledge to be tolerant and open-minded, you'll have a place at my court."

He nodded fervently. "Yes, Your Grace. I swear."

"Very well. Natalia will assign you to a job that she sees fitting for your talents. And our healer will tend to your wounds to ensure you haven't contracted an affliction."

Alec bowed, a bright, charming smile spreading across his face. "Thank you, Your Grace."

He was escorted out of the tent by Commander Gris. As he left, I turned his story over in my mind. He'd been attacked by *something.* But a witch who could turn into a wolf? It didn't make sense. Tyson was right, it was a legend amongst Diana's Moon Witches. Some saw transforming into beasts as disgusting, akin to becoming nothing more than a familiar like the Witches of the Darkness bound. Others argued the power was necessary to winning the war against dark magick and were always on the hunt for a way to shift.

If Angelina Prideaux found a way... No, I dismissed the

thought. She was a thorn in the side of the Unified Territories, but that kind of magick was ancient and far too powerful for her to wield.

I dismissed my council, ready to get back to Claire, but Natalia lingered—her quill still in hand.

"What is it?"

She gave me a half-grin that I didn't like. "We arrive in Roselyn tomorrow. And seeing how you've been... *occupied* of late, we haven't discussed the details of Miss Donadieu's accommodations."

I rolled up the nearest leather map, feigning indifference. I knew Natalia was suspicious of how protective I'd grown of Claire, and how much time I was spending with her.

"Miss Donadieu will be cared for just like any other," I said, offhandedly, fixing the leather strap around the map and reaching for the next one. "She'll take the room adjoining mine, and will have attendants, and dresses, and anything else she desires."

Natalia hummed as she scribbled notes. I stood, ready to leave, when she added, "And what about her consorts? We can ask if Tibitha's pillow whisperers are willing to stay on staff, but something tells me she'd like to pick her own. Maybe Alec will be to her liking."

I froze mid-step. Every protective instinct roared to life. Despite knowing I shouldn't give this order, I did. "Miss Donadieu doesn't require a consort."

Natalia let out a chuckle. "I'm tired. It's been a long trip on horseback. I'm not in the mood for your dark humor at the moment, Uncle."

I turned around, temper rising. I didn't like that she thought this was a joke. I'd never been more serious about anything in my life. No one would touch Claire. No one.

"She will not have any lovers."

Natalia raised an intrigued brow. She was twice as smart as any man on my council and equally as observant. "And why not?"

I knew I had to think logically here. I couldn't risk Natalia discovering the truth. As a member of the vampire nobility, if she knew Claire was my mate and did nothing, she'd be culpable in my crimes, and I didn't want that for her. I'd chosen to take my mate as my sanguine partner, against the laws, and I was the only one who would suffer for it.

"Because," I explained, "I don't think she wants one."

Natalia narrowed her eyes. "Did she tell you that?"

I considered lying, but instead, gritted out, "No."

This was an impossible situation, and I was beginning to understand why there were laws around leaving your duchy and returning to the capital when you found your mate. Having them around made a vampire impulsive and distracted. I was strong enough to keep my urges in check. I wasn't giving in to her. I was just... *watching over her*. Keeping her safe. When the year was up, I'd send her off to a palatial home in the south where she could live a happy and well cared for life far away from me.

"Your Grace, not that I trust this woman or even really like her, but it's your job to ensure she has all her needs met. That includes this *particular* need. You can't have her sneaking around with random strangers in dark corners, putting herself in mortal jeopardy. Or trying to leave the castle for a midnight rendezvous."

I turned away from her, trying to imagine a situation where Claire ran into the arms of another man, and I didn't rip that man to shreds.

"If she keeps consorts," Natalia continued, "her lovers will be well-vetted and paid handsomely for their services."

My hands were shaking and I shoved them into my pockets

to keep her from seeing how angry I was. How could I refuse when my other sanguine partners had consorts? It would show her I thought Claire was different, and I couldn't have that.

"Fine," I said at last. "Make the arrangements. But this is the last I want to hear of it."

Natalia made a note, then closed her book. "Very well, Your Grace. I will meet with Claire when we arrive at Château Rose, and we'll select her consorts." She laughed, and I gritted my teeth. "I always enjoy this part of my job."

"I'm sure."

I pushed the heavy tent flaps open and stormed out. I stared at my tent for a few moments, breathing hard, trying to decide what to do or how to proceed. Did I go in the tent and feed from her, knowing that any day now, she would have another man between her legs? Feasting on parts of her that I wasn't allowed to taste?

I couldn't stand the idea. If I saw her now, I'd do something I'd regret. So, I didn't return to my tent. Instead, I secluded myself in one of the feeding tents. I needed to release some of the pressure building inside me before I saw her again. I needed to work out this primal urge to fuck her. That's all this was. *An urge.* An urge that I could satisfy myself.

Undoing the buttons on my pants and letting them fall to my ankles, I sank onto one of the cushions. My stiff cock sprang free, ready and waiting. Fisting my length, I told myself this was truly unhelpful to my cause. Imagining Claire's hands and mouth, so supple and sweet, fitted around me, wouldn't make being around her any easier. But despite everything, it's what I wanted. *What I needed.*

Stroking myself, I gave in to every desire I had about my mate. I imagined pulling her into my lap, watching her ride me. Her tits bouncing up and down as my hips bucked into her sweet center. Again and again. Claiming her as mine. Mine. All mine. Hearing her moan my name as I sucked one of her nipples into my mouth.

"Claire." I whispered her name inside my head, working my stiff length harder. Faster. *"I'm going to come so deep inside you. I'm going to give you all of me."*

CHAPTER 19
DÉCOUVRIR
CLAIRE

An unexpected gust of cold wind howled through the tent. I closed my book and rose onto my elbow, causing one of the heavy furs I was cuddled beneath to slip off my shoulder. I hadn't anticipated the council meeting running this late.

"Your Grace?" I called, anticipation tightening in my belly.

For the past two weeks, I'd been doing my best to get closer to the Duke. Every night, after camp was made and he'd finished his council meetings, we'd stay up late, talking about the types of plants he grew in the glass greenhouses at Château Rose.

My love of flowers and working in the dirt and his love of science intersected, and I found I could talk to him for hours about how he managed to grow anything that far north. Last night, he'd sat beside me and sketched out one of his greenhouses, telling me how difficult it was to lay each massive pane of glass. I hung on each word, impressed with his dedication to growing food and herbs for the surrounding villages and his human staff, even though he ate neither.

"It sounds like a lot of work," I'd said, meeting his ice-blue eyes, which held a measure of warmth I hadn't seen before. Like the sky over an ocean on a clear summer day.

"It was," he replied. He watched me for a moment that stole my breath, then canted his head to one side and ever so carefully pushed a stray strand of hair away from my face. My cheeks heated at his touch. "But," he said softly, "I'm not afraid of hard work. Especially when the result is something that could last forever."

His words opened a chasm in my chest, and I swore he wasn't talking about a greenhouse, but about something else. Something that I didn't quite understand but that I felt in my bones.

The ghost of a kiss we only shared in my dreams warmed my lips, causing my breath to stutter.

"You want to say something," Bastien said. Leaning in an inch.

It wasn't words I craved. I ached to close the distance between his lips and mine. Was desperate to curl his long hair around my fingers and pull him closer against my body. To devour him. To let him devour me. Bite by bite until my eyes rolled back and my body shuddered, and he finally showed me what it meant to be wanted.

I'd decided to woo him into trusting me so I could kill him, but it was getting harder to reconcile what I'd grown up understanding about his kind with the things he said and did. Bastien was forcing me to see him for who he was, night after night, and it was all very confusing. Especially with the heady way his presence affected me.

"I think I'm ready for bed," I said.

The Duke pressed his lips together, nodding once, then set aside his sketchpad and graphite and scooped me up like he had the first night we'd met. Surprised, I gasped, wrapping my arms around his neck to steady myself.

Our eyes connected, and my mouth softened for him. I knew if he kissed me now, I wouldn't stop him. I'd fold like a house of cards. Desire and anticipation had my skin tingling with need. But it wasn't my kiss that he wanted. It was my body. *My blood*. That's why I was here.

Gently, he lay me on the pile of furs that served as my camp bed. My hands reluctantly left his neck, gliding down his shoulders and grazing his chest before tucking them back at my sides. He stared at me for a long moment as I lay there. His hungry gaze trailed over the swell of my breasts, continuing down to my navel. Down, further still. Lingering around the place where my sleeping shift had ridden up, showcasing my bare thighs. I guessed what he wanted. And if truth be told, I wanted it too.

Without looking away, I spread my legs apart, watching him as he watched me. I was so needy for him. So vulnerable. Spread open wide and exposed. Ready to be licked and kissed and nipped at in the only way I'd ever been. "Eat, Your Grace," I said in a thick voice I almost didn't recognize—spreading my legs wider, ready for him to crawl between them and drink from me as we'd done every other night in this twisted, dark exchange I'd come to thirst for as much as he. "I don't want you to go hungry."

Bastien grabbed my wrist, stopping me from pulling my shift up around my hips. My eyes grew wide with surprise. "No," he said sharply, even though the shadows under his eyes had appeared, and his transformation was imminent. He drew a measured breath and released his grip on me, then said, "I mean, *not tonight*. I've kept you up too late."

His denial stung more than I thought it would. My body ached for him, *for his touch*. And it didn't like being told no. A million thoughts tumbled inside my head, all of them screaming at me for being a failure.

He covered me in furs and sat beside the bed reading. Leaving me alone and frustrated. I turned away from him. When the anger and shame twisting inside me finally let me sleep, I closed my eyes and curled beneath the thick furs like I was retreating into a cocoon.

My sleep was fitful. Marred by dreams that felt too real. Of kisses. Of hands pressed into the bedsheets. Of that hardness between his legs pressed against my soft middle. Then, the scene shifted to a chilly autumn night, a full moon, and the shrill howl of a wolf.

I awoke the next morning feeling shameful and made the no-nonsense choice to rededicate myself to my mission. It was time to take things to the next level. I needed information about the relics he was stealing from the Lawless Lands.

Another gust of wind blew through the tent, bringing me out of the reverie and back to the present. I sat fully up, holding the furs against my chest. "Your Grace?" I called again. But only the wind answered.

I frowned. Had he gotten sick of me? Had he found another's tent to warm him? What if he was there right now? It would make sense. I was just his sanguine partner, and it wasn't my job to see to any of his *other* needs.

Maybe my plan to woo him had been stupid. Jealousy like I'd never felt before sprouted in my stomach, and suddenly I didn't want to be sitting here, waiting for him. I forced myself to leave the warmth of the bed, wrapping my arms around my middle as I strolled through the expansive, multi-room tent, only to find one of the ties had come loose.

I went to refasten it when I saw Bastien's nephew, Tyson, staring at me from a few paces away. He looked resplendent in his royal blue cloak with gold stitching. His dark hair pulled back, and his bronze skin shining under the glow of the moon. He ran a thumb across his lower lip, looked both ways, then made his way over to where I stood.

I braced myself, unsure what to expect. Bastien had allowed him and Okeri to ride with the guard the past few days, allowing me some alone time, and we hadn't said much to each other except to exchange pleasantries.

"Good evening," the vampire said, bowing at the neck.

I curtsied politely, giving him the honors he was due as a viscount, but I felt uneasy speaking to him alone.

"I couldn't help but hear you calling for my uncle."

I closed the folds of my robe as tendrils of embarrassed heat raced up my neck.

Tyson offered me a charming smile then he tapped the side of his ear. "Us vampires have very good hearing, as I'm sure you know. A blessing and a curse, if truth be told. Especially in a camp this small. We hear *everything*. Every stubbed toe, every moan of pleasure." He pursed his lips and leaned conspiratorially in. "Be grateful for the limits of your mortal hearing."

"Oh," I said as heat crept into my cheeks. He'd heard our whispered conversations in the dark. And my moans of pleasure as he fed.

"Is there something you wanted? From my uncle, that is?" Tyson asked, and I couldn't tell if he was fishing for information or trying to be helpful.

If his hearing was as good as he boasted, he knew things I didn't. Perhaps forming an alliance with the young vampire wasn't a bad idea. "That is very kind of you to ask, My Lord." I shivered from the winter chill, and Tyson unfastened his cloak and offered it to me.

"Please. Take it. I can't stand to see a woman shiver."

I accepted it hesitantly, setting it over my shoulders and

sighing into the warmth it provided. "Has the council meeting finished yet?"

Tyson raised a mischievous eyebrow, and a smirk settled on his face. "It has."

That jealous snake in my stomach started writhing once again, and I looked over Tyson's shoulder, hoping to see a hulking, stoic blond vampire stalking through the night, making his way toward me, but he wasn't.

Tyson leaned in closer and cupped a hand to his mouth, inviting me in for a secret. Nervously, I bent forward, allowing him to whisper in my ear. "My uncle has secluded himself in a feeding tent. Just over there."

I followed his finger to a cluster of small tents. Why would he be in a feeding tent? We had our own tent that we'd been making good use of. "Should I—"

"Join him?" Tyson offered, finishing my sentence.

I nodded.

He lifted a shoulder, feigning indifference. "If I were my uncle, I'd very much like to see you. But, alas," he said with a sigh, "I am not him, as he constantly reminds me, and therefore cannot give you very good advice."

The sudden urge to find Bastien overtook every other thought in my head. He hadn't fed from me last night, and I wondered why he hadn't come to me tonight. I reached for my gloves, which were just inside the tent, and slid my hands into the fur lining, then laced up my boots. The younger vampire stepped out of my way as I left the warmth of the tent and shivered again. Despite the chill, the heat generated by the jealousy twisting in my stomach was enough to keep me warm.

"Which tent?" I asked.

He bit his lip before pointing to a small clustering of tents closer to the edge of camp. "One of those."

Hugging my arms to my chest, I thanked him, then stormed off. Not caring if Bastien and his excellent hearing heard my approach as I crunched through the thin layer of snow. If he was feeding from another or... or doing *other* things, he could be just as embarrassed as I was.

Two of the tents had the curtains drawn, and with halting steps, I peered through the flaps of the closest one, but immediately backed away when I saw a man from Bastien's council with another. Both of them shirtless. Definitely not feeding.

I curled my hands into fists and made my way over to the tent. My breaths became shorter the closer I got. Forcing myself to verify my worst suspicions, and satisfy the voice in my head that was telling me I was a complete and utter failure, I peered through the closed flap, and had to hold my breath at the sight before me.

Bastien. *Naked from the waist down.* Sitting on a cushion. Head tipped back. Fisting the hard length of flesh between his legs.

He wasn't with anyone else, and he certainly wasn't feeding. He was... well, I didn't know *what* he was doing. All I knew was that it was the most decadent thing I'd ever seen. The sight of him doing *whatever it was made* me clench with desire. I struggled to look away from the action of his hand. The way he massaged himself up and down in a fevered way. Like he was chasing something. Something I wanted to chase, too.

"Claire," he whispered through our bond like he was speaking in my ear, pumping himself harder. Spreading his legs wider.

The way he said my name had every nerve standing on end. I gripped the tent flaps to steady myself, thankful that his eyes were closed and that he was completely lost in the moment.

"I'm going to come so deep inside you. I'm going to give you all of me."

With those words ringing in my ears, Bastien moaned, and hot release spilled over his hand. I couldn't look away. Transfixed by what he'd said and what he was doing. Continuing to work himself up and down.

I told myself to leave, to go back to our tent, but I was frozen in place. Chest heaving. Body trembling. The ache between my thighs pulsing. *There was nowhere else I wanted to be.*

The snow crunched beneath my feet, and his eyes flew open. For a heartbeat, neither of us moved. I could tell by the look of mild surprise on his face he hadn't realized I'd been watching him. Which meant I had two options: turn around and leave *or stay.*

CHAPTER 20

VOULOIR

CLAIRE

I stood there, holding the tent flap for dear life, indecision holding me in place. I knew leaving wasn't an option. There was no way I could pretend I hadn't seen what I'd seen. I swallowed hard.

Or what I was still seeing.

Bastien didn't move to cover himself. No. He was still gripping his thick shaft, slowly pumping up and down, *up and down*, then squeezing right around the tip in this slow, seductive rhythm that I wanted to learn. Like maybe he *wasn't* finished.

He never looked more like a prince than he did right now. Sitting on a cushion with his legs spread. Unashamed and unhurried. Like there was nothing to be embarrassed about. Like he didn't care that I'd caught him with his pants around his ankles.

Moaning my name.

I needed to know why he'd opened our connection and said my name. The desire held me in place. Maybe he'd been imagining kissing me the way I'd been imagining kissing him. And if he was, maybe I was doing something right after all.

This was all for a good reason, I reassured myself. The more he trusted me, the closer I could get. And the easier it would be to kill him. Because that was still my mission. Right?

On my next shaky inhale, I removed the cloak Tyson had given me and dropped it in the snow, along with my gloves, knowing the sight of royal blue would infuriate him. Then parted the curtains and stepped inside the tent. Bastien tracked my movements as I closed the curtains and did up all the ties. I didn't want an errant breeze to interrupt this conversation.

When I turned back around, my breath caught. He was beautiful. Spent and glistening. And the desire to touch him like he'd been touching himself made sweat collect along the base of my neck. I wanted to run my fingers over him and bring his hard length to my throbbing middle while he kissed me into oblivion. I didn't know why, or where the idea came from, only that there was a primal need inside me to be filled with him. It was shameful, but I was already a ruin.

Bastien reopened the connection between us, which only drew me deeper into the fantasy. Pulling my attention into him and forcing me to unburden my worries as I listened to the sound of his voice.

"Why are you here?"

My stomach tightened and my muscles clenched. *Why was I here?* The answer was simple, yet very, *very* complicated. I couldn't tell him that I'd been worried he was feeding from someone else or that he was in another's tent. Lusting after her. I barely wanted to admit that I had those thoughts to myself because why should I care what he did so long as I could get information from him? But for whatever reason, *I did.*

Clearing my throat, I responded with the most basic yet honest answer. *"I was looking for you."*

There was a beat of silence.

That ache between my thighs crested to new heights when he released himself to grab a handkerchief and began wiping off his thighs, allowing me to look at him fully. At how hard and long he was. How thick this part of him was.

He tossed the soiled handkerchief on the floor, his gaze never leaving my face. The line of his dark blond brows pushed together in question. *"Why?"*

"You're in a feeding tent, and considering I am the one you are supposed to be feeding from, I thought you would want to see me."

"Feeding tent is nickname we use for tents designated for fucking."

"Oh."

He glanced down at his hard length, then back up at me, nonplussed. *"When you saw I didn't require a feeding, why didn't you leave?"*

The question needled me, and an embarrassed flush rushed back into my cheeks. Maybe he didn't want me here. Maybe he hadn't meant to open our connection and say those things.

I twisted my fingers together and looked over his shoulder at the brazier hanging in the corner—it was the only thing warming the small tent, except for the fire in my cheeks. *"I-I don't know."*

He said nothing, and neither did I. After a moment, my curiosity got the better of me. If he wanted me to leave, he wasn't making a show of it or even moving to cover himself.

He was simply questioning me, like he always did.

"What were you doing in here?"

It was the first time his lips moved—one corner lifting into a smirk. I would've been irritated that he found my question funny, but he had the most beautiful lips I'd ever seen, and they were rather distracting.

"I'm assuming this is a rhetorical question," Bastien drawled, *"because you saw what I was doing."*

Another fresh flush of embarrassment filled my cheeks, and it was so frustrating that I had been as sheltered as I was. I'd never been given the words to articulate myself properly.

"You assume I have a name for it."

Bastien quirked a brow this time. *"You don't?"*

"I'm assuming that must be a rhetorical question," I began, mocking him, *"because you know I grew up in a convent. And that,"* I pointed in the general direction of his stiff length, *"wasn't covered in my lessons on worshipping the Moon Goddess."*

He didn't laugh like I thought he might. No. He raked his teeth over his bottom lip and rubbed at his long chin. Contemplating me. His silence did nothing to stop my desire for him. If anything, it *intensified*, and I had to shift my weight, needing to move some part of me.

His smirk fell flat. *"You're curious."*

Curious didn't quite cover what I was feeling, but I supposed it was close enough for his understanding. *"Yes. I am."*

"You stayed out of curiosity? Nothing more?"

No.

"Yes."

I bit my lip. It was one of the few outright lies I'd told him, besides, of course, about my upbringing at the Nightfall Convent and Mama's choker. But those lies were necessary to my espionage. This one *wasn't*.

"And what are you curious about?" he asked. His hand slowly inched up his thigh, closer to the part of him that held all my attention.

My breath came out in a stutter. *"I-I'm curious about a lot of things, Your Grace."*

"Like what?"

My brain went momentarily blank when his hand found himself again. Slowly massaging his length as he watched me.

"Does that feel good?" The question exploded out, causing the vampire to grin a wicked, delicious grin that had my heart beating even faster.

"Yes," he said casually. *"That is the point."*

More questions rose to my tongue, and I took a half step closer.

"Do you do it a lot?"

He made a satisfied sound in the back of his throat, grinning sheepishly. *"Define a lot."*

"Every day?"

"If I have the time."

I looked away from him again. Feeling unsure of myself and way out of my understanding. These things weren't talked about. But still, I wondered if he satisfied himself like this because he had a mate he hadn't found? Was he only allowed to touch her? If not, I wondered if he wanted to do that with someone else. With me, perhaps.

The sound of his voice inside my head brought my attention back to his face. *"Miss Donadieu,"* he said thoughtfully, *"have you ever touched yourself?"*

His look of genuine concern had a whole new flurry of emotions swirling inside me.

"Touch myself wh-where?"

He contemplated me before rising to his feet and pulling up his pants, but didn't fasten the buttons. They hung low on his hips, open, doing little to conceal his hardness.

Closing the distance between us, he captured my hand, holding it gently, and with the other, lifted the hem of my shift.

I was trembling as he pressed my palm to my stomach and slowly, without breaking eye contact, dragged it down, stopping only when he reached the aching place between my thighs, and encouraged me to cup myself.

A hiss of breath left my lungs, and I thought I might fall forward.

"*Right here,*" he said, working my hand back and forth, *back and forth*, then pressing on one of my fingers until it parted my flesh.

My lips parted. My breath stuttered. He let me squirm under my own touch while his gaze tracked every twitch of my face. Meanwhile, his mouth curved in a dark smile.

"*No. I haven't touched myself like that.*"

He leaned forward, letting his lips graze the shell of my ear. His breath against my skin had me dizzy. "*Do you want to?*"

Yes. Yes. I did. Only...

"*I wouldn't know what to do,*" I explained, glancing up at him through heavily lidded eyes. "*No one taught me. In fact, they'd probably say it was sinful.*"

I wasn't sure what they taught at the convent, only what I'd been told at home. Intimacy was for marriage and for producing heirs. Since I was fit for neither, no one had explained I could do *this*.

Bastien looked angry for the first time. He cupped the side of my face with his free hand, holding me so tenderly. "*I know those convent sisters spent years trying to extinguish your flame, Miss Donadieu, but they could never fully do it. Do you know why?*"

He paused, like he was waiting for me to answer, but I said nothing. There were no convent sisters, only my family. And he had no idea the reason why I was treated the way I'd been treated. Because I deserved it.

"*There is a fire burning inside you. I can see it behind your eyes, burning hot and bright. I'm sure they saw it too and it scared them.*"

You scared them because they knew you were made for more, so they decided to stomp that fire out."

I didn't know what to say or think. Not when he was making declarations that he didn't understand. But... I so badly wanted to believe he could see something in me I couldn't see myself.

He pressed his lips together, studying my face like he could see the fire inside me. It was breathtaking.

"But what they didn't anticipate when they were trying to douse your flame was that they could never stop you from burning. You are fire."

I was a failure. A disappointment. *Not fire.*

"Miss Donadieu," Bastien continued, coaxing my finger to move over my center again, *"feel the fire inside you. Feel it."*

His fingers spread me open so that I could more easily access that sensitive little spot. And *oh, Diana.* I let out a staggered gasp as the pad of my middle finger grazed over it. I leaned forward to steady my forehead against his chest.

"You can pleasure yourself. Just like this."

Tentatively, I traced the spot. Once. Twice. By the third time, my hand was slick. I let out a strangled gasp.

"Good," he encouraged. Then he slowly guided me to the cushion, and lowered me onto his lap so my back was reclined against his chest. My body was alive with new sensations. The scrape of wool against the back of my legs. The feeling of his hardness pressed against my backside. The heady scent of pine and bergamot radiating all around me.

"Now keep going," he told me. Holding me around the waist. Encouraging me. *"Don't stop."*

He guided my hand back down my stomach until our fingers connected with that place again. Once I was there, he removed his hand, placing it on my thigh.

"What do I do?" I asked.

"Whatever feels good."

I swallowed. *"Tell me what to do. Please, Your Grace."*

He whispered encouragement and instruction through our connection. Holding the bond between us open, allowing me to push out everything except this. Except him. Us. This feeling. Then forcing me to linger when it felt too good, telling me to enjoy every sensation. Showing me how to draw this out until my body *begged.*

Maybe he was right. Maybe I was fire. Because right now, I felt *ablaze.* I was close to being swallowed by some inferno.

I rolled my hips, and felt his hardness slide behind me. His bare skin flush against mine.

"Your Grace," I whimpered.

"Bastien," he corrected. *"Use my name. Say it like it's yours."*

"Bastien," I said, gasping his name, *his real name.* "Am I doing this right?"

Breath hitching, Bastien groaned, *"If you keep rolling your hips against my cock, you're going to make me come. Is that what you want?"*

I recalled the way he looked moments ago with his hand around his length. The way pleasure was etched onto his face. *"Yes."*

"Then don't change a thing." His hand guided mine lower, until one of my fingers was nearly inside. *"Play with yourself, chérie. Do what feels good. Nothing is wrong."* He kissed the side of my neck, watching me as I slowly worked a finger inside myself. I'd never felt anything like it. *Nothing.* *"Watching you play with yourself is a gift from the gods."*

My mind raced back to his hardness. The stiff length of him that was pressed up against me. That was smearing warmth onto the back of my shift and across my bare skin. I rolled my hips against him again. And again. He moaned for me in a way that sent me spiraling with desire. I circled that sensitive little spot. Pressing harder. Faster. All the while, rubbing myself against him.

His jagged breaths against my ear had everything inside me tightening. *Tightening.* I was chasing something, some release, just like he'd done, but I didn't know exactly what that was. I moaned again when his lips pressed against my neck.

"*Claire,*" he whispered my name. And the intimacy of it nearly broke me. "*I can feel what you're feeling through this bond. I can feel how badly you want to come. How badly you need this.*"

"*Then help me.*" I grabbed his hand and pressed it to me. Nothing prepared me for the feeling of his skin on me like this. Not our feedings. Not my own touch. Not his gentle guidance. Nothing. His hand felt *right.*

He froze, and I could tell he'd stopped breathing. "*I'm not your lover, I'm your prince. Your duke. I'm supposed to take care of you and keep you safe. Not—*"

"*Then take care of me,*" I demanded, feeling frustrated and needy. "*Bastien, please.*" I grabbed his hand like he'd grabbed mine, pressing him against me, coaxing his finger to move against me.

He started slow. "*You're sure?*" he asked, still toying with me, barely touching me, driving me mad with need.

"*If you can feel what I need, then help me.*"

He groaned against me. "*You're so wet. I shouldn't—*"

"*Don't stop.*"

"*As the lady commands.*"

Slow, soft strokes that had only teased and frustrated me turned more deliberate. More demanding. One finger dipped inside me, curling, beckoning me toward some end that had stars exploding behind my eyes.

I knew I had finally found the feeling he'd spoken about. Something that felt like the building climax of a piece of music.

"*That's right, Claire,*" Bastien said, not letting up, even when I spread my thighs wider for him, draping my legs over his. *"Come undone for me."*

He'd taken up a punishing pace, working me harder and faster until I wondered what could feel any better than this. But each time I had that thought, that tingling, demanding, intense feeling grew, until I knew there was no turning back.

Something was coming.

My breath was jagged. My heart pounding. I lifted my arms to wrap them behind his neck, holding on to him as I watched him pleasure me. He drew his finger in and out. In and out. His other worked me in tight little circles. So cold, yet so thrilling. I rolled my hips against him, each time feeling the dampness spread over my back.

Faster. Faster. *Faster.*

We moved together as one. My body tightened. My fists clenching in his hair. My back bowed.

"You're going to come for me," Bastien rasped. *"Give in to the pleasure you were made for."*

I was right there. Teetering on an edge. But I couldn't seem to walk over it.

He buried his face in my neck, shuddering, before he gritted out, *"I'm coming—fuck, Claire—coming. Come with me, my moonflower."*

A jagged breath left him. And that was all it took to let go. I screamed through our shared connection as everything inside me unraveled. Pure, unadulterated pleasure tore through me in waves. I shook, I moaned, but Bastien didn't stop. He played with me until I was completely done and the little tremors happening low in my core had ceased.

A moment of stillness passed. The sound of our breaths filling the small tent. A satisfaction I'd never known settling over me. His hand floated up my stomach, holding me in place, holding me against him. When I didn't think I was capable of feeling an ounce more pleasure, he lifted me off his lap and set me on the cushion, dropping onto his knees in front of me.

I thought we were done, my body still humming with aftershocks—when he caught the back of my legs. For a knee-weakening moment, I thought he meant to lick me. *There.* But instead, the shadows under his eyes darkened, and he lunged for my soft flesh, his fangs latching onto my thigh, drawing my wet center against his cheek as he feasted on me.

There was no kissing or licking or nipping. This was a feeding. Raw. Impulsive. And it was exactly what I needed. His finger slid back inside my heat, working in quick pulses that drove me right to the edge.

"Bastien," I moaned. The word slipping from my lips. Not through our connection. Everything too intense to remember not to speak.

The pleasure of him drinking from me caused another, even stronger release, and I came all over again, shaking and moaning until he was done.

"Now we're even," Bastien whispered against my skin. He leaned back on his heels and wiped his mouth with the back of his sleeve. Taking a fresh silk towel from a basket, he cleaned the mess between my legs. I found I was sensitive to even the lightest touch.

"What do you mean?" I asked, half delirious.

He simply grinned in response. "Let's get you back to our tent. You need supper and water." His gaze darkened as it fell on my bare shoulders. "Where's your cloak?"

CHAPTER 21
COMMANDER

BASTIEN

Claire undid the ties of the tent to retrieve her cloak. I watched her, knowing I was getting too close. Taking too much of her blood. Of her. Allowing myself to be consumed mind, body, and soul. Muddling my duty to protect and honor her with the pull of the mate bond. And now, I was feeling what she felt through our connection, which had never happened before.

She plucked a cloak and a pair of gloves from under a pile of newly fallen snow, but even with the material covered in thick snowflakes, I recognized the royal blue color. "Don't be angry," she began.

I ripped the cloak from her hands. The sight of it—of her holding my nephew's color—made the world narrow to red. With all the calm I could muster, I slid a finger under her chin and lifted her gaze to mine.

"Why do you have my nephew's cloak?"

She trembled. "He-he gave it to me."

Is that so?

I found another desire rising inside me—the one to slay my

own kin for daring to cloak my mate. A low growl resonated in my chest, and Claire recoiled from me. I was scaring her. I needed to calm down.

I tried drawing in a slow breath to no avail. "Why did he give you his cloak?"

She swallowed hard, and I could tell she was nervous, but instead of letting it speak for her, Claire did this thing she sometimes did when I questioned her sharply—she rose to the challenge and answered with conviction. "It is cold, as you said, Your Grace. It was the gentlemanly thing to do."

Your Grace. So, we were back to formality.

I let go of her chin and folded my arms across my chest. Tyson's cloak puddled to the floor in a wet, useless heap. "You saw my nephew before coming to see me?"

She shook her head. "No. He came to visit me."

As hard as I tried to hide my anger at this revelation, it was impossible. My voice shook with barely leashed fury. "He was inside our tent? With you? *Alone?*" I gritted out. "And you were dressed like this?" I asked, letting my gaze trace the slope of her shoulder. "In nothing but a nightgown?"

"No," she said, shaking her head harder. "He was outside. The tent flaps blew open, and when I went to check to see if it was you, I noticed him across the way. I asked if he'd seen you."

She was *looking for me?* That knowledge satisfied something deep down inside me. Relaxing a tightness I didn't know was clenched until now. I didn't think the tent opened from the wind. I'd tied those ties myself. Tyson had wanted to draw her attention. He'd wanted to draw her out. But why? He couldn't be foolish enough to make a move on my sanguine partner. Could he?

Then, understanding dawned.

"He's the one who told you I was in a feeding tent, wasn't he?"

She nodded. I turned around, needing a moment to think without looking upon her face. He told her I was here to force an uncomfortable interaction. He gave her his cloak—not to keep her warm—but to mask her scent so I wouldn't sense her coming. I wasn't sure why my nephew had pulled this little stunt, but I suspected it had something to do with me kicking him out of my council meeting. Or perhaps he wanted something to hold over my head.

Either way, he was smarter than I was giving him credit for. He wanted my castle, after all, and the prestige that came with my title. I had to tread carefully. If nothing else, it was a good reminder that I was getting far too close to Claire. I wasn't making sound decisions. What I'd done with her in this tent, for anyone to hear, was expressly forbidden. I needed to get a handle on this mate bond, and there was only one person who could give me guidance.

Imogen.

I had to get back to Château Rose.

"I don't understand why you're so angry," Claire interjected, her voice cutting into my thoughts. She grabbed my arm, wheeled me around to face her, and somehow reopened the internal communication line between us, speaking to me inside my own head. *"Explain it to me."*

The way the world around me went silent stopped me cold. I stared back at her in confusion. This power should only be one way, initiated by me.

With the connection between us reopened, I was experiencing all her feelings again. The confusion. The frustration. *The desire.* She might be angry, but, Gods, if I wanted her, she'd let me take her right here. Right now. On Tyson's cloak. But that couldn't happen. I had to put more distance between us. I couldn't allow her to impose her emotions on me at any given time. This had to stop. There were other, more important things that required my attention. I had to remind myself of that.

Gathering my strength, I replied through the connection, *"I broke the rules for you once. To indulge your curiosity. I won't be doing it again."*

A harsh truth, but a truth nonetheless. With it came a rush of emotions, all hers, and the intensity of them was like being held underwater. I felt... *ineptitude.* A belief that she'd never be enough for anyone. I hated that I was making her feel that way, or that those sisters even put the idea in her head, but there was no way around it. This had to end.

"Didn't you enjoy yourself?" she asked.

I knew she must not be able to sense my emotions, otherwise she never would've asked that question. Pleasuring Claire did more than satisfy a carnal desire. It drew me in to her completely.

I'd always felt detached during intimacy. It was all transactional. Whether I was with a man or a woman, it didn't matter. But this—feeling her desire while I was touching her—was the opposite. I was engrossed in her. Invested in her. Breathing in tandem with her.

All I wanted was to be with her. Slowly, I fit my hand around her waist, drawing her against me. She sucked in a sharp breath as our bodies collided. Nothing was more satisfying than having her warmth pressed up against me. Nothing.

I realized, *too late*, it was happening all over again. I was losing myself in her, and I needed to focus. I couldn't give in to our mate bond again. I released my hold on her. *"Whether I did or didn't is of little consequence. Rules are in place for a reason. When we reach Roselyn, your consorts can pleasure you all day and night if you wish."*

As soon as the words were out of my mouth, I wished I could take them back, but I couldn't. She was allowed to be pleased. It just couldn't be with me.

Her brows knitted together. *"What's that supposed to mean?"*

I couldn't be the one to explain this to her. If I tried, she wouldn't need to feel my emotions to know how I felt about it.

"Go back to our tent," I told her. *"I'll have supper sent to you."*

I closed our connection, and it immediately shut off the flow of emotions coming from her, allowing me to breathe again. I opened the tent and stalked toward my horse, Lucien, who had been tied up for the night.

Claire followed after me, not abiding my command.

I forced myself to face her, intent on demanding she return to our tent, but when I did, I found myself speechless. Under the glow of the moon, she looked *otherworldly*. The strands of her hair alight like stars. Her eyes, molten gold. Her skin, like Diana herself. Bright and glowing.

She was the song inside my heart. The beat that brought me back to life and made me feel almost human again. But I wasn't human, and I never would be. *I was a vampire.* And I had a job to do.

"Your Grace, where are you going?" she demanded. Then, more quietly, "And what in Diana's name is a *consort?*"

Gods, I couldn't do this. "Lady Natalia!" I called over my shoulder.

A few moments later, my niece was at my side, looking rather annoyed at being summoned. "Yes, Your Grace?"

I cut a glance between Claire and Natalia, then began untying my horse. My decision made. "Pack up the camp. We leave for Roselyn immediately."

I mounted Lucien and fitted my feet firmly in the stirrups, avoiding Claire's gaze. If I looked down at her beautiful face, illuminated by the moon, I might not have the strength to do what needed to be done.

"But Uncle," Natalia argued, "everyone just got settled."

"Then get them unsettled!" I snarled back, baring my teeth. "We travel faster at night anyway."

I didn't wait for her to reply, knowing she'd follow my orders, and whirled my horse in a tight circle, intent on putting more distance between my mate and I, but paused, needing to say one last thing.

"Natalia!"

"Yes?" she said with irritation. One hand landing on her slim hip.

I kept my gaze trained on her, not wavering to Claire. "Don't let Miss Donadieu out of your sight until she's safe inside her room at Château Rose. And make sure she eats before you leave."

"Why can't *you* babysit her?" Natalia asked. Then she realized what I had planned. "Are you leaving now? Alone?"

"You have your orders." Without another look, I tore off, encouraging Lucien to race into the night. If I didn't get away as fast as I could, I was worried I'd lose my nerve and return for my mate.

I assumed distance would help dull my need for her, but I discovered it didn't. In fact, the opposite happened. Thoughts of Claire consumed me, plaguing each inch between us. The hours it took me to make the trek up to Château Rose were painful. It would be another half day before I saw her again. The coach and the other riders would move slower over the rocky terrain.

When I reached the familiar outline of my home at last, I dismounted and held Lucien's muzzle between my hands. "Good boy. Now, go to your stall." He pinned his ears back, snorted at me, then trotted off. Clearly unimpressed with being ridden so hard and for such little thanks. I'd let him rest for a while before bringing him a bushel of apples from the garden.

I didn't enter through the front gates, choosing instead to use the secret entrance on the south side of the castle that was designed to allow none but the Duke of Roselyn passage. When I reached the entry point, I freed the gold chain hiding inside my shirt and regarded the bloodstone dangling from the end.

All vampires were gifted a bloodstone at birth. Their magick fueled by the Blood Treaty—the accord made when Light and Dark Witches traded war for peace. With this accord, they used their magick to create creatures who were strong enough to keep the peace between them.

Twelve of us were made that night. Six from families of dark magick, and six from light. Some of us were warriors, gifted in our craft. Others renowned for nurturing peace when the world was breaking. Brothers not in blood but bound together, destined to protect the balance of magick on earth. To keep the peace when others would end it.

I pressed my bloodstone against the outer wall, then stood back as stone morphed into an archway, welcoming me home. Once I crossed under the arch, the wall reformed behind me.

Now, all that was left was to seek out Imogen and ask for guidance on how I could break this mate bond before it ruined everything I held dear.

CHAPTER 22
CHERCHER
BASTIEN

Imogen's chambers were in the darkest recesses of the castle, far below ground. She never emerged from the caverns, preferring to soak her ancient body in the salt pools. When I came to call, I found her amongst the steam. Her jade-green eyes piercing through the dark.

"I've seen your journey in the waters," she said in her paper-thin voice, barely audible over the echo of my boots on the stone floor. "It seems you found more than your sanguine partner in the capital, didn't you, boy?"

She laughed, and the sound was like the croaking of a toad. I crouched beside the pool, as I often did when seeking her counsel, and tossed a handful of shells into the murky depths. An offering to the only known Water Witch still living. She snatched them up in her bony hand, inspecting them carefully before setting them on the ledge behind her. "What can I help you with, young master?"

I hesitated, dropping my chin to my chest as thoughts of Claire filled my mind. From the first moment I saw her across the ballroom to the moment I left her at camp and every moment in between. She was never far from my thoughts, and that was the problem. I needed my life to return to how it was before.

Imogen waited with her hands steepled under her chin. Her thin lips pulled into the suggestion of a smile. I had the sneaking suspicion the old witch already knew what I'd come to ask.

"Is there a way to break a mate bond?"

Humidity beaded my brow. Water dripped from the damp stone overhead. My question hung heavy in the air.

"Your mate is determined by your Gods," Imogen replied. "Such were the terms of the treaty you made with them. The only way to break your bond *is to break the Blood Treaty.*"

Breaking the Blood Treaty was a ridiculous suggestion. My whole purpose in life was to preserve the balance of magickal power on earth, not destroy the only thing keeping the peace. Frustration had my fists curling into tight balls. "There has to be another way," I demanded. "Something. *Anything.*"

Imogen didn't balk at my anger like others might. She'd seen too much in her extraordinarily long life to be bothered by my temper. "When you sacrificed yourself for this so-called peace, your Gods required limitations to check your power. It's why the sun drains your strength, why you must feast on blood, and why you become consumed under the pull of a mate."

I waved her explanation away. "But there has to be a way to break this bond without breaking the Treaty. I cannot be tied to Claire. This is not the right time for me to be *consumed.*"

The witch turned her attention to the stack of seashells around her pool, and selected one. The torchlight caught on its iridescent sheen, reminding me of the way Claire's hair shone under the light of the moon.

The witch held it out for me, and reluctantly, I allowed her to place it in my palm. The shell was curled like a tusk, and was quite beautiful. "There's never a right time to fall in love," Imogen said softly.

Love. What a ridiculous notion.

I curled my fist around the shell, letting the sharp edge bite into my skin. "This isn't love," I gritted out. "It's cosmic punishment to keep me from being the man I need to be."

"And you know better than the Moon Goddess? Is that it?" she asked. "Or the God of the Underworld? Your gods chose your mate."

As my temper rose, Imogen remained ever the same. Her tone mild and unaffected as she sat soaking in shoulder-deep water.

"I didn't come for a lecture," I said, rising to my feet, intent on throwing the shell back into the murky depths of the salt pool. For whatever reason I kept it curled in my hand. "I came here for a spell or a sacred ritual to break her hold on me. Your advice has never failed me before."

Water Witches were renowned seers in their time, though their talents had become their undoing.

She offered me one of her rare smiles that showed a row of chipped yellow teeth. "She is your mate, Bastien. Your fates are intertwined. Which means you hold just as much power over her as she has over you."

Impossible. It was impossible. If she felt the way I did, we'd already be properly mated, and my life would truly be over. There was no doubt in my mind. Especially after the way she'd come alive when I'd touched her. The way I'd come alive. But I was able to compartmentalize that tryst because she'd been curious. That's all. She didn't care about me; she only wanted to feel pleasure she'd never experienced before.

Claire blamed me for her father's death and for her upbringing at the Nightfall Convent, where she was taught heinous things about herself and the world. And she was right to hate me. I led many soldiers into the Lawless Lands, and couldn't protect them all.

"I'm sorry you wasted a handful of good seashells to hear nothing can be done," Imogen said, "but that's the answer you're going to get."

Desperation had me crouching down beside the pool again. "Imogen, please. I've protected you all these years and have never asked for anything in return."

She let out another toad-like croak of laughter, and, behind the tendrils of steam, I saw something shift in her eyes. "You think my life matters that much to me?"

"That's not what I meant."

She pushed herself off the ledge and swam closer to where I sat crouched beside the pool, looking less human and more like a creature of the deep. "My people are gone," Imogen said, her bony hand gripping my ankle. The look on her wrinkled face was pained. "My goddess is in hiding. I sit here in these waters, waiting for a sign that might never come. So excuse me if I find your request *annoying*. What's fifty years of matrimony to an immortal?"

"Those fifty years might seem trivial to you, but if I leave and return to the capital with Claire, the witches of the Lawless Lands with whom I've made alliances with will all be dead upon my return, and who knows who will have replaced them."

Extremists. Sycophants. Those who would seek to increase their power in unnatural ways. Young witches like Shayla, who rose against Hector's level hand. Those who desired the power of the wolf. Who wanted to find a way to kill Witches of the Darkness.

The echo of the word *werewolves* sounded in my head. I opened my palm, staring at the tusk-shaped seashell. From this angle, it looked like a tooth. I didn't want to believe it was possible.

My voice softened. "I'm so close to bringing more people under the protection of the Blood Treaty. I can't abandon them."

She released her hold on my boot, but stayed close. Something like a smile crested over her thin lips again. "You are too noble for your own good."

"I'll take that as a compliment." I expelled a strangled laugh, which seemed to break the tension that had been brewing between us. Rubbing my thumb over the shell, I asked, "Is there anything that can be done? Anything at all to reduce the bond's effect on me? Imogen, please, I'm desperate."

"Desperate, you say?" The old witch floated back to her place across the pool, not meeting my gaze as she toyed with her collections of shells. Rearranging them into little stacks with her long, bony fingers. "Desperate enough to summon one of your gods?" A charged silence filled the cavern. "Diana will not speak to you nor offer any way out of this bond. She is a romantic. And besides, her witches have the advantage in these aggressions your kind are ignoring."

"We are *not* ignoring them," I told her as calmly as I could.

She shot me a glare that told me she thought otherwise. "Moon magick doesn't require a limited resource, like the demonic relics. You can't banish the moon from the Unified Territories the way you have banished demons. She will see no benefit in helping you. But," she said, "perhaps Damien could be persuaded. Summon him, tell him you wish to break the Blood Treaty."

"I can't do that."

"This accord was made to prevent war, but tell me, Bastien, are we at peace?"

"This is your advice? That I break the very treaty I died to create?"

Imogen pointed to the shell in my hand, turning her strange eyes on me once again. Eyes that saw things that weren't in this cavern. "It seems you've done a fair few things that go against the rules, *Sebastien,* in the name of preserving your *noble quest.*"

"The way you say *noble quest* makes me feel like you don't think it's very noble at all."

She turned her back to me. "If you wanted to ask more questions, you should've brought more shells."

I took my leave of the cavern, climbing the spiraling steps that led back to my chamber. When I reached my room, I threw the heavy black drapes open and was rewarded with the sight of the moon hanging over the snow-capped pines—refusing to bow to the rising dawn.

It reminded me of Claire. The stubborn look of defiance she'd given me when I'd left her alone. She was fire. But she was also soft and delicate.

A moonflower.

Could Imogen be right? Could Claire feel a pull toward me too? Was she as tortured as I was? I swallowed down guilt and shame. I'd left her alone, making her vulnerable to the elements and my nephew and any number of dangers that could befall her on the half-day journey. All because I couldn't keep my feelings for her at bay. I didn't want this—*her*—and at the same time, she was all I wanted.

CHAPTER 23
JE NE TE FAIS PAS CONFIANCE
CLAIRE

Natalia stood beside me, glaring into the darkness, as if she, too, was cursing him for being such an arrogant bastard.

Guilt, shame, and frustration had me clenching my jaw and balling my hands into fists. Bastien had pulled me into his lap and unraveled me like a spool of thread. Now he was punishing me like this was all my fault—and everyone else's too.

After the sound of hoofbeats died, Natalia whipped around, her long braid nearly smacking me in the face. "Come on, Claire. Dinner time."

I didn't move when she stepped toward the circle of tents. My body trembled from the cold and the wind, but I continued to stare into the darkness, making my own kind of oath. One that hardened my heart to him. If he never wanted to touch me again, then so be it. I never wanted him to touch me again, either.

This whole thing proved just how much of a monster the Duke truly was. It also proved how stupid I was for thinking my plan to woo him might actually work. My shoulders slumped, and the hot press of tears burned in the back of my throat. Mama was right. *I wasn't smart.* Now, more than ever, I needed to stick to what my family had told me to do—gain enough of his trust to sneak around behind his back. To listen. To find allies in his court.

"Did you hear me?" Natalia prodded. "I have orders to follow, and so do you."

Her demanding voice grated on me, and I struggled to harness the sweetness I was supposed to be showing these vampires. I was too frustrated. Too angry. Too bitter.

A breeze blew over my shoulder, and I could feel the presence of another vampire. Behind me, Natalia groaned. "What do *you* want?"

I turned to find Tyson had joined us at the edge of camp. He looked wholly out of place among the trees and tents. A shiny coin at the bottom of a dark well. He casually ran a hand through his black hair. Glancing my way, he winked. "I thought I heard someone ask what a consort is?"

I narrowed my eyes at the Viscount. I was angry with him for causing trouble.

"No one asked *you*," Natalia shot back. "Come on, Miss Donadieu," she grumbled, grabbing my arm and yanking me roughly forward. I slipped on the icy snow and nearly toppled into Tyson. He steadied me with one hand, and with the other, grabbed Natalia at the wrist, just above where she held me.

"Just a moment, Cousin."

My gaze darted between the two of them. Natalia stared at the place where he was touching her like she might bite his hand off. Which I wasn't opposed to after he sent me to that *feeding* tent.

"I can see you're rather busy," he said casually, "so how about we split the duties? I can give the order to strike camp. You ensure Miss Donadieu has something to eat and gets all her important questions answered. She's half frozen, standing there in nothing but a nightgown."

Despite my annoyance with Tyson, if given the choice, I'd rather eat dinner with him than spend more time with her. Which was saying something.

A beat of silence passed before Natalia shoved me backward. I stumbled over a pile of snow and landed squarely on my backside, gasping as she drew a knife from her chest scabbard, elbowing him in the ribs in the process. He doubled over, and just as fast, she whirled around behind him, grabbing his hair and fitting the blade against his throat. A wicked smile spread across her face.

"I'd love to see you order our guard around," she said with a humorless chuckle. "Gods, it would make me laugh so hard to watch them tell you to *fuck off* like the green little boy you are."

Tyson reached for his own blade, drawing with lightning speed and twisting out of her grip, reversing the hold on her. His blade pressed to her throat.

I gasped again, unsure who I wanted to win in this fight. Or if I wanted anyone to win. I hugged my arms around my chest, trying to stop shivering.

"What makes you think you're so much better than me?" Tyson questioned. "I'm the one who has been named heir to Château Rose."

Natalia slipped free from his grip, and lunged, slashing at him with her dagger. Teeth bared. Eyes black. "I don't think I'm better than you. I know it."

I wasn't sure why, but watching them argue had my thoughts drifting to my little sister. Sera was younger than me, but had been named my mother's successor because I lacked the magick necessary to lead our coven. I wondered if Tyson possessed any special skills, like Bastien's ability to slide into minds, and if that's why he had been chosen over Natalia. Or if it was simply because he was a male.

Natalia kicked Tyson between the legs and then punched him in the jaw. He flew ten feet through the air and landed in a snowbank. It gave her enough time to draw the sword at her hip. The two stared at each other. Her—standing her ground. Him—flat on his back. Both breathing heavy. Natalia let out a bellowing scream and attacked—racing to where he lay and pointing the tip of her sword at his neck.

"Diana!" I gasped. Was she going to cut his head off?

I crawled toward them, trying to get a better look. My fingers were like icicles, and, without a cloak, my clothing was soaked through.

She pressed her weight forward, and the tip of her sword pushed against his skin. "These people are more than just family to me. We've fought together, shoulder-to-shoulder. Taking curses. Carrying dead bodies back to the wagon. Watching friends burn on the pyre. I've lived in the north for a hundred years, and the people of Roselyn know my worth." She bent low, teeth bared. "You're nothing to them. They won't respect your title—*or you*—until you do something worth respecting."

Tyson scowled, and something inside me twisted. I felt a little bad for him. Yes, he was haughty and spoiled, but it wasn't his fault. He was eighteen. I mean, my sister could be reckless at times too, but wasn't she supposed to learn and fail and grow as a leader?

I might envy her gifts, but I would never treat Sera the way Natalia was treating Tyson. Even if she was adored while I was ignored.

Natalia eased her weapon back into its scabbard, and Tyson got to his feet—brushing snow off his back. He dipped his chin in the smallest bow. "I'll pack up my tent." He strode off, only stopping to look back at me once before he disappeared into his tent.

Some part of me admired him. Even if he had caused trouble.

Natalia grumbled something under her breath in Sanguisi, then gestured for me to follow her. This time, I was cold enough to listen. We cut our way through camp, heading toward a spit where a wild boar was roasting. Natalia cut off a hunk of meat and placed it on a piece of bread. She was beautiful. With perfect cheekbones and a long, slender neck. Thick brown hair that always stayed in place. But there was a hardness to her. Like she picked up a shield a long time ago and never set it down. Not for anyone. I needed to do the same. Put a shield around my heart and stop acting so damn emotional.

She handed me the food, then gestured for me to follow her. As we walked through camp, she called into each tent we passed, informing them it was time to pack up and move out for the night. Her order was met with groans, but swift action.

Once we got to the largest tent, the one Bastien and I shared, I sank onto a pile of furs, wrapping myself in one. Natalia took a seat across from me, elbows propped on her knees while she watched me eat. The meat was juicy and hot, and I ate without manners.

"What did you do to anger His Grace?" she asked. "Did you slap him like your sister slapped me?"

"Are you always this... *intense?*"

"No," she snapped back, another wicked smile spreading across her face. "Sometimes I'm worse." Her look darkened. "Now answer the question, Miss Donadieu."

I told myself to be sweet and control my temper, but it was impossible at the moment. Returning her glare, I said, "I didn't slap him."

Natalia didn't seem convinced. Her little nose scrunched.

"Maybe not, but you've done *something* to him. Ever since he met you, he's been acting strange. You're not a witch in disguise, are you?"

I busied myself with a piece of meat, tearing off a hunk and shoving it in my mouth. "Of course not. Don't be ridiculous."

"When I find out what it is," Natalia continued, "there won't be a law in this land that keeps you safe. Do you understand me?"

I had no doubt she'd make good on that promise if she ever discovered my treason. Barely tasting the meat, I swallowed hard, forcing myself to meet her critical gaze, wondering how I was going to convince her I wasn't here for nefarious reasons, when I was.

"I haven't done *anything* to him. The Duke is simply..." I searched for a word to describe him without being too disrespectful and landed on, "moody."

Silence followed, and I wondered if I'd gone too far—if she was going to raise her blade to my throat too.

Natalia cracked a reluctant smile. "He is moody, isn't he?"

We both shared a small laugh, the tension breaking. When the laughter died, it got quiet again. I shoved another piece of meat in my mouth.

"Moody as he may be, there isn't a better vampire in the land. He's worth three of his brothers. And six of the *Viscount*." She spat on the ground, then shook her head. "I still can't believe that *idiot* was named heir. Of all my cousins, they had to choose *him*."

I realized Natalia and I might have more in common than I thought. It seemed she didn't have many people to talk to either. I could learn a lot from this warrior vampire.

"Who is your father?"

She crossed her arms, reclining back on the furs. "The Duke of Nightfall. Prince Josse."

I didn't know much about vampires, but I knew the Duke of Nightfall. He governed the lands of my family home. Mama had a drawing of his face that hung outside the barn where they practiced throwing axes. She was fond of saying how incompetent and arrogant he was. I kept that last part to myself.

"Château Blanc is far from here." I leaned sympathetically in. Setting my food aside. "Do you miss your family?"

She made a disgusted noise in the back of her throat. "Why do you care?"

"I'm just making dinner conversation," I offered.

Natalia removed her blade and started cleaning it with the edge of her black tunic. "My dinner usually doesn't talk."

"Neither does mine," I snapped back.

She regarded me with mild amusement, and I hoped this meant she found me funny and wasn't about to stab me.

"The Duke told me about that necklace. The way it tried to kill you. He said it was meant to tease him into choosing you by drawing fresh blood." She made another disgusted noise. "Who does something like that?"

I met her angry gaze with wide eyes. "You've never done anything desperate to protect someone you love?"

Natalia went silent, and I went back to eating. Finishing most of the tender meat and starting on the bread before the vampire spoke again. "Choosing your consorts is the best part of your job. Besides the money."

She was changing the subject, which I took for a good sign, and I followed her lead. "But what are they?"

She gave me a foxlike grin, then crossed her long legs. "Well paid lovers who have been trained in the art of seduction."

Oh. *Oh.*

"You get to pick three, but know you're required to treat

them just as kindly as they'll treat you. Or face my Uncle's wrath."

"Three!" I gasped, my cheeks reddening. "Why so many?"

She eyed me. "We don't want you becoming too attached to one person. Sanguine partners aren't allowed to be courted during their employment. So, keeping multiple lovers ensures your needs are met without it developing into a relationship."

So, this was why Bastien had said my consorts could take care of my needs. They were there to *pleasure* me. I didn't *need* pleasuring, so to speak. But, having three people at my disposal might be good for other things. Like discovering more information about His Grace and the demonic relics. The idea had promise.

"We'll sample the applicants when we arrive at Château Rose," Natalia told me.

"Thank you," I said, giving her a genuine smile. "For the food. And the dinner conversation."

Her grin flattened into a scowl. "Stay put until we give the order to load the coach. I'll come back to collect you."

I nodded, standing when she did out of respect. Trying to prove to her that I wasn't the enemy. Even though I very much *was*.

CHAPTER 24
JALOUSER

CLAIRE

Château Rose's towering iron gates opened as we approached. Although the grandeur of the castle loomed in the distance, my attention narrowed on Bastien, who was waiting to receive me.

I quickly closed the curtains and drew in a calming breath. I hadn't expected him. Not after the way he'd left last night.

The coach door was opened, and an army of goosebumps rose across my arms. The wind biting through my thick black cloak. A footman offered me a hand, which I took with trepidation, and slowly made my way down the stairs. Another gust of snowy wind sent pieces of my unbound hair flying around my face. With measured steps, I made my way to where the Duke of Roselyn stood.

Others joined me. Tyson. Okeri. Natalia. I took little notice of them. I only had eyes for *him*. Bastien wore a black knee-length frock coat, its lapels and cuffs embroidered in gold thread. A simple black cravat framed his throat. One hand rested on the head of his cane, the other tucked neatly behind his back.

He looked like an inkblot against the majesty of his castle, which was hewn from black stone. The tops of each turret frosted with snow. I was drawn to him, despite how angry I was, in a way I couldn't quite understand. Seeing him now, here, felt like coming home. However, I knew better than to be tricked. It was just the allure of him. A deadly predator who sought to set their prey at ease with their beauty. Now, I knew much more about this vampire than rumors or gossip.

And I was prepared to bring him to his knees.

My attire matched his. Layers of black lace and chiffon detailed with gold appliqué on the bodice—one an attendant had stuffed me into during our last stop. I lifted the hem of my dress as I took the castle steps one at a time, careful not to trip on my way up the long set of stairs. When I finally reached him, I was taken by the color of his blue eyes. They were as brilliant as the frozen streams crisscrossing the land outside his castle.

Dipping my chin, I curtsied, as was expected of me. Bastien bowed at the neck.

"Welcome to Château Rose, Miss Donadieu," he said in his deep, melodic voice. "I believe a tour of your new home is in order."

He extended his hand. I looked up at him through my lashes, not sure what to make of this gesture. Last night, he'd told me he didn't want to touch me ever again.

I realized he thought me weak. Nothing more than a simpering girl who was ready to lap up whatever attention he was ready to give me. On his terms. Well, I wasn't the same girl he'd met before the last full moon, and I certainly wasn't going to let his looks or his manners rule my actions from now on.

"Actually, Your Grace," I said, glancing at Natalia, "The Lady Natalia and I have plans."

"That's right, Uncle. Remember, you'd said we'd be selecting her consorts upon arrival."

Bastien tucked his hand behind his back. "I've already made arrangements to have the applicants brought up to Miss Donadieu's room after supper," he explained, holding my gaze. "Until then, Miss Donadieu and I will be taking a tour of the castle and the grounds."

He was trying to force me to play his game. Well, games involved more than one player.

"I'm not particularly hungry, Your Grace. I'd rather meet them now, if it's all the same to you." Lifting my chin, I added, "Afterward, if she's amenable to it, Lady Natalia can take me on a tour of the castle. I don't want to bother you. I know you're very busy."

I smiled as sweetly as I could and, in doing so, was able to watch Bastien's polite pretense crack. This wasn't what he was expecting from me. Good.

Tyson eagerly said, "Lady Okeri and I would love to take the tour with you, Uncle."

I nodded at him, encouraging this suggestion with a smile.

"Well, that's settled then! You two can take the tour with His Grace," Natalia said, gesturing to Okeri and her cousin, "and I'll speak to Lena to see if Miss Donadieu's selection can be moved up."

She laced her arm with mine, and we started up the next step, when Bastien held out his cane, stopping us. "*I* will accompany Miss Donadieu."

It was a command, nothing less. The low tenor of his voice went right through me, making the fine hairs on my forearms stand on end. I wasn't sure why he was taking such an interest in my consorts. He'd made it clear how he felt about me. Regardless of how frustrated I was with him, I wasn't going to start an argument in front of his staff. No. Mama wouldn't want that. I'd made my point, and he'd made his.

"Whatever you wish, Your Grace," I said, adding another curtsy for good measure.

His jaw clenched again, and for whatever reason, his displeasure caused me inordinate amounts of happiness. I wanted him to be just as frustrated as I'd been last night when he'd gotten on his horse and left. He withdrew his cane and turned to his nephew. "Tour the grounds with Natalia, but be ready for the council meeting at eight bells."

Tyson stuttered out his thanks, but Bastien ignored him. He attention focused on me. I tried to maintain my dignity under the intensity of his eyes by remembering how fickle he was. And how hurt I'd been.

He didn't offer me his hand again. He simply turned on his heel and strolled through the large open doors and into the grand entrance. His cane striking the marble floors with each step. I followed after, taking in every detail of the entryway. Long, plush carpets lined the floors. Flickering sconces dotted the walls. Pausing, I let my gaze drift up to the iron chandelier hanging from the top of the vaulted ceiling. This place felt uniquely like Bastien.

Not opulent, but impressive.

He made small comments to me here and there, noting where the kitchens were located as well as the library. Staff bustled about, bowing and curtsying to us as we passed. I noticed most of the people here didn't seem to fear him, but greeted him warmly.

We climbed a long set of stairs clad in deep red carpets that led to a quieter section of the castle with fewer staff. Portraits hung on the walls, and fresh-cut flowers sat in vases on small side tables. "This is the Royal Wing," Bastien explained as we continued down the long hallway. "Our personal residence. It's secluded from the other suites." He gestured to a large wooden door. "This is your room."

He stopped in front of the second-to-last door on the left, and withdrew a key, unlocking it. He held it open for me, and with interest, I stepped inside.

Floor-to-ceiling window panes stretched across the entire back wall, showcasing the snow-capped mountains surrounding the castle. The view was as spectacular as the rest of the room, which was furnished with a four-poster bed, a seating area, a large claw-foot bathtub, and a wall of book-shelves packed with books. Lush green plants were tucked into every nook, and pots of lilac moonflowers were placed on every flat surface. Their sweet aroma filling the air, giving off notes of jasmine and vanilla. It was a place I could spend days inside. Every detail perfect. More than I ever could've asked for.

Bastien, who had been walking in front of me, stopped so abruptly I nearly collided with him. Before I could catch my balance, he caught my wrists and pressed my back against the glass wall.

"Your Grace!" I gasped.

He was close enough to catch each one of my tight breaths. Close enough to feel my chest rise and fall, straining against the confines of my dress. Close enough to feel the heat pouring off of me. A heat only *he* could coax. He looked like he wanted to shake me and kiss me all at once—like he was one wrong move away from breaking his own rules.

"Are you trying to punish me?"

I studied the harsh line of his jaw. The tightness around his mouth. The wild light in his eyes. "Of course not, Your Grace. I'm simply following your orders."

His grip on my wrists tightened, and he slid my hands up the cold glass. My breath hitched. There was something about the power he possessed—his dominance. Knowing that I was at his mercy. Knowing that I was the one driving him to act this way. It was nothing short of intoxicating, but I wasn't going to be like a reed in the wind, bending to his whim. Not this time. Even when his gaze lingered on my mouth. This was about defeating the Dark Witches who'd murdered my grandmother and who this vampire loved so well. And a little about my pride.

My back flattened against the cold glass when he inched closer. The hard line of his body pressed through the soft folds of my skirts, reminding me how very little space existed between us. If he wanted to stay away, why was he always getting so close?

"I-I thought you didn't want to touch me again."

Bastien held my gaze for a tense moment, then released my wrists. My hands fell limply to my sides, brushing my skirts. He didn't step back. Instead, one of his hands braced the glass beside my cheek, the other gripping his cane, which was flush against my hip. Caging me in.

"I regret taking my temper out on you last night. That wasn't gentlemanly of me. Nor was my *other* behavior. I apologize if I made you feel like any of it was your fault. To be clear, it wasn't."

I nodded once. Swallowing hard. "Thank you, Your Grace."

He studied my face like he was searching for something. If he found it, I wasn't sure. "No matter what Lady Natalia has told you, you are not required to select consorts today. In fact, you're not required to have any at all."

I was playing a dangerous game with Bastien, one that I had to play carefully if I wanted to earn his trust. So, I decided to give him another truth. A dangerous truth. "Last night, you showed me *something*. Something... I am very grateful for. But I understand our relationship must remain professional. So, now, as a twenty-five-year-old woman whose femininity has finally been awakened after a life of seclusion, I am excited to explore more of who I am outside of prayers."

His eyes fluttered shut and he muttered something in Sanguisi under his breath. "You deserve that."

Our eyes met. I nodded. So did he. An understanding passing between us. "Before you meet these applicants, you should know there are a few rules. First, *and most importantly,* no one can touch you if you've been drinking."

"Why is that?" I replied as sweetly as I could.

"It's for your safety. There are no exceptions. Do you consent?"

I considered pushing for a better explanation but decided there wasn't a point. I didn't drink very often, so he could have his way.

"Fine."

"Second, if I desire your presence, my request trumps any *fun* you may be having, and you must attend me. Is that understood?"

I raised a brow. "How often do you plan on exercising this right?"

"As often as I please," he gritted out. "You are a vital part of my life—of keeping me alive," he quickly corrected himself.

"Are there any exceptions?" I asked. "Let's say if it's not life or death. You're fine, just hungry, and I'm with one of my consorts. If we're *together,*" I forced myself to say, cheeks reddening with heat. A low growl emanated from Bastien's chest. "and you knock at the door, am I allowed to finish?"

"Miss Donadieu," he growled.

Something inside me purred with satisfaction. "I'm only asking to clarify, Your Grace."

He rolled his lips together, leaving them wet. "I will wait outside your door for three minutes. After that, if you don't answer, I'm coming in."

"Well, if they are as skilled as Lady Natalia says," I replied offhandedly, "three minutes should be more than enough time."

Another growl came, and I wondered what he planned to do. If he'd smash one of these glass windows or throw his cane across the room like he'd done at the inn. But he did neither. He simply asked, "Do you have any other concerns?"

I had many concerns, but I kept them to myself. For now. I shook my head. "Not at the moment, Your Grace."

Slowly, his hand dropped from beside my face, and he backed up a pace, allowing me space to finally draw a full breath. "Should I send them in?"

Our eyes met, and once again, a flash of tortured pain swept across his face. I could feel it land inside my chest too. He didn't want this arrangement. He didn't want me to have consorts. And neither did I. Not really. I wanted his mouth on my throat, his hands on my skin. I wanted him to unravel me until there was nothing left. But more than that, I wanted his company—to sit with him until late in the night, talking about his greenhouse, his roses, the things that made him human.

I wanted to strip away all the rules and let him show me exactly what I'd been missing my whole life.

But that was impossible. There was no future where my revenge, my mission, and my happiness all lived quietly together. I lifted a hand to the choker around my neck, and released a pent-up breath. There was no turning back. No room for fantasies of me and him. This was the next step in collecting more information.

"Yes, Your Grace. I'm ready."

CHAPTER 25

REGARDER

CLAIRE

Ten applicants filed into the room, all wearing long, silky black robes with hoods that shadowed their eyes. They formed a straight line in front of me, and I tried my best not to fidget or appear nervous as Bastien closed the door.

His attention never strayed from me as he made his way to my side, brows furrowed and jaw set. He opened our connection, sliding inside my thoughts. *"Are you sure you want to do this?"*

"Absolutely." My smile widened until my cheeks hurt, and Bastien finally relented, addressing our guests.

"You have the pleasure of meeting Miss Donadieu, my new sanguine partner."

"Your Grace," I said, setting a patronizing hand on his arm, "thank you for the kind introduction, but there's no need for such formalities with me. I'd prefer for them to call me Claire."

The muscles in his jaw ticked and irritation curled up one side of his mouth. My attempt at warmth clearly annoyed him. Bastien was incredibly handsome when annoyed.

187

"I'd like you to know a little about me before accepting an offer. I'm twenty-five years old, and I have very little experience when it comes to intimacy." I paused, heat flaming everywhere. "However, despite my lack of experience," I glanced at Bastien, "I am eager to learn."

He looked like he'd been stabbed. Like he was ready to send them all away. But, instead, he continued with his duty. "I have found Miss Donadieu to be stubborn and hard-headed. However, she is incredibly smart and is a lovely conversationalist. She also has an interest in gardening and books."

Coming from him, I took that as a compliment.

"Starting on the left," he continued, "if you would be good enough to remove your hood and state your name, we'll begin."

My chest tightened as my gaze wandered to the line of hopefuls. I did my best not to let my nerves show, fisting my hands into the folds of my skirt to keep them from shaking.

Again, Bastien canted his head in my direction, as if to ask if I'd had my fill of this spectacle so he could send them away. And again, despite my anxieties, I smiled pleasantly back at him like I was completely fine.

The first applicant removed her hood, revealing hair as white as Seraphina's that fell down her back in a long braid.

I had to swallow a gasp. Why was a Witch of the Light in Bastien's castle? Was she a spy?

"My name is Tansy," she told me in a cheeky voice.

She undid the sash on her robe, and the folds opened just enough to reveal her slight muscular frame, the swell of her small breasts, and the soft v between her thighs. Her skin was a beautiful shade of brown.

I wondered what coven she was from but held my tongue. There'd be time for questions later, away from Bastien. I knew without a doubt she needed to be one of my consorts, if just for companionship. Besides, it would be nice to have someone who reminded me of home.

"It's nice to meet you," I said.

"It's nice to meet you too."

"Next!" Bastien called. I got the sense he was trying to hurry this along.

The tall man beside Tansy slowly untied the sash of his robe, allowing the folds to open until his well-honed chest was visible, as well as... My eyes widened, and my cheeks flamed with embarrassment. *By Diana.* The hard length of flesh between his legs was *pointing* at me, which wasn't half as concerning as what I saw when he lowered his hood. His hair was as red as the flames crackling in the hearth. He was a Witch of the Darkness. And he was standing in my room. *Naked.*

He didn't have a wand on him, at least not one I could see, but that didn't mean he wasn't dangerous. I moved closer to Bastien.

"I'm Devlinn, Miss Claire. It's good to meet you."

"Yes, we can all see that. Thank you, *Devlinn,*" Bastien said through his teeth.

I was still trying to process how in Diana's name a Dark Witch had come to be here, when I caught the slightest smirk twisted around the vampire's lips. *This was his doing.* He knew I would never take a Dark Witch to bed. I didn't find his little joke funny in the least.

Bastien could tell I was flustered, and his gaze returned to mine, a question in his pale blue eyes. *"Have you had enough yet?"*

I shook my head. He could have his joke. I wouldn't select Devlinn, and that was that. But as each of the remaining applicants undid their robe, I found every male had a shade of auburn hair ranging from bright red to strawberry blond.

Once all of them were introduced, I glared at the vampire beside me, who was now openly grinning. What a slimy, manipulative toad.

"Is there a problem?" he asked, replying with the same overly sweet voice I'd used with him.

I had two choices. The first was to scream at him for being so controlling. So manipulative. Or, I could swallow my fear of these witches in order to prove a point. Besides, Bastien had unknowingly given me a gift. Witches of the Darkness knew the location of relics. They would be useful to my mission.

Steeling my nerve, I rolled my shoulders back and raised my chin."There's no problem at all, Your Grace. These applicants are all wonderful." I swallowed hard, watching as the smile on his face shrank. Keeping my tone as pleasant as possible, I raised a brow and added, "Don't you agree?"

Bastien frowned, and he ripped open the connection between us while ten half-naked strangers watched on. The force of it left me disoriented as his voice sounded inside my head. *"Has your opinion of Dark Witches changed since you threw a chair at one?"*

My hands landed on my hips. *"Did she tell you I threw a chair at her? Because I very well did not."*

I told myself to keep my cool, but I was boiling on the inside.

Bastien lifted his cane, waving it between us. *"Are you willing to take one as a consort?"*

"As long as they're good at their job, I don't care."

He slammed his cane against the floor so hard that the sound reverberated off the vaulted ceilings, but I didn't move. I stood toe to toe, hating every inch of him.

His love for the dark craft knew no ends. He kept at least nine Dark Witches at his castle, and he pledged to retrieve demonic relics from the Lawless Lands for the likes of Shreesa.

Yet *I* was an abomination to him. *I* was something to regret.

"Fine," he said, fixing his cravat. *"Make your selection."*

I closed the connection between us like I was slamming a door. Bastien glared back at me but didn't move.

I realized ten sets of eyes were staring at us with a mixture of humor and confusion. I supposed it would be strange to watch two grown adults have a silent debate. Sheepishly, I smoothed a hand down my bodice, attempting to regain my composure as I reengaged with the group of people before me.

Bastien, however, did not. His hair was a mess from running his fingers through it and he was gripping his cane like it was a sword. I shrugged off his reaction and turned my attention back to the task at hand.

Who to choose? I had no way of knowing which one would skin me alive or curse me in my sleep. My gaze rolled over to the woman standing on the left, and an idea struck. I trusted no one's opinion more than one of Diana's chosen. She would know who to pick. "Tansy," I said, taking a step closer. Mindful of the horde of Dark Witches staring at me.

"Miss Claire," she said, dipping into another curtsy.

Trying to maintain composure, I asked, "Which of these men would you say is the best?" Her brown eyes met mine, and I wished she could speak inside my head like Bastien could. "If you were me, which one of these men do you choose?" I clarified when she didn't respond.

Without flinching, Tansy replied, "Devlinn, Miss Claire." My gaze shifted to the man beside her. "He's funny, clever, and he has a tongue like you wouldn't believe."

The two exchanged a heated glance, and the red-haired witch beside her grinned like the demon he was. Tansy spoke as if she had firsthand experience with him, and I couldn't believe a Witch of the Light would ever... *kiss* a Dark Witch. But apparently, I had much to learn about the world outside Prideaux Hill.

"That's good to hear," I forced myself to say, throat dry. "I choose Tansy and Devlinn as my consorts, so long as they're willing."

They both looked at each other and nodded. "Yes, Miss Claire. We'd be honored."

"I'll reserve selection of my third for another day."

Robes were tied and hoods were raised, then eight of the original ten filed out of the room as quietly as they came in. Once the four of us were alone, Devlinn and Tansy removed their robes fully, shamelessly puddling the black silk at their feet.

"Oh, I..." I started, not knowing how to tell them I wasn't ready for this. My fear rose, twisting in my stomach, and I tried not to look to Bastien for help. But I didn't need to. The vampire's voice was tender against my ear, and his cool breath tickled over my skin.

"You don't have to do anything you're not prepared to do. You can simply *watch*."

I regarded him with new curiosity. "What do you mean?"

"I mean," he said, pausing, "they can touch each other. If that's something you'd like to watch and they'd like to do. You don't have to participate."

I swallowed hard. That was an idea I hadn't thought of.

Tansy had seemed amenable to this Devlinn, and she'd named him as her favorite of the group. And while I was unsure about this whole thing, I couldn't deny I was curious to know how people moved together. To learn more than what Bastien had shown me.

"Is that... pleasurable?" I asked him. My words slow and barely audible. "To watch?"

His nearness had my pulse pounding in my ears and my heart fluttering in my chest. Something about him did that to me. No matter how much I despised him for marching nine Dark Witches into my room.

"Some find it very pleasurable."

"We don't mind at all, Miss Claire," Devlinn said. He took Tansy's bare waist and dragged her against his hard, muscled frame, pressing her close in a way Bastien had done to me before.

She looked eagerly up at him as she wound her fingers through his red hair, twisting the strands until her fingers were threaded in it. Then, slowly, he lowered his lips to hers. Kissing her like he wanted nothing else in the world. I lifted a hand to my lips as the ghost of a kiss I didn't remember tingled. A song of gasps and sighs began as his hands explored her body, cupping her backside and squeezing. Molding his hands to her flesh.

Bastien and I had become very still. His lips were hovering beside my ear, like he had more to whisper, but the only thing I could hear was the sound of his breath. I turned toward him, the slightest movement of my head, and found he wasn't watching them, *but me.* And the look in his eyes was anything but gentlemanly.

I quickly turned back. My breath coming in jagged little sips. Desire ignited between my thighs as I continued to watch them. Their kisses became rougher. Their cries sharper. Until he had her bent over, and... and... *slid inside her.* Tansy's cry of pleasure made my legs too wobbly to stand. Bastien's hand found the small of my back, and he let me lean against him. He tucked a strand of hair behind my ear so his lips could press flush against my skin. Everything inside me clenched.

"Should I tell them to stop?"

I bit my lip hard. Watching. Feeling the way Bastien's cool hand drew circles on my back. It was too much and not enough at the same time. But did I want them to stop? "No, they can keep going."

CHAPTER 26
PROPOSER

BASTIEN

After the performance was over, Claire and I were alone again. She was standing at the window with a hand pressed to the cold glass, silently staring at the mountains beyond. Her heart rate had settled; the reassuring beat pulsed inside my bloodstone.

I wished I knew what she was thinking, but that wasn't one of my gifts. As casually as I could, I plucked a moonflower from a crystal vase and stood beside her at the window. She drew in a deep breath and blew it out, her warm breath fogging the glass, but otherwise didn't acknowledge me. Awkwardly, I offered her the flower. "Would you care to see the greenhouse where these moonflowers were cut?"

"No," she said, softly shaking her head. "I want to be alone, Your Grace." Alone? But she looked so... *sad*. Standing in front of this window. I took a step closer, but she recoiled. "Please, Your Grace."

I studied the lines of tension around her eyes. The way her lips pressed together in a quivering line. There was something wrong. And by the way she was acting, it was my fault. "You're upset with me."

She faked a smile. "No, Your Grace. Just tired."

She might be tired, but that wasn't the only thing bothering her. She wouldn't have recoiled from me if she was sleepy. "Claire..." I said as tenderly as I could. Unsure what to say or how to frame my thoughts, when tears welled in her eyes and frustration furrowed her brows.

"Of course I'm upset with you," she said, refusing to look at me.

I'd caused her pain. Not physical pain, but emotional pain. It lodged itself in my chest like a knife. "Is there something I can do?"

Hugging her arms to her chest, Claire shook her head. "Just leave, Your Grace. Please. You've done enough today."

Every cell inside my body told me to go to her. To comfort her. To hold her. To take away whatever pain she was experiencing, but that's not what she wanted from me. She despised me, and there was nothing I could do to change her opinion.

My gaze fell to the black lace around her throat. The cursed necklace that she couldn't take off. The one she'd bought to try and make a better life for her sister. She was selfless. And here I was, being selfish. Just like everyone else that made her feel less than perfect. That realization nearly brought me to my knees.

I might be a prince, but I wasn't the right person to be this woman's mate. That much was plain. The gods had gotten this mating wrong. I couldn't make her happy. She was far too sweet to be mated to a man like me. But I could promise her one thing. "I promise I will not force Dark Witches on you again."

I backed away, step by step, wanting to do as she asked, but I stopped halfway to the door, needing to say something more

—then thought better of it. She didn't turn around, not even when I whispered, "I'm sorry."

Once I closed the door, I couldn't make myself leave. I lingered, torn between returning to explain our bond and tending to the other matters awaiting me. I reminded myself that Claire wasn't the only thing that needed my attention.

I was awaiting word about the state of my continued negotiations with the witches of the Lawless Lands. If they agreed they were ready for peace, I'd need to meet with them in person. It involved negotiating the construction and placement of new châteaus and selecting representatives from each coven who would move to the capital of the Unified Territories to speak for their people.

But, again, it was tenuous.

They battled as we once battled. Summoning demons at will and using Diana's light to burn villages. Practicing the kind of magick that the Blood Treaty had outlawed in our land. I knew these negotiations could turn bloody if I wasn't careful. But all the same, Claire inhabited my mind like ivy growing into crumbling brick. Twisting around every inch of me until there was nothing left—only thoughts of her.

For a moment, I allowed a twisted fantasy to unfurl. Wondering if I could keep Claire as my mate here in Roselyn, and still be the duke the people needed. Wondering... for the first time... if we could keep it a secret.

Through her door, I heard the muffled sounds of her crying. She was crying... because of me.

The fantasy I'd dreamed up died. She didn't want me. She hated me. And she should. I was poison to her. She deserved to be with someone far better than me. I touched her door, letting my hand linger there for a beat. A silent goodbye. Then I made my way down the grand staircase to visit Lena, an older woman who'd been a consort for many years and now helped me manage the staff. She was an advocate, ensuring they had sufficient rest, medical treatment, and were properly trained.

She seemed surprised to see me twice in one day. "How can I help you, Your Grace?"

The pain the next words caused me was nearly unbearable, but I forced myself to speak them. "Have those who volunteered to dye their hair red wash it out. If any are amenable to being reconsidered by my sanguine partner, have them present themselves to her chambers."

The thought of Claire surrounded by this many lovers was like taking an arrow between the shoulder blades, the pain so sharp I couldn't draw a full breath, but this was the right thing to do. I had to treat her like a sanguine partner, not a mate.

She made a note in her ledger, then glanced back up at me. "She only needs one more. Are you sure this is necessary, Your Grace? I don't like wasting the consort's time."

"Pay volunteers triple their salary," I said between my teeth. "And tell them there will be a buffet. Food and desserts. And musicians. It will be a party."

Lena made another note. "I think this sounds like the kind of fun many would be interested in, Your Grace. I'll speak with the staff straight away."

I offered her my thanks and departed, intent on taking out my pent-up frustrations in the training yard.

The sun was shining despite the frigid temperature, and I knew it was ill-advised to cross swords with my Master-at-Arms while distracted, but I didn't care. I met blow after blow for hours until I could barely lift my arm, and the sun's rays had drained my strength.

"What's got you all pissed off, Your Grace?" Sir Gavin finally asked when I threw down my sword and wiped the sweat from my brow. "You're fighting like an angry young man, not the warrior I know you to be."

I ignored the comment and winced as I touched my aching lip.

He'd punched me hard enough to split it open before I'd decided enough was enough. I licked the wound; Claire's blood coated my tongue. Tantalizingly sweet. I cast my gaze toward the tower where her room was and wished I hadn't. The pain of knowing she was up there with *whoever*, doing *whatever,* was more than I could bear.

You can bear it, and you will.

"Out with it, Your Grace. What's bothering you?" he asked in his gruff voice.

I forced a grin to put him at ease. I didn't want him to think I was troubled. I needed to be their commander. "I fancied a scrappier fight after spending all that time at the capital," I told him, forcing my attention away from Claire's room.

I wasn't sure if I fooled him into believing all was well, but the old Master-at-Arms let out a chuckle. "Speaking of the capital, that lad of yours, Lord Tyson, he came by the training yard just before you did."

I raised an interested brow. Tyson may be palace-trained, but Sir Gavin's opinion was the one that mattered. "And?"

He shrugged and offered me a reluctant smile. "His style is formal, but he isn't without talent. A trip past the mountains will do him good. Rough up his *smooth* edges."

I laughed with him.

Sheathing his sword, he added, "His sanguine partner is a fighter, too. The Lady Okeri crossed blades with him and held her own."

My laughter died as I considered his statement. A trip over the mountains might be good for Tyson, but I wondered if it would be good for Claire. How was she going to fare if we went to battle? More importantly, what would happen if she was injured? What would I do?

Shaking his hand and offering him my thanks, I left the training yard and headed for my council chambers, which were as far away from Claire's room as I could get without sitting in Imogen's salt pools. I pored over maps and scratched down notes and did everything I was supposed to do to prepare for my meeting at eight. Including researching more about werewolf sightings in the last millennium. If Alec's story was true, there was a new threat loose inside the Unified Territories.

Yet, I was distracted, cutting my attention between what was required of me as the Duke of Roselyn and being Claire's mate. I cursed the gods. Cursed my wretched life as a vampire.

I had too many responsibilities to be mated. And yet, the fantasy of living with her as my mate twisted its way back into my thoughts. Unhelpful and unwelcome. I rubbed my temples in frustration, trying to see a way forward. If Tyson was half the leader Natalia was, there would be a chance I could trust him. Because the one thing that would pain me more than hurting Claire would be to sit idly by, watching him fail to negotiate peace. Especially if my absence from these negotiations meant the people of Roselyn—my people—would be standing on the front lines if the covens of the Lawless Land attacked.

CHAPTER 27
QUI ÊTES-VOUS?
CLAIRE

I couldn't stop crying. Heavy sobs shook my shoulders and tears poured down my cheeks.

My desire to know what it meant to be close to a man had kept me watching Tansy and Devlinn, but somewhere along the way, it became less about my curiosity and more about disbelief.

How? How could a witch blessed with the powers of Diana forsake her people and give herself to a Witch of the Darkness? *Willingly and happily.* Sighing and gasping with pleasure as he moved inside her.

I was a ruin.

I had no magick.

I was an embarrassment.

But Tansy wasn't. She had white hair, which meant she had power. If Tansy could be with him without remorse, it made me question *everything* I knew about the world.

I sank onto the ground, back pressed against the cold glass just to feel something real. Wiping my tears, I wondered if Tansy's family didn't have cemeteries filled with the bones of those who died by dark magick? If maybe, they weren't at war with the darkness like we were.

My thoughts bounced around, flitting between the stories I heard from my family and what I saw at Shreesa's Inn. Bastien insisted that they practiced their craft within the bounds of the law, and I'd seen no reason to doubt that. My back was slick with condensation from the glass and numb with chill, but it wasn't the cold that made me shiver. *No.* It was my next question.

What if—I'd been lied to?

Sickness rose in my throat, and I swallowed hard, forcing the sour taste back down. No. No, that *couldn't* be true. *It couldn't.*

Light flashed across the gilded surface of a floor-length mirror. I forced myself to crawl toward it, unwilling to trust my unsteady legs, just to see the lace choker Mama had fastened around my neck.

Sitting up on my knees, I pulled back my long silver-lilac hair and tilted my head to inspect it—something I hadn't done since we left the inn. The scabs beneath the lace were almost healed, but I'd never forget the sickening pain of the barbs as they pierced my skin. Nor the way the vampire had tried to save me by cutting it off. His first instinct had been to protect me.

Sniffling, I let my hair fall back around my shoulders and stared at my reflection in the mirror.

I didn't recognize the girl staring back at me. Dressed in the black and gold of House Allard, sitting in a room that catered to my every need, my femininity awakened by the touch of a vampire.

Who was I? Really? Fresh tears rolled down my cheeks.

The only thing I'd ever known about myself was that I was a witch devoid of magick. I was cursed with hair the color of pale purple orchids, as if to show everyone how different I was —how alone I was.

I knew I wasn't the eldest daughter Mama had hoped for, not by a long shot, but she wouldn't have asked me to take on this burden, to make a vow to discover the location of the demonic relics if the circumstances weren't dire. I touched the black lace as a question rose to my mind. My lip quivering.

Would she?

I closed my eyes and a memory of the ceremony surfaced. Of the vow she made me say. Of the way the magick burned on my lips. At the way the choker sealed itself around my throat. The way she looked into my eyes and told me that I wouldn't be able to escape my fate. That if I tried to take it off, it would kill me. That if I tried to seek help, or breathed a word of who I really was or who sent me, it would bleed me dry. It was either fulfill my mission or die.

I opened my eyes, looking at myself, really looking. Where Bastien saw fire, Mama saw a worthless girl. *Useless.* Could she have sent me on this mission just to rid herself of me?

My breath caught on something painful and sharp, and tears blurred my vision all over again. Heavy sobs flooding out of me until I doubled over, on hands and knees, willing the sick feeling to leave my body.

I was her blood, her daughter. She wanted to see me rise despite my lack of magick. She wanted to push me to be stronger, better, than I'd been. And I was doing just that, wasn't I? Proving at every turn that I could do this. I wiped my cheeks and forced myself to take a deep breath. So what if I met a handful of witches along the way who were different? I couldn't doubt my loyalty to my family.

If I did my job, Sera could be the first witch who didn't need to worry about dark magick. That's the goal I needed to hold in my heart. I couldn't fall to pieces. I had to act.

There was a knock at the door, and I startled, hoping it wasn't the vampire. I didn't want him to see me like this. Pushing to my feet, I made for the vanity and powdered my nose. Then, rolling my shoulders back, I strode across the room to the door. I found an older woman with kind eyes staring back at me. "Can I help you?"

She let out a titter of laughter. "No, my dear. I'm here to help *you*." She curtsied, then regarded my puffy eyes with a sympathetic smile. "I know you're a long way from home, Miss. But hopefully you won't be sad for long. My name is Lena, and I'm here to bring a bit of cheer your way."

She turned, revealing a host of people lined up behind her. Two were carrying a long table, others silver trays laden with food. Sweet and savory scents drifted into the room, making my stomach twist with hunger.

Lena slipped inside, fluttering into the room and directing everyone where to place the table and how to arrange the dishes. I followed after her with slow steps, not knowing what to do as two men with musical instruments hurried past me. Those who weren't carrying trays were wearing robes. *Black silk robes.* Just like they'd done this morning.

"What's going on?" I muttered more to myself than anyone in particular.

"We're having a party!" replied a male voice. *Devlinn.*

He and Tansy appeared at my side. No longer wearing robes, but beautifully tailored clothes. A dress for her made of gold silk that offset her deep brown skin and white hair, and a smart pair of black trousers and a gold tunic for him that fit his long, muscled frame.

Tansy linked her arm with mine. "His Grace put together a party in your honor! He even tripled our salary!" She squealed with delight then offered me a wicked smile. "You must be quite special to him."

My mouth fell open. "Really?"

She nodded. "His Grace is most kind, but this is truly extravagant!"

Kind wasn't the word I would use to describe him, but I was surprised at this turn of events.

Tansy fitted her hand under my jaw and urged me to close my mouth, then rubbed a soothing hand down my back. "Miss Claire, you're a sanguine partner. You've been chosen to be the life source of one of the most powerful vampires in this land. Step into your power."

Step into my power. The words drifted into my head and settled there.

Musicians began to play. The silver trays were arranged in a beautiful display on a long table. People filled the room. I might not recognize myself anymore, but I wanted to step into my power. To be the woman I wanted to be. Confident and poised. Not someone who swooned at the mention of blood or questioned every move she made. But how did I do that?

Tansy playfully bumped her hip against mine, and I met her gaze, which was gentle and warm. "Come, let me introduce you to my friends."

By *friends*, she meant the men and women wearing black robes. Any of which would willingly make love to me the way Devlinn had made love to her.

Everyone's attention was on me, just as it had been the night of the Sanguination Ball when Bastien had led me onstage and spun me into a dip so low my hair fanned out across the wood floor. Something inside my stomach tightened, but I rolled my shoulder back and told myself I could do this. For the next hour, Tansy and Devlinn led me around the room, stopping to chat with each person wearing a black robe.

Some were flirts. Some made my cheeks burn with nervous heat. Some were a little too self-involved for my taste. But they all seemed to have two things in common: great respect for the Duke and a passion for their job as a consort.

I wasn't sure if any of them would be any help. Except *one*.

"What do you know about him?" I pointed to the only man they hadn't introduced me to. The one with the charming smile who'd been sitting alone by the fire. His skin was nearly as dark as Tansy's, and his eyes were the warm reddish brown of tea. His soft black hair cropped short at the sides.

"He arrived this morning, with His Grace's party," Devlinn said. "I thought you'd know him."

I shook my head. "No. I don't."

"Personally, I can't believe Lena allowed him to come with those scratches on his arm," Tansy added.

"Scratches?"

"On his left forearm. Deep ones. I thought he needed rest, but he was very insistent on coming."

I was kept out of many conversations at Prideaux Hill, and as a result, I'd become very good at reading body language and ghosting around the outskirts of whispered conversations. I knew this man was one I wanted to speak more with.

Step into your power.

Excusing myself, I snatched two bite-sized tarts from a silver tray and made my way over to where he sat. I offered him a tart and a smile. He grinned back at me then leaned in, taking the sweet from my fingers with his lips. I had to hide my surprise.

"You honor me with your presence, Mademoiselle." He lifted my hand to his lips and placed a kiss there. I knew I was blushing, but I pretended like I wasn't. The woman I wanted to be had her hand kissed all the time and didn't bat an eye.

"Please, call me Claire," I instructed him. "Would you care to dance?"

I didn't really want to dance, I just wanted an excuse to talk closely.

"Again, you honor me." He offered me his hand, and I allowed him to lead me out to the dance floor. We swayed in time to the music. I had no idea what I was doing. It was my first dance. But I tried not to let it show. Even when I accidentally stepped on his foot.

He laughed it off, and so did I, but as I gazed into his eyes, I saw a hollowness. "I don't remember seeing you on the journey north."

"That's because I joined late." I waited for him to clarify. He glanced toward the windows, at the mountains, then back to me. "His Grace offered me a place at his court. After hearing my story."

He twirled me in a circle, and when I was back in his arms, I asked, "What story?"

His smile shrank and he pulled me in close. So close that my body was flush against his and I could feel his breath against my skin.

"One that isn't fit for parties." He paused, then said, "Besides, I think the better story is how His Grace asked for volunteers to dye their hair red." He leveled a look at me, along with a charming grin. "I know I'm no Dark Witch like Devlinn, but I hope you'll consider me just the same."

My feet missed a step. *Dye their hair?*

Bastien hadn't paraded nine Dark Witches in front of me— only one. He just wanted me to think they all were. Why? Why was he intent on treating me this way? It was almost like he didn't want anyone else to touch me. Like... he wanted me to himself. But if that was the case, why not just say it? Because of the laws? He didn't seem the kind to follow rules.

Still, he'd told me he didn't want me, and I certainly didn't want him. And yet, I couldn't stop my thoughts from drifting to him, again and again.

During those quiet nights together in the tent, when we'd talked late into the night before he lay me over a pile of furs and sank his teeth into my thigh, licking and tasting my skin like I was the only thing in the world that could satisfy him.

"I'm sorry if I upset you," Alec whispered.

"There is nothing to apologize for," I reassured him. "I just was thinking about... something else."

Alec spun me in another circle, but this time, when we came back together, he wasn't being the flirt he'd been before. "They told you about my scratches. Didn't they?"

I stilled. "Tansy mentioned you'd been hurt."

Slowly, he pulled up his sleeve, revealing a set of angry red scratch marks that had been covered in thin linen bandages. My hand shot to my mouth. "What happened?"

He held my gaze, then said, "I was attacked during the last full moon... by a werewolf." Disbelief cinched my brows together. A werewolf? "I know it's a mad story, but I'm not crazy. I know what I saw. I know how I got these scratches."

"Of course. The good news is that you're safe now." I knew without a doubt that Alec was my third. I needed more time with him. Alone. To hear his story. If not to spy on Bastien, then to learn what he knew. Mama would want to know. "I want you as one of my consorts. That is, if you'll accept."

"It would be my honor," he said.

His fingers slid up my spine until they cradled the back of my head, thumb brushing the base of my skull. His other hand cupped my cheek, thumb ghosting over my lower lip. And still, maddeningly, Bastien's face flashed through my mind. His lips at my throat, his voice in my head. I drew in a stuttering breath, which made him smile. But it wasn't for him.

"Thank you for being so kind when others would shun me.

I promise to repay each kindness in turn as one of your chosen."

His comment warmed my cheeks. He was very handsome, that was hard to deny, but I knew this was his job, and he had to say things like that. I'd never been kissed before, even though the heavy sense that Bastien's lips had been on mine once before lingered with me, but I had a tingling suspicion that Alec was about to kiss me.

He tilted his head. His lips angling closer. So close. Did I want him to kiss me? A little voice said *no*. Because my body wanted someone else. Another said *yes*. Because it would prove Bastien didn't own me.

The sound of a door slamming sent my heart into a wild flutter.

CHAPTER 28
DÉPOUILLER
CLAIRE

I pulled away from Alec, putting a foot of distance between us. Only...it wasn't His Grace in the doorway.

"Lord Tyson of House Allard, Viscount of Aurenne. And his sanguine partner, Lady Okeri Djannelle," the attendant announced.

"I can't believe you're hosting a party and didn't invite your favorite traveling companions!"

A whoosh of breath left me.

Tyson wagged two bottles of amber-colored spirits in my direction. "Miss Donadieu, this is the perfect opportunity to play a proper game of *Dépouiller!*"

Excited applause and giggles went around the room at the mention of the card game, and I swore the temperature rose as everyone's attention shifted to me. I recalled the game they'd taught me to play on our way to Roselyn. The one that took me the better part of a day to learn and the one they'd abandoned, explaining it was only fun with more people and... *strong drink.*

Tyson kicked the door closed behind him and the pair strolled inside without further invitation. "Never, ever choose your consorts without playing Dépouiller with them first," Lady Okeri told me, sauntering up to where I stood and pulling a deck of cards from the satchel around her waist. "It's practically an unwritten law amongst sanguine partners."

Okeri and the Viscount were both dressed in royal blue trousers and tunics that bore evidence of swordplay. Her curly hair had been braided in tight rows with gold beads threaded into the ends. She was so beautiful and fierce, it was hard not to be intimidated by her confidence and the way she just *knew* things. Especially about this role I was supposed to be filling.

"Isn't drinking with your consorts... illegal?" I asked Okeri.

She gave me the strangest look. "Says who?"

I promised Bastien I wouldn't drink with them. He'd told me there was no exception to this rule, and I thought that meant it was codified for *all* sanguine partners, but I guessed that was another rule crafted just for me. I bit my lip. "Never mind."

Okeri playfully tapped Alec on the shoulder. "Go find some chairs for the table, my darling."

"Of course, My Lady," he replied excitedly, bowing. Then turned to me. "It would be an honor to be on your team."

My team?

Okeri and Tyson hadn't taught me to play the game with teams. I wasn't sure what that meant, but didn't want to seem foolish. Besides, I wanted him to feel like he could tell me anything.

"Who else's team would I be on?" I replied.

He grinned that too-charming smile, then scurried off to find more chairs. My attention shifted back to Lady Okeri, who posed the same question to the room. "Who wants to be on *my* team?"

Many hands rose, and after careful perusal, she selected a pretty brunette with curvy hips and full breasts. Deferring to me, Okeri asked, "Miss Donadieu, do you mind if this one plays with me?"

"I think she is the one you should be asking."

She agreed, asking the woman, who heartily consented. Meanwhile, Tyson had ordered the buffet table cleared of food and was sloshing amber liquid into little crystal cups. Once again, I was way out of my comfort zone and had no idea what I was getting myself into, but everyone seemed excited to play, including Tansy and Devlinn, so I committed to enjoying myself despite my reservations.

"Don't let me drink too much, 'Keri," Tyson said, downing the contents of his glass before refilling it.

She raised a brow. "And why is that?"

"Because I have a council meeting tonight, and I don't want to be sweating booze from every pore. My uncle won't approve."

A few people giggled, but I didn't. If he strolled into the council meeting drunk, and Bastien asked where he'd been, he'd be livid. At him. At me. I stopped that line of thinking and reminded myself I was a grown woman who was allowed to make her own choices. Who could stand in her power. And all these special rules Bastien had for me were nothing but over-protective nonsense.

If I was so special to him, then he would treat me like a princess, not a prisoner. Everyone was taking their seats, and the pretty brunette was being pulled into Lady Okeri's lap. Her twin on Tyson's. Alec had chosen a seat between them, and he beckoned me over. Oh. *Right.* I was going to be sitting on his lap since he was on my team. That was going to be... interesting.

Smoothing a hand down the front of my dress, I took Alec's extended hand and lowered myself into his lap. The black satin robe he wore was doing a very poor job of covering his legs, or anything else. I folded my hands anxiously on the table, not allowing all my weight to rest on him, and fixing my attention on Okeri as she shuffled the cards around the woman on her lap.

I needed to be confident like her. Flirty. Happy. It's what I wanted. To feel good and enjoy the moment, but something was holding me back. Something... *or someone.* That needed to stop.

Reaching for a small crystal glass, I threw back a shot of amber liquor, and immediately regretted it, coughing into my arm as the flavor burned down my throat.

"Look at you downing the hard stuff!" Alec said encouragingly, and copied me, drinking a shot of liquor.

Both of the cups were refilled by Lena, who was fluttering around the room, ensuring everyone was having a good time.

Tyson set his arm on the back of our chair and leaned conspiratorially in. "You're going to love this version of the game. The only difference from the one we taught you in the coach is that if a Jack is on the river, everyone takes an article of clothing off, regardless of if they're winning or not. You do a shot if someone plays a spade. And of course, all the losers have to remove an article of clothing for each number of tricks they're short."

I stared blankly back at him. "Most of the people here are only wearing robes."

He winked. His dark hair not quite shadowing the mischievous look in his eyes. "Exactly."

It would seem the point of this game was to get all of us naked and drunk as quickly as possible. And I was sitting on Alec's lap. I closed my eyes, dragging in a breath through my nose, trying to steady myself.

The last time I'd been pulled into a man's lap, Bastien had undone me with a single hand. Touching, teasing—driving me mad with a need I hadn't known I could feel. But this... this *wasn't* the same. This didn't feel intimate and inevitable, like it had last night. In fact, this felt like the opposite. I was tense, and I wasn't sure I wanted to strip in front of all these people, especially Tyson. On the other hand, I didn't want Bastien to be the only one who could make me feel that way, because he'd told me he would never touch me again. And I was supposed to be spying on him.

So, here I was, surrounded by beautiful people who were allowed to touch me. This had to be good enough. Alec was very handsome, and if I had never met Bastien, I might've thought him the most handsome man I had ever seen.

Cards slid across the table. Two to each team. Three were turned face-up in the center. A ripple of anticipation passed around the circle; the promise of losses and wagers more intimate than coin. I tried to remember all the rules I'd learned, but it was so loud. Lilting strings competed with the hum of conversation and the occasional gasp of pleasure. Bursts of laughter broke my thoughts.

Alec's arm slid easily around my waist, warm and steady as he tugged me closer. I let myself rest against him, if only because the liquor in my veins and the noise in my head made it easier than resisting."Look out for the Lady to the right. Everyone I've played Dépouiller with from the capital cheats," he announced, voice pitched just high enough to draw another ripple of laughter.

"It's not cheating if you don't get caught," Okeri fired back.

More laughter circled the table.

I tried to focus on the game, but it was all a blur of cards, clinking crystal cups, and flushed faces. My attention wavered —half on the numbers in my hand, half on the couples already partaking in the spoils of pleasure. Fingers disappeared beneath silken robes. A woman's head tipped back as her partner's mouth found her throat.

As if caught in the tide of desire, Alec bent his head close to mine, his voice a low purr meant for me alone. "Why so tense?" he murmured, as if coaxing me through a dance. "You may be the Duke's sanguine partner, but you're allowed to have fun. And it's my job to remind you of that."

The words were gentle—a trained reassurance designed to make me feel safe. And damn him, it worked. A little. Maybe it was the liquor warming my stomach, or maybe it was the way his breath tickled across my ear, but some of my dread eased.

"We've got a good hand," he said suddenly, tapping the cards before sliding his palm up the curve of my stomach. His touch halted just beneath my breasts, suggestive but not forceful, as if waiting for me to grant permission. "What do you think? How many tricks can we make? Six?"

I caught his hand before he could rise any higher, threading our fingers together. My heart thudded against my ribs, like it was trying to shove him away because it only wanted the touch of someone else. Someone who didn't even have a pulse.

"Two," I said firmly.

He chuckled, lips brushing the line of my neck in a way that made me shiver despite myself. "Two? Where's the fun in that?"

"If we lose..." My protest died on my tongue as I turned and caught the foxlike glint in his eyes. His grin said he'd already calculated the risk, already imagined the inevitable loosening of my corset strings. "Three, then," I amended, heat crawling up my throat.

He conceded, and bets went around the table, laughter and teasing flying as fast as the cards. The first hand stretched on longer than the game in the coach, spades being thrown twice, which meant another two rounds of liquor.

My head grew lighter with every swallow. The burn leaving my chest warm. My lips loose. My laughter spilled out unguarded, rising with the chorus around the table. I stopped caring whether Alec's hand rested on my stomach or not; I leaned back against him, letting the firm line of his body mold to mine. I let myself imagine—for a fleeting moment—that maybe this was enough.

Cards slapped down one after the other until Lady Okeri leaned back with a victorious grin. She was declared the winner, and the room erupted with groans, cheers, and *another round of shots*. I winced when Alec revealed we'd only taken one trick. That meant two articles of clothing would need to come off. One for me. One for him.

Okeri clapped her hands like a drumbeat and shouted, "Take it off!" Others joined in, the chant swelling as more guests banged their hands on the table. I laughed and whooped with the others, taken by the sultry spell the liquor had woven. And I *wanted* to be caught in it. For once, I wanted to feel free. I wanted to feel like I belonged. I wanted, for the first time in my life, *to have fun*.

Alec rose, lifting me gently from his lap as if presenting me to the table. Everyone clapped and cheered, but his attention never wavered from mine, steady and playful, daring me to laugh along with him as he tugged at the ties of his sash. The black silk slid loose under his fingers.

The sight jolted me, and I stopped laughing. As if Bastien had slipped inside my mind, the world around me dulled until all I could think of was *him*. I thought of Bastien in the steamy bathhouse, kneeling in front of me, and the way he twirled my sash around his long fingers. The way his eyes had devoured me. Worshipped me.

I forced myself back to the present. To the music and the man in front of me. Bastien wasn't here, which I was very happy about. If he was here, no one would be having this much fun. He was the darkness that swallowed fun. But if that was true, why did my body ache for him as soon as Alec's robe slipped free?

There was no denying he was very attractive. With flawless bronze skin, unmarked by war. Save for the angry scratch marks on his arm. So soft to touch and warm under my palms. He was nothing like Bastien. I couldn't decide if it was his best quality, or his worst.

"Your turn," Alec said, coming closer and running his hand along my curves, stopping when he reached my corset strings.

I wasn't wearing anything underneath my skirt except a petticoat and undergarments. When the corset was off, my breasts would be bared for everyone.

I should be nervous, but right now, the liquor was making me feel braver. Many others were completely naked, and I wanted to feel like I belonged. But more than that, I wanted to silence the questions I'd asked myself earlier. If I'd been fed lies about Dark Witches and vampires.

Slowly, he started pulling on the strings, loosening the front of my corset with each tug. His lips skimmed over my bare skin, tracing up one arm, across my shoulders, then down the other. I couldn't believe I was doing this—Bastien would be furious—but the alcohol dulled my inner voice.

I'd drink anything—kiss anyone—to stop the whisper of *what if? What if it had all been a lie?*

With Alec's urging, my corset slid down my hips. With another wiggle and a tug, he pulled it over my head and tossed it beside his robe. I cupped my chest and let out a burst of ridiculous laughter. This was mad. I was mad.

"I was wrong," Alec said, slowly easing one of my hands off

my breast so he could spin me around. "You are more than beautiful. You're *radiant*."

Our eyes locked, and the anticipation that he was going to kiss me settled over me once again. Cupping my face, Alec pulled me close. His hardness pressed against my belly. For whatever reason, another bubble of laughter crested my lips.

"Say the word, and I'll give you whatever you want."

I hummed in response. I wanted... *what did I want?* For the room to stop spinning. For everything to stop being so funny.

Giggling, I closed my eyes, and pretended he *was* Bastien. I couldn't say why, but the vampire's frustrating image formed behind my eyes and wouldn't leave. Or, maybe... *I didn't want it to leave.* I swayed where I stood and chuckled as Alec righted me.

"I want you to kiss me." The words just... came out. I wasn't sure who I was talking to, the man inside my head or the one standing in front of me, and right now I was too drunk to care. Just as he lowered his lips, nearly touching mine, the unmistakable crack of Bastien's cane struck the floor.

"Your Grace!" someone gasped.

Alec let me go so that he could bow, just as everyone else did.

I didn't.

Slowly, I turned to face him. He was impeccably dressed, of course, with a cravat tied at his throat. I dropped the hand banded over my chest. If he'd come to see me, then he could see *all of me.*

CHAPTER 29

PROPOSER

BASTIEN

A hush fell over the room, save for beating hearts and nervous breaths that grated against my patience.

So what if they were afraid? *They should be.* I'd kill them all where they stood for daring to *look* at my mate's bare chest. None of them mattered to me the way *she* mattered.

Claire was the curling ivy inside my heart. The gravity that held me to the ground. The moon on my darkest night. As much as I wanted to deny her hold on me, it was real.

I was beholden to her.

And right now, the woman who captivated all my attention was exposed for every wagging tongue in the room to see— including my whelp of a nephew. Heir to my lands and titles, and yet still a reckless boy. How foolish was I to even consider stepping aside? This wasn't the kind of behavior expected of the next Duke of Roselyn.

Parting the sea of people standing between me and her, I removed my jacket, then settled it over her shoulders. Claire glared up at me, and I glared down at her. Furious that she could make me feel this way.

"Your Grace, the point of Dépouiller isn't to put clothes *on*," she seethed. "It's to take them *off*."

I caught the scent of whiskey on her breath and the hazy look in her eyes. She was drunk with her consorts, even though I forbade it. "I know how the game works," I replied, trying to keep my head.

I didn't want to play nice in front of all these people. I wanted to rage. *At her*. At them. At myself. Without breaking eye contact with Claire, I told her guests that the party was over. The room emptied quicker than if I'd announced the château was on fire. Men and women tripped over themselves to get dressed and get out as quickly as possible. A flutter of robes and arms rushing out the door. All except my nephew, who sidled up beside me, clearly intoxicated.

"Don't be upset. We were just having a bit of fun, Uncle," Tyson said, clapping a hand around my shoulder. "The journey here was painfully boring. You understand, I'm sure."

My fury was a living, breathing thing. Had Tyson been anyone else besides *mon sang*, my blood, he'd already be dead. My fangs lengthened, and the shadows under my eyes darkened. "If you don't want your mother to receive your severed head in a box, *boy*," I said around a snarl. "I suggest you shut your mouth and *get out*. You've caused enough trouble for one night."

The color drained from his face, but he said nothing else. Just as quickly as the others, he vacated Claire's room, closing the door behind him. I had a mind to shove him in a coach and send him back home. But it wasn't him I wanted to think about. It was *her*.

Once again, I found myself alone with Claire. And despite my anger, something inside me relaxed, knowing that it was just the two of us. I drew in a deep breath through my nose, trying to calm my temper. When I turned my attention back to her once again, I found her angrily collecting playing cards.

"Have you been harmed?" I asked. "Did *he* coerce you to do anything you didn't want to do?"

If he had, even the goddess wouldn't be able to save him.

She expelled a loud breath, marched over to where I stood, and, without warning, threw the cards in my face. They fluttered to the ground like tree leaves. I didn't react, except to pick one of the cards from my collar and toss it on the ground.

"You are such a spoil sport!" she screamed, poking me hard in the chest. "And confusing! I mean, what is actually wrong with you?"

That was an excellent question. One that I had been asking myself ever since I met her, despite knowing the answer. I folded my arms across my chest. "You're drunk."

"And you're an ass!" she countered, poking me in the chest again.

This time, I grabbed her wrist, if only to steady her. She was teetering like we were on the deck of a ship. "I'm an ass? I'm the one trying to keep you safe. You're the one disregarding your own welfare."

She laughed and rolled her eyes. "We were just playing a game!"

"And drinking. Which I specifically prohibited with your consorts," I reminded her.

At this, her sarcastic laughter ceased, and she poked me again with her free hand. "You can shove all your rules up your entitled ass!"

I captured her other wrist and drew Claire closer to me until her body was flush against mine, and her heat burned into me. "Those rules are for your safety."

"That's bullshit. None of them would hurt me. Especially when you're always looming at the door."

Both of us were breathing heavily, and the tension between us seemed to double when her gaze shifted down to where my bloodstone was glowing through my shirt. Pulsing in time to her heart. She'd been chosen for me, and I for her. I didn't know why, but it had happened all the same. We were fated. When Claire glanced back up at me, her lips were parted, and her eyes were wide. For the first time, I wondered if she'd guessed my secret. If she knew that I was tied to her and she to me.

I'd never felt the bond between us as strongly as I did right now, and it was getting harder and harder to control my instincts. Because the truth was… I didn't just need her. I wanted her. All of her. Her sharp mind and her vulnerability and her bravery. Somewhere along the way, I didn't just need to protect her—I'd come to enjoy her company. Even now. Even angry. And, against all odds, I'd started questioning if I could give everything up just to be with her.

Which was why it hurt so bad when I saw her pressed against Alec. Her lips nearly touching his. I'd been stabbed many times before, but this was a pain I'd never forget. Releasing her wrists, holding all that hurt and anger and fury inside, I asked, "How did you expect that game to end?"

"In a *fun* way," she replied.

"What would've been fun?" I asked. Each question fueled my jealousy. "Did you want him to *fuck* you?"

Say no. Tell me the thought disgusts you.

But she didn't. Instead, she laughed again and refused to meet my eye. "So what if I did?"

How? How could she even consider another man when she was mated to me? If she felt an ounce of what I felt, the idea of getting close to anyone would be *impossible*.

I told myself to leave it alone. To walk away and let her do whatever she wanted. If she didn't care, then why try? But I couldn't make myself leave. "You spent thirty minutes in his company, and, in that time, decided Alec was the first person you wanted to take to bed?"

She set her hands on her hips, and as she did, the folds of my jacket that was draped around her shoulders parted, exposing the curve of her breasts. My jaw ached with the effort of restraint. "Why are you concerned with who I take to bed, Your Grace?"

The thought of another man between her legs, taking his pleasure with her, had me ready to put my fists through the stone wall. I couldn't stand it. "Your first time should be with someone who knows more about you than your name."

Claire took a step closer, her eyes narrowed. One finger accusatorially pointed at my chest like she might poke me again. "And why does that concern you?"

I couldn't tell her the truth. I couldn't. No matter how badly I wanted to. No matter how much easier it would be to explain my actions.

I'd done what no vampire was allowed to do—what no vampire should be able to do—drink from their mate. Claire wasn't just the heartbeat inside my bloodstone. She ran inside my veins. She was everything. *Everywhere.* Consuming me from the inside out.

When she realized I wasn't going to answer, she came a step closer until her nail sank into my muscle. "I'll tell you why," she said, unflinching. Her eyes glassy with unshed tears. "This is payback. You *hate* me for making you choose me as your sanguine partner. You're punishing me."

If only I could hate her. If only I could forget about our bond. But I wasn't about to summon a god or break the Blood Treaty on the chance it would work, so I was cursed with my wanting. Slowly, I lifted a hand to her face and traced my thumb along her cheekbone. "I do not hate you."

I hate myself for hurting you.

I hoped this declaration would soften her. Hoped she'd see the torment on my face at being torn apart on the inside. But it didn't.

"If you don't hate me, then why are you being like this? Making up rules for me? Pushing me away only to act like this. I don't understand."

I withdrew my hand from her face and clenched it into a fist. Frustrated. Annoyed. Why was I trying to be vulnerable with her? It was foolish. But I'd done many foolish things since meeting Claire, including letting the next words out of my mouth. "If you want to continue this conversation, allow me to remove the alcohol from your veins."

Her pretty lips fell open. Anger melting into shock. "You can do that?"

I nodded, desperate to get close to her in the only way I could. To do something for her.

"Won't it make you drunk?"

A half-smile rounded my lips. "Not as drunk as you."

She considered me for a moment, swaying slightly, then said, "Fine."

"You should lay down," I said, gesturing to the settee beside the fire. "Maybe on the—"

"I know what to do," she replied, full of drunken confidence. "This isn't my first time." I watched her with a bemused expression on my face as she staggered toward a settee, nearly rolling an ankle when she tripped on the gauzy hem of her petticoat and stumbled forward. "Stupid skirt!"

I thought to help her, but knew she'd just rebuff me. Besides, I was enjoying watching her too much.

Letting out an exasperated huff, Claire undid the buttons on the front and let the slip of fabric fall to the ground, revealing every curve I'd been dreaming of, then collapsed on the couch, naked save for my jacket, which had fallen open, a scrap of black lace covering her sex, garters holding up black thigh-high stockings, and high-heeled leather boots.

I wasn't much for prayers, but I said a silent one now, asking for some amount of strength because this wasn't fair. Why did the gods see fit to mate me to such an exquisite temptress? I bit down on my lip, knowing I should look away, but I was unable to stop myself. Taking in each line of her body. Memorizing every inch as I stalked toward her. The black stockings and lace stark against the creamy color of her skin. Her lilac hair framing her heart-shaped face.

I lowered onto my knees, and the scent of my mate's arousal had my cock thickening, needing to serve its one purpose, which was to bring this woman as much pleasure as possible.

"What are you waiting for?" she asked, crossing her arms over her chest. "Let's get this over with."

I hummed low in the back of my throat. "When you've been alive as long as I have, you learn there's no reason to rush every little thing, *chérie*." I ran my hands up her calves, letting my palms trace the nylon stockings. Her breath hitched, and *by the gods*, there was no better sound. "In fact," I continued, "you come to understand that the best part of being alive is the *anticipation*."

I caught her behind the knee and guided her leg over the back of the couch, spreading her open for me. My fingers traced the path down her thigh, unhurried, until they pressed against the wild beat of her pulse. I watched with pleasure as she gripped the couch, breath coming in and out, making her chest heave. Her nipples turning into tight little peaks. The fire in her was burning hotter than ever.

Our eyes locked. "Unlike you, I'm not immortal," she said. "I can't live that way, or I'd never get anything done."

I ran my fingers up and down her thigh. A barely there touch that had her biting back my name. "If I want something," she said, all gasps, "I have to... t-take action."

I lowered my lips to the sensitive flesh just below the apex of her thighs, and my mouth watered. Anticipating the sweet taste of her blood as I transformed into the hunter that I was. Fangs lengthening."I'm well-versed in taking action, chérie, make no mistake."

I licked her skin with long strokes of my tongue to soften it. Her back arched, and her hip slid down an inch. If only I could pull the lace to the side and lick her center the same way.

"Bastien. *Please.*"

My name, so sweet on her lips.

"Easy, Claire," I purred, kissing her thigh once again. "I need you to hold very, *very* still."

Fitting one hand under her backside, I gripped her hard, lifting her to my mouth and sank my fangs into her. The taste alone nearly undid my sensibilities. She was... *delectable.* Claire writhed beneath my touch, moaning softly. My eyes rolled back as the flavor of her blood raced down my throat, but I needed to focus on the alcohol, not the taste. It took only a few minutes until her blood ran clean. Once I was done, I released my hold on her but was careful to catch the soft dribbles of red running from the already healing wound with my tongue.

The buzz of alcohol swam in my head, and I couldn't believe how much she'd had to drink.

Claire lay sprawled across the couch, her eyes hazy, her cheeks pink. "You *are* trying to punish me."

Something deep inside me purred with satisfaction. I knew exactly what she meant. But that little tease was not punishment. Not compared to the sharp pain I'd felt after catching her half-naked with another man. "I swear, I'm not trying to punish you."

She pushed herself into a seated position and asked, "Then why are you making all these unfair rules for me?"

I hesitated. "May I?" I asked, gesturing to the space beside her.

She nodded.

I sat. Daring to brush a wild strand of hair aside. Our eyes met, and hers were wide, dark pupils like twin moons. Without the alcohol swimming in my veins, I struggled to deny her. But with it, I found myself admitting a dark truth.

"I make these rules because I am protective of you. I—" My breath caught on something sharp lodged in my chest. "You and I shared a special moment—have shared many special moments. I've gotten closer to you than any other sanguine partner. I can't stand the idea of your first time being with a man who doesn't know how precious you are."

My voice was a bare whisper. Told as only dark secrets were. But it was only a half-truth. What I truly meant was that I couldn't stand the idea of anyone else having her... *but me*. No one could care for her the way I could. We were bound by blood and a fated bond.

What we would share could never be replicated.

For the sake of my duty, I was trying to tell myself she could be cared for well enough by others. She was right. Who she took to bed was none of my business. But I couldn't shut off my feelings. The part of me that was mated to her wouldn't allow it.

"You don't have to pretend with me," she said dejectedly. "I know I'm not precious. I'm—"

"Don't you dare say worthless, Claire Donadieu. You are fire. Remember? *Fire.* Who else dares to defy my orders, in my own castle?" She gave me a half-hearted grin. "Only you."

"And Lord Tyson."

"Don't mention his name. Not now."

A moment of charged silence stretched between us. Her, staring into the hearth. Me, staring at her. "So this is about preserving the sanctity of my first time? Nothing else?"

No. It wasn't about honor—it was about wanting her for myself, even though I couldn't have her. I had a moment of weakness where I wondered if a different life was possible, but tonight proved I couldn't trust Tyson. The instant I stepped away, he'd torch Château Rose in some misconceived plot. I swallowed that dark truth. "Yes. Exactly."

The words were like sandpaper on my tongue.

Neither of us said anything for a long moment. She simply studied me, like she was trying to solve a complicated problem. "What about you?"

"What *about* me?" I asked. Slowly, haltingly, her hand found my shoulder, pushing me back against the couch. "What are you doing?"

She didn't answer, except with a look. Then she slid her leg over my lap, easing herself down on me. Straddling me. The tips of her breasts pressed against my shirt. My cock straining against her heat.

Every instinct in me howled to take her. To mark her. To stop resisting. All I could do was look up at her like I was staring into the face of a goddess.

"You could be my first."

CHAPTER 30

DITES-MOI DE PARTIR

CLAIRE

Bastien was staring at me like a war was raging behind his eyes. I hadn't forgotten what I'd heard him say last night when I caught him touching himself. The way he fisted his hard length with my name on his lips.

"Claire, I'm going to come so deep inside you. I'm going to give you all of me."

Now, after watching Tansy and Devlinn, I knew exactly what that meant—what it looked like and how good it would feel. It made me lean into him, pressing that hardness against me and exhaling a luscious breath as images drifted in my mind. His breath mingled with mine in the inches between our lips. His intoxicating scent of bergamot and fresh pine winding its way through my senses.

Carefully, I set my palms on his chest, letting them mold to hard muscle beneath his vest. He reacted to my touch, inhaling deeply. Muscles flexing.

"Claire." My name spoken so softly, so sweetly, and laced with so much desire. It lifted goosebumps across my bare skin.

It was time to step into my power.

My fingers danced to the first button on his vest, and I pushed it through the hole. He didn't move to stop me. Didn't speak. Just stared at me as I worked until it was open. Next, I untied his cravat, letting the fabric slip free of his throat. Watching the cords of muscle flex in response to my touch.

All the while, his gaze remained locked on me.

The shirt was next. I freed the first button, then the second, until, at last, I saw his necklace—the one with the pulsing dark red stone. I ran my finger over the edge of the gem, which was set inside a gold pendant and was warm despite the cool temperature of his skin. A wave of déjà vu settled over me, leaving me lightheaded. The memory of a kiss I couldn't remember tingled on the edges of my consciousness.

"What is this?" I asked, my eyes crinkling at the corners as I tried and failed to remember something that was just beyond my ability to recall.

He rolled his lips together. "My bloodstone."

I'd only seen it twice. The first time was at the Sanguination Ball when it was glowing through his shirt. The second time was... *at the bathhouse.* Funny. I'd grown up around witchcraft—crystals and moon magick went hand in hand—but I'd never seen a gem pulse.

The choker around my throat squeezed my airway as if in warning: say nothing about your past. *Or else.* I shook my head to clear the thought, refocusing on him.

"Does it always pulse like this?" I asked.

Bastien studied me for a moment, his full lower lip caught between his teeth. After a few seconds passed, he said, "A bloodstone beats with the pulse of a vampire's mate. So long as they draw breath, it beats."

My gaze sank back to the stone while my thoughts spiraled. Was this why he kept pushing me away? Because he had a mate? Jealousy curled inside my stomach at the thought of someone else being fated to Bastien. I didn't understand why. It's not like I cared for him. I had plans to deceive him. But all the same, something inside me despised the idea of him touching or kissing anyone... *but me*.

"Do you know who she is?" I asked.

He hesitated. Then nodded once. "I do."

A chill swept over my skin. "Does she know you're fated to her?"

He regarded me with that tormented expression. "I'm not sure that she does."

I looked away as a strange mix of emotions tumbled inside me. Who was this person? And was she the reason why he looked so tormented? Because he was here with me even though he was fated to another?

Bastien cupped my jaw, guiding my attention back to his face. It was hard to believe anyone else was on his mind besides me. His eyes roved over the lines of my body, lingering on my breasts. The hardness between us twitched, pressing against me, and as it did, his hands found the small of my back, gently holding me to him.

The feeling was... indescribable. Wrong. *Right*. Sinful. *Bliss*. I tipped my head back and closed my eyes, enjoying it. Savoring it. Our bodies fit together like pieces of the same puzzle. I didn't know why touching him felt so right, but it did.

I wanted more than just this. I wanted him. Closer. So close. As close as Devlinn and Tansy had been. I wanted him to be all around me and inside me until he forgot the person he truly belonged to.

Opening my eyes, I leaned forward, letting my hands cup his cheeks, my fingers stretching into his soft blond hair. When our lips were a breath apart, I whispered his name. "Bastien."

"Claire." The low rasp of his voice went right through me. I wanted to kiss him. There was no question in my mind. No doubts. No wavering. It felt as inevitable as the tide meeting the shore. As if drawn to him by a string, our lips brushed against each other in one chaste touch.

My heart was pounding and my hands shook. We'd touched before, but this felt different. It *was* different.

"Claire. I want—*I need*—*more. More of you.*"

"I need you too," I choked out.

He groaned, then brought my face to his again, sweeping his lips over mine and capturing my lower lip with his teeth. A gentle bite. This kiss wasn't anything like the heady desire of last night. He pressed our foreheads together. Breathing coming fast. "Before this goes any further, there's something I need you to see."

I wasn't sure what he meant, but I waited, still trembling from the intense emotion building in my chest. He opened the connection between us, pulling me deeper into him, like it always did. I waited for what he wanted to show me, when suddenly, a picture formed behind my eyes.

It was dark, save for the light of floating candles. Steam curled off the surface of the water. I saw myself across the pool, shampooing my hair. Then the scene panned away from me, and to Bastien's pulsing stone.

I realized I was watching a memory. His memory of the night he took me to the bathhouse. And with it, I felt his emotions like they were my own. His frustration and anger were there, but it was nothing compared to the deep affection he had for me. For... the desire.

When the scene panned back to where I'd been standing, I wasn't there. Now, fear crowded into my chest. I felt like I couldn't breathe. I was looking around, but couldn't find me. And the bloodstone... it wasn't glowing anymore. Panic. Blind panic. With shaking hands, I dived under the water, swimming hard and fast, until I saw myself floating.

The sleeping draught. I must've fallen asleep. I must've *drowned.*

I scooped my lifeless body out of the water, praying to the gods as I stared at my face. There was a momentary hesitation before he decided to bring me back to life. Breath by breath. Begging me to live. *He saved me.*

When the memory was over and I opened my eyes, I was back in my own body. Tears were running down my cheeks. Slowly, he wiped them from my face. He'd saved my life, and never said a word.

"You saw what happened that night?" he asked.

I nodded, unsure what else to say. His lips *had* touched mine. Somehow, even in death, I'd felt him. He could've let me die and rid himself of me, but he didn't.

Unlike Mama.

She would send me to die for her war. My family, too. They watched her place the choker around my neck without a word against it. All because of the shame I held. Because I was a magickless witch—a burden. It sat on my chest, pressing down on me until it felt like I was drowning all over again.

The pulsing light of his bloodstone gave me something to focus on besides the shame, and I let the rhythm ground me when everything felt too heavy to hold.

Beat. Beat. Beat.

I swiped my finger over it again.

"Do you know why I saved you?" he asked. I shook my head. Still choking back tears. "If you think hard enough, you'll understand."

I sucked in a shuddering breath. "Bastien—" was all I managed before he kissed me again. The touch of his mouth awakened something inside me. Saving me. Bringing me back to life when the weight of who I was and who I wasn't threatened to drag me under.

Bastien slanted his mouth against mine like he wanted to savor every piece of me. Like nothing was too much for him. His smooth tongue swept over the seam of my lips, encouraging them to open for him. When I did, he traced mine with his. I was floating again. Lost in his tide. Wanting to swim to him and hold on tight.

Kiss by slow kiss, I fell deeper into him. Our bodies moving together. My hips and his. My hands and his. Rolling together and gripping tight. I gasped. He moaned. The hunger increasing until Bastien abruptly pulled away, leaving my lips wet and swollen and tasting of him.

"We shouldn't be doing this," he said, shaking his head, breathless. "It will only strengthen our bond."

Did he mean the connection between our minds, or something else?

Again, I saw the war raging behind his eyes, and I wanted to understand it better. I probed our connection, and found his guilt. His hesitance. And a need to protect me at all costs. But on top it was an intense desire. A desire that matched my own. Heat prickled in the back of my throat. How could he feel all these things for me at once? Unless... My gaze fell back to the bloodstone.

Beat. Beat. Beat.

In his memory, it had stopped pulsing when I was under the water. Bastien said the stone came to life while his mate drew breath. My own became shallow, and as my heart raced, the bloodstone pulsed faster.

Beat. Beat. Beat.

I saw the answer waiting in the frozen blue ponds of his eyes. One word resonated through our connection.

Mine.

My head swam with dizziness. No, it couldn't be. *It couldn't.* It didn't make sense. I was a witch, born of the Prideaux line.

How could a witch be mated to... "Bastien," I said, voice trembling, "are you saying...?" I couldn't finish the question.

He trailed the edge of my lips with his thumb, and, despite the coldness of his skin, left a trail of heat behind. "Claire..." My name came out as a sigh, and the guilt that hit me after it was said was so thick it made it difficult to breathe. "Nothing between us has to change," Bastien reassured me.

He hadn't been able to control his feelings for me in the weeks I'd known him. Even now, at the party, his protectiveness had never been about my first time. It had been because I was *his mate*. He'd been sending confusing signals, affectionate one minute then cold the next, because he was fighting against our bond.

My shock slipped into anger. He'd known this whole time and said *nothing*. "Why didn't you tell me?"

He pressed his lips together, and a crease formed between his brows. "Because I hoped you wouldn't be drawn to me in the way I'm drawn to you. Because you hate me for who I am and what I've done to your family."

He had no idea about my family. And the thought of Mama made me sick all over again. She'd say *this* was the reason I was born without Diana's light. Because I had been fated to an *unnatural monster*. The choker squeezed again, tighter this time. A reminder there would be no mention of my family to him. Not my *true* family.

My head swam, and I shook it to clear the haze. "After last night, you should've known that wasn't possible," I said. "You could've told me instead of *abandoning* me." Those last words tore from my throat, leaving behind a raw feeling. I shifted off his lap, coming to stand in front of him. Needing to put more space between us.

"Last night, I didn't tell you the truth because I had the ability to walk away," he said, pushing off the settee and standing before me. Bastien was so tall I had to tilt my head back just to look him in the eyes.

"What about now? Do you have the power to walk away?"

He bit his lip. Staring at me hard. "No. I don't," he admitted. His attention burned a trail of desire that settled between my legs. He wanted me so badly I could taste it on my tongue. And despite all that I'd learned tonight, *I wanted him too.* Because he was my mate. The vampire I was fated to.

"I need you to tell me to leave," he said, the words breaking into a million pieces, looking like he was on the verge of losing control. "Because I'm trying to do the right thing. To give you a choice. To let you live your life."

I should be scared. I should push him away. But... I found myself saying, "And if I asked you to stay?"

He was quiet for a long moment. The fire in the hearth crackled, and I tried to find a steadying breath. Finally, Bastien said, "My thoughts are consumed by you. Every moment of the day. Right now, I am barely getting by. If we seal this bond and become truly mated, I have no idea how I'll run this château or what I might do to protect you."

Cupping my face with both his hands, Bastien looked at me so tenderly it stole my breath. His thumbs tracing lines over my cheekbones. I could feel everything he was feeling. The deep, endless desire. The care. The admiration. The need to protect me. All of it.

"Had we already been properly mated and I walked in to find Alec's filthy hands on you, he'd be dead. And anyone else who'd looked at you like this would be dead, too. Is that what you want? To unleash me?"

There was a part of me that wanted to unleash him. On me. On everyone. I wanted to see Bastien Allard completely out of control.

But... there wasn't a world where Bastien and I could live as mates. Not while the choker bound my voice. Not while Mama's orders bound my life. Even at the end of my time in Bastien's service, if I hadn't killed him, I'd have to return home. If I didn't, Mama would come looking for me. And when she did, she'd tell Bastien the truth that my choker prevented me from admitting.

Despite that fact, or maybe in spite of it, I laced my hands around the back of his neck and rose up on my toes, letting his hard shaft slide down my belly.

"Claire," he said, his hands trembling as they circled my back. "I need you to tell me to leave."

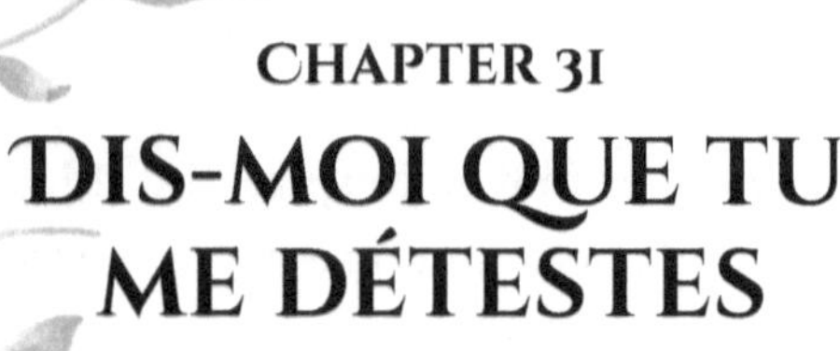

CHAPTER 31
DIS-MOI QUE TU ME DÉTESTES

BASTIEN

I should've left for the council meeting already. Decisions waited. Documents waited. But with Claire's hands locked behind my neck and her breasts pressed to my chest, everything else fell away.

My palms skimmed down her spine, curving over the smooth rise of her backside, a thumb catching on the black lace of her garter belt. I'd already divulged too much tonight, and I had no idea what else I might say or do the longer I stayed. "Tell me to get my hands off you."

Her nails bit into my skin and her back arched, but she said nothing. Only gasped my name. "Bastien."

My cock was heavy with need, straining against her as I steered us slowly across the room toward her bed. Every step pressed her tighter to me, her body molded against mine. I was consumed with the need to please her. To give her exactly what she wanted.

And the closer I got, the less everything else seemed to matter. When the back of her knees hit the bed, I lifted her up and tossed her on the mattress. Her tits bouncing as she landed on the quilt. "Tell me you didn't mean what you said. Tell me the thought of me between your legs disgusts you."

One easy motion and the buttons on my trousers were undone; my aching cock sprang free, the tip already slick with need. Claire propped herself up on her elbows, legs spread, unable to tear her eyes away from my hard length as I gripped it and stroked it up and down. I tried to restrain myself before I did something foolish. "Dammit, Claire! Tell me to stop."

She wetted her lower lip. "No."

I had to bite my lip to keep a groan from slipping out. Working my length up and down, I tried to make the want, the need, go away. If I just finished, then it wouldn't be so hard to be around her.

Claire rose up onto her knees. All her silver lilac hair flowing loose down her shoulders. Cheeks pink with a pretty flush. "Do you want me to lie?"

Why would she put that idea in my head? Just tell me the lie and push me away. But she didn't. No. Instead, her warm hands eased down my chest, tracing scars. Her lips only inches away from mine. Her scent intoxicating as it surrounded me. She set a hand on top of mine, squeezing me. I groaned, my head falling forward against her shoulder.

"Lie to me if that's what it takes," I begged as we both slid our hands up and down my cock. Squeezing at the top. Pausing every time. The pad of her thumb rubbing over my slickness.

With her lips brushing my ear, Claire whispered, "Go, Bastien. Leave."

The sound of her low voice and the gentle sigh of her breath had every one of my nerves screaming her name. I was a dying man, pleading for the mercy of a quick death, but only getting a cup of water. I lifted my head, needing to see her. Needing to see if she wanted to stop, but the look of pure ecstasy on her face undid me. Slowly, I tangled my fingers in her silky hair, grasping the strands and tilting her head back—exposing her throat to me.

"Tell me you hate me," I rasped, gazing into the depths of her eyes. "*Say it.*"

"I hate you."

The admission was breathy. Her chest rising and falling in heaving gasps that told me she didn't hate me or what I was doing. No, not at all. She was enthralled by me. By the attention I was lavishing on her.

By the feel of my cock in her hand.

I leaned forward, pressing my lips against her throat, kissing her deeply. Sucking when she gasped as another bolt of pleasure tore through me. If she kept going, I was going to come all over her pretty stomach and ruin the black lace.

Each kiss had her squirming for me. Trying to get closer, to move my cock closer to her sweet center, but by some miracle, I held her hair fast in my grip, not allowing her to get that close. "Say it like you *mean* it," I said in a commanding voice as my mouth wandered down to her cleavage

"I hate—" The words broke on a shuddering cry of pleasure as I licked one nipple into my mouth. I sucked on her, letting my tongue toy with the hard little peak. Flicking it back and forth in my mouth until she cried out, then giving the other the same attention. Drawing her into my mouth again.

"What was that?" I prompted her. "Be a good girl and tell me what you hate, my little moonflower."

She grabbed my wrist and moved my hand off my cock, taking over with both of hers. I growled like the beast I was. "I hate when you touch me," she said.

I released her hair and leaned forward, guiding her backward to the mattress. Caging her hips with my knees. All the while, she held onto my cock like it might save her life. Working me up and down until I was so close. I grabbed her wrist, stilling her. Not wanting to finish just yet. There was no going back for me, now. Not unless she told me to stop. No matter how bad of an idea this was for everything and everyone around me, she was a cosmic force. Gravity. The sun. The moon. Pulling me in.

My kisses floated down, down, *down*. Past her belly button. Not stopping until I reached the hem of her undergarments.

"I hate the way you feed from me," Claire whispered, without a drop of anger. "Hate the way you drink from my thigh."

"It doesn't sound like you hate it," I said, covering the damp heat of her sex with my mouth, and reveling in the taste of her through the thin material.

She moaned louder. "Please. *Bastien*. Please."

"Convince me, Claire." I ran the flat of my tongue over the lace, dragging it back and forth before carefully sliding the damp fabric aside.

"Hate—" was all she could say before it tapered into a moan. She twisted in the sheets. Her thighs snapping around my neck. I pressed them open again and held them down. Licking her, tasting her. "Oh, Bastien!" she cried.

"Will you let the man you hate make you come?"

Her chest rose and fell. Her hips rocked forward. "Please. Please, Bastien! Don't stop."

I'd been between her legs dozens of times, it had never been to taste *this*. The forbidden sweetness of her.

Mine. Mine. Mine. She was *mine*.

My cock wanted to be where my tongue was, but we weren't there yet. No. Not even close. I wanted her to have every experience she'd been missing out on. Starting with this one. Licking. Sucking. Dragging out her pleasure until she was quivering and whispering my name like she was talking to her moon goddess, begging for a long-held wish.

Gently, I slid a finger inside her tight pussy, just far enough in to tease her. "Give it to me, Claire. Give me all that hate."

Quicker strokes. Gentle, but fast against her clit. Rubbing. Moving my finger inside her heat. Over and over. Back and forth. In and out. Until my hand was covered in her and she finally screamed. I slipped inside her mind just to feel the pleasure—the ecstasy of her release. Like a depraved man, I grabbed my cock and worked my own free, pumping hard, pushing my pleasure to her so she could feel it. Feel how good she made me feel.

"Show me," Claire gasped. "Let me see you."

I sat up, unable to deny her anything, and worked my cock hard with her release on my hand, until I groaned and thick, hot lines shot across her belly. Her breasts. Covering her in my mark. My breath was locked inside my chest. My head swam with sensations and feelings I'd never experienced before. It wasn't just a release, but a coming home.

Claire ran her fingers through my cum, and I imagined her licking them. Her eyes met mine. "I'm ready now."

Ready for me to fuck her. To be her first. Her last. Her only. I teetered on the edge of a decision that couldn't be undone.

"Please, Bastien." She hooked her hands around the back of my legs and pulled me onto her. My length slid through her wetness. Her hips bucked into me, pressing my tip *right there.*

One movement, and it would be done. One little thrust, and she'd be mine. I grabbed her knee, and opened her up wider for me, draping her leg around my hip.

"This is what you want?" I asked, my body trembling with the restraint needed for this moment.

She nodded. "I want to feel you. All of you."

Gently, *foolishly*, I sank a breath closer, barely nudging her open. Her mouth rounded in shock, and tears gathered in her eyes. I bit my lip. She was so tight. Too tight. But that wasn't what was holding me back. If I did this, I'd be more than just her first time. If I did this, I'd be more than mated to her. According to our laws, if I did this, I'd be making Claire my wife.

"D-don't stop," she said. "I can take it." I was so lost in her eyes, lost in the war raging inside me, that I almost didn't hear someone knocking at the door. Claire stilled. "Someone's here."

I blew out a long breath. "It's *Natalia*." She was looking for me. I knew without slipping inside her mind and asking. I was late for my meeting. All it would take was one look at me and she'd know the truth.

My gaze settled on Claire, whose cheeks were bright red, and who was covering her chest with her hands. "You should go."

She was right. I shouldn't have even let it go this far. Kissing her was torture, but I could endure it. Sealing my bond, making her my wife, was selfish. I needed to go. However, I couldn't just leave her like this. Alone and questioning what happened. Thinking I meant to abandon her again after intimacy just to hurt her. She knew of our mate bond now, so it felt imperative that I give her more than just words.

If I was going to be able to maintain any sanity inside this castle, I was going to need to know she was safe. And there was one way to do that. Another knock. More impatient this time. I returned my attention to Claire. Lacing my fingers through hers, I pulled her into a seated position. "I have something for you."

Her eyes connected with mine, and in the soft light of the fire, they looked like liquid fire. I unhooked the chain from around my neck, and carefully turned my bloodstone over, opening the locket and removing the small necklace that had been stored inside. With care, I removed the thin gold chain with a pea-sized red stone attached, then donned my own necklace once again. Taking her hand in mine, I let the chain coil into her open palm.

"What is it?" she asked, staring at the red gem.

"It's a bloodstone."

A bloodstone that was harvested from the mountains surrounding this very château and imbued with both light and dark magick.

She drew in a surprised breath before suspicion creased her brow, touching the lace choker that had nearly taken her life. She was leery of collars, and I understood why.

"This necklace isn't like yours. It's not meant to hurt you. For centuries, vampires have given their mates a bloodstone. A twin cut from mine. If you need me, touch the stone and say my name." She said nothing, only stared at the stone. Her eyes going glassy with tears. "Is something wrong?"

"It's just... no one has ever given me something like this before."

"If you don't want it—"

"No, I do. I do want it."

Hesitantly, I asked, "May I?"

Once again, she nodded.

Pulling back her long hair and gathering it in one hand, I draped the necklace around her delicate neck, fastening the clasp. As soon as I did, I felt the tether between us strengthen. Our bond deepening. The gem sat just above her cleavage, and it brought me unimaginable pleasure to see her wearing it. I wondered if she felt the same thing. If she could feel how this tied us tighter together. "Keep it concealed," I told her. "Under your dress, if possible."

Another, more insistent knock came. I gritted my teeth. "Why do I need to conceal it?" she asked.

There was so much more to explain but now wasn't the

time. I had to speak with Natalia and tend to the council. "I promise I'll answer all your questions. But right now, I need your word that you'll keep it out of sight."

Nodding, she said, "I promise."

I took her face between my hands and placed a slow kiss on her lips. One that stirred more than my desire, but my deep and growing affection for this brave, beautiful creature. When I pulled back, I found it difficult to leave, even though I knew I had to.

"Goodnight, Claire."

"Goodnight, Bastien."

With that, I buttoned up my shirt and fastened my trousers, then made my way to the door, casting one last glance at her before leaving her alone. At least I knew she would be safe. If she needed me, she'd call for me. And if she didn't, well, I'd always know how to find her.

CHAPTER 32
MONTRER
BASTIEN

The gravity of what I'd just done and the decisions I'd made settled over me when I came face-to-face with Natalia. As soon as the door was closed, she rounded on me. "What the hell was going on in there?"

Despite the sound-dampening spells on Claire's room, she knew I was doing *something* I shouldn't have been. My niece knew the law just as well as I did. Vampires aren't allowed to make sexual advances on their sanguine partners.

From her perspective, what I was doing wasn't just foolish. It was illegal. But she didn't know the truth. So, instead of being honest, I brushed past her, making my way across the hall toward the council chamber, irritation collecting at my temples.

Undeterred, Natalia grabbed me by the arm and whirled me around. When she did, her eyes fell to my chest. "Bastien!" she gasped. "Your bloodstone!"

I looked down, realizing that I hadn't put my jacket or cravat back on, and the bloodstone was glowing right through the buttonholes. Pulsing away for all to see. "Leave it alone," I said, slapping her hand away and turning to fetch a new jacket and tie from my room.

Natalia followed at my heels. The door of my private apartment—which was carved of ebony-stained wood and bore the sigil of House Allard—opened at my approach. The magick of the castle allowing only its master passage.

She followed me inside, and the door closed behind us. "Gods, this makes so much sense!" she nearly shouted once we were safely behind the wards. "This explains why you've been acting so... so *weird*."

I glared at her. I'd been called many things over the course of my life, but never had I been accused of being *weird*. I could feel my temper begin to rise, and the part of me that was a predator awakened, just as it had done in Claire's room.

"Uncle, you know what this means," Natalia continued. "The implications alone of taking your mate as a sanguine partner are severe. You could be dethroned! Or worse, *exsanguinated!*"

"Don't you think I know that!" I shot back.

If she could figure it out in a matter of weeks, it was only a matter of time before others did as well. Marius might've forgiven me for tasting Claire's blood before the first bite, but he would have no tolerance for this. He'd demand my return to the capital, or he'd be duty bound by the Blood Treaty to kill me.

My carefully composed life felt like it was unraveling at the seams. I was acting careless and impulsive—wholly unlike myself. But there was nothing I could do to stop the effects of our mate bond. I knew I was risking everything by telling Claire about our mate bond and giving in to my primal urges, but I didn't know how to resist her. It was like asking a vampire not to crave blood. It was... impossible.

Unless, of course, I was willing to summon a god. *Which I wasn't.*

When I saw the tears in Natalia's eyes, I realized she was less angry at me for keeping this from her and more afraid. Still, I couldn't find it in me to ask for her help. "I'm sorry," I told my niece. "Trust that I know what I'm doing."

When she didn't respond, I made my way toward the back of my apartment, to the bedchamber I never used except to store my clothing. "I do trust you," she said, as I grabbed a fresh jacket and shrugged into it. "More than anyone else. But this is different. You're *mated*. To her of all people. By the gods, Bastien—you have new responsibilities. Things you're supposed to do. Like, create an heir that isn't Tyson!"

"My heir wouldn't be ready to lead for decades."

"The longer you wait, the longer it will take to replace Tyson!"

I glared at her. "I don't mean to leave Château Rose and start a family. I'm staying put."

She stood there, mouth agape. As if I needed to be reminded, the weight of those responsibilities followed me wherever I went. For a vampire, being mated wasn't just a responsibility. It was a way of life.

But one thing was for sure: *I would not create an heir with Claire.*

For the longest time, I'd thought I was a mateless vampire. Forgotten by the gods and glad for it. In nearly five hundred years since I'd been turned, all of my brothers had succumbed to their mate bond multiple times over as their mates were reborn again and again.

All but me.

I'd put the idea of a mate and a child so far out of my mind and turned to helping other children. Lost souls who came to my castle needing safety and food. I employed them. Housed them. Tried to make this world a little safer for them by negotiating with covens on our borders.

"You can't stay here! It's against the laws. Mated vampires are impulsive. You've been thinking of nothing but her for weeks."

"Never, *ever* accuse me of putting myself before my people."

"Fine. But—"

"What would you have me do?" I asked, fastening a new cravat. "Return to the capital? Leave Tyson to lead the negotiations between Hector and Chastity in the Lawless Lands?"

"No. Of course not," Natalia replied. Deep down, I knew she was just as unhappy as I was to have an heir named for me. "That's why you should petition to become the High Prince. Then you can force them to listen."

Since the moment I'd seen my niece swing a sword, I'd known she was a warrior, and I needed help leading and ruling here in the north. But she wasn't my heir. And as much love as I had for her, I was only one man amongst twelve brothers.

"I'm sorry, Natalia, but you know I have no desire to take Marius's position. I've done everything I can to get your titles reinstated or to name you my heir, but they are obstinate and refuse."

Fury burned in her eyes. "They think I'm just being difficult. That one day I'll grow up and stop pretending to be a girl. Then, and only then, will I be treated like an equal."

Yes, Natalia might've been born a male, as all vampires are, but she knew she wasn't meant to be called '*lord.*' When she confided in me the truth, I'd been *proud.* Proud of her for insisting to be seen for who she truly was. While our family accepted her new name and dress, they couldn't allow a female to rule. So they stripped her titles, and with them, her rightful claim to lead.

"If my brothers want to shun you for who you are, it's their loss."

"It's not just *their* loss," she said quietly. "It's mine. I'm the one who suffers. And so do our people when they get Tyson instead of *me*."The words scraped from her throat, torn from some pain she rarely spoke of.

"You're right," I said quietly. I blew out a long breath. "Listen, I know you're upset about many things right now. Tyson. Claire. The fact that things are changing. But you are my most trusted advisor, my second-in-command, and I will not abandon you. I need you to trust that I have everything under control."

We stared at each other for a long moment. I needed her to believe that I could do this in order to believe it myself.

"I *do* trust you." She crossed her arms. "It's *her* I don't trust. Even if she is your... you know, *mate*."

Not this again. Her skepticism about Claire. I shook my head as I brushed past her, checking my reflection to ensure no one could see the bloodstone. "Not everyone is an enemy," I reminded her as I straightened my tie.

"But some are," she hissed. "There's something about her and her sister that I don't like."

I'd had my suspicions about Claire at first, but now I understood why she'd bought that necklace. She was scared, and besides, she was my mate. "Claire has given us no reason to mistrust her. You heard the report from the scout. She returned to Nightfall Convent. How much more proof do you want?"

"What about Alec's story? He was attacked by strange men and scratched by a woman who turned into a werewolf—a woman who'd been at the same inn. A woman who matches her sister's description."

"Except for the hair."

"It's close enough!" Natalia snapped.

I leveled a look at her. "Claire is not an enemy. End of story." Natalia's opinion appeared to be unchanged despite my reasoning. Even though I trusted her judgment, she could be just as pig-headed and stubborn as my brothers when she thought she was right. "Can I trust you to keep this information confidential?"

She turned away from me. "You know I will."

"Thank you."

Natalia let out an annoyed breath. "Don't get all sentimental on me. I'm not your mate."

I grinned. "Thank the gods."

We shared a laugh that relieved some of the tension, but I could tell she still had her doubts. To be fair, so did I. I doubted how I was going to earn her trust. And more importantly, how I was going to walk the line between being mated and being the Duke of Roselyn.

The two of us left my apartment and made our way to the council chambers, where my advisors were waiting, looking grim.

"What news?" I asked, taking my seat at the head of the table.

I noticed my nephew, drunk and disheveled, was seated in a chair in the corner, which I found annoying. Yes, as my heir, he needed to be involved, but I was still furious with him for getting Claire drunk. This could have been avoided had he not involved himself.

"A raven has arrived," Laurent announced. He was Grand Advisor—a largely ceremonial role, but he often served as a level-headed voice in a room of hotheads.

"From the Lawless Lands?" I asked, leaning forward. I'd been waiting on a reply from my last letter.

"No, Your Grace. From Devonelle. More attacks have been

made by Witches of the Light. The Kemp family states their defensive spells were breached. One of their own is dead."

An uncomfortable silence followed. It seemed the troubles Shreesa described were following me north, leaving behind a trail of increasingly heinous carnage. I leaned forward in my seat, my fists curling into tight balls.

"Who was killed?" I asked.

Laurent set the letter down. "Temperance, Your Grace. Temperance Kemp."

Grumbles and whispers went around the council room. My worst suspicions confirmed. The matriarch of an incredibly powerful coven was dead. A level-headed woman that had kept her coven's practice within the bounds of the law, even when those inside it, like her daughter, Hera, had advocated for retribution. Her death was a tragedy in more than one way. Perhaps Imogen had been right when she counseled me down at her salt pools. Perhaps the war I so badly wanted to believe the Blood Treaty settled had never really ended.

"Will you be attending her funeral? Hera has requested your presence for the funeral rites."

Taking Claire to the home of Dark Witches during a funeral ritual might be too much. Yet, I was loath to leave her alone. Rubbing a frustrated hand over my face, I sat back in my chair. "Let me think on it."

I contemplated the maps laid out in front of me. I was sworn to protect this land. This fragile peace. That was our mission. That's what the covens had created us for. Staring at the mark labeled *Witches of the Light Territory*, I wondered what to do. They'd attacked my people on my land. Killed one of my own.

Laurent let out a sigh that seemed to capture my own feelings on the matter. "Some will never listen to reason, no matter how much peace you keep, Your Grace."

The room went quiet again, and I didn't need to ask which coven had attacked the Kemps. There was only one still causing problems.

The Prideaux Witches.

"Old debts get inherited. Even ones that date back to The Choosing."

Over the centuries, I'd considered obliterating the entire coven, but there were still those who quietly supported the old ways, and killing one unruly coven could rally others to their cause, pitting more against us.

"I'm sorry, Uncle," Tyson interjected, "but are you saying this grudge goes back to The Choosing?"

The night my brothers and I were selected for this task— six Witches of the Light and six Witches of the Darkness chosen to die a mortal death and be reborn as vampires. Immortal protectors of peace.

My gaze wandered to my nephew, who had risen out of his chair and had wandered over to the stone table. He looked so much like his father in this light, it was shocking. Hair so black it was nearly blue and olive skin, tanned from the southern weather. I wondered how much he'd been taught about our histories or if the entirety of his education was conducted either in the training yard or at fancy dinner parties.

"Yes. That's correct," I replied. "During the run-up to The Choosing, there was a coven who thought they deserved to provide a tribute more than any other. At the time, their matriarch believed her strongest spellcaster, a witch named Dorian, should be chosen as one of the twelve." If I closed my eyes, I could still see Dorian's face. His pale hair and smug expression. "But Dorian was an extremist. Just like the rest of his family. And so he wasn't chosen."

"And five hundred years later and they're still bitter about it?" he asked with a quizzical look on his face. So innocent in his belief that old grudges would ease with time.

"Grudges ripen, like grapes on a vine, becoming sweeter and juicier. After a time, the younger generations have no idea who planted the vine or why they must pick its fruit, but it's become such a large part of their culture that they stop asking questions. They live hate, drink hate, and spread hate."

Grunts of agreement made their way around the room. Tyson settled back into his seat, chin in hand, lost in thought.

Natalia banged her fist on the table. "If you won't say it, then I will. Angelina Prideaux is a relentless buffoon, and to keep the peace you promised to uphold, we must take her out."

Many nodded their agreement.

"She may lack the resources to start a war, but damn if she's not going to try," Gavin, my Master-at-Arms added.

I folded my hands, thinking how best to handle this attack. Marius's blood ran just as hot as Natalia's, and if I told him of this most recent attack, he very well may reach the same conclusion. This kind of war required a gentle hand. The last thing I wanted to do was radicalize the neighboring Witches of the Light.

Natalia leaned in. "And what of Alec's story? What if the Witches of the Light have learned how to transform into werewolves?"

CHAPTER 33
APPARTENIR
CLAIRE

For a long while, I sat in my bed, staring at the door, absently toying with the little red gem, wondering what it meant to be fated to a vampire.

A vampire I was supposed to be spying on. One that I had committed to killing.

One question rose above the chaos churning inside me: Did he actually care about me, or was this all about keeping me quiet? Maybe none of it was real, but simply *instinct*. A little voice in the back of my head reminded me that he'd saved my life—breathing air back into my lungs when I was already dead. I felt his fear. He'd been scared to lose me. If he wanted to keep me quiet, he could've let me die.

I touched my lips, recalling the way he touched me. The way he kissed me. The way he looked at me. The things he said.

"Claire, you are fire."

Sadness and confusion mingled with my anger, and I twisted in the sheets, trying to find a comfortable position despite how luxurious the bed was.

In a moon's turn, he'd done more for me than my family

ever had, showing me kindness when cruelty would've been easier. He wasn't perfect, but I understood why he'd been so conflicted. Only... it didn't change anything. Even if he cared, and this wasn't all just a way to keep me quiet, I still had to help Sera. If I didn't follow Mama's orders—if I never found the location of a single relic besides the one at Shreesa's place—what would happen to her? She'd be forced to go into the homes of Dark Witches, hunting for relics to smash without a map. The weight of that secret pierced me harder than the choker ever had.

I brushed the scratchy black lace at my throat, my stomach turning. If I could only tell him the truth, he could help her. But Mama had ensured I could never break my silence. This *thing* wasn't just a necklace, but a muzzle. There was no way to tell Bastien the truth without it killing me.

So where did that leave me? Caught between wanting to help Sera, needing to continue my espionage in order to stay alive, and the unending pull toward the man at the center of it all.

I waited for him to return, staring at the bedroom door. Waited for an explanation or a revelation that would help me make sense of these warring emotions. I stayed up, thinking about everything, until the sky turned into the bruised purple of dawn. Eventually, I lapsed into a light sleep, peppered with dreams of him that ended the moment the sun rose over the snow-covered mountains, sending delicate pink light into my room. I awoke, tired and weary, but some small part of me was excited to find Bastien sitting beside my bed, reading a book like he'd often done on our voyage to Château Rose.

But he wasn't here.

I fell back against the pillow and stared at the bed canopy. I told myself it didn't matter if I was alone. I was used to it. In fact, I was always alone, even around my family. *A ghost in every sense of the word.*

I clutched the bridge of my nose as the sudden urge to cry came over me. What was the point of questioning my life—*my family*, my identity—if the only thing that would change was that I'd inherit a bigger house to haunt?

An emptiness settled over me, hollowing out the pit of my stomach. *This* was what it meant for *me* to be mated to a vampire. Yes, he had pretty words. And yes, he gave me this necklace. But there was nothing else. I'd be here for him when he needed me, and when he didn't, I'd be alone. And when the year was over, I'd be sent back to my family.

I allowed myself to give in to the tears, sobbing over everything that I'd lost, everything that had changed, and everything that remained *exactly* the same.

I missed Sera. I missed knowing who I was.

When my pillow was wet and my throat was sore, I knew I needed to get out of bed and do something to take my mind off the sadness. I couldn't collapse in on myself. But what? What did I have to do besides sink into the mattress and wait for breakfast?

A wave of sadness hit me again, and I curled into the sheets. I could just stay here and read. There were plenty of books to keep me company. I drew in a deep breath. Or, I could continue to face myself and the beliefs I was raised with. I might not be able to tell Bastien the truth about who I was, but I could learn more about the war Mama was always fighting. I just needed to *get up.*

When I was at home, and a depression settled over me, I leaned on my routine. First, I'd get ready for the day and then tend to the ravens and the garden. I needed to find a schedule here as well. I eyed the large claw foot tub and decided to take a bath.

After soaking in the soapy water until the warm water ran cold, I lotioned my skin, then found a brush inside the ornate vanity beside the tub and combed out my long silver lilac hair. While I did, an attendant cleaned up the bath, then left a hot curling rod on a tray beside my vanity. I took it as a sign she thought I should do something more with my hair than leave it an unbound mess. But, I'd never done anything more with my hair then put it in a simply braid.

I looked at myself in the vanity mirror, and *by Diana*, I looked like hell. My eyes shadowed with dark circles and rimmed red from tears. My gaze shifted away from my face, not wanting to stare at every imperfection, and I found myself drawn again to the little red bloodstone Bastien had given me. The one that marked me as his mate.

I brushed my thumb over it, remembering that all I'd need to do was say his name, and he'd come back to me. One whisper, and I wouldn't be alone. He could stave off these thoughts with his hands and his mouth and his teeth. But, he was the Duke of Roselyn, and he had other, more important things to tend to than me. Meetings to take and people to glare at.

But did I really care if I bothered him? He called on me whenever he liked. Barging into my room and ordering everyone to leave. Staring at my body like he wanted nothing more than to devour me. Kissing me. Touching me. Unraveling me like a spool of thread. Making me feel desired and feminine. Begging me to make him leave because he wasn't strong enough to do it himself.

My thoughts returned to last night. To the way he'd almost made love to me. The prickle of desire was back, throbbing between my thighs. My body longing for him to take this emotional pain away and make me feel desired. My lips parted. My breath becoming heavier.

All I needed to do was say his name, and he could make me forget everything else with one touch.

Thoughts of his smooth tongue gliding over my heated skin and his thick length stirred my need. Opening my thighs, my fingers drifted down my abdomen until I found that same sensitive place he kissed. The place he'd encouraged me to touch the night I found him alone in the tent. I recalled that encounter now. How seeing him like that had awoken something dark and needy inside me.

"Claire, have you ever touched yourself?"

I rocked into my own touch, moving back and forth, circling, just as he'd showed me, until heat crested inside me. I dared to sink one finger inside my heat, gasping when I did, then moaning as I dragged it in and out.

It felt so good. But I didn't stop. I knew I could feel more than this. My nipples peaked, tightening into hard points as heat continued to course through me. If a finger felt this good, I could only imagine how good *he* would feel. The hard length of him stroking inside me. Just the press of him against me last night had been world-shattering.

I dared to try a second finger, and found there was pain, but also pleasure hidden behind it. Just like his bite. I thought of him now, of his cold breath against my neck. His hands tangling in my hair. I tipped my head back and spreading my legs wider. Seeking out the release I so desperately wanted, teasing myself until it was nearly unbearable.

"Bastien," I breathed, panting as I imagined him thrusting into me.

He gripped my hair. His eyes tortured. *"Claire, I'm going to come so deep inside you."*

His words pushed me over the edge, as I imagined him doing just that, spilling his hot release inside me. My body quaked as I came, throbbing out my own release. I reveled in the feeling. In the way nothing else mattered. When it was over, I squeezed my thighs together, feeling the aftershocks. I couldn't believe I'd just done that.

Someone knocked, and I startled, quickly adjusting the folds of my robe and wiping my hand on a towel, silently cursing every interruption. "Who is it?" I asked, trying to even out my breathing.

"It's Tansy!"

I expelled a tight breath.

"I've got breakfast!" she added in her musical, teasing voice.

At the mention of food, my stomach growled. "Come in!" I shouted over my shoulder, then went back to brushing my hair.

I watched Tansy in the mirror as she danced inside the room and kicked the door closed with a slippered foot, all while balancing a tray covered in domed silver dishes.

It was still so strange to me to see a Witch of the Light in this dark Château. "I hope you had fun night last night," Tansy said, offering me a bright, cheeky grin that made me ache for my sister.

"I did. Thank you," I answered.

It wasn't the whole truth, but it wasn't a complete lie either. I noticed she was sidestepping the fact that Bastien had ended the party by throwing everyone out in a fit of rage. She set the tray down on a small dining table and made her way over to where I sat. "Good—they left the iron," she said with a wink.

"This was your doing?" I asked.

"Of course," she replied, taking the brush from my hand and running it through my thick strands. I watched with a shocked expression as she smoothed my hair, then reached for the small curling iron on the tray.

I snacked on the fruit she'd brought while Tansy took a narrow section at my temple, wrapped the tip in cloth, wound the hair around the heated rod, and clamped the tongs shut. A faint smell of singed steam rose where the warm metal met the damp hair. I flinched at the heat but held still as she twisted the section into a ringlet, coiled it into her palm, and pinned it flat against my scalp with a silver hairpin. She repeated the motion, over and over.

"You have to tell me what you use to make your hair this color. It's such a gorgeous shade of lilac."

I laughed awkwardly. The color wasn't pretty. It was revolting. "This is the color I was born with."

"Come on," Tansy said, rolling her eyes, "you can be honest with me. I won't tell."

Shame and embarrassment flushed hot in my cheeks. I'd give anything to have Tansy's color. "I *am* being honest."

She simply shook her head, tucking a stray curl behind my ear as she worked. "Claire, I've traveled all over the Unified Territories and I've never seen anyone with this shade."

I bit my lip, forcing myself to look into the mirror once again. Mama had told me my hair color marked me as magickless, but I hadn't realized I might be the only person in the Unified Territories with this color hair. The lone mistake.

"Alright, fine, keep your secrets," she said with another teasing smile, twisting the last curl into place and fastening it with a tiny ribbon so the ringlets would hold. "I have a little secret of my own."

I was grateful that she didn't pursue the topic any further, but her mention of having a secret of her own had another question rising to my lips. Maybe she wasn't a Witch of the Light at all.

"Is your hair dyed?"

She let out a laugh that held little humor. Shaking her head again, she said, "Sadly, no. I'm a full-blooded witch."

"What do you mean *sadly*?" Perhaps the question had been too forward, because Tansy kept her lips pressed together as she smoothed the pinned curls into an elegant crown. The rest of my hair flowed down my back in soft waves. The overall effect was quite pretty. *Despite the color.*

"Let's not ruin our day before it begins with talk of my life." I frowned, wanting answers to the questions burning inside me, but I wasn't willing to push Tansy to tell me things she didn't want to talk about. "I'm taking you on a very special tour of Château Rose."

Tansy was going to give me a tour? I wondered what this was about. The breakfast. The hair. The tour. Why was she being so nice to me? She was a consort, not an attendant. "Did His Grace tell you to do this?" I asked. "Or Lena? Because I have attendants. You don't have to—"

"No," she said, cutting me off. Taking both my hands in hers, she pulled me out of the chair. "I just wanted to get to know you better and show you around." She squeezed my hands and gave me a sincere look. "That's what friends do."

I stared back at her, unsure what that meant. "Friends?"

She nodded. "Yes. Friends."

I'd never had a friend before. I wondered if Tansy would still want to be my friend if she knew the truth about my birth. If she discovered I'd been shunned by the very goddess who'd given her magick, she'd never want to be my friend.

"Come, let's pick out one of the dresses His Grace had made for you." She grinned, adding, "I saw them get brought up before you arrived and there were enough to fill a whole closet."

I let Tansy lead me to a door I hadn't noticed before, and as

I did, a warm feeling I wasn't wholly accustomed to spread through my chest, and the ache of loneliness eased.

If only just a little.

CHAPTER 34
EXPLORER
CLAIRE

Arm in arm, Tansy led me around Château Rose, showing me the grander parts of the castle while explaining what she knew about each room and introducing me to members of the household staff. I soaked in every detail, trying to learn all I could about this place.

"Do you like living here?" I asked her.

"The weather is shit, but you get used to it."

"But do you like it? Are you happy?"

"Truthfully?" She gave me an affectionate look. "As happy as I've ever been. Mostly because of the people. His Grace demands acceptance and respect of all who come here. They're values I've come to cherish."

Acceptance and respect.

I swallowed hard. Acceptance wasn't a value I was raised with. In fact, I'd been taught the opposite. "You know," she said, setting her hand on mine, "I think it must be one of the reasons why His Grace likes you so much."

"Oh, I don't know that he *likes* me—"

"He is very protective of you. I think it's because you're not just here for the money. You're running from something too. Aren't you?"

I stilled, my breath catching in my throat; the lies I was trained to recite about the convent refused to come. Instead, the night Mama sealed my life to the choker and my mission came screaming back. She'd packed me and Sera into a coach and sent us off to the capital like I was nothing more than a lamb to be sacrificed. It was only by chance that I was still alive. Chance... and my mate bond with Bastien.

"I'm sorry," Tansy said. "I didn't mean to assume."

I shook my head. "No, don't be sorry."

What I couldn't say was that I couldn't run away. I tried to put on a reassuring smile as we continued the tour, but the knot in my throat refused to loosen. I needed to know the truth.

Tansy squeezed my hand. "I think it's time for my little surprise."

I eyed her suspiciously. "I don't really like surprises," I admitted, not quite sure what she had planned.

"Well, if it will put your mind at ease, I'm taking you to the ballroom so we can dance like real ladies."

I stopped walking, my eyes widening. "Oh, I don't think that's a very good idea. I don't know how to dance."

"Neither do I!" she said, tugging on my arm to restart my feet. "But after a few sips of wine, it doesn't matter what you know and don't know. Besides, Devlinn and Alec are waiting for us, and I told them to bring lunch."

I let her lead me to the ballroom even though nerves twisted inside my stomach. Wine. Dancing. A huge room all to ourselves. Alec. The combination would surely draw Bastien, who seemed unable to spend time with me unless it was to intervene on behalf of my virtue. Well, if he showed up just to lecture me, I resolved to ignore him or send him away when he inevitably appeared.

He could accept and respect that.

After what felt like a mile of walking, we arrived at a set of massive double doors stained black and inlaid with gold roses.

"Welcome to the ballroom," Tansy said, throwing open the doors and revealing an awe-inspiring expanse of a room.

The walls were black. The floors were maple. The chandeliers were crystal. The windows shaped like arches that stretched all the way to the ceiling. A smile pressed itself onto my lips as I marveled at it all. I didn't know how to dance, but this room made me feel like anything was possible.

I spied Alec and Devlinn standing beside a small table in the corner of the room, laden with candles and desserts. Neither of them wore shirts beneath their gold-and-white–trimmed jackets, exposing well-honed musculature. I accepted the wine glass Alec offered me, and we all rang the crystal together in a toast, silently sipping the smooth vintage.

One glass. I could have one glass and keep my head.

Once I drank my fill, and I was feeling less self-conscious, I let Alec lead me out to the dance floor while Devlinn put on a record that began playing a slow waltz. I laughed harder than I had in years as he tried to teach me the steps. However, I mostly stepped on his feet

"You're too stiff!" Tansy shouted, prancing over to me and taking my hips in her hands, working them back and forth as I giggled.

"There's no such thing as being *too* stiff," Devlinn remarked, which caused everyone to explode with laughter.

I quit dance lessons not long after, drawn to the table by my growling stomach. I knew they had been trained in the art of lovemaking, but I enjoyed just spending time with them. Even Devlinn. I might not know about his wicked tongue, but he was funny.

I knew my consorts were paid handsomely to spend time with me. For them, this was employment. But all the same, as I sat with this impossible little quartet, I wondered why there was fighting between Light and Dark. If we could all get along, enjoying ourselves, sipping chilled herbal tea with lemon and honey and snack-sized sandwiches, why couldn't everyone else?

What made us special?

"What brought you all here?" I asked, taking another sip of tea to help dilute the glass of wine.

The energy around the table shifted as I watched their expressions change, and a pit of guilt opened in my stomach. Devlinn and Tansy glanced at each other while Alec focused on his glass.

"You've already heard my story," he said. "I tried to help a girl who was being attacked by strangers, only to earn this scratch when she turned into a wolf." He took a slow drink. "I'd still be working at the inn if the Duke's scout hadn't found me and insisted I accompany him back to Roselyn."

The Duke's scout? I hadn't heard that part of the tale. "What do you mean, *his scout*?"

He shrugged. "I think he must've been following someone who was staying at the Veraleese Inn, but he found my story worth bringing to His Grace. So we left Nightfall and now I'm here."

I bit my lip, wondering if the person the scout had been following was Sera. I wouldn't put it past Natalia to give the order. Or Bastien for that matter. Either way, his story raised more questions.

"You said she was a Witch of the Light. The girl who scratched you," Tansy said.

Alec nodded. "That's right. White hair and all. I saw her transform into a wolf right in front of me. It looked painful, the way the claws shot out of her hands, and when I asked if she needed any help, she scratched me and ran."

Tansy shook her head. "My mother prayed all the time for such gifts. I wonder if it was a girl from my coven."

My breath was caged in my throat. I wanted to ask her for more details, but I found I couldn't speak. Had he really seen a werewolf?

"It sounds like it's only getting worse out there. I'm glad we left when we did," Devlinn said.

Silence passed between us. I couldn't stop myself from leaning in and asking, "What do you mean?"

Devlinn rumpled his red hair, then reclined back in his seat, taking Tansy's hand and setting it on his thigh, their fingers twisted together.

"All I'll say is that *magick* ruined our lives." My brows cinched in confusion. Magick was a *gift*. "Neither of us charge our powers anymore. At this point, we're as magickal as you and him."

My mouth fell open. Witches, regardless of *where* they drew their power, had to charge their magick. Witches of the Light performed sacred rituals when the moon was full. Witches of the Darkness had their own rituals with demonic relics.

But... I couldn't imagine why they'd choose to be... *normal*. I'd give anything to have their power. I waited for him to say more, but that seemed all he was willing to offer.

"I heard a rumor that His Grace keeps a mermaid locked below the castle," Alec said abruptly. With a charming grin, he added, "Is that true?"

Tansy snorted out a laugh. "Oh yes. She tends to the dragon, who heats the hot springs with his fiery breath."

Laughs went around the table, the mood lifting, but I couldn't work free the knot of tension I was still carrying.

"There's probably not a mermaid or a dragon," Alec admitted, "but what about the greenhouses? Are those magick? I mean, how can they grow things in the winter?"

"It's not magick. It's *science*," Devlinn answered. "The sun warms the glass, and the heat gets trapped inside."

"Be nice, my love. Science is magick by another name," Tansy said, reciting one of Mama's favorite phrases.

"My mother says the same thing," I admitted. My stomach dropped at the slip. "*Said* the same thing. Before she died. May the goddess bless her soul."

Tansy's eyes met mine, I could see the curiosity sparkling. "Where did you say you were from?"

Swallowing hard, I realized I'd offered too much. I was just as foolish as Mama said. Her voice echoed inside my head, scolding me for being so stupid.

"These people aren't your friends. One is a Dark Witch. The other is a traitor. And that one is an imbecile who thinks he can smile his way through the world. You're supposed to be spying."

The hate I'd grown up on was like venom in my veins. I fell back on the lie I was supposed to tell them. "Nightfall Convent."

She gave me a sympathetic smile. "Looks like we both escaped Diana."

I nodded, knowing I *hadn't* escaped Diana. Not by a long shot. My hand floated to the lace choker around my neck, reminding myself of the spell I was bound to.

"Us misfits should stick together," Tansy said, rising from her chair and sauntering around the table toward me. Her hand grazing Devlinn's shoulder as she passed by. "We should celebrate our liberation."

"Here, here!" Devlinn cheered, raising his glass.

She came to stand behind me, her hands finding the slope of my shoulders, her fingertips trailing up my neck to cradle my face. "We brought pillows. And blankets," she said. "Enough to make a cozy little pile on the floor." Her voice was a coo in my ear. "Can we please you? I promise we'll be gentle."

Nerves and uncertainty curled in my stomach as my gaze trailed the table. There were three of them. Three very skilled pillow whisperers. I didn't doubt their skill. But the truth was simple: I didn't desire them in the deep, needy way I craved *Bastien.*

"I am grateful to you all, truly I am, but I only want your friendship. Nothing more."

I stared at the ballroom doors, wishing I could see Bastien. To—what? Ask him questions about the wolf? My sister? Kiss him? I didn't know. My head was pounding with the evil words I was raised on and this new, quieter, darker part of me that didn't care if I was a ruin so long as I was his.

In that inner war, I heard whispering in my ear. *Murmuring* I couldn't quite understand but that I knew no one else could hear. Little words spoken just for me.

"If you'll excuse me, I need to use the restroom," I told Tansy. I didn't know where I was going, but I knew I would find him if I went looking.

"Nearest one is back through the doors and to the right. Do you want me to come with you?"

"No, thank you."

As I left the table and began walking to the door, I felt like I was underwater once again. It was as if our connection had reopened, and he was whispering to me inside my head.

"Claire. Claire."

Beckoning me toward the door. When I lifted my hand to the handle, I heard his ragged breath like he was standing directly behind me. I wanted to see him. Despite *everything*.

The door cracked open before I could touch the handle, and when I pushed it open an inch, I didn't find the hallway behind. No. What I found had me gasping and scurrying through the opening as fast as I could.

CHAPTER 35
FIER

CLAIRE

The castle had transported me to... *a greenhouse.*

Bright sunlight, blooming flowers, and fragrant herbs enveloped me in a kind of happiness I hadn't experienced since working in the garden back home. But it wasn't a stalk of rosemary that had drawn me through the ballroom door so quickly.

It was him.

Shirtless.

Working only in a pair of dark trousers and tall boots. His blond hair had been gathered at the nape of his neck, and messy strands fell around his face as he worked.

Bastien was a painfully beautiful creature, that much was true, but there was something different about him out here among the plants. He seemed more alive. More free. He stabbed the earth with a spade, muscles flexing, and I accidentally let the door slam shut behind me. Our eyes locked. My breath stilled. I had so much I wanted to say, but I found I couldn't speak. Not with him looking at me like a rare gem he'd found while digging in the soil.

"I thought you were with your consorts," he said, breaking the silence.

So, he'd known exactly where I was and who I was with, yet hadn't barged in on us. I wasn't sure if this knowledge made me more or less angry with him. I was stuck between wanting to rage at him for leaving me alone last night after telling me I was his mate, and wanting to seem unaffected by his absence.

"I was," I replied, clasping my hands together and glancing around the greenhouse.

I could feel the warmth of his attention even when my back was turned. It made me hot beneath my dress, and sweat prickled on my skin. I tried to focus on the plants in order to keep my composure. The greenhouse shelves filled with potted herbs and flowers, which lined the glass walls. Small, well-manicured trees bearing citrus fruits grew in the corner, the leaves teeming with ripe lemons, limes, and oranges.

Alec was right: despite the frigid temperatures there was no ice on the windows, only a heavy layer of condensation that hid the view from anyone outside. I turned back to the vampire, who had begun adding fresh soil to a garden bed.

"What are you doing?" I asked, still trying to sound casual.

"Presently?" he said. A rare smirk tipped up his lips. "I'm clearing out space in these beds so you can plant what you like."

My mouth hung open for a full second before I had the wherewithal to close it. He was taking the time to do something... *for me.*

If he had the time in his busy schedule to do this, why didn't he return to my bedchamber after everything he'd said and done last night? I pulled a blood orange from the nearest citrus tree, bringing the fruit to my nose and inhaling the deliciously sweet aroma.

"I could tend to these plants," I said. I dug my nail into the peel of the fruit, and cherry red juice welled up. "You don't need to go to the trouble of clearing space for me."

"The best part of gardening is watching the seeds sprout from beneath the dirt." His voice was tender and low, and it caused all the fine hairs on the back of my neck to rise. "That's what you told me."

My attention shifted back to him. I hadn't expected him to remember such a fleeting comment. He cleaned his hands, then stalked toward me, eyes trained on mine. "This greenhouse is yours to do whatever you like with."

"The *whole* greenhouse?"

He nodded. "Unless you prefer another."

It was an absolutely massive space. Narrower than the ballroom, but perhaps just as long.

"No. This is perfect," I said breathily, meeting his gaze.

He plucked the fruit from my hand, then carefully peeled it with a dagger and handed me a slice. Juice ran down my fingers as I lifted it to my mouth. "Where will these plants go?" I asked, slipping the slice between my lips and savoring the deliciously tart flavor.

He watched me as I ate, his attention on my lips. I swallowed, feeling the weight of his gaze. "I'm sending them to Roselyn."

He cut another slice from the orange; red juice dripped down his hand. Sudden desire rose in my core. I knew what else he could do with his hands. "We've finished constructing a new greenhouse for the public that could use more plants."

He lifted the slice of orange to my lips. Instinctively, I opened my mouth. Slowly, he fed it to me. My lips closed around the tip of his finger before he drew it away. I moaned, savoring the taste as it slid over my tongue.

His lips parted as he watched me.

I was drawn to him in a way I couldn't explain, but I felt in the deepest recesses of my soul. "That is very thoughtful of you."

"Caring for my people is my responsibility."

Just like Seraphina was mine to care for. To protect. Alec's story had unsettled me. I was worried about my little sister, and I couldn't shake the feeling that something was very wrong.

"You're upset," Bastien said.

I met his gaze, not wanting to look affected, but I was. "Why didn't you come to see me?" He tilted his head, waiting for more. I closed my eyes hard, trying to force the words out. "Last night. You left a lot unsaid. You told me you'd be back to answer my questions, and I *stupidly* expected you to return. But you didn't."

"Do *not* call yourself stupid," he said flatly. Then, softening, "It was not stupid to expect me to return. I said I'd answer your questions, and I didn't."

Bastien expelled a long breath, and as he did, he undid the ties on my fur stole, carefully peeling it off and revealing the bloodstone. He took the small gem between his fingers, regarding it for a moment before his eyes found mine.

"I am not a man of many words, and I've lived a solitary life, so I don't often need to explain myself. But I'll try." He squinted, like the next thing he wanted to say was distasteful or painful. "I asked you to keep this bloodstone hidden because it is unlawful to take your mate as your sanguine partner. If anyone realizes who you are to me and what I've done, it would upend our lives. Marius might kill me, or he might force me to move to the capital with you. Either way, the more people know, the less choices we have. Does that make sense?"

I nodded, my head spinning with this information. If I really wanted him dead, all I'd have to do is expose his lies. It was that simple, and, at the same time, that complicated. "That's why you offered to let Marius kill you."

"Yes. Exactly. I thought death might be an easier choice than the truth." He paused, and I realized I wasn't breathing. "I know you don't want to stay with me forever. I've already inflicted enough pain in your life, and I refuse to cause more by forcing you into this mate bond. I'm trying my best to give you space because you deserve to live the life you want. I promise, when your contract is up, I'll ensure you and your sister are well cared for."

The force of his pledge shook something loose inside of me. I couldn't help but wonder how much fate had led me to him. A woman, who was rarely allowed outside the confines of her family home, sent out on a mission to become his sanguine partner, with a magickal choker around her neck, spellbinding her to the task.

Again, I wondered how much Mama had known. Was our mate bond the reason why I was born without magick?

"Claire," he said, my name so sweet on his lips, "you will always be my *everything*."

No, that couldn't be possible. I wasn't anyone's *anything*. I was Claire. *Magickless*. Useless. Good for nothing but dangling in front of a vampire like bait. The shame was back, and this time, it was hot in my throat. My inclination was to disbelieve him, because how could I be his everything, but I could feel the hurt and the anger and the powerful need to protect me at all costs, emanating off him in waves.

And... there was something else there, too. Another emotion. Something I'd never felt before. A strong emotion that made me feel warm and tingly and... safe. I was feeling all these things from him, and we didn't even have our bond open. We were speaking plainly. What did that mean? I wasn't sure what to say or do.

"I wasn't exaggerating when I told you that I'd kill a room full of people in cold blood if I believed they'd hurt you or wronged you."

"Bastien, I don't know what to say."

He touched my cheek. The barest brush of his knuckles. He would do anything for me, anything, *except be with me.*

"Does this adequately answer your questions?"

Tears pressed into my eyes. There was so much I wanted to say, but I was unable to speak through the knot in my throat. I nodded, holding his hand to my cheek. The tenderness in his eyes nearly broke me all over again.

"Now that I've answered your questions, there's something else I want to discuss."

I swallowed back the emotion threatening to overwhelm me. "Last night I learned of a disturbing attack—one that had been plaguing me for half a day. To be honest, it was one of the reasons I didn't come back to you. I'd been trying to figure out how to handle the situation."

This time, I cupped his cheek, holding him. "Tell me what happened."

He grabbed my wrist and turned his face into my palm, kissing it. A thrill raced up my arm at the feel of his lips. "I know you don't care for Dark Witches, but a coven under my protection, the Kemps of Devonelle, were attacked. Their matriarch is dead."

The Kemps were the worst of the worst, as far as Mama was concerned. I'd eavesdropped on enough meetings to know killing Temperance Kemp was a high priority. Once, I would've celebrated this news, but now, all I could feel was a strange sense of loss. "Who was responsible for the attack?" I asked. "Do you know?"

"I know you grew up at Nightfall, so I'm sure you've heard of this coven. The Prideaux."

My head spun, and pressure sat in my chest. Mama had come this far north and attacked the Kemps? Maybe the strange feeling of dread I'd had about Sera had nothing to do with werewolves, and had everything to do with this attack. What if she was hurt? What if...

"I know this is shocking news. Especially when you grew up revering this coven, but... perhaps now you can see that not everything is just light and dark." He paused, then added, "I need to pay my respects at the funeral ritual tonight, but I can't bring you with me. I said I wouldn't force Dark Witches on you again until you were ready, and I meant it."

He was choosing me and my safety over carrying out the responsibilities of his role as the Duke of Roselyn? Disbelief circled my features. It was hard to believe someone would choose me over their responsibilities, especially when that person was a vampire. A creature who I'd been taught was ruthless. But... who were the ruthless ones now? Bastien was right. I was starting to see that the lines separating good and evil were blurring.

I wanted to tell him to go without me. I would be fine alone. But the part of me that was still my mother's daughter and beholden to the spell cast on my choker bade me to give another answer—one that would place me in a position to find the location of another demonic relic.

The girl in me hoped I would see Sera there. Even if just a glimpse from the shadows. A wink from behind the trees. I'd feel better knowing she was safe. "I'll come with you."

"Are you sure? These funeral rituals are dark, and the magick used could be... off-putting."

"Bastien, I know I'm safe with you."

CHAPTER 36
ENSORCELER
CLAIRE

We spent the remainder of the day in the greenhouse, clearing out garden beds. I enjoyed the peace that came with Bastien's quiet nature. I was accustomed to being alone, and so was he—but together, even in silence, I found I wasn't lonely.

From time to time, our eyes would lock, and he'd give me the most beautiful smile. There was something about seeing him among the vibrant blossoms and lush green leaves that made Bastien seem alive.

When we first met, I thought he was nothing but an entitled, smug vampire. Sure, he had a prickly exterior, but he was showing me there was also a softer side to him.

We waited until the last rays of light disappeared over the snowy peaks surrounding Château Rose before I dressed in thick wool and fur for travel and Bastien's shaggy black stallion was brought around. I approached the beast with no small amount of trepidation. Truthfully, I'd never ridden a horse before. Not properly. Horses were expensive, and riding was a warrior's privilege. Granted to the likes of my sister and other true Witches of the Light.

From time to time, when I'd been allowed off my family's land, I'd traveled in the back of a wagon, feeling every bump as we rolled toward the falls or some other important spot for rituals. Not that I was invited to participate. Even though I was no warrior and never would be, things were different now. Tonight, there would be no wagon or coach to pull me along. I was riding with Bastien.

The horse's breath was a visible puff in the frigid night air. Bastien patted his neck, whispered a few words in Sanguisi, and then turned his attention on me. His pale eyes blazed with blue fire, almost like he had just harnessed magick to cast a spell. For a moment, my breath caught in my chest, mesmerized as I was.

The longer I was in Bastien's presence, the more I believed there was something magickal about him. I wondered if it was the same dark magick that he fancied protecting or if he was something else entirely.

"Don't worry," he reassured me, taking my waist and making my breath catch all over again. "I've never had any trouble on Lucien."

His closeness had the same effect that it always did, causing heat to fill every corner of my body, but it didn't stave off the frigid night air that had already begun to seep into my bones. Taking hold of a leather strap, I hoisted myself up. Once my foot was in the stirrup, Bastien lifted me onto the saddle, which was also cold. The horse shifted its weight, and I grabbed its mane for dear life. Worried Lucien was about to throw me off. "Bastien!" I cried.

A moment later, he was sitting behind me, his chest pressing against my back as he tightened his grip on the reins. "He's just excited to run, that's all."

His body enveloped me, protecting me, and it quieted the worst of my fears. But the horse was the least of my worries. I was going to the homestead of Dark Witches who were burying their matriarch. Bastien whispered a word to the horse, and we lurched forward into the night, his hooves striking hard against the frozen ground.

"Don't we need a guard?" I asked as the gates of Château Rose slammed shut behind us, separating us from everyone inside the castle—like Natalia and Tyson, vampires who could stand and fight if necessary.

Wrapping one arm around my middle and pulling me tighter to him, Bastien fitted his lips against my ear and said, "I'm the most terrifying thing in these woods, *chérie*. You have nothing to fear when you're with me."

Dark trees raced by as we rode and I wished I could believe him. I wished he could keep me safe from every scary thing. But no matter how strong or fast or gifted with a sword he was, Bastien couldn't break the vow I made to my mother, nor could he remove the choker around my neck.

He might be my mate, but that didn't mean he was my savior. However, I could still be Sera's. "What about... werewolves?" I asked him as we rode.

A beat of silence. "Alec told you about his attack?"

"Is it true?"

"He seems to think so, and I have no reason to believe he's lying. But... it requires more investigation. I wouldn't let it trouble you."

We were quiet again. The sound of Lucien's hooves and the wind filling in silence. For hours, my mind ran through everything I'd learned about dark magick since leaving Prideaux Hill.

I told myself tonight was a turning point. If I didn't find any issue with these witches, then I knew I'd been lied to. I'd know that the war I'd grown up learning about was very one-sided. If it was... maybe I could somehow get Sera away from Mama and bring her to Château Rose. It was just a fleeting, rebellious thought, but it was there.

We rode so long and hard that my back and legs ached, and I thought I might never feel warm again. But thankfully Lucien slowed to a trot as we approached the wooden gate to a crooked manor nestled in the foothills of the mountains.

A healthy layer of fog stuck to the grass, obscuring the view of the grounds. A powerful charge in the air made the hairs on the back of my neck stand on end. A sweet smell lingered all around us. *Dark magick.* And by the feel of it, much more than resided at Shreesa's.

"It's unnatural," Mama was fond of saying. *"Demonic power isn't meant to be wielded above ground. One day, you'll understand what I mean."*

Fear had me pressing my back more firmly against Bastien's hard chest.

"This coven has a reputation for being a bit standoffish and rather old-fashioned, but I don't want that to make you fear them. They will not hurt you."

My old fears rose up, reminding me of all I'd been told about Dark Witches, but I committed to having an open mind. We stopped before the gate, and two witches dressed in long black robes appeared from the thick fog. One was short and squat, the other as tall and thin as a willow branch. Both of their wands lifted in warning. Red eyes shone from beneath black hoods. The sight was unsettling, and my heart responded, racing faster in my chest, slamming against the bloodstone.

"What business?" croaked the shorter witch.

I tensed as Bastien encouraged Lucien closer.

"I'm Prince Bastien of House Allard, Duke of Roselyn, and I am here by invitation."

The two witches exchanged glances. "And who is she?" the taller of the two inquired, pointing the tip of his wand at me.

I told myself to be brave, but I trembled, struggling to find a steady breath as flashes of Gran's charred flesh and the graveworms in her chest raced through my mind.

Bastien fitted an arm around my belly, holding me to him, and a sense of sureness and safety rushed over me. "This is Miss Claire Donadieu. She is my sanguine partner," he explained in a commanding voice. "She goes where I go and will be shown the respect that accompanies her title." There was a pause. A charged silence. No one moved. "Now lower your wand before I dismount," Bastien growled. The sound of his voice told me he'd transformed. Fangs bared and eyes shadowed.

Could he move faster than a spell? I wasn't sure. Thankfully, I didn't have to find out. With a twist of their wands, the gate flew open, allowing us passage. The shaggy stallion trotted forward, and I told myself not to gawk as we went by, but it was impossible. They looked like demons, with their red eyes and puffs of frozen breath billowing from under their hoods.

Once we were past the gate, I could make out the sound of chanting. I glanced around, wondering if my family was somewhere in the woods. Hiding. Waiting. *Watching*.

CHAPTER 37
LE RITUEL
CLAIRE

We trotted past an estate that nature seemed to be reclaiming. Thick, brambly bushes and twisted trees dusted with snow clawed at the outer walls. Dead vines crawled up the sides. It didn't look like a happy place.

Bastien brought his horse to a halt. In one graceful movement, he dismounted and quickly set about tying Lucien to a tree. I was so cold and stiff that I could barely shift my weight when I tried to swing my leg over Lucien's back, and I let out a groan of pain. Bastien had me by the waist and lifted me out of the saddle like I was a doll. Our eyes locked as he set me on the ground, and a thrill raced through me, just like it always did when he was close enough to kiss.

Brilliant, warm light from the moon settled on his shoulders. Diana's glow made his blond hair look nearly white. There was something breathtaking about seeing him surrounded by it. It was difficult to focus on anything except the way he came alive in the garden and here under the moon.

Almost like he was... no, that was silly. I readjusted the hood of my cloak, settling it over my head.

Bastien offered me his arm, and I wrapped my gloved hand around the crook of his elbow. He shortened his long strides so my stiff muscles could keep up. "Let's get you in front of a fire, then I'll find something warm for you to drink."

We followed a stone path around the house to an old family graveyard that was encircled by a tall wrought-iron fence and *filled* with Dark Witches. Fear raced up my spine and clawed at my chest. I had to keep it together, no matter how afraid I was. I was going to give these witches a chance to prove Mama wrong.

Two floating braziers illuminated a sign just above the gate that read, *Kemp Family Burying Ground*. Another shot of fear had me struggling to draw in a full breath. Ghosts of witches long dead surely lingered, as they lingered in our family plot.

Bastien set a hand atop mine and squeezed. I heard his voice inside my head, offering reassurances that no one would hurt me. But I also felt his emotions: sadness, regret, and nervousness.

I glanced up at him and found he was already staring at me. It took one look to send my heart skittering around in my chest, but it didn't quell my nerves completely. As we passed beneath the gate, I took in the scene. Most of the witches were dressed in long black robes that hid their faces. However, some braved the chill and were dancing naked around a bonfire. Others drank from bubbling cauldrons hanging between marble statues that seemed to watch me. While others sat on the ground, holding hands, chanting around a lifeless body.

Instead of being a solemn affair, as was the case at our funerals, the graveyard was filled with the sweet smell of dark magick and life. *All kinds of life.* There were just as many *creatures* in the graveyard as there were witches. Snakes as thick as my arm. Goats. Chickens. Bats with leathery wings. Owls hooting from atop gravestones. One white raven squawked from atop a statue, and I watched a curvy witch with long red hair arguing with it to come down.

Acceptance and respect. Those were the values of Roselyn. I wanted to try to be more open-minded than I had in the past. I could accept that they were different from me, even if I was afraid.

When the gates slammed shut behind us, Bastien led me across a path of crushed seashells toward the large fire at the center of the graveyard. We stopped at one of the cauldrons along the way and he handed me a cup of steaming hot liquid. "Drink," he said.

I couldn't deny that the warmth of the cup on my hand was very welcome after hours on the back of a horse. But... this was straight from the cauldron of a Dark Witch. She'd probably cooked human bones and flesh inside it before this drink.

I drew in a breath, remembering that I was keeping an open mind. I looked into the cup skeptically. "What is this?"

"It's sweet cider, chamomile tea, and whiskey. It'll warm you."

I forced myself to lift the cup to my lips. The scent was sweet and spicy. I took a sip, allowing the elixir to coat my tongue. The flavors were *delicious.* Notes of cinnamon mixed with the oaky flavor of the whiskey, but didn't overpower the floral chamomile.

We continued up the path, nearing the fire, but were abruptly stopped by a witch in a hooded black cloak who seemed to appear out of nowhere. She lowered her hood, revealing a face that was both terrifying and beautiful at the same time. Her nose was pointed, her cheekbones razor-sharp, her eyes a strange smoke color, and her hair was as red as the flames. "How good of you to join us, Your Grace," she added without a smile, just the slightest curl of her lips.

"You have my condolences, Hera. Your mother was a thoughtful witch and a good leader," Bastien said. "I hope your reign as matriarch of the Kemp Coven will be just as long and harmonious as hers."

She lifted her eyebrows and inclined her head toward a giant black spider that was sitting on her shoulder as if they were sharing a private joke. "Harmonious? Yes, of course, Your Grace. It's what Mother would've wanted."

There was a moment of awkward silence,, but I couldn't take my eyes off the spider. How could I when its eight beady eyes were staring right at me?

When the witch didn't seem to have anything else to say, her mouth flattened into a hard line, then she clapped her hands. Everyone stood straight up, even the woman who had been arguing so vehemently with the raven on top of the statue.

"Now that His Grace has arrived, it's time to begin the ritual."

A magickal charge pulsed through the air, and I glanced at Bastien, who didn't seem surprised by this turn of events as every witch in the graveyard joined those chanting around the body, including a great panther that padded forward and laid its massive head on her chest. Witches of the Light didn't bond familiars. Seeing animals act like this was… strange, but not unwelcome. I could imagine an owl or a cute little kitten would be excellent companions. Hera stood at her mother's feet and lifted her hands into the air. Everyone did the same. Everyone… except Bastien and me.

I watched as witches chanted, swaying back and forth. Young. Old. Cloaked. Naked. The smell of magick became so strong I could feel it inside my lungs. Through our connection, I said to Bastien, *"What's going on?"*

"Witches of the Darkness have a unique relationship with death. Damien, the God of the Underworld, doesn't take a witch's magick when she goes to his lands. Instead, through ritual, the power of the witch who died is passed on to another."

The chanting rose. Dry leaves whipped around the loose circle that had formed around the body. A sense of dread rolled through me. *"You're not just here to pay your respects. Are you?"*

He pressed his lips together, and by the expression on his face, I knew the answer before he said anything at all. *"Magick this powerful requires balance."*

The wind howled. The witches beside me were bumping into me as they swayed back and forth. The tide of magick so strong that it penetrated through our connection. *"What do you mean?"*

Slowly, Bastien's hand fitted around my jaw, cupping my face like he was fond of doing. Holding my gaze as he contemplated me. I could feel how badly he wanted to tell me everything he was thinking, but there was fear.

Fear... he would... *scare me.*

"The moon is a flame fed by night. Her shape is made visible because of the darkness."

I narrowed my eyes, trying to make sense of his words. *"I don't understand."*

"Let me show you."

Animals hissed and clucked and screeched and growled. The chanting was nearly as loud as Bastien's voice inside my head. He drew our foreheads together as the chaos unfolded around us and closed his eyes. Suddenly, an image filled my head, just as it had the other night. I was standing in a circle with a group of men when a silver cup was pushed into my hands. The liquid was red and thick and I was ordered to drink it by an old wizened witch.

There was excitement and pride but also... *apprehension.*

"Prince Bastien!" came the shrill voice from outside the memory. The scene faded away and all that was left was the hundreds of eyes staring at us. "Your Grace, if you will, step forward!" Hera called.

My eyes went wide, my breath refusing to come. "She doesn't mean—"

"Stay right here," he said, stroking my cheek. "I'll be back."

I covered my mouth with a shaking hand as I watched him cut through the mob of witches with tears in my eyes. What was he doing? What was going to happen to him? I might be trying to accept and respect their ways, but a sudden rush of dread filled me, and I knew he trusted these witches *too* much.

The bloodstone nestled against my breastbone throbbed like it wanted to be back with its mate.

In the distance, past the fence line, I saw a pair of glowing yellow eyes that seemed to be staring right at me. I didn't know if it was one of the familiars... *or something else.*

CHAPTER 38
CHANGER
CLAIRE

I swallowed hard, my breath shallow. I needed to know what was waiting out there in the shadows, but the yellow eyes disappeared.

The chanting rose again, a low rope of voices tightening around the fire. The air hummed with the scrape of feet on shell and the wet, hungry answers of beasts. Smoke braided with the scent of herbs and iron and pushed into my face, and every sense dragged my attention to the circle where Bastien stood, a pale silhouette lit from below.

Was it truly his duty, as the Duke of Roselyn, to participate in a funeral ritual? I'd never seen the Duke of Nightfall at my family's estate charging moon crystals. Not that Mama would've invited him. *But still.*

More than a prickle of jealousy raced through me when he clasped hands with Hera. With her long pointed black nails and blood-red lips, she was everything I feared and longed to be. Clearly, there were things about the Duke I didn't know, like who he was before he became a vampire prince of the House Allard.

The vision he showed me made me believe he wasn't born a vampire, like his niece and nephew, but was made into one through a blood-drinking ritual. What was I missing?

"We invoke the powers granted to us by the God of the Underworld!" shouted Hera. The ground trembled beneath my feet. "Send our beloved's magick into the body of the worthiest witch in our presence!" shouted Hera, raising their clasped hands into the air. Her eyes glowed a demonic red. His caught fire like sunlight on a frozen pond.

It was like I was seeing him for the first time. My hands were trembling, but not from the cold. Bastien had been a witch—*a Dark Witch*. Duty had brought him here. Duty to help *his* people. "Hear our plea, great shadow spirit!" shouted Hera. "Give us the strength to fight back against the threat that plagues our people!" She meant... my people. *My family.* "Infuse Temperance's gift inside a warrior who will protect us."

So it was true. There *was* a war. A sick feeling sat in my stomach and angry tears pricked at the corners of my eyes. It seemed Bastien had already chosen his side.

Power swirled around the two of them, popping and hissing, while the cold wind blew the sweet smell of dark magick through the bare trees. I had no weapons. No magick. No coven. No means to defend myself when their warrior appeared. I had nothing except my desire to keep my sister safe from all of this. To prevent her from being just another skeleton in our family graveyard. There was no mistake. These witches and their beasts were coming for her.

A sob lodged itself in my throat. Beautiful, reckless Sera. So full of life and talent. She deserved every good thing in the world. I wished I had been born with magick so I could lead the coven instead of letting all this fall into Seraphina's lap. If only I had power.

The bloodstone around my neck warmed against my skin, throbbing like a second heartbeat. Bastien might preach acceptance, but I couldn't accept *this* was Sera's fate. To fight and die in this war.

Feeling lost, alone, and *so, so stupid*, I backed up a pace, and then another, needing space and time to think. To do something to warn Sera about what was coming. Running away wasn't an option. It was too cold, and Bastien would only catch me. And besides, if I left his service before our contract was up, I'd die. I had to come up with a plan that wouldn't blow up in my face like the others.

My attention snapped to the four objects sitting on flat stones around the circle. A curved horn of a sheep. A piece of snowflake obsidian. A wilted wild rose. And a feather that looked like it once belonged to a goose. Demonic relics were once owned by a demon or imbibed with demonic power. The Dark Witches used them to channel demonic energy to fuel their magick. So many of my family members died trying to destroy these stupid little trinkets.

I glanced up at the moon for guidance. *Please, Diana. Give me the strength to be better. To protect my family. To understand the way forward.*

The chanting of the witches was deafening. Louder. Faster. The ritual was coming to an end, and someone was going to receive new powers. *I could feel it.*

If Diana heard my plea for help, she wasn't answering.

I glanced around the graveyard, looking for some kind of sign pointing me in the right direction, but... there was nothing. *Nothing.* Nothing... except a deep, low growl that came from behind the casting circle. I found those same strange yellow eyes peering at me through the darkness.

Something had me in its sights.

Another tide of dark magick swirled around the circle, but I didn't let it scare me. I was so tired of cowering. So tired of being afraid. So unbelievably sick of watching others and wishing I was different. I was so fed up with being... *me*.

Step into your power. Tansy's words.

You are fire. Bastien's words.

I squeezed my eyes shut, letting them infuse me, strengthening me. If I wanted the world to change to keep Sera safe, then the old version of me, the one who didn't believe these things, had to die. When I opened my eyes again, the beast was still staring me down, waiting.

"Show yourself."

The eyes blinked, and then the creature padded forward. Torchlight illuminated it for what it was—a *massive gray wolf*. Its shaggy fur wet with snow. It's muzzle slick with blood.

Rumors of echoed in my head. Alec's story of the werewolf. I should be scared of the beast, but nothing in me told me to run. A calm settled over me. *A knowing.* The wolf was said to be the Moon Goddess's sacred companion. Her spy. The one who told her secrets when it howled each night.

Maybe the beast Alec saw wasn't a werewolf, but one of *Diana's wolves.* Maybe the woman he saw wasn't a woman at all, but our goddess walking amongst her people?

I locked eyes with the wolf. *Did Diana send you?*

If the wolf could hear my thoughts, it didn't move.

Wind whipped graveyard dust into my eyes, and I had to shield my face, but I didn't let it stop me. I took a tentative step forward, when a brilliant light filled the graveyard, like a star had fallen from the sky. Warmth flooded my veins, and the last thing I remembered was the sound of my name being shouted as I fell headlong against a gravestone, before everything went black.

CHAPTER 39

UNE CHOSE SOMBRE ET CONTRE NATURE

CLAIRE

My head. *Hurt.* My chest. *Burned.* My blood felt like it was boiling in my veins. My skin felt like centipedes were crawling all over me.

What was happening? Why was there so much pain?

I couldn't remember what I'd been doing just before I blacked out. It was like trying to remember a dream just after waking. Every time one detail surfaced, it disappeared.

All I knew was that *Bastien was one of them.* He was helping them fight against Sera. I needed to find the strength to get up and fight back. The thought helped my consciousness return, and I held on to it like the tail of a kite. I followed it as I slowly opened my eyes and found my vision was blurry. I blinked, trying to clear the image, but everything was a blob of red, orange, black, and gray.

Then everyone was shouting at once. Gritting my teeth, I lifted my head, squinting until I could make out the big blurry shapes in front of me.

Wolves.

Not just one, but five. A pack. And by the looks of the tight circle they'd made around me, they were... protecting me.

But why?

One voice penetrated through the cacophony of others. "That was *my* gift! It belongs to me! I'm the worthiest witch in this graveyard! She did something to the spell!"

A growl and the snapping of teeth followed.

My head spun, and my stomach was sick. Sweat trickled down the side of my face. I didn't understand what was going on. I wondered if the throbbing spot on my eyebrow was to blame or if it was something else.

"Call off your beasts, Hera! If you don't, so help me... I'll kill every last one."

I'd recognize that voice even if it were pitch black, and I was on the brink of death. I'd heard it inside my head more times than I could count. It was Bastien. And he was *furious*.

With that one look I knew deep in my core that he might've been one of them, he might've even helped them do this, but no matter what, I was *his*. He would always, *always* stand with me. Something clicked inside me, like a key in a lock, and it opened a new emotion in me. One that fought back against every evil thing I'd ever been told about his kind. One that burned inside me.

The wolves growled, and they tightened around me, bristly tails brushing against my legs and arms.

I could only watch what was transpiring from between their feet.

"They aren't *my* wolves!" the witch screeched. "They're *hers!*"

Hers? As in... mine? Then it all came back to me. The wolf in the graveyard—the one with the yellow eyes. It was *my* beast? And so were the other four? Pride swelled in my chest. My family might not be here to help me, but Diana had sent me a another.

The vampire lunged forward, eyes dark as night and fangs lengthening, but the wolves moved in unison, snapping and biting his limbs.

My heart cried out, *"Don't hurt him!"*

Helplessly, I reached for him, and when I did, heat gathered under my skin, and a pulse of static energy raced through me. My hand burned like someone had set fire to it. I screamed in pain, inspecting it, sure my flesh had turned black. I knew I must've been hit by one of their spells. But there was nothing. *Nothing.* I was unharmed.

Confusion and fear set in, my pulse quickening. I looked to Bastien for explanation, but he was on the ground, flat on his back, and the wolves were reforming their circle around me.

Had I... Had I done that?

"She can't control the power!" someone shouted.

"Only a true born witch can handle the gift of darkness!" exclaimed another. "Temperance's power was unmatched!"

Grunts of agreement followed. My eyes found Bastien's as he clambered to his feet. I'd seen him angry. I'd seen him lose his temper. But this was something *different.* This was a man unhinged.

Hera's voice rose above the madness. "Kill the wolves! *And bring me the girl!*"

Bastien opened the connection between us, speaking to me as only he could. *"Run for the woods behind the house and make for the caves. I'll be right behind you."*

I was in no condition to run. Not with the gash on my head. I could barely find the energy to stand. On top of that, I was scared. Scared of what happened in the graveyard. Of who that power went to. They couldn't mean... *me.*

Flexing my fingers, I cast my gaze down to my hand.

"*Bastien,*" I said, my voice small, "*what is happening to me? Why do they want me?*"

I felt the fear and regret stirring inside him even though his face remained impassive. "*Right now, all I need you to do is run.*"

The truth settled in my gut. I didn't need him to tell me what happened. I could feel it. He was just as nervous and afraid as I was. This was why I felt like my blood was boiling. Or like something had taken residence in my chest and refused to leave. With shaking fingers, I pulled a few strands of hair free, revealing a burnished shade of copper.

No. No. This couldn't be happening. It couldn't. I couldn't be...

I cast my gaze around the graveyard at all the witches shouting for my blood. Maybe I should let them kill me. Because I could never go home. Never. I'd become the thing my family despised. The thing my sister despised.

A Dark Witch.

How? *Why?* I was born from the light. This shouldn't be possible.

"*Claire, we will figure this out,*" Bastien reassured me. "*But right now, I need you to climb on the biggest wolf's back and go. I'll take care of the witches so you can escape.*"

Concern knitted my brows together, making my gash sting. He couldn't possibly fight them all. I knew he was a battle-tested vampire prince with the scars that prove his skill, but even in his monstrous state, there were too many of them.

If I was his to protect, then he was mine.

"Stop!" another voice shouted as a girl who couldn't be more than twenty flung herself in front of us. "The wolves are sacred. The penalty for killing a familiar is death! This is Damien's chosen leader. We should be on our knees, thanking her."

It was the witch with the white raven. The bird had hopped

down from the statue and was sitting on her shoulder, and now she was standing between her family and my wolves.

"You simple-minded fool! She's stolen your grandmother's gift, Cora! And you protect her?"

The girl's bird hooted dolefully. "The law is the law, Mother, whether you uphold it or not. We'll have to face the consequences from The God of the Underworld if you kill them. Gran wouldn't have wanted this." She raised her wand. "Those loyal to Temperance, stand with me."

No one moved. *Except Bastien.*

"Listen to sage advice and stand down. You dishonor the memory of Temperance with your actions. She stood for peace. My sanguine partner is not responsible for the result of your spell. Damien, in his wisdom, names her the worthiest in this graveyard. As your liege lord, as the protector of the peace the Blood Treaty demands, I command you to *stand down.*"

The sentence landed and the world tightened. Animals hissed and growled, but they didn't attack. And for a moment, I thought this meant I was safe. That we could leave and Bastien could figure out how to get rid of this magick. Maybe if he drank enough of my blood, it could be removed like alcohol.

Hera sauntered forward, approaching Bastien with her wand drawn. "I don't think we will." Her red eyes skimmed Bastien's shoulder, then landed on me, and that look was a knife's edge. "If you stand between us and our gift, we'll do whatever it takes to retrieve it, *Your Grace.*"

Bastien's jaw tightened, but he didn't flinch. "I came here in peace. I don't want to kill anyone tonight. But if you don't lower your wand, *I will.*"

His vow swallowed the remaining noise, along with every doubt in my heart. He was standing *against* them, *and with me.* For all to see. The moment stretched and stretched until I was hopeful Hera would see reason and stand down. Her lips lifted in a grin, and somewhere deep inside me, I knew she would never, ever stop hunting me for the power she believed lived inside my veins.

I had a choice. Run, like Bastien said, knowing he'd die protecting me. Or, I could stand and fight.

I'd wished for magick every day since I understood I was different. Now I had it. Freshly charged magick burned hot in my veins. If I just gave into the darkness, if I let this demonic power in, I could finally be useful. It might not be the gift I'd wanted, but it was the gift I got.

"Run!" Bastien shouted, dropping into a defensive crouch.

The white wolf raced to my side, but the biggest of the wolves, the gray one, snapped at her. He flattened to the ground, offering me his back.

The graveyard erupted with the sounds of battle. Bolts of fire and flashes of light illuminated the darkness around me. Bastien snarled as he threw one of the cloaked witches into a copper statue, and they landed with a sickening crack. He landed his dagger into the neck of another.

I twisted my fingers into the wolf's shaggy fur and, using all the strength I had, pulled myself onto his back. Something warm trickled down from my cut, but I swallowed my fear.

I couldn't let that stop me now.

Hera wanted to kill me and start her power-grabbing spell all over again. Or maybe she'd eat me whole so she could imbibe her grandmother's magick like a snake eating a chicken egg.

Bastien wanted me to run to the woods to hide from the fighting, just like my family when they left me to haunt Prideaux Hill alone.

I drew in a deep breath and my eyes glowed red. Power coursed through my body like lightning. I wasn't useless anymore. People didn't need to protect me. In fact, they were afraid I didn't know how to control the darkness inside me. Maybe I didn't. But that didn't matter anymore. I didn't need to be ashamed or afraid of the dark thing inside me.

I *was* that dark thing.

Me and my wolves weren't going to leave. No. Not without Bastien. I was going to unleash all my anger on these witches who did this to me. This was their fault. And they were going to pay.

CHAPTER 40
COMBATTRE

CLAIRE

Deciding to stay and fight was the easy part. Living long enough to escape this graveyard was going to be much harder.

I swallowed hard as sweat broke out across my feverish skin. I didn't know how to use my power. Earlier, when I'd pushed Bastien away, it shot out of my hand, but I thought Dark Witches needed a wand to focus their magick.

Through the pain throbbing in my head and my blurry vision, I watched as Bastien continued to battle the murderous witches surrounding him. Opening my hand, I willed the dark thing inside me to crawl out once again.

I wanted to hurt them. I wanted to make them pay.

I chanted those words over and over again. Curling my fingers in anger, I begged the magick to come, but nothing happened. Frustrated and beyond disappointed with myself, I let my weary head fall against the big wolf's neck. Why couldn't I do it again?

The pack tightened around me, each warm body pressing against some part of me—legs, arms, shoulders—adding their strength. The white wolf pushed closer to me, resting her muzzle against my hand. Even though my wolves couldn't speak, one word filled my head. *Fight.*

"You condemn your family with each passing moment, Hera!" Bastien roared.

His cloak was gone, and his shirt was in shreds. His blond hair hung in wild streaks around his face. One of his hands was around a woman's throat. "Stand down, or the Wicked Kemp Witches will be nothing more than an inkblot in the history books. A once powerful and sensibly led coven wiped out over a misunderstanding."

Hera didn't respond, and Bastien seemed to take her silence as a dare. With a sidelong glance in my direction, he lifted his hand to her chin, and I squeezed my eyes shut.

Screams filled the graveyard, along with the unmistakable crunch of bone. Whoever he'd been holding was dead. He'd told me he'd kill for me, and he'd made good on that promise. Maybe not Shreesa and her kitchen witches, but anyone who would threaten me. Even if they had been allies moments ago.

A shrill laugh broke the silence, and it caused the fine hairs on my arms to rise. "From now on, the Kemp Coven disavows your kind as our protectors."

A breath of sweet-smelling wind shook the bare trees, and the gravestones around us seemed to shiver. Words held magick. I'd always known as much. And hers felt like an incantation. I could feel them in my chest, burning and snapping some long-held magick that bound this family to the vampires. Around the graveyard, the others seemed to feel it too. They stopped where they stood, hands raised to chests.

I closed my eyes and reached out to Bastien through our connection, and when I did, I could feel his fear and his betrayal. More than anything... he felt... betrayed. Like whatever great sacrifice he'd made by becoming a vampire had been for naught. Whatever Hera had done was undoable.

"Stop! Please!" a strangled voice said. I opened my eyes and saw the witch with the white raven sitting on her shoulder. She was standing in the space between my wolves and her kin. Her wand held aloft and trained on her family. "This is wrong!" she said, pointing at me. "She was chosen! And His Grace has always been good to us."

I couldn't believe that this witch was standing up for me. And Bastien. *Against her family.*

It seemed unthinkable that she would speak against the coven leader. No one ever spoke against Mama. What she said was law.

"You've always been a stupid girl, Cora!" Hera screamed. "But now I see you're a treacherous one, too!" A spell flew at the girl like a whip. She deflected it, but the force of the casting knocked her off her feet, and she landed on the ground hard and didn't get up. As soon as she was down, the other witches refocused their attention on Bastien. Hundreds of red eyes peering in the dark like a horde of murderous insects.

No. No, please. Leave him alone.

"The girl!" Hera shouted, pointing one of her long finger-nails in my direction. "Get the girl! I'll take care of the vampire."

My wolf growled as the red-eyed witches turned in my direction.

"Over my dead body," Bastien said in an ominous voice.

Then he was running toward me. Shoving witches aside. His face was the only thing I could focus on. The only thing that wasn't blurry. Just him. As he ran, he reopened our connection. This time, instead of screaming at me to run, he showed me a memory. The night in the feeding tent when he touched me for the first time.

When he'd awakened something dark in me that I hadn't known was there.

"There is a fire burning inside you. I can see it behind your eyes, burning hot and bright. I'm sure they saw it, too, and it scared them. You scared them because they knew you were made for more than the life they could give you. So they wanted to stomp that fire out. But what they didn't anticipate when they were trying to douse your flame was that they could never stop you from burning. You are fire."

He'd been able to see the darkness hiding inside me the entire time. Waiting to be unleashed. On him. On them. On everyone. And this time, I didn't hold back because I didn't have experience with battle or a name for the spells I wanted to cast.

I didn't doubt myself.

I let go of everything inside me. All the anger and sadness and feelings of inadequacy that had been festering for years. The pain I'd held at not being blessed with Diana light. None of it mattered. I could fight back with the fire inside me.

The bloodstone around my neck throbbed, wanting to be reunited with its mate, needing to protect him. I reached out my hand like I was waiting to take his, and a great wall of red and orange fire formed around us, bathing the graveyard in a deathly glow. It locked out the witches and encased us in flames, like we were safe inside the eye of a storm. *I'd* done that. *I'd* called the flames. My hands and my chest and my lips warmed from the inside out as I marveled at the magick.

For a stolen moment, Bastien and I smiled at each other. He was a beautiful nightmare of a man. Dangerous and dark. Brutal when necessary. But... there was a softness to him. I saw it in the curve of his lips and the way he was looking at me.

"You are finally starting to believe in your fire," he said over the roar of the blaze around us.

I nodded, tears prickling in my eyes. Too terrified and relieved to speak. There was blood all over him. It dripped from his brow like sweat. I forced myself to look into his eyes, those endlessly pale blue eyes that reminded me of a bright, clear dawn that followed a burning sunrise.

Lowering onto his knees in front of me, Bastien took my trembling face in his hands and tipped my head to the side, gently inspecting the cut on my brow. His own drew together in concern.

"I'll kill every single one of them for doing this to you. I swear it." His thumb swiped across my cheekbone, and my cheek fell into his palm. "I'll never forgive myself for allowing them to hurt you."

The wall of fire popped and hissed. Witches shouted around us. But it all felt far away and scary. And right now, my magick was protecting us. I touched the side of his face. His skin was cool, which felt nice against my hot skin. He was trembling—because of rage or one of the other emotions stirring inside him, I wasn't sure.

"You should've left," he said in his firm, direct way.

"Not without you."

He gave me an exasperated look that melted into something more tender. "Does this mean you're starting to like me?"

My cheeks warmed, and it wasn't because of the fire I'd conjured. "I suppose I've gotten used to your face."

It was a ridiculous thing to say, but I had gotten used to his face. To him. But for the first time, I was starting to understand him. Bastien wasn't just an evil vampire who loved Dark Witches. He was... complicated. No. He was mine. My mate.

"I've grown very fond of your face too," he admitted, then drew our mouths together. The kiss was soft and slow and greedy.

The white wolf whined, which made me chuckle against his lips.

"You might be warming up to me, but she isn't," Bastien said, eyeing the beast warily.

He was probably right, but I didn't say as much. Not now. Not when everything was starting to make sense. It had gotten eerily quiet, and the sound of their frustration outside the circle of fire had stopped. "Do you think they're gone?" I asked.

Bastien pressed his lips into a hard line. "Hera is not going to leave you alone. I need to kill her. And then I am going to get you as far away from here as possible." His thumb stroked against my cheek again. "Don't worry. I have a plan. All we need to do is—"

He froze mid-sentence, and at first, I thought he was being silly. But after a few moments, I realized Bastien wasn't playing around.

"Bastien! Bastien!" I shouted, tapping the side of his face. "Come back to me. Come back!"

My wall of flames parted, revealing Hera. In all her wicked glory. Her wand pointed at his back. He was under a wicked spell. Hera whirled her wand in the air and pulled him backward, closer to her.

"The vampire said I could take you over his dead body. I plan to make good on that."

CHAPTER 41
TENTER

CLAIRE

The words "dead body" tugged at something sealed inside me—a trunk in the attic of my mind. It shuddered, lid lifting just enough for a single, brittle memory to fall into view. A shallow river ran as red as wine, choked with dead bodies. In the distance, a woman screamed while a small child cried. An icy chill racked my bones. There was so much blood. *Everywhere.*

As quickly as the memory came, it left. I wasn't sure if it was mine or the old witch whose power now lived inside me, but I didn't have time to make sense of it. My fire was shrinking, and without Cora or Bastien to help me, there was no one to stop the swarm of witches with wands raised and spells on their lips. They wanted me dead. They wanted to take the only power I'd been deemed worthy to wield. If I was going to survive, I was on my own.

The wolves growled and scratched at the frozen ground, restless for a fight, and determined to remind me that I would never be alone again while they drew breath.

Hera twisted her fingers in Bastien's pale blond hair like a lover might, devilishly grinning at his frozen form. Feral magick flowed through me. I opened my palm and welcomed the heat coursing through my veins. The magick pounded against my flesh, waiting to be unleashed. My body vibrating with the power.

"Let him go!" I shouted. "Or I'll burn this graveyard and *everything in it* to the ground!"

Cackling, Hera said, "Vampires might be hard to kill, but even they aren't above a good beheading." She removed a short dagger from her belt. "And with this little thing, I'll be sawing at his neck for a long time before his pretty head pops off."

She pressed the blade against his skin, and I sucked in a sharp breath as a bead of red welled up. I wanted to hurt her for hurting him. I wanted to hurt them for turning me into this... *thing*.

"You'll surrender yourself to me, *or he dies*." A few witches inched closer, and my wolves snarled. Growling and showing their teeth."You know you don't deserve the gift you've received."

The tiny hairs along my arms stood on end. Her voice carried the same cruel edge as my mother's. The same dismissive tone. Designed to make me feel small and stay small because I wasn't like her. It was a weapon. It had always been a weapon. And in a single sickening instant I felt every childhood lesson sharpen into a blade aimed at my heart.

I tightened my jaw and let something colder than fear settle into me. This was not the night to be small. This was the night to be terrible and whole. I whispered to my pack, "Kill them all," without a shred of remorse.

I wasn't sure what I'd done to bind such powerful beasts to me, but I was glad for them when three attacked, their teeth finding purchase in soft flesh. Witches raised their wands, but the beasts were already inside their fear. Screams rent the night; the sight and smell of blood made me dizzy, but I didn't swoon.

The big gray wolf crouched, and I vaulted onto his back, fingers digging into his mane. He already knew what we needed to do: *get to Bastien.* He cut a path through the chaos, slamming into a witch's ribs and sending her skidding across the grass. He bit another's sleeve clean off from shoulder to elbow.

A witch flung her wand in the air and cast a crimson spear at us. My wolf pivoted. The bolt smashed into his muzzle with a wet crack. He yelped and staggered, but still his jaws found her boot and dragged her down, shaking her like a rag.

A witch slipped past the white wolf at my right, and she shot a spell in my direction. A jet of angry light hurled toward me. I closed my eyes and braced myself for the pain that would surely come, but at the last second, my wolf reared back on his hind legs, knocking me off his back. I landed on the cold ground with a thud, my lungs unable to pull a breath in, just as the bolt struck him in the chest.

"No!" I screamed, clambering to my feet as the wolf crumpled to the ground. He'd taken the spell to protect me, and now he was *dying.*

Tears filled my eyes. His brethren howled into the night air, but when they regrouped around me, there were only two left standing. I hadn't wanted them to die for me. I hadn't wanted anyone to die. I'd come here trying to see things in a different way, to accept and respect, but everything had fallen apart. The war I'd wanted to believe was a lie was here.

And... *Hera still had Bastien.*

Angrily, I reached for my fire, my power, but nothing came. Calling it wasn't like calling to the beasts. It was different. Almost like I was trying to pry open that locked trunk where half-recalled memories lived. I curled my hands into fists, demanding it to answer, feeling the rage, the loss, the need to set things right, but whatever magick I had didn't come.

"Pity," Hera said, eying me. "I thought you'd make the right decision and come quietly, but it looks like I get to be the first witch to kill a vampire. Which is why *I'm* the one who deserved my grandmother's power."

The sharp end of her dagger dug into Bastien's throat, and more blood blossomed.

"No!" I shouted. My throat raw. My head throbbing.

I might've wished for Marius to behead Bastien when we first met, but things had changed. He'd saved my life. He'd killed for me. He'd been kind to me when he didn't have to, and trusted me even though I'd been lying to him the whole time.

I... didn't want him to die. I wanted him to live. I owed him that much for saving my life. The untamed feelings I had for him felt like the closest thing to love I'd ever felt.

I touched the choker around my neck. I'd been a woman marked for death, ready to die in order to protect my family. Was I ready to do the same to save Bastien? Tears rushed to the corners of my eyes because I already knew the answer. If my death would unleash his vengeance on the Dark Witches, then surely that would protect my sister. If I could die to save him, *and her*, then I would. With my eyes locked on his face, I walked forward.

Hera removed the wet dagger from Bastien's neck. "That's it, girl. Do the right thing. You know how this is supposed to end."

I was incensed. I was devastated. But... she was right. I knew how this was supposed to end. I'd *always* known how it was supposed to end. With me as a sacrifice. Hera beckoned me forward with a finger, and I struggled to find a steady breath.

The clouds shifted overhead, and a thick shaft of moonlight illuminated the statue and the patch of snowy grass where she held Bastien, and I knew it was Diana's light shining down on him. "I know I'm not your favored daughter," I whispered to the moon, my eyes never leaving Bastien. "But give me the strength to do what is right."

After I'm gone, release him from the spell and give him the power to seek vengeance in your name. Keep your daughters safe.

The two remaining wolves joined me, padding quietly at my side. My fingers brushed over their soft fur.

"You dare pray to the Moon Goddess with my mother's magick in your veins!" Hera shouted.

My attention stayed on Bastien. Tansy's words rang in my ears. *Acceptance and respect.* He'd been teaching me this lesson all along. I knew how heavy it was to carry around hate so thick it ruled your life. It wasn't her magick that made her evil. It was the way she wielded it.

I might have dark magick inside me, but that didn't mean I couldn't do good things.

Blood trickled down Bastien's neck. His skin was the color of cream, except for the bruises forming under his eyes. His cheeks hollow. It was like the life was draining out of him. I drew in a shuddering breath that did nothing to stop the tears from dampening my lashes.

"If you let him go," I said with as much confidence as I could muster, "you can have me and no one else needs to die."

CHAPTER 42
SACRIFIER
CLAIRE

The wolves didn't take kindly to my hands being bound, but they seemed to understand that I was voluntarily being taken prisoner.

The purple light of dawn was rising in the distance. A cold, clear morning that promised to be my last as my back was pressed against a frigid graveyard statue. Fear of what came next was there, but it was overshadowed by the sickness that had settled over me. Cold sweat dripping down the side of my face. A rush of dizziness. Disorientation.

A dead body lay in a pool of blood. The sight reminded me of that bloody river and the absolute carnage I saw in the memory. While the sight and memory of blood was bad enough, the smell was inescapable. It lingered all around me. Coming from the wound on Bastien's neck, the gash on my brow, and the jaws of the wolves at my side.

I fought through another crashing wave of dizziness to look at his face. Everything about him was still frozen, except for the warm drips that ran down his neck.

My bloodstone tugged me forward, begging me to go to him. To be with him. To hold him one last time. But that wasn't my fate. I was never going to touch him again. A lump formed in my throat when I thought about all the things I'd never get to learn about him or all the questions I'd never get to ask. I didn't have time to grieve the loss of that future. Bastien needed to leave as soon as possible in order to feed. With each passing second, he looked more gaunt. More pale. More unlike himself.

I needed him strong enough to ride to his castle, where he could meet with Natalia, Tyson, and Okeri and avenge what was about to happen here, which meant I needed to end this quickly. Mustering my courage, I forced myself to meet Hera's eyes. "You have me," I told her. "Now release him from the spell."

Silence.

Then, a small laugh that sent a shiver through me. My heart pounded out a furious rhythm that seemed to say, *Live, live, live,* like some cruel joke.

She glanced at the spider on her shoulder, like they were sharing some private joke. "How could a girl as foolish as you be the worthiest witch in this graveyard?" she wondered aloud. Her head canted to one side.

"Doing the right thing isn't foolish. Now let him go! We made a bargain."

Another pause. Another heated silence. All of a sudden, I started to feel *very* foolish because I realized what was happening. Bastien was under a spell. My hands were bound. She had no responsibility to fulfill her promise to me.

My gaze darted to Bastien, and even though the sight of him broke my heart into a million tiny pieces. *I'd failed him.* And now, because I was so foolish, my family would suffer.

Sera—sweet, wild Sera—would suffer. Because I wasn't the witch anyone needed me to be, I was too weak.

The beat of my heart was frantic and adamant, begging me not to give up. *Live. Live. Live.*

I had nothing left to barter with except...

"The High Prince will avenge this treason."

I didn't know Prince Marius very well, but I knew he loved his brother. It was likely the reason he showed him mercy when he'd believed Bastien had broken the law and tasted my blood before a contract was made. However, the witch seemed unconcerned.

"That's the thing you don't understand about these creatures. Once upon a time they were members of great covens. But they've grown soft and lazy. They aren't our immortal guardians. Castles and wine and parties. That's all they care about."

So I was right. They were once witches. Bastien had been a witch. And now more than ever, I believed that he'd spent his immortal life trying not to show favoritism. Because that's the man that he was. And all along the way, he'd been trying to show me that Dark Witches weren't all bad.

Present company excluded.

"I can't speak of the others, but that's not true about Prince Bastien."

Hera patted the side of Bastien's face with the flat side of her blade, leaving a red trail across his cheek. I breathed in. And out. Swallowing down the dizziness.

"This one loves war. Fearless. Deadly. Except, of course, when he's stuck in a full-body bind. But that doesn't make him better than the others. No. It just makes him... *different.*"

And she was right. He was different. But that didn't matter to her.

"You won't be able to cover this up," I told her as desperation started to rise. "And those soft, lazy vampires will come for you and your family."

"Well, if the High Prince comes to call, we'll just say we haven't seen our dear duke in some time."

I smirked. "The others knew we were coming. Bastien's council. They'll tell the truth. You won't get away with this."

She considered me carefully. "Well, perhaps I'll tell the High Prince that Bastien had his throat ripped out by a wolf that only seemed to obey the commands of his new sanguine partner."

She eyed the two giant wolves sitting nearby. "We, as his loyal subjects, took justice into our own hands. As they say, dead vampires tell no tales." She shot a glare at me. Red eyes blazing. "And neither do dead witches."

My hope was cut like the string of a trap. This was it. I was going to die. And it was all in vain. I wasn't going to save anyone.

Hera gestured to someone behind me, and they fisted their hand into my hair. My neck strained as my head was pulled back to open my throat. The lace collar around my neck biting into my flesh. I squeezed my eyes shut against the pain. Clenching my jaw as I waited for what came after her blade.

My gaze circled their faces, ready to argue with whoever thought I wasn't telling the truth when I caught sight of the witch with the white raven—the one who had defended me. She was crouched behind a gravestone, with her bird perched atop her shoulder, and pointing her wand my way.

She lifted a finger to her lips, as if to tell me not to react. I had no idea what she intended to do, but I had to trust her. I had no other choice. Swallowing hard, I watched her twist her wrist and mutter some silent spell. I was hoping Hera would burst into flames or she'd break my binds, but... nothing.

For a moment, I doubted my decision, but as soon as the

thought entered my brain, it was shoved aside by another. A feeling swept over me—as if I were underwater, safe and far away from here. The only thing I wanted to do was swim to him.

Then I heard it. My name. Faintly. Calling to me.

"Claire."

CHAPTER 43
AIMER

BASTIEN

I'd always been a man of few words. They mattered little to me. Instead, I cared about actions. No matter what my mate may have believed about me or my kind in the past, I knew from this moment on that she was mine. Our bond ran deeper than forbidden kisses or carnal desire. We were willing to die for each other.

I intended to spend the rest of my life ensuring that she would never be put in that position again.

She was my new Blood Treaty. Her body my sacred land. Her breath my oath. Every inch of her mine to protect. To worship. Which meant there was only one thing left to do: kill Hera and take Claire away from here. Everything else would have to be figured out after she was safe.

I locked eyes with her and opened our connection. I tried to convey how sorry I was that she was about to witness the ruthlessness inside me as my fangs lengthened. My thirst for blood was almost too much to ignore, but I had to. I had to protect her. To save her.

"Your Grace," called a faint voice. Reluctantly, I tore my gaze away from Claire to find the witch who had come to our aid whispering from behind a gravestone. "I'll bind the ones holding Claire. Then you attack."

I would've offered her my thanks, but I didn't have it in me to thank anyone. I was too thirsty to think of anything else but my vengeance.

With one quick movement, I leapt to my feet and clamped my hands around the back of the nearest witch's throat.

After that, the monster in me took control. Killing one after another. As I moved from body to body, time slowed, or perhaps it sped up. I wasn't sure as the blood coated my chin and stained my clothes.

I wasn't biting to drink, but to kill, and the taste of vengeance was sweet. And before long, the witches whose bodies had once filled the graveyard with music and song now lay in a puddle of their own blood or had run for their lives.

All except the woman who was shoved against the same statue Claire had been bound to. As I stared into Hera's eyes, I trembled with rage. An unhinged monster. I wanted to rip her throat out as I'd done to the others, but this one wouldn't get a quick death.

She was going to burn.

"Go ahead, Bastien, make me a martyr," hissed the witch. "Kill me, and it will start the very war you swore you'd prevent. It goes against the sacred oath you took as part of the Blood Treaty."

I glared back at her, barring my teeth. "It's a good thing you revoked my protection."

My reminder stilled her tongue, and I went back to work tightening her binds. Once she was secured, I began piling sticks at her feet, stealing them from the bundles that had been neatly stacked beside the bubbling cauldrons.

"Kill me, and other covens will rebel!"

Grabbing a nearby lantern, I walked over to the pyre and tossed it on. Watching as the flames caught. Her threats were nothing to me. They quickly turned to screams as the flames rose higher.

My job was done.

"Bastien!" Claire shouted, and the sound of her sweet voice did something to me that I couldn't explain.

I turned to find her running toward me with her arms spread open wide. There was nothing more beautiful in the world. Nothing that I ever wanted more.

She jumped into my arms, and I squeezed her around the waist, holding her against me as I lifted her off the ground. There were no words to describe how good it felt to hold her, to know she was all right, to feel her reassuring heartbeat thud against my chest.

"I was so worried," she whispered. "You're covered in blood."

"I'm fine," I reassured her, rubbing her back in circles as I held her in my arms. "Does the sight of me like this make you ill?"

"The sight of you alive and standing is the only thing I'm focused on right now."

I carefully set her on her feet long enough to take a red handkerchief from inside my pocket and wipe the worst of the blood off my face, then tended to the cut on her head. Dabbing away the sticky red trails.

"Better?" I asked, wrapping my arms around her waist again.

Claire grinned up at me. "A little."

For a brief second, I forgot about everything else except the pull of her warm brown eyes and the way the rising sun made her copper hair shine.

Our reunion was interrupted when Cora appeared beside us, and I managed to tear my attention away from Claire for a moment to thank her. She saved me against her family's wishes. And for that, I was in her debt.

"What will you do now?" Claire asked. "Where will you go?"

Cora shrugged, and I noticed she was holding a demonic relic in her hand. The others were stuffed inside a bag.

"Not sure," she replied, casting a forlorn glance at the burning witch. "All I know is that I can't stay here."

I offered her a place at my court, but she only shook her head. Then she handed the curved sheep horn to Claire.

"This was my Gran's favorite relic. Charge your powers. Learn the ways of our people. Make her proud." Then she snatched up her broom and stalked out of the graveyard without another word, her white raven squawking after her as she mounted the broom and took flight.

"I didn't know dark witches could fly," Claire breathed.

"Most can't. It's a rare gift. Much like the fire you possess."

We watched her silhouette disappear on the horizon in silence. Our breaths mingling in frozen puffs. We were truly alone. Not another soul around. For the first time ever. Standing in the middle of carnage.

Claire bit her lip. "Hera was right. I can't control it."

Something had changed in her. I wasn't sure if it was her new magick, but I could feel the difference.

"You don't know how to control it. Yet. But you will learn."

She nodded, then gathered her red hair at the nape of her neck and tilted her head to the side. "Drink," she whispered. "You need it."

I knew she thought I looked weak. It struck at my insecurities. I'd let myself get hit by a spell, and because of it, she'd nearly died. If it hadn't been for Cora, we'd both be dead. She dropped her hair and took my face between her hands. Holding me even though I was a ruin of a man. A cold-blooded murderer. She looked at me like I was still an honorable prince. "You need to eat."

Her blood wasn't the only thing I wanted. No. Far from it.

I pressed a kiss to the corner of her mouth. Then another to her jaw. Feathering kisses until I reached her earlobe, teasing her with the promise of teeth, but never biting.

"Take what you need," she demanded. "Don't be stubborn."

I couldn't help the smile that curved my lips. "There's only one thing I need from you, my darling."

Slowly, haltingly, I slanted my face to hers and brushed our lips together. As soon as our mouths connected, it was as life giving as drinking from her veins. Her. Just her. It was all I needed.

She was the only thing I craved more than blood.

"Please, Bastien," Claire said, breaking off our kiss. "I need you to live. This can wait until after—"

I swallowed her words with another kiss that was anything but halting. It was demanding. "This can't wait."

Sliding my hands down, I cupped her beneath the thighs and lifted her higher, coaxing her legs around my waist.

"Bastien," she gasped as I sidestepped gravestones and bodies and began walking us toward the now-vacant house. Kicking open the back door, I strode inside the darkened kitchen, kissing Claire's neck as I searched the first floor for a bedroom. Her wolves padded in behind us and curled up beside the door. "What are you doing?" she asked breathily. "Please, you need to eat."

Pausing, I eased her back against the nearest wall and ground my hips between her thighs, letting her feel just how well I was. How very alive I felt. She tried to say my name again, but it turned into a moan when I kissed the soft spot just below her ear. I braced my hand against the wall, rocking into her, but it wasn't enough.

I caught her lips in a kiss that consumed me and somehow made me even hungrier for her. Slowly, I fisted sections of her heavy skirts and dragged them up until my hand could slip between her warm thighs. Like the starved man that I was, I massaged her sex over her undergarments while she moaned in my mouth. I swallowed each little sound like it was the sustenance I needed to survive.

I'd resisted Claire as long as I could. But now, after what we went through together, I didn't want to wait any longer.

"Bastien, please," Claire gasped between kisses. "Please."

I didn't know what she was begging me for. To let me drink from her or for something else. Something deeper. Something that would seal our bond so we could never be torn apart. Something that would twist our souls together.

Tucking my hand inside her undergarments, I found the slick seam of her sex and ran my finger through it, dipping the tip just inside her tight entrance. The sound that escaped her lips was delectable.

"I want to make love to you on the bed of our enemies," I whispered. Letting my breath fan across her skin as I continued to curl my finger inside her, coaxing more little whimpers from her. "I want to bury myself inside you, filling you with all the pleasure you deserve while the woman who dared to hurt you burns outside. That's what I need."

I searched her face for disgust or hesitation but found neither. Still, I asked, "Tell me now if you're not ready or don't want the same thing."

"I do," she rushed to say. Those two words helped to put my reservations at ease. "I want you in the same way. But…"

Claire hesitated, biting her lip in a way that made it difficult to concentrate on anything else.

"But you told me that you were going to send me away when our year was up. That you could never be with me because of the laws." She swallowed hard and cast her gaze down to the floor.

I cursed myself for making her feel this way and for putting anyone or anything in front of her. If she let me, I was going to spend a lifetime making it up to her in a million little ways.

"Claire, look at me. Look at me." When she refused to meet my eyes, I grabbed her chin, forcing her to look into my eyes. She needed to see the truth. She tried to look away again, but I held her in place. "Do you truly believe some law could keep me from you?" She didn't answer. Just stared back at me. I knew I needed to try harder and be more honest, even if words were not my strength. "You're more than just my mate. Claire, I love you with every shred of my soul."

She relaxed and stopped fighting against my grip. Her eyes widened. Cheeks pinked with a fresh flush. She was silent for a long moment. I waited patiently for her to find her voice, and when she did, each word came out haltingly.

"I-I don't really know what love is," she explained with sadness in her eyes. "I've lived so long without it that..." Her words broke my heart. How could she not know love? "Bastien, this feeling between us is what I *think* love should feel like. It's warm and exciting and drives me crazy most of the time, but it's there."

I kissed her once. Hard. Then again, softer. Her mouth opened for me, and I slid my tongue inside, rubbing it against hers just like my fingers were rubbing against her swollen clit.

She loved me, too. In a deeper way than just because we were fated. That knowledge made her next words even more meaningful.

"Bastien, I need you. Now. Please."

I couldn't disobey her. Not anymore. Reluctantly, I pulled my hand from her undergarments, and only after licking her sweetness my fingers, did I open the door to the room beside us. I lifted Claire into my arms and carried her inside, shutting the door behind us.

CHAPTER 44
ROUGIR

BASTIEN

I lowered her down until her back was resting against the mattress and her head was cradled by a pillow. She gazed up at me with so much adoration and trust that the weight of this moment sank deep into me. This might be her first time with a man, but she wasn't a meek girl waiting to be deflowered on her wedding night, unsure of what was going to happen.

She knew.

The pull to seal our mate bond demanded that I take her hard and deep, devouring her until I was completely spent and my cum dripped out of her, slicking her thighs. My instincts were driving me to make an heir, but that couldn't happen. I couldn't burden her with the pain of carrying a vampire child.

Her fear of blood would make it impossible. Especially after the babe was born. No, I had to be careful. I had to prioritize her well-being. She was mine to protect. This was all we could have. Each other. And it was more than I could ever want.

My moonflower. So beautiful. So alive.

Distracted, I traced the sharp edge of her cheekbone with my finger until I reached the curve of her lips. I coaxed them open, parting her lips ever so slightly until they pursed around me. All warm and wet. Sliding it deeper, my finger trailed over her tongue before I pulled it out. Watching her take me, even in this small way, had me thickening for her until I was painfully hard.

"Are you going to make love to me?" Claire asked, looping a finger through my chain and dragging me an inch closer.

Holding my bloodstone in the palm of her hand like she held my heart. I gazed down at her with the same adoration and made a pledge to make this moment one she'd never forget.

"Oh yes. I'm going to make love to you," I said, parting her lips and sliding my finger in and out again. I dropped my voice to a rasp. "And when you're ready, I'm going to fuck you like you were made for me. Because you were, Claire. You were made for me, just like I was made for you."

I pulled my finger out of her mouth and kissed her hard, swallowing whatever she wanted to say, then broke off the kiss just as quickly, leaving her breathless.

"Don't stop," she gasped, reaching for me.

I kissed the top of her knuckles, then said, "Close your eyes."

She did not obey, and her obstinate frown made me grin. She'd always been fearless, but now my little witch had confidence. She was bold and fierce with fire in veins, not just her heart. Gently, I ran my hands down her face, encouraging her to do as I asked. When her eyes fluttered shut, I leaned forward and pressed my lips against the shell of her ear, expelling a breath against her skin, just like I had the night of my Sanguination Ball.

She reacted in kind, arching her back and pushing her

breasts into me. My hand melted around her, holding her against me. I had to bite my own lip to keep from sinking my teeth into her. For so long, I'd been teetering on the edge, holding back the primal desire for her. I wanted her to know the torturous pleasure that accompanied having to wait for what you so desperately wanted.

"I want you to need me so bad you can't hold still. I want you to need me so desperately that you can't focus." One of her hands twined into my hair, twisting the strands. "I want the anticipation of our first time to fill your mind and steal your breath until the only word you can speak is my name. And when you say it, it's a strangled gasp that only I could understand."

My hand slid around her waist until it found hers and guided it down, *down, down,* over the thick wool of her dress until she was cupping the warm spot between her thighs. A cry of pleasure left her lips when I squeezed her hand. "I want you to touch yourself to dull the need so you can make it through another second without my cock inside you." My next breath caressed her skin, and I gripped her harder. "I want you begging for me. Then, and only then, will you know how I've felt. How I have felt since the moment you stormed into my life."

"I'm already there," Claire gasped, squirming under my touch. "I already can't stand it. I'm already begging."

Humming in the back of my throat, I let go of her hand and backed away from the bed, watching the need and want blowing her pupils into dark chasms. Breaking eye contact, I went about removing what was left of my clothing and tossed it on the floor. I could feel her warm gaze tracing the lines of my back, heating skin that had been cold for centuries.

"I thought I told you to close your eyes," I teased, as I made my way over to the washbasin to scrub the smears of blood and sticky sweat from my body. Rivulets of water ran down my stomach and puddled onto the floor until I was someone I recognized in the mirror once again. Not the bloodthirsty monster I'd become.

Claire was propped up on her elbows, watching me with a delicious flush running from her cheeks to her throat. All her copper hair loose around her face and cascading down her shoulders.

"You're not closing your eyes."

"I want to watch you," she said. Chest heaving. Flush spreading. "I want to watch you watching me. I want you to see how tortured I am."

I fisted my hard length as I drank her in. Rubbing it up and down like a depraved man, because I was a depraved man. My need thick and hard and already dripping for her.

She tracked the movement of each stroke as I made my way back to the foot of the bed. "Show me," I demanded, my voice thick with pleasure. "Show me how tortured you are."

Claire pushed herself onto her knees and undid the clasp on her black cloak, letting it slip off her shoulders and fall to the bed. Next came the buttons running down the front of her bodice. With each one, she showed me more and more skin until she could remove her arms from the belled sleeves.

My breath stilled. Time stilled. The whole damn world may have stilled, and it wouldn't have mattered. I longed to touch her. To taste the peaks of her nipples. To draw each one in my mouth, sucking gently while her body writhed beneath me. "Oh, Claire," I managed, as a fresh bead of slickness rolled down my tip. "You torture me."

A wicked grin spread across her face as she reached behind her back and began undoing the buttons of her skirt until it inched down her hips. The petticoat was next. Both bunching around her knees by the time she was done.

Finally, I had a perfect view of the thin undergarments covering her sweet little cunt. With her eyes locked on mine, Claire tugged them down her thighs until the soft v between them was bare for me.

She was everything, all at once.

"I am not worthy of such beauty," I explained, one hand braced against the footboard of the bed to keep me in place. "Of such perfection." I drew in a ragged breath. I was dying to hold her. To lick and taste her. But I stayed put. Knowing it would be worth the wait. "But I will do my best to earn you over and over again."

"For a man of few words, you've given me many."

This woman would be the death of me. I was sure of it. But she wasn't wrong. I couldn't help it. Everything about Claire drew me, whether it was because we were fated or because I'd want her even if we weren't. "Do you want me to stop?"

"No," she said faintly. One hand cupping her breast. Squeezing it. "I like it."

I let out a groan. "Keep playing with yourself. Let me hear how tortured you are. How badly you want this."

Slowly, Claire reclined back on the pillows. I moved her skirt out of the way so I had a better view of her hand snaking between her thighs and parting her slick seam.

She gasped, and so did I as I opened the connection between us. Feeling everything she felt as she explored her body. Finding pleasure in each little circle of her finger. Moaning. Sighing. Trembling. Breathing my name. Unable to stop myself, I climbed onto the mattress, and gently coaxed her legs open.

My fingers glided down her thighs, leaving behind a trail of goosebumps as she continued. I'd be right here so many times, but this time, I wasn't between her legs for a feeding. I was here to devour her. To satisfy her. To make her my wife.

Wrapping my hands around her thighs, I ran my tongue along her sex, and her legs snapped shut around my neck.

"B-Bastien, please," Claire moaned, her fingers twining in my hair.

I knew what she wanted. I knew what she needed to come. I could feel it. Soft, slow strokes of my tongue, teasing her first, before picking up the pace. Then licking, licking, licking. Lapping every drop of her. Her hips circling as she chased her pleasure.

I felt it building inside me. So close. So close. But she needed more. I crawled on top of her, rubbing the heavy weight of my cock over her center, sending bolts of pleasure through every inch of me.

"Claire..." Her name whispered like a prayer almost too precious to be spoken aloud. "Come for me. Come all over me."

"I'm-I'm. *Oh, Bastien!*"

"I know, darling. Let it go."

Gripping my back so hard I was sure she'd drawn blood, Claire screamed my name as she trembled beneath me. She ran her hands up my back, pulling me closer against her. I relished the feel of her skin against mine. All the waiting was over. We were finally, finally giving in to each other.

I trailed my cock down until it pressed against her entrance. She was so wet, and I was so hard. She wrapped her legs around my hips and coaxed me deeper, but I resisted.

Nuzzling my nose against the side of her face, I pressed a kiss against her jaw, then whispered, "I've ached for you. Burned for you. Dreamed of you even though I haven't slept in hundreds of years. I need you. All of you. My love. My *only* love. Are you ready to become my wife?"

CHAPTER 45
JOINDRE
CLAIRE

In the heat of the moment, it took a second for me to process what he'd just said. His hands slid into my hair, holding me so tenderly.

"When a vampire takes his mate, they are married under the laws of the Blood Treaty," Bastien said, kissing me again. "If we do this, you will be more than my mate. You'll be... *my wife.*"

Married?

I'd be the wife of a man who commanded an army and lived in a snow-covered château in the wild mountains that separated the Unified Territories from the Lawless Lands. A man who'd kill for me. A man who'd do anything for me. But I thought he wasn't allowed to do any of this with his sanguine partner. "Isn't this forbidden?"

"Yes. Very," he confirmed, trembling as he hovered over me. His hard length traced lines over me, a barely there movement that was impossible to ignore. "If we do this, it would have to stay a secret. There's too much at stake now. Too much I need to do to make this world safe for you."

He couldn't give up his title, just as I couldn't give up my mission. Both of us committed to other goals, but unable to deny what was right in front of us. His length stroked over me again, and I tipped my head back, circling my hips to feel more. He was so hard. So, very hard.

He pressed my hands into the bedsheets and laced our fingers together. "I know it's hard to ignore the pull, the gods know I've been fighting it, but we don't need to do this. You don't need to marry me."

He sat back on his knees, dragging me up with him, relieving me of the feel of him against me and giving me a moment to think. I knew he was right. I shouldn't do this. Not because I didn't want to be with him, but because of the secrets dangling between us. He had no idea he was asking *Claire Prideaux* to be his wife, not an orphan girl.

If he knew that I was sent here by the woman who killed Temperance Kemp, the catalyst of tonight's events, would he still want this? I wanted to believe the answer was yes but I wasn't so sure. "Bastien, there are things you don't know about me. Things I can't tell you."

He pressed his forehead against mine. Our breaths tangling in a jagged embrace. "I don't give a damn. I love you, and I trust you. If you want this, then we'll figure everything else out."

It wasn't perfect. It would never be perfect. Not until Mama's choker was removed and this war was over. I swallowed hard, staring up at him and all his haunting beauty. I should say no, but I didn't want to.

After tonight, after nearly dying for the second time in a month, after watching that blade to his throat, I knew there was no going back for me.

"I'm already yours," I whispered. "I've been yours. Even

when I didn't want to believe it. Even when I fought it. You're the only thing that's ever made sense."

As soon as the words left my mouth, our bloodstones snapped together like two magnets joined by some supernatural force. There were no rings or vows. No priestess of the moon to bind our hands and speak the sacred spells. This was our ceremony, and I was proclaiming that I accepted his protection and love. That I wanted him, and only him. My darkness and his, twisting together forever.

"I am yours," he gritted out. "I will always be yours. Every single piece of me."

I smiled a real smile. And so did he. With my heart fully open to him for the first time, my hand came to rest on the swell of his chest as I gazed into the depths of his eyes. My thumb stroked a thick band of scar tissue that slashed across his muscle. If he was made for war, and I was made for him, what did that say about me? About who I really was?

So many questions, but the pull of desire in my core was undeniable. I wanted to be filled. To be satisfied. To know what it truly meant to be mated to him. Body and soul. To be joined as one.

His hands slid into my hair and tilted my face to deepen our kiss. Our tongues twining together in a seductive dance I'd never tire of. I gasped with pleasure as a sense of surety rocked through me. He lowered me back against the mattress and angled himself so he was pressing against me. *Right there.*

He kissed me once. Twice. Catching my lip and sucking gently. "We'll start slow."

I nodded, my breaths coming quicker as anticipation twisted inside me. His hands shook as he eased himself in, slightly parting me. A gasp caught in my throat as pain and pleasure rocketed through me. He was so thick. So hard. So big.

Bastien held my gaze, both of us breathing heavily, as he slid himself deeper.

Tears burned in my eyes. A strangled cry tore from my throat. More from surprise than pain. He stilled, holding himself just inside me. "Do you want me to stop?"

I bit my lip and shook my head. "No. Keep going."

Inch by inch, he sank into me. Giving me space to breathe as his thick length went deeper. So deep. As far as he could, burying himself inside me until there was no space between us. Then slowly, tortuously, he pulled himself out.

"You're doing so good," he said encouragingly.

I panted. Sweat beaded down my face. *Then he did it again.* Slowly in, letting me feel everything. Lights exploded behind my eyes as I cried out in the most deliciously satisfying pain I'd ever felt. My nails sank into his skin, needing to ground myself. My hips lifted, wanting more friction. Wanting more of him.

He opened our connection, allowing me to feel what he was feeling. The blinding passion, the lust, the pleasure, the need to take me hard and fast tempered by the fear he might hurt me. The endless love.

I felt it all.

Bastien held himself all the way inside me, grinding against that sensitive place. The one that was throbbing with desire. Needing release. It was all so new, yet I couldn't get enough of him.

"Claire, you're so tight around me. So tight. If I'm hurting you—"

"You're not," I choked out. "I want more. More."

"Are you sure?" he asked through his teeth. His desire and need to hold back warring inside him.

"Yes, I'm sure."

With his face buried in my neck, he dragged himself out of me, only to slide back in, harder and faster than before. This time, I screamed his name. Not from pain, but from the unexpectedness of it.

"That's it, darling. This is just the beginning."

My hands wrapped around his neck. My fingers tangling in his hair as I moved my hips to feel him in every way. Our bodies sliding over one another. Sweat turning our skin slick. Bastien held perfectly still, allowing me to explore every sensation. Gasping when I found the place that felt so good. Heat built inside of me, that need to chase something.

A throaty groan escaped his lips. "Look at you, already squirming on my cock. Trying to make yourself come." He slid out slowly once again, lingering, teasing that one spot until my eyes rolled back and my throat ran dry from panting, *'more'* over and over again. He thrust back inside me. Filling me. Taking me. Holding himself all the way in again. "Go ahead," he rasped. "Rub that tight little pussy all over my cock. Use it. Don't hold back. Make yourself come."

Everything inside me was trying to obey his command. To find the sweet, hot release that was building inside me. Gripping his shoulders, I worked myself up and down on him. Breath hitching and moaning his name the closer I got to oblivion. But something was holding me back.

His hands melted around my waist, and he flipped us over so I was sitting on top of him. Breathless and so needy, I stared down at him and saw the hunger in his eyes as they drank in the curves of my body. His bloodstone throbbing with my erratic pulse.

Sitting astride this vampire, covered in scars, I felt so powerful. So wanted. So... loved. And so hungry for more.

His hands cradled my hips. His fingers dug into my backside. "Go on, *chérie*. Fuck your husband."

My husband. *Yes.* I was going to fuck my husband. Pressing my hands into his shoulders, I moved my hips up and down on him, my breath breaking on gasps and moans, until I found that place again, the warm spot that begged for release.

"I love watching you use me," he said. "Keep going. It's all yours. Only yours. Always yours."

I moved faster, watching him as I slid up and down. And oh, Diana, it was coming. My release. I could feel it cresting like a wave. Harder and faster than I'd ever felt before. With him inside me, it was different. Hitting places his tongue and his finger alone couldn't. A torrent of pleasure and deep emotions that I had only dared to dream of.

He gripped my backside and helped me, guiding me up and down until the pleasure reached a peak. Fire burned behind my eyes. The release unlike anything else. I fell forward, clutching the strands of his hair in my fists, shaking and trembling for him. Every part of me touching every part of him.

"Good girl," he purred in my ear when I finally finished. "I nearly came watching you come on my cock."

He smoothed back my hair with his cool hand then let it travel down my back, gliding along the furrow of my spine and over the swell of my backside until he was touching the place where we were joined.

Kissing the side of my cheek, Bastien said, "Look how wet my wife is. She's dripping for me." His fingers ran through my wetness, massaging me, eliciting a whole new kind of pleasure.

He thrust his hips up, making the space between us disappear once again, filling me up until I lost my breath. "I love hearing all the little sounds you make when I'm all the way in."

Another thrust of his hips. Another moan I couldn't hold back. Now that I'd come, I felt everything so much more intensely and the pain was gone. Bastien promised that he wasn't going to make love to me like it was my first time. He promised to fuck me like I was made for him. I wanted him to make good on that vow.

The more I thought about it, a deeper, darker desire swirled inside me. He cupped my breasts, gently squeezing before bringing one to his mouth, toying with my nipple.

"Take me like I was made for you. I'm ready."

Bastien was quiet for a moment. "I don't want to hurt you."

"You won't," I insisted. Yes, there was a sweet ache in the place where we were joined but not pain. "You wouldn't. Just—"

My voice broke off when I felt his teeth against my neck. Scraping down the column of my throat. He moved inside me again. A slow, lazy thrust of his hips made me moan for more. Through our bond, I could feel his thirst. His desire wasn't to just to take me, but to fulfill both of his desires at the same time. To have me in both ways.

"Drink, Your Grace."

His hand went around my waist, and Bastien flipped me over, putting me on my hands and knees, his body hovering behind me.

His hard length glided between my legs. He rubbed his head over my sweetest spot, teasing me with slow strokes before tucking himself back in. I gasped as he filled me. The new angle was different from the first two and made me feel like I was his in a primal way.

"I shouldn't drink from you. Not while I'm inside you. It's—"

"What?" I managed. "Forbidden?"

"Claire," he roared, sliding in and out. In and out. In and out. "I'm already breaking so many laws."

"Exactly."

He gathered his arms around my waist and pulled me up so my back was resting against his chest. His thick length still inside me. One of his hands cupped my breast. The other found my sex, and I arched into him as he played with me.

"I shouldn't," he breathed against my ear. "It's wrong. And I'm already fucking you like no man should fuck his new bride."

"Please, Bastien," I said. "I want it."

He groaned. "You know I can't resist when you beg."

He licked a trail up my throat, then came the pressure of his teeth. Bastien moaned against my skin as his bite deepened. So deep that I lost myself in him. My body limp in his arms as he continued to pump into me, raw and wild. Thrusting in and out. Not slowing down. My pleasure deep and desirous as he rubbed his finger over me in tight little strokes until I was panting out his name.

Sweat rolled between my breasts. Slick heat dripped down my legs.

"I'm going to come!" I screamed.

He didn't stop. He kept drinking and taking me until I was seizing around him, coming hard and fast with his cock inside of me and his teeth on my neck. When I finally finished throbbing, he licked my neck.

"Now, I think my wife is ready to be fucked," Bastien rasped.

He released me so I fell forward onto my hands. His fingers trailed a line from my neck to my backside. Then gripped my hips as he gave one hard thrust.

There were no words for the feeling of *this*. Of him. Unhinged. Mine.

"If you want me to stop, just say so," he gritted out.

I was shaking, so locked on his emotions that I couldn't think of anything but him. He wanted me so badly, it was inconceivable. The need and desire so overwhelming that all I wanted to do was satisfy him. I wanted to give him that release. To take him fully and deeply until his need was dripping out of me.

His hips smacked into my backside with each hard thrust. I gripped the bedsheets, silently whispering prayers. His hands molded to my flesh, squeezing me. It was teetering on the edge of too much, but the ache was what I wanted. The feeling of him pushed out everything else. Burning it all away.

I bit down on my lip to keep from screaming out again. He fell forward, one arm wrapping around me as he kept up his pace, bucking into me like he couldn't stop himself.

"You're too sweet. Too fucking sweet for me. I don't deserve it—don't deserve you—but I'm going to come so hard anyway. Come so hard all over you."

Hearing how desperate he wanted his own release triggered something inside of me. That darkness. The magick. The fire. I spread my legs wider so he could take me deeper. Feeling into each thrust. My skin tingled with heat. My hands burned against the sheets. Lines of smoke rose along with the smell of smoldering fabric.

I was feeling everything. Letting the magick flow. Feeling the burn of my internal flame. Bastien moaned my name before he pulled out of me. He shook as he set his thick length on my backside, working himself hard until warmth coated my back, marking me as his. Holding on to my hip to keep himself upright until he was completely spent.

I felt the pure unadulterated pleasure course through him. Felt the bone-deep satisfaction of the moment and knew that I'd made him feel as good as he'd made me feel. Only then did he let go of me long enough to clean the mess off my back and gently wipe between my legs.

When he was finished, I collapsed onto my stomach, drenched in sweat and with an ache in every muscle. Bastien lay beside me, one of his legs possessively hiked over my bottom. His arm draped around my middle. He kissed my shoulder. My neck. My cheek. Then he just held my gaze, watching me as I took in all the lines of his face, memorizing each one. Burning the picture of him into my mind so that it could never leave.

"I love you," he whispered. "I love you with every shred of my soul."

I ran a finger across his lips, wanting to savor the moment. Allowing the love he felt for me to seep into my heart. Smiling, I pressed a kiss to his lips. "I love you, too."

CHAPTER 46
ÉTREINDRE
CLAIRE

Bastien and I lay just like that—our legs intertwined—for a long time. Him, absently playing with a lock of my hair, and me, staring out the small bedroom window that looked out onto the graveyard. I glanced over at him and caught him watching me so intently it nearly stole my breath.

I didn't need to read minds to guess what he was thinking. My attention drifted to the hair in his hand. *To my red hair.* I had to squeeze my eyes shut against a sudden wave of nausea. Now that the adrenaline had worn off, along with the heady desire, I was left with my messy emotions about my new identity.

He didn't say anything when I looked away. He understood I was conflicted about these new powers. We were married, joined. There should be happiness and celebration. But instead, a heavy feeling of guilt was lodged in my stomach. I'd married him even though I was lying to him about my family.

If they could see me now, with my red hair and my vampire husband, they'd be more than disgusted with me. Giving myself over to him meant my lie became my truth. I was an orphan now. I wasn't sure if Sera would look at me as a sister again. A sob caught in my throat, and Bastien settled his hand on my lower back, dragging his fingers along my bare skin in comforting lines.

My toes curled into the rough cotton sheets, and I turned my attention back to my mate. His pale blond hair falling into his eyes as he watched me. Despite his stony exterior, Bastien was the only person who made me feel loved. I liked being the person he believed me to be.

Intelligent. Stubborn. Beautiful.

His cool fingers traced lower, traveling down until they reached the sensitive skin of my backside. His touch raising goosebumps over my legs. Each caress tantalizing and new. The temperature of his skin and the stillness of his heart were the only signs that he was different from other men. Besides his lust for my blood.

I swallowed hard as soon as the word came to mind. Since meeting Bastien, I'd been forced to be around *it* more than ever before. And while I was nowhere near unaffected by it, the sharpness of my symptoms was beginning to diminish.

So much had changed. For me. Around me. About me. I wasn't the same weak girl that arrived at the capital. Something thick settled in my throat, making it difficult to swallow.

I called Bastien's name through our connection. I needed reassurance that he hadn't changed his mind. Just because we were bound together didn't mean he'd always love me. I'd learned long ago that family didn't always mean love.

He offered me no words, nor did he ask what I was thinking, but his steady presence filled the little bedroom until he was the only thing I could think of. I allowed myself to get lost in the pale blue of his eyes. His hands were as grounding as the earth. His hair shone the color of sunshine. And his lips... So soft and delicious, they made my breath hitch in my chest. His lips were godly. Holy. Sacred in the way they moved over my skin and claimed me as his own. Benevolent in the way they gave pleasure.

I wished we never had to leave this room. That he could keep me in his arms. Locked away. Where we could live out this fantasy together.

Bastien's deep voice broke me from my thoughts. "You're sad."

It wasn't a question. I knew he could feel it. A crease settled between his brows as he contemplated me. His head tipped to one side.

"You have something to say, but you're afraid that bringing it up will make me even more sad," I said.

He lifted a hand to my hair and spun a lock around his finger, rubbing his thumb over the strands, yet his attention never left my face. His cool eyes focused on mine, drawing me into their depths. He drew in a deep breath, and his gaze dropped to the swell of my breasts, heating my flesh with his full attention.

"Then let's not talk," he said. His cool breath fanning over my heated skin. He lowered his mouth to my breast, sucking my nipple into his mouth.

My body reacted on instinct, arching into the press of those godly lips, offering myself to them. Letting them move over my skin like they were reading from a sacred text. Showing me with more than words that he wanted me. Wanted to satisfy me. Deeply. Carnally. As only a mate could.

Being wanted in this way spurred my desire.

Wrapping a hand around the small of my back, Bastien pulled me against his body, bringing us together once again. Lying side by side, his hardness pressed against my thighs as he licked his way across the valley of my breasts. Finding my other nipple and drawing it into his mouth.

My fingers sank into his forearms. His shoulders. His back. His hair. There wasn't enough of him to grab. To hold. To get as close as I wanted to be to him. He was the only thing I had left, and right now, I wanted him to fuck me like no one else mattered.

I didn't have to be sad when he was inside me. I was just his.

Bastien's hand slid down my leg, gripping me by the back of my knee and spreading me open. He didn't waste time with words or asking me what I wanted. He dusted kisses over my thighs and over my heat. Tasting me. Slowly rebuilding the fire inside me. I didn't think it was possible for me to find release again, not with all the thoughts weighing heavy on my mind. Until he circled my clit with his cold tongue in painfully soft little strokes.

A low moan escaped me.

Heat pooled between my thighs, melting for him.

When I was twisting in the sheets, he crawled on top of me, his thick length pressing against me. He caught the back of my knee in his hand, and with a gentle thrust, he slid inside me.

Bastien didn't hesitate this time. Didn't ask if he was too much. He just gave me what I needed. My hips rolled with each of his deliberate thrusts, meeting each one until we found a steady rhythm. He held me. Kissed me. Was so present. His attention never drifting from my face. Catching my lips with his as he thrust in and out. In and out. Our chests rising and falling in tandem as we moved together.

Our first time was a rush of firsts. Of exploding emotions and whispered promises. This time, we were making love. He rested my leg over his hip, and his hand came to cup my backside, squeezing my flesh hard as he dove deeper. It felt so good

I moaned into his mouth, and he swallowed the sound like it was all he needed to survive.

I kissed him back with everything inside me. Our teeth clacking together, lips mashing, tongues twisting. The friction between us building with each steady beat.

He pushed our foreheads together and showed me what he was seeing, what he was feeling. How close he was to coming because of how good I felt.

"Does my wife want to come?" he said against my mouth. His forehead pressed to mine. Breath ragged.

Bastien's hands left mine to fit under my hips, angling me up so that each thrust landed against my swollen spot, giving me the friction I needed to push me over the edge. I screamed his name, and the sound echoed around the room and inside the chambers of my heart. Begged him for the release I so desperately wanted.

"That's it, come for me," he said. Eyes blind. Lips pulled tight. Just as lost as I was.

His command opened the gates of my pleasure, and another scream tore from my throat as I came, my fingers gripping the bedsheets and my back arching off the mattress.

As soon as I was done throbbing around him, Bastien pulled himself out and crawled toward me, his hard length gripped in his hand; he rubbed the tip over my lips, coaxing them open.

"I'm going to come down my wife's pretty throat. Open up for me."

Submitting to him, I took him into my mouth as far as I could, my tongue tasting the sweet flavor of my pleasure on him. Gently gripping the back of my head, he thrust inside my mouth, and a guttural groan of pleasure followed.

Warm, salty liquid filled my mouth, and I did my best to swallow it all down, taking him deep inside me. Letting him fill me in every way. Running my tongue over his tip as more leaked out. When I couldn't swallow any more, cum dripped down my chin and coated my lips.

He pulled out of my mouth, and the look on his face was indescribable.

"My beautiful wife," he said, his thumb skating over my cheek before holding my chin in his hand with so much tenderness. "Let's get you home."

Home.

The word settled deep in my chest.

He was my home now.

CHAPTER 47
DÉFENDRE

BASTIEN

'd made Claire my wife.

My world.

Mine.

It was foolish to pursue this, to consummate our bond, but I couldn't make myself regret it. The pull toward her so strong it was as if I was under a spell. Her spell. A spell I had no wish of breaking.

My grip on Lucien's reins tightened as we continued to climb the treacherous path to the castle. Château Rose reminded me that I couldn't get lost in her completely. I had to find a way to keep my wits about me. Fully succumbing to the pull of our mate bond wasn't an option. No matter how much I wanted to.

I was the Duke of Roselyn. I commanded the largest army. And war was coming to the Unified Territories. I could feel it. Imogen had told me as much. I couldn't ignore it anymore.

My arm snaked around Claire's shoulders, flattening her protectively against my chest as we climbed the last of the snow-slick rocks that led up to the main gate. She'd fallen asleep some hours ago, and as loath as I was to wake her, I had to. The hour was late and I feared there would be little rest for us once we arrived at home.

I pressed my lips to her cheek, which seared hot against my cold flesh. She was warmer than she should be. Something told me the dark magick that had awakened in her was the cause.

After her transformation, I had more questions that needed answering about who she really was, but now wasn't the time. I had to focus on the task at hand.

"Claire," I whispered.

She stirred, eyes fluttering open. So big and brown and wide, they were easy to get lost in.

She glanced around. "How long was I asleep?"

I gave her a half smile. "Not long enough."

"What are we going to tell them?" she asked.

She didn't need to explain the question further. I knew what she meant. And as difficult as it would be, there was only one answer.

"Nothing more than they need to know," I replied.

Claire nodded with a mildly terrified look fixed in her brown eyes. My hand fell back to her waist. My palm pressing protectively against her stomach.

"What if they find out? What if they tell Prince Marius?" she asked. "What if—what if you get in trouble?" She drew in a shaky breath. "Bastien, I can't lose you."

I halted Lucien so I could take Claire's face in both my hands. Pressing our foreheads together, I made her another vow.

"Nothing will take me away from you. Nothing. Not my brother. Not some law. Not anything. I swear it by all the gods. Do you understand?"

She nodded, and even though I could sense her hesitance, I

kissed her hard. Claiming her mouth in a way that pledged my body and life to her. So long as I stood, it would be by her side.

I broke off the kiss, and the cold mountain air skated across my wet lips. How I'd explain this to my council and ask the impossible of them was a question I'd been contemplating the whole ride here. How did I reassure my people that I was still a competent ruler?

"I trust you," she said.

Her belief in me filled me with the promise of hope, and I encouraged Lucien on, up the last of the rocks until the castle was in full view.

Once we were past the gates, my full council was braving the harsh weather, standing on the narrow steps ready to receive us. Grim expressions on their faces. Natalia looked murderous. My raven arrived ahead of us, explaining what transpired at Kemp Manor. But what none could've anticipated were the two shaggy wolves that dogged Lucien's heels. The familiars had bonded themselves to Claire after she'd received her powers and they were nearly as fierce of protectors as I was.

These were no normal wolves. I could smell it. They were twice as big as any wolf I'd ever seen. If these were the breed of wolves that Alec had seen, then I could understand how he'd thought them werewolves.

Claire sucked in a sharp breath and gripped my forearm in pain, and guilt lanced through me. I didn't need to ask what was wrong as she shifted uncomfortably in the saddle. My mate had been through so much in the last twenty-four hours. And I was to blame for nearly every ache that pained her.

As much as I wanted to allow Claire a bath and rest, I had to ask her to accompany me to the council meeting. The strained look on my second-in-command's face showed that she was more than outraged by the Kemp attack; she was afraid for me.

They all bowed as we came to a halt and I dismounted. Grabbing Claire around the waist, I lifted her off Lucien's back and set her carefully beside me. Then retrieved my cane from the saddlebag. She'd insisted on covering her hair with her cloak, but there was nothing to do to hide the wolves.

When my hand found Claire's and I laced our fingers together. Unsurprisingly, Natalia glared back at us. Clearly shocked that I would make such a brazen move.

"Miss Donadieu has been injured," I explained. "She needs to lean on me."

Together, hand in hand with her wolves trailing behind, we climbed the stairs and made our way to the council chamber. None questioned why I was leading my sanguine partner inside, nor did they question why I seated her at the place of honor, directly to my right, where Natalia usually sat.

I could hear her teeth grinding as I pulled out her usual chair for a very nervous looking Claire. I offered my second-in-command the chair to my left, which forced everyone to rearrange their usual spots.

I cared not as they bumbled about the room, arguing over who should sit where now. Once we were all settled and the door to the council room closed, I set my cane down on the carved wood table in front of me. My gaze sharply trailing the room.

"Your raven was scant. What happened, Your Grace?" Laurent asked.

I was not a man to dance around the truth or mince words, and I knew neither would sit well with the leaders of Roselyn. They were a tough people, who lived and labored in the northern mountains.

"The funeral ritual didn't go as Hera anticipated, and Temperance's magick went to Miss Donadieu."

The room went silent. Natalia's nostrils flared. I looked to Claire, noting how the color raced from her cheeks.

"Why didn't you *tell* us you were a Witch of the Darkness?" Natalia said.

"She *obviously* didn't know," I shot back, answering for Claire. "What's important is after she received the magick, Hera disavowed the protection of the Blood Treaty then tried to kill her. And me."

More silence. Footsteps approached just outside the door, and when it creaked open, my nephew breezed inside. I'd nearly forgotten about his smug and unwelcome presence. A sign of just how entranced I was by Claire. Because he was a very important piece of this tenuous puzzle.

"Sorry I'm late, Uncle," Tyson said casually, shutting the door behind him. Running a hand through his coal black hair. Then he cut a hard look at Natalia. "I wasn't informed there was an emergency council meeting."

Natalia scooted her chair back, the screeching sound ringing through the room, then stood.

"I thought you didn't want to be bothered when you were playing *Dépouiller* with your consorts."

At mention of the card game that had caused me to find Claire half naked and drunk, I felt the change happen. My fangs lengthened, and thirst burned in the back of my throat. My vision tinted red. He'd seen my mate in a compromising way. He'd fed her alcohol. Got her drunk. Defied my orders. He didn't deserve to draw air in her presence.

I nearly lost hold of every restraint keeping me from slaying my kin when I felt Claire's hand on mine. The gentle pressure and the warmth drawing my attention to her face. Her beautiful face. She was everything all at once.

"Your Grace?" she whispered.

The sound of her voice gave me something else to focus on besides blind rage. Opening our connection, she stared into my eyes, and I was able to find a steady breath again surrounded by feelings of love.

When my senses returned, I found everyone staring at me. Confused and afraid, I shook my head and gripped the bridge of my nose to clear my thoughts.

"Sit," I instructed my nephew.

Cautiously, he pulled the nearest chair out and did as I commanded. But he didn't miss the way Claire's hand was still covering mine. His eyes lingered there for a moment before folding his hands on the table.

"What did I miss?" he asked as if he hadn't nearly had his head ripped off seconds earlier.

My teeth gnashed together. "We were discussing the rupture in the Blood Treaty. The Kemps chose to disavow and attack during the funeral. A fact you'd already know if you were here on time."

His mouth hung open in shock. "I can't believe it. And after the letter we received from Shayla? What's happening?"

Shayla was a Witch of the Light from the Lawless Lands. One who vehemently disagreed with signing the treaty. She wasn't in charge, however. Hector was. And Hector was the one I'd been communicating with.

The rest of my advisors shifted uncomfortably. I narrowed my attention. "What news did we receive from Shayla?"

"While this news with the Kemps is most terrible, I fear we cannot hold word from the Lawless Lands, Your Grace."

Laurent gestured to an attendant who set a wooden box on the table in front of me. The smell of rotting flesh filled the air. My Grand Advisor passed a letter to me.

It read simply, '*Negotiate this.*'

My gaze shifted to the box, and my stomach sank. I knew without opening it what was inside, but I had to look. It was my duty to see the carnage. To witness it. I lifted the lid, and found Hector's severed head staring back at me. Claw marks slashed across his face. The size and shape resembling Alec's wound.

Sorrow buried in my heart. He'd been a friend. A man who wanted peace for his people. And who died for it. Unlike me, he didn't get a chance at a second life to watch that peace flourish and fail for eternity.

Claire gagged, and I placed the lid back on the box, resting my hand on the lid and saying a prayer to Diana, hoping that his spirit found his way to the stars.

"See that he receives the burial he deserves," I ordered my council, and the box was taken away.

Something was happening within the Witches of the Light. In the Unified Territories and the Lawless Lands alike. What happened to Temperance Kemp and Hector weren't isolated incidents. I could feel it. I started to reconsider Alec's story, wondering if perhaps he'd actually seen a werewolf. If the Witches of the Light were making these moves because they'd learned how to harness the ancient power of shifting.

In light of this news, things would need to change. I needed to find a way to keep the peace and prevent war from spilling over into our lands. That was my main duty. That, and keeping Claire safe. I'd told her I was only going to tell the council what they needed to know, which, at the time, didn't include our marriage. But know, I needed them to know, because I couldn't do this alone. I had to lean on their advice when I wanted to make rash decisions to protect Claire. It couldn't all fall on Natalia.

The peace we'd worked so hard for was being tested, and I wasn't going to let it fall apart because of my pride.

"I've been keeping something from you all that I can't hold any longer." Natalia shook her head in warning, but I pressed on. "On my recent trip to the capital for my Sanguination Ball, when I met Miss Donadieu, I realized that I'd found my mate."

I set my hand on Claire's shoulder to bolster her strength as collective gasps went around the small room and all eyes went to her.

"While I resisted the bond due to my obligations here, it became unavoidable. I love her. And now, she's my wife."

The following silence was deafening. "From now on," I announced, still standing, "when we are in session, Miss Claire Donadieu shall be known as Lady Claire Allard, Duchess of Roselyn."

That was her name now. *Claire Allard.* But she had so much more than just my name, but my heart. My soul.

Claire appeared more than shocked at her new title, which caused a small smile to curve up one side of my mouth. A show of softness just for her. She was, after all, my lady.

When I turned back to the assembled, my lips were pulled tight. My niece looked incensed and I snarled to still her tongue.

"She is the lady of this castle, and you will show her all due courtesies and respect." I grabbed my cane and slammed the point down hard on the marble floor, breaking the silence. "Did you hear me? This is your new duchess."

CHAPTER 48

CONTRAINDRE

BASTIEN

I didn't want to lead by fear, but sometimes I had to remind people of my strength. Words of fealty and welcome passed around the table, but it wasn't a happy announcement. I might've told them all I was cutting their pay in half instead of announcing my marriage.

The council room grew silent, save for beating hearts and tapping feet, but it didn't remain silent for long.

My nephew—unsurprisingly—was the one to speak first.

"But she's your sanguine partner. Uncle, the laws clearly state—"

I growled, low in my chest. He abruptly shut his mouth and swallowed whatever he was going to say. To have my decisions questioned was not the issue. I welcomed dissent. But I could not abide it from *him*. Not when I knew how poor his own decision-making was.

"I know what the laws say," I said.

My Grand Advisor cleared his throat, and in his kind way, offered, "Of course we desire you here, leading us as you have done for centuries, Your Grace. Surely when you return to the capital with the Lady Claire, you'll be welcomed warmly."

Tyson stifled a laugh.

My lip curled at his obvious disrespect. I wanted to rage at him for it, but I rather agreed with his sentiment.

"I don't believe my brother will be so forgiving. I've already crossed him once, and even he has limits."

My Grand Advisor rose from his chair and set his hand on my shoulder, gazing up at me with a warm smile. "You should go to the capital. Beg for his mercy. Face-to-face. Man-to-man. He is your brother." Yes. Marius was *mon sang*. My brother in blood. This was true. But just because we were brothers didn't mean we always saw eye to eye. Laurent continued, undeterred. "The Viscount can serve in your place as steward until the duchess bears you a *child*."

The word *child* pulled on everyone in the room. They all knew the power of an heir. The rising tension was so palpable and alive I could offer it a seat at the table. I'd taken Natalia in when she refused to be the heir Josse demanded. Tyson had an older brother who ruled his father's duchy while he remained at the capital with his mate.

Those who were born in Roselyn, my human advisors, did not follow the patriarchal rules set forth in the Blood Treaty, and thus did not understand the need for a male heir. Any heir would do.

And then there was Claire.

My new bride. A woman raised in isolation at a convent filled with other women. And who feared the sight of blood so deeply she couldn't wield a knife or even bear hearing the word spoken aloud. The birthing bed was no place for her.

Despite all of this animosity, a fuzzy image flashed in my mind's eye. A young boy with silver lilac hair and ice-blue eyes. He was the most wondrous thing I'd ever seen. No more than two years old, but strong. He looked just like me, save for his mother's iridescent hair. The color she'd been born with.

I wished to hold him more than I'd ever wanted anything. But the woman whose lap he sat on, my wife, looked... ill. Blood wept from the bites on her neck, and her breasts were covered in gruesome bruises. A mother was always the sanguine partner for the child until he reached school-age.

I watched the little boy as he wiped a drop of red blood from his lips. My throat grew thick and tight with emotion. He was killing her. No, I told myself. *I would not allow it.*

I gripped the table, disoriented by what I'd seen and what it foretold, and tried to regain my composure. If that fantasy was not a premonition, it was surely a projection of things to come.

Claire could not survive it.

Besides, having a child was a dream I'd given up on long ago. A wish that would never come true. Not if he hurt Claire.

I caught sight of my wife sitting with her head bowed, one hand pressing against her stomach. I wondered if she'd seen the same thing. If the image had drifted through her mind too. I reached out through our connection, probing her emotions. Needing to know how this was affecting her. All I could feel was fear and panic. The emotions so strong they made my chest clench. But there was also intrigue. Pride. And...

I drew in a deep breath, and the scent of her arousal filled me with desire I shouldn't have. I'd already taken my fill of her twice today. Too much for her to endure. And yet, I wanted more.

She lifted her gaze to mine, her brown eyes blazing with flecks of molten gold, and the need to fill her with every last drop of me became overwhelming.

Gritting my teeth, I forced my gaze back to those assembled. Willing myself to have the composure of a level-headed leader and not be sucked into some misbegotten fantasy. I was stronger than these base desires, and I was going to prove it.

My nephew rose from his seat across the table, and in that moment, he looked so much like my brother Josse that I might have trouble distinguishing the two if they were side by side, especially since Tyson still insisted on wearing the royal blue of his father and styling his black hair in the slicked back way of the South.

"I am prepared to lead in your absence," Tyson confirmed with all the arrogance of youth.

I scowled back at him.

I would not be distracted or swayed. This was my mantle. My task. Marius had said as much. He needed me to see this through. More than that, I needed to lead our armies to ensure Claire's safety, so no one would hurt her again. *No one.* Including a child.

"We," I said, in a forced calm, my lips trembling with the intensity of my anger, "are not leaving." I caught Natalia's eye and I saw the fear and anger welling there. I knew she still didn't trust Claire any more than she trusted Tyson, but I would make her see reason. "I am asking *all* of you to commit treason by supporting my decision and keeping our secret. No one outside this room will know the truth of my mate bond. My private residences will be closed to all staff."

A hushed silence swept around the room.

With slow steps, I began walking around the table. Pausing behind each chair as I spoke.

"We have a mission," I reminded them. "A mission the High Prince sees as crucial to the stability of the realm. A mission that is even more vital after the *despicable* events at Kemp Manor and the rising threat Shayla poses."

I struck the tip of my cane against the ground to emphasize

my point. Just thinking of the danger Claire had been in and the useless way I'd failed to protect her egging me on.

Anger turned to rage, and I felt my change occur again, my fangs lengthening.

"I've been treating the symptom for too long, as Lady Natalia often reminds me. It's time to stop turning a blind eye to the war still brewing between the Witches of the Light and Darkness. The time has come to investigate the presence of werewolves." My eyes locked with Claire's. She was gripping the table, leaning all the way forward. This was for her. And for my people. To maintain the balance of power. "We must remind the witches of the Unified Territories," I said ominously, "that vampires still have teeth."

My Master-of-Arms clambered to his feet and, drawing his sword, shouted, "I swore fealty to you, my Prince. And I'll follow whatever order you give. The laws be damned!"

The other warriors stood and grunted out their agreement, drawing their swords in solidarity. Pride and gratitude swelled in my chest.

Natalia, emboldened by their show, stood as well. Her gaze found Claire's before landing on me. "We are with you, Uncle. And to prove it, let us all make a blood vow to you, promising to safeguard this secret."

She drew the short knife holstered across her chest. The blade glinting in the candlelight. The room grew silent once again. I'd never asked my people to make a blood vow, choosing instead to inspire loyalty over forcing it. But Natalia had a point. This secret and their loyalty were of utmost importance.

My Grand Advisor dumped his chalice of wine on the floor and offered his hand to Natalia, who made a cut in the fleshy part of his palm. The delicious scent of blood filling the room.

Laurent dribbled blood into the cup. Then they swapped hands, and Laurent cut Natalia's, adding hers to the cup.

Claire abruptly turned away.

One by one, I watched in awe as my advisors allowed their blood to spill in silent solidarity with me.

When Natalia presented the cup to my nephew, he hesitated. "Uncle, I can lead a werewolf investigation," he insisted stubbornly. "Then you and Claire can avoid treason and seek your own peace in the capital."

My nostrils flared at his continued indignation. "And how will you do that? What will you do if your search takes you into the Lawless Lands?"

"Well, I—" he stammered.

Had I not been so angry, I might've laughed. "I hope your sword arm isn't as limp as your cock, Nephew. Because stuttering like that in front of lawless witches will get you and everyone you wish to lead killed." To make my point, I pointed to the council warriors, Destine, Gavin, and Levi. "Are you ready to let them die for your arrogance?"

Tyson squeezed his fists into tight balls before banging them on the counter. "Then teach me what to say. That's why I'm here. To learn from you."

My response was swift. "If you wish to rule in my place, or in any place, you should listen more often than you speak. Read more often than you speak. And drink only with those you are supposed to drink with. You've already proven that you make choices based on self-interest alone."

"Aren't you doing the same, Uncle?" Tyson asked.

I paused, appraising this tenuous situation. I knew Natalia wasn't happy with me, but she was loyal. Tyson would never be appeased with anything less than his new inheritance. Yes, I could kill him now and be done with it. But that would not win

Marius to my side or make Claire any safer. I needed to think and act like a strategist.

"Make the vow," I said, taking the knife from Natalia, "afterward, we will discuss this matter further in private. I swear it." Each word cost me a piece of my dignity.

Tyson wavered like he meant to argue, but whatever he saw in my eyes stilled his tongue. Begrudgingly, he offered me his hand, and I sliced the blade across it, causing red tears to well, which I squeezed into the cup.

A breath of relief escaped my lips. It was done. Tyson would keep our secret, or die. I reached for the cup, ready to drink and seal their vow, but Natalia held it out of my reach.

"Just a moment, Uncle," Natalia bit out. "We still need a drop from *the Duchess.*"

CHAPTER 49
LE VŒU
CLAIRE

My attention darted between the dagger and the cup and the cold look in Natalia's eyes. I had no idea how to handle her, or the threat she continued to pose to my secret. *And my life.*

"The Duchess should vow, like the rest of us," Natalia continued—her hips swinging as she sauntered closer. "She should swear to *never* reveal the secret of your marriage. And never, *ever* betray you. Or keep *any* secret from you."

A vow I couldn't keep without *dying*, which was exactly what she wanted. My hand flinched toward the choker necklace, but I caught myself before actually touching it. Natalia didn't miss the movement, though. She could read me in a way her uncle couldn't. I cursed my younger sister's impulsivity. Had she not slapped her, perhaps Natalia wouldn't be so suspicious.

"Nervous?" she asked in a devilish way. Her tiny nose crinkled.

I didn't know what to say. Fear had me by the throat,

unable to speak. I knew Bastien could sense my emotions, and with each passing moment, they grew stronger.

He knew I was afraid.

Frantically, I looked around the room, noticing the faces of those who had already pledged loyalty to Bastien, including Tyson. If his nephew agreed, how could I get out of this? I couldn't. Arguing against it would seem even more suspicious.

My life depended on how well I could keep up my lie. I knew Bastien would never forgive the truth of my family's mission and my part in it, so honesty was out of the question.

I swallowed hard, staring at the cup. I supposed I was faced with death yet again. In my moment of hopelessness, when I didn't know what to do, the dark thing inside me flickered to life. The part of me that was a Dark Witch.

Live. Live. Live.

The words calling to me with each beat of my heart. The darkness reluctant to be snuffed out.

The heat of magick warmed my blood and snapped against my skin like it was begging to get free. I was ashamed of it, disgusted by it, but I couldn't deny its power. In the graveyard, the darkness had broken past whatever was keeping it at bay, allowing me to create a wall of flames out of nothing to protect Bastien and me from the witches before retreating back inside me. It was back now, called forward by my desperation. Only this time, I didn't need fire—not exactly. I just needed *strength*.

The magick filled every corner of my body, coaxing my nerves to relax and my swirl of thoughts to settle. When they did, I realized honesty or death weren't the only ways. I rolled my shoulders back and lifted my chin, facing Natalia with courage I did not feel, but that seemed to possess me like a demon.

Pulling back the hood of my cloak, I revealed what I'd been

hiding: my burnished copper hair. Even though they'd been told, this was undeniable proof. I let them all stare.

Yes, I was a ruin. *A ruin that was still standing.*

"What *are* you suggesting?" I asked the vampire in a sharp voice that didn't sound wholly like my own. "That the gods erred when they fated His Grace to me? Do you believe you know more than Diana or Damien? And that you see things in me that they did not?"

Whispers went around the room. I only caught clips of what they were saying, but it sounded like:

"Out of line."

"Too far."

Good.

A smirk rounded my lips when I caught sight of the mild look of surprise on Bastien's face. He didn't like me meek and soft, as I once thought. He liked seeing me show my teeth. I canted my head to one side, taking in the lines of frustration creasing Natalia's forehead. She was on the defensive now. As a warrior, she must know her position wasn't good. As much as they respected her, I was the Duchess of Roselyn now. The wife of their liege lord.

"Of course not," Natalia said, glancing between Bastien and me. "The only thing I'm suggesting, Lady Claire, is that you ally yourself fully with my uncle. As we all are."

I made a noncommittal *hmph* and then crossed my arms. I had no idea where my confidence was coming from or whether this side of me was good or not, but I did know the darkness inside me was elated. It urged me on. Told me to press my advantage.

"I was with the Duke at Kemp Manor, accompanying him as he requested, when, by some fate, Damien named me the worthiest witch in the graveyard, granting me Temperance Kemp's powers. When the witches turned their cloaks and came for our heads, I stood by his side and fought with him when he told me to run. And when they came for me, I offered to trade my life to save his." Hot tears collected in my eyes at the memory of that blade to his throat. "We trust each other. And whether you like it or not, His Grace and I are one now. Fated by the gods."

"I understand that—"

I pressed on. "What you seek is to make a mockery of me by suggesting that I cannot be trusted. To drive a wedge between us where none exists."

More whispers followed. Bastien looked as if he wanted to intervene but was too intrigued to do so.

Then I delivered my final point—the one that I knew would keep them all from questioning my loyalty again. I leaned in, lips pulled back over my teeth and said, "The Duke drinks from me whenever he wishes. I do not need some cup and knife to make a vow to him. I have already done so, time and time again."

"Yes, but—" she started, but Bastien cut her off.

He was at my side, one arm wrapped protectively around me. His tolerance for this was clearly at an end.

"That's enough, Lady Natalia," he said between his teeth, seething. Roughly, he took the cup from her, causing a bead of red liquid to slosh over the side and run down his long, pale fingers.

"Claire is my wife, and she has demonstrated her unyielding loyalty to me in more than one way. I will not tolerate hearing her questioned any further."

My heart swelled as I watched him lift the gold cup to his lips and drink. However, the pride and adoration I felt was tinted with guilt.

"With your blood, your vow is sealed. None will speak of my mate bond to Claire, or death will be your consequence."

A breath of magick, carrying the familiar fresh scent of garden herbs, trailed around the room, weaving between each one of his council members before it collected around him, the spell binding them all together.

The scent his magick left behind reminded me, shockingly, of home. I'd thought him a Dark Witch, but now I knew that wasn't true. He had been born of the light. And I was the darkness. The thought caused the magick in me to retreat, and I shivered as my inner flame disappeared.

Bastien set down the cup and took my hand, then lifted my knuckles to his lips.

I'd grown up a ghost. Ignored and left out of important meetings. Shunned for years because of my lack of magick and made to believe I wasn't good for anything. Told I wasn't smart or strong. But Bastien believed in me. Where others saw weakness, he saw strength. He raised me up, offered me a seat at his his table, made me powerful in ways I'd never imagined. However, it wasn't the power of my new position that had my throat burning with emotion.

It was him. Just him.

The blue of his eyes and the fierceness of his gaze when they looked upon me. The careless way his golden hair was pushed to one side. I reached for his face, taking the soft strands between my fingers. Then slowly pushed it back behind his ear. Bastien leaned into my touch, and the feeling was heavenly and sinful at the same time.

He cupped my jaw and leaned in slowly, our eyes locked even when he pressed our lips together like he couldn't bear to keep me out of his sight for even a moment—even in the middle of this meeting.

His lips tasted of the coppery flavor of blood. My head swam, but I breathed through the feeling, and thankfully, it passed. Bastien touched the corner of my mouth, trailing his finger along the line of my lower lip, then let out a sigh.

"Would you return to our room and wait for me there?" He glanced at Tyson. "My nephew and I have a few things to discuss."

I wasn't sure what Bastien was going to offer Tyson in return for his secrecy, but I knew whatever it was would cost him dearly.

"Of course," I replied. "I would like to bathe."

He smiled and pressed a kiss to my forehead, just beside the painful gash on my brow. "I will send a nurse to tend to this cut."

I nodded, and so did he, and I knew this was goodbye for now.

With my hand still clasped in his, Bastien addressed his niece. "Lady Natalia, escort the Duchess to our rooms. Ensure she has a bath drawn."

Natalia narrowed her eyes. "I'm not her attendant."

"I do not care."

The usual warmth between them was absent, and I wondered if it would return any time soon or if my darkness and the need to protect my secret at all costs had severed their bond. For that, I felt guilty, because Natalia wasn't wrong. Not at all. But I had no other choice when she kept pushing.

"And what of her dogs?" Natalia asked. "Should I bathe them, too? Or should we put them to the question for our werewolf investigation?"

The two great wolves howled outside the door to the council room, which gave many in the room pause.

"They are familiars, not dogs, and not werewolves. I witnessed them bond themselves to her after she received her magick," Bastien said.

My gaze found Natalia's, and no part of me wanted to be

burdened by her sour mood or to be the target of her insults for the next half hour. I'd experienced enough of that at the hands of my family to know how sour moods festered. Instead, I squeezed Bastien's hand, drawing his attention back to me. "I don't require an escort. I have my wolves. I can find my way to our room by myself."

Pressing his lips together in a hard line, Bastien nodded, then touched the gem hidden under my dress. "If you need me, you know how to reach me."

I nodded. "I do."

"Then go. Bathe," he said. "Get some rest. I will join you later. I swear it."

With one last look, I exited the council room to find my two familiars waiting patiently for me. Their eyes alight with magick. I ran my hands through their thick fur, and a spark of heat tickled my palms.

CHAPTER 50
FAIRE
CLAIRE

The sheep's horn relic Cora had given me sat on the vanity beside my ink and parchment. Even sitting still, it throbbed with latent demonic power. The poison of hate that still ran in my veins told me I should smash it. That I was an abomination for considering to use it.

I fought back against it and dipped the quill, the scratch of ink on parchment loud against the hush of the room. My hand shook, though whether from exhaustion or fear, I couldn't be sure.

Dearest Sera,

I'm learning that strength doesn't always look like moon magick. Sometimes it looks like surviving when the world tries to end you. Sometimes it looks like writing this letter and trusting you'll forgive me for never being the sister you deserved.

In the time I've been away from home, I've learned many things about the world. And I can say that the hate we grew up with isn't shared by everyone.

I paused to glance into the mirror. The girl who stared back at me, with her red hair, still surprised me. I could only imagine what my sister would think of me now. I gave the barest shake of my head and continued.

If you ever think to leave, know that you'll always have a place here at Château Rose.

Things are changing faster than I can keep up with, but one thing has not changed and never will: my vow to you. I will keep you safe, whatever it costs me. Even if I can't walk beside you, I'll find a way to make this world safer for you.

With all my love.

I signed my name and folded the parchment, tying it with black thread before slipping it into the raven's satchel. Beside it, I tucked my small coin pouch—my earnings as his sanguine partner for the month. Enough to help Sera if she decided to run. Enough, I hoped, to prove I was still thinking of her.

The black raven clacked its beak as I fastened the pouch to its foot. My chest tightened.

The white wolf whined and stepped in front of me, her golden eyes flashing with something like warning. She nudged the satchel, as if begging me not to send it.

"I have to," I whispered, stroking her thick ruff. "She has to know."

The wolf pressed closer, trying once more to block my way, but the brown wolf growled low, as if reminding her of her place. I lifted my hand, and the raven spread its wings. With one strong beat, it vanished into the night beyond.

The fire cracked. My shoulders sagged. Both wolves settled at my feet, one watchful, the other restless. I retrieved the relic and held it to my chest, staring at my reflection in the mirror.

Cora had told me to charge my powers and learn the ways of dark magick, but something inside me was resisting it. I'd struggled to truly connect with it in the graveyard.

A familiar presence filled the chamber before I even looked up.

Bastien.

"Claire?"

The sound of my name, spoken so softly, unraveled something in me.

His stride cut through the shadows, his pale eyes catching firelight as they found mine. I couldn't look away from his face. The intensity of what lay between us—love, devotion, duty—was stronger than anything I'd ever felt. Stronger, and so much more dangerous.

"I've sent word to Marius, explaining what transpired at the Kemps, and my desire to lead an investigation about were-wolves. I wish we had more time to rest, but time is not on our side. Not with the way things are moving."

I nodded, though my hand tightened around the sheep's horn like it could somehow solve our problems, but the tension in his posture told me there was more. "Something else is on your mind."

He let out a long breath, and slowly closed the distance between us. "I believe there's someone in the Lawless Lands who can help you. Someone who can remove the cursed choker and free you from its bind."

The words should have filled me with hope. Instead, dread coiled in my chest. Only a Prideaux could break the choker's curse. If this witch told him as much and he finally found out the truth, he'd know I was the enemy all along. That I'd been lying since the moment we met. And I would lose him.

"I don't know, Bastien."

He stepped closer, his hands gently circling my waist. "Do you trust me?"

The truth that came out was the one that had been burning on my tongue all along. "Yes. Of course I trust you."

He pulled me against his chest, grounding me. But beneath the gentleness of his touch, I swore I felt the phantom pinch of barbs around my throat. I knew now that Mama was just as bad as Hera. If I was going to protect Sera—if I was going to protect him—I had to break free of this curse on my life.

Bastien's voice drew me back. "I swear on my life, I will do whatever it takes to keep you safe."

ABOUT THE AUTHOR

Ainsley James writes darkly romantic fantasies steeped in forbidden love, magic, and heroines who discover their power. She loves Halloween and struggles to resist a graveyard tour. She lives in coastal Virginia with her incredibly patient husband, four children, dog, and two cats. *Fated to the Vampire Prince* is her fiction debut.

In addition to her books, Ainsley offers private coaching for authors, helping writers break through blocks, develop stories, and cultivate authentic, unforgettable voices. You can learn more about individual coaching programs on her website or by sending her an email. She also runs a Discord for writers called Hype Girl Besties, where she hosts writing sprints and monthly craft talks.